Perils of Sea And Sky

Lilian Horn

Text copyright © 2022 by Lilian Horn

All rights reserved. For information regarding reproduction in total or in part, contact Rising Action Publishing Co. at http://www.risingactionpublishingco.com

Cover Illustration © Jon Stubbington

ISBN: 978-1-990253-15-7

FIC009100 FICTION / Fantasy / Action & Adventure

FIC009030 FICTION / Fantasy / Historical

FIC009120 FICTION / Fantasy / Dragons & Mythical Creatures

#PerilsofSeaandSky #TheFastAndThePerilous

Follow Rising Action on our socials!

Instagram: @risingactionpublishingco

Tiktok: @risingactionpublishingco

RISING ACTION

I wrote this story for myself,
but I couldn't have done it without the people around me.

KATSHOV

NOVAL

VALO ALTEEN

SALIS

ORLAND

BOGMIN OTALLO

BUNNSBOROUX

elderness baitunge

QUEENSLAND ST. EMMANUEL

KVENCHESTER

GERNERA

THE GREY VEIL

PERILS OF SEA AND SKY

AUTHOR'S NOTE

Perils of Sea and Sky takes place on an earth-like world not unlike our own in a time that resembles the early 1700s. Mysterious forces surround the oceans in a perpetually foggy hellscape that, while dangerous to any who seek to traverse them, supply the world with the means to make ships airborne. Technological advancements happened well before their time, shooting colonial trade and plasma-based weapons into the age of powdered wigs and piracy.

Welcome to the United Colonies of Terra.

CHAPTER 1

THE TWO-FACED QUEEN

Light spilled into the tavern from the sun-lit streets, the door creaking shut without disrupting the casual mull of patrons caught in banter and plots. Nelson Blackwood covered his nose with his hat to hide the stench of sour sweat and stale beer, far stronger than he was used to. It was the kind of beer one bought when seeking comfort rather than quenching thirst.

He clutched his faded, red-leather satchel close to his chest with his other hand. Sweat beaded on his forehead, threatening to run down his face and unbalance the thin wires of the spectacles on his nose. Freeing his forefinger from the hat, he pushed them back to their place and fanned himself.

A woman in her mid-thirties sat hidden under a wide-brimmed cavalier with a broken feather. This was whom he was looking for.

"C...captain Drackenheart?" he asked. It came out as a croak, forcing him to repeat himself, this time a little too loudly.

Her glow and prominence of youth disappeared when she turned her head to look at him. Her lips stretched into a thin line, and her gaze pierced Nelson. He tried not to squirm as she studied his hot-pressed coat, youthful face, and carefully trimmed dirty-blond hair. She wrinkled her nose.

Unnerved by her silence, Nelson let his eyes wander to the rumbustious group distracting him with boisterous laughter. For a moment, he reconsidered his trip to this ransacked dump at the bottom of the skyport and wondered whether the journey was worth the grime on his shoes.

Captain Drackenheart set the ale cup down after what was likely a deliberately long chug and belched.

"My name is N-Nelson Blackwood," he finally mustered and balanced his hat and satchel in one hand. "I'm a lawyer at Parkson and Blackwood. I have come to you because I've heard you might help." He dug a finger into his cravat and gave it a tug. He didn't know what to make of this person, the infamous 'demon of the sky' whose exploits he had only heard about through whispers. Captain Rosanne Drackenheart's indifference accentuated her already terrifying reputation, but her current beer-influenced state made Nelson question its validity.

Why was she among Valo's rabble when she had access to perfectly fine drinking quarters at the skyport's top disk? This tavern was no place for a woman of her stature and family, even if she downplayed herself to the level of common drunks.

"Get lost, boy."

Nelson turned his gaze about the room to see if he had drawn attention to himself, but none of the other patrons were paying him any mind.

"Please, listen." He sat down at the table despite her command. A sticky wetness on the stool seeped into his trousers. Nelson shuddered. His blunder drew a chuckle from the relaxed captain as if she anticipated his misfortune.

Brushing the discomfort aside, he fiddled with the straps on his satchel and produced a photograph. Posed in front of a three-spire mayfly battleship stood a crew and captain dressed in straight yellow lines of the royal navy's blue jacket. They were dwarfed by the ship.

"This is Captain Ernest Blackwood of the *Retribution*. His ship went missing during a reconnaissance six months ago, and no one has heard or seen any signs of the ship or its crew since," Nelson explained.

Drackenheart picked up the weathered photograph and gave it an apathetic, half-drunken stare.

"Mid-sized corvette, light armour plates and three square-rigged masts," she stated. A bitter smile crept over her lips, and she flicked the photo across the table. "Didn't think the Royal Defense of Aerospace still used those outdated aero ships for coastal patrol." Her narrow eyes locked with his. "Listen kid; I'm a merchant ship captain, not some clam-baked marine investigator. You'll have more luck at the RDA." Her tone turned snide. "Take the central elevator all the way to the topmost disk. You do know where to find it, right? Good luck." Drackenheart took another swig from the cup, emptying it. She tipped her hat as she rose to leave, but Nelson blocked her path with his scrawny frame.

"Please wait. I have exhausted all my options. No one wants to look into the disappearance of the *Retribution,* and every time I ask, I get the boot."

She stared, blinked, and moved around him.

Nelson bit his lip and racked his brains.

"February thirteenth, Gellivar," he blurted.

Captain Drackenheart paused, turned on her heel, and fixed her hazel eyes to Nelson's cowering shape. Her lips curved into a smirk, daring him to say another word.

"February sixth, Haddon," he continued in a whisper and watched her lips tighten with the barest hint of a twitch, and her confidence wither. He cleared his throat. "I hear you sail the Grey Veil and other unconventional routes no sane captain would attempt." He kept his voice firm. The sudden hushed silence in the tavern alerted Nelson that he had said something he shouldn't have. The captain snorted and grabbed him by his shoulders, giving them a petulant squeeze, making him wince.

"Mr. Blackwood, you drunk fool. You can't jump from the skyport to swim in the ocean. You'll freeze to death even in the summer if the fall doesn't kill you first," she exclaimed with a roaring laugh. The surrounding patrons turned their attention back to their drinks, chuckling at the commotion.

"Wha—" Befuddled, Nelson squealed in the woman's strong grip, and he grabbed the table to steady himself. Captain Drackenheart leaned in, so close he could smell the strong stench of sour ale on her breath.

"Shut your trap before anyone hears you. Meet me at The Captain's Quarters at twenty hours sharp. That is the only chance you'll get." She smacked him merrily on his back, making him tumble to his seat.

The singular central strap on his satchel broke, opening its expanding compartments and spilling documents everywhere. In his attempts to recollect the yellowed papers, his glasses tumbled toward the grime-stained floor. He caught them with a deft hand.

In his periphery, Nelson spotted Captain Drackenheart's amused grin as she tipped her hat to the patrons and exited the building.

In his momentary distraction, his foot caught in the stool and sent him sprawling to the floor, where his glasses landed in a shallow puddle of stale beer.

VALO SKYPORT SWAYED with the high northern winds. The vast, circular, floor-like structures, referred to as disks, were without walls and could house hundreds of ships from many floating docks. Thousands of buildings scattered across the levels. With its three disk spire, it was considered one of the largest trade ports on the northern coast of Noval, neatly positioned on the Southern tip of Valo's elongated island.

The massive skyport would have toppled over if not for anti-gravity technology. Its shadows danced over the factories below, throwing half the industrial district into darkness. On the lower disk, cranes hauled cargo from small and broad ships onto transport belts, their quick rhythmic clacking of gears accompanied by the barking of orders heard all around the port.

Nelson had never been to this section of the tower before. The dizzying array of winding staircases bypassing packed buildings made him double-take for each corner he rounded in search of the central tower unit connecting the entire structure.

Along its fringes hovered docks for aero ships of all kinds. Some quays were massive and reserved for men-of-war and large transport vessels, while smaller berths were packed so tightly together that pilots required skill and finesse to dock without causing an insurance claim.

Nelson squeezed himself into the passenger elevator, a large square platform surrounded by tall, rusted metal bars. A man dressed in a stiff blue and yellow skyport uniform armed with a whistle closed the gate behind him while people shuffled for elbow room.

The evening bustle was stifling, and people were cranky and prone to snap at each other like chickens in an overfilled coop. The man blew the whistle twice, and the elevator lowered itself to the disk below. Nelson struggled to keep his balance as the elevator came to a bowing halt.

People pushed past him and stepped on his feet when they scurried off to whatever business they had on the main cargo level. The elevator descended another disk. Nelson stared out at the docks where naval ships rowed in from the seaside, slow-paced and merry compared to their evolved cousins floating above.

The underside of the first level disk reached over the sprawling vista of factories, marketplaces, and cobbled roads running under the swaying tower. Years of industry had resulted in an accumulation of smoke and grime, coating the underside of the lowest disk; it created a nasty chance of black rain on the hottest of summer days. Splotches of tar littered the streets, and Nelson gingerly watched his step as he hailed a two-seater cab.

"Dunhill Main Street, please," Nelson said to the driver as he gave him a bronze quid. The driver pocketed the coin and urged the horse out from the marketplace and up the streets. Nelson settled back to the pleasant sound of the clatter of wooden wheels, hooves on cobblestone, and the crack of the whip as the driver snapped the horse to attention. They travelled north on the island for fifteen minutes before clopping over an arching bridge to the mainland. The skyport pierced the white dotted sky like a needle. The seas below surrounded the island like an inky mirror, with the meandering shoreline between the mountains and the city stretching for miles in either direction. Nelson wouldn't trade this view for anything in the world.

At the very top of the skyport stood the communication tower which directed traffic to different docks. If Nelson squinted, he could make out the numerous antennas jutting from the structure's roof. The topmost disk was pristine and gleaming in the mid-afternoon sun, choked with oncoming traffic of heavy-bowed ships and enormous golden aethersails.

The cab rolled into the valley between two peaks on the mainland and set him off at Dunhill Main Street, where the city unofficially ended. The living districts with the occasional shop expanded along the coastline. The chill mountain breeze seemed to blow right through him, and Nelson buried his exposed neck in his coat.

Snow clung to the mountaintops, and the western coastal winds didn't help the late spring the city suffered every year. He ducked out of the way of a small pack of reindeer which crossed the street. A passing cab driver shouted at the young boy herding the animals. The boy replied in a sharp sing-song tone and stuck up his nose as he ushered the reindeer along, presumably further into the grassy valley. With many locals clinging to their cultural heritage and lands, letting flocks of reindeer run between the plots was common. Despite the city's official status and trade hub of the north, if you lived in Valo, you remained a country bumpkin.

A paperboy at the corner of the two converging main streets waved the latest news. "Fire ravages the capital! Coffee prices expected to rise," he proclaimed in local

Novalian, and was immediately surrounded by a group of people vying for his papers.

Blast. Another fire. Most of the coffee imports came through Ottalo in the south and if another fire ravaged the capital, he couldn't afford another meeting with unwilling sailors. Coffee was still too expensive for everyday consumption. Yet it resonated well with the Novalian spirit, warm and dark during cold winter months with a dash of bitterness.

Nelson checked his timepiece; five hours remained until his meeting with the infamous Captain Drackenheart. He had time to assemble all the paperwork the captain might be interested in. She was his last chance to get to the bottom of the *Retribution's* disappearance. With a bit of luck, she was mad enough to undertake his task.

THE CAPTAIN'S Quarters was a quaint angular building with broad doors, smartly dressed guards, and black-heeled servants. The austere architecture was a stark contrast to the new-Gothic style the town had taken on in recent years, where every jagged detail of the buildings could end one's life with the slightest misstep on the spire-rooftops. It was reserved for officially appointed captains of the Royal Navy and Aerotrade Association, which took a certain percentage of their paycheck in exchange for lodging.

Captain Rosanne Drackenheart caught the doorman staring at her rounded hips. Her tailored trousers fit so snuggly she fooled people into thinking she had changed skin colour. She loved the attention, but she hid her smile beneath her faded-brown hat.

She ascended two bare staircases, entered a numbered door, and shut it behind her. The one-bedroom apartment doubled as a living room with a designated seating area for guests in front of the tall windows. The ensuite was decent sized for its simplicity but did its job in terms of privacy and hygiene—

rather luxurious compared to most living quarters on the skyport.

Rosanne relieved her feet of shoes and socks, digging her toes into the thick carpet. Despite the outside temperature being shy of twelve degrees centigrade, her tunic was damp. To her, the term *cold* meant warm and *frigid* was comfortable, all the makings of a true northerner. Soon enough, she would be up in the sky, and the spring weather promised no light clothing. Spring in the north meant four seasons a day, two if lucky.

Fanning herself, she unbuttoned the jacket and all other clothing too warm for comfort, strewing them about the room as she moved through it.

A ship's horn drew Rosanne to the window. The lumbering hulk of a passenger ship sailed in from higher altitudes to dock at the port. A flow of people exited the broad aeroship as the crew worked quickly to secure the shimmering sails and fetch portable cranes on tracks. Further down the disk rested a two-mast brigantine undisturbed by cranes, crew, and passengers. Its sleek, sharp design and blue painted hull stood out among the late afternoon traffic.

Royal Aero Navy.

Rosanne fetched the spyglass from her bag, extended the rounded metal tubing and pointed it at the ship. The lens was a blurry mess, and she twisted the dial at the outermost configuration, zooming in on the ship's letters. The unreadable text made her adjust a second dial.

"*RDA Arctic Pride,*" she muttered to herself. The brigantine was a lightly armed military ship that kept trade routes free of pirates. Its fresh coat of paint told her it had recently scuffled with another ship. Why else would the RDA invest in a makeover of one of their vessels for any other reason than to cover up the damage?

Rosanne recalled the young man who had confronted her earlier today. *What was his name? Backwash? Blacksack? No, Blackwood.* Young, foolish, and a lawyer.

"Blabbering so openly about the Grey Veil. Does he want to be jailed?" She tapped the spyglass thoughtfully and regarded the *Arctic Pride*, then averted her gaze to the papers in her satchel.

After Blackwood's ambush at the tavern, Rosanne had sobered up in the Magistrate of Trade's archives digging for any information pertinent to the RDA's interest regarding trade routes. Her findings were sparse but intriguing.

Still, something gnawed at her gut.

The foolish Mr. Blackwood must be desperate to seek out her of all people if the Royal Navy and Aerotrade Association refused to investigate the disappearance of one of their ships. She was keen to learn how he had come across her name and her connection with the Grey Veil, for such information was costly and dangerous. She better hear what this clever bastard had to say. Never underestimate a lawyer.

Chapter 2

A Fool's Errand

Nelson eyed the terrace building and corrected his spectacles. The sun still clung to the sky above the surrounding mountains despite it being evening. Yawning, he shifted the weight of his bag from one shoulder to the other, waiting for no reason other than to gather courage. The front doors creaked as they opened, and a greying man stepped outside. Caught in his nervousness, Nelson marched towards the door before he lost his mettle. Once inside, he gave the receptionist a wide-eyed glance before the man asked if he needed any assistance.

"Captain Drackenheart sent for me. Nelson Blackwood is my name." He stood before the desk while the young man checked a book hidden under a wooden top.

The receptionist stretched out an open palm towards the staircase. "Right this way, Mr. Blackwood."

Nelson was escorted up two floors and down a hallway with identical doors lined up like a hotel. The servant knocked on a door twice, and although Nelson couldn't hear the approval for entering, the servant clearly did.

The door swung open in silence, and he stepped aside to let Nelson pass. Rosanne sat on a tall, cushioned chair with her legs crossed. The dainty porcelain cup in her hands looked out of place with her steel gaze, which quickly softened.

"Mr. Blackwood. Please, come sit." She smiled and motioned to the chair across the round table. "Bring us coffee. The strong kind," she ordered the servant, who gave a curt bow and closed the door behind him.

Nelson clung to his overly large bag as if it protected him from a vicious beast. The beast in question was well-dressed in brown trousers that fit her curves too well. She wore only a simple white tunic under a brown vest, with her mahogany curls loose so they covered most of her shoulders and chest. Without the hat, there was nowhere to hide from her hard eyes. Nelson gulped and took off his coat, then noted that she wasn't wearing any shoes despite being dressed for a formal meeting. He unlaced his shoes and placed them on the shoe rack next to her boots.

"Miss Dracken—"

"*Captain* Drackenheart," she corrected.

"Yes, of course. Captain Drackenheart. I have a proposition which might interest you, and I apologize for the inappropriate assault this afternoon."

Her cup clinked on the table as she set it down. "Cut to the chase, Mr. Blackwood. You come into a seedy tavern at the lower disk and blabber about the Grey Veil. Let me ask you, are you out of your goddamn mind?"

Nelson chuckled and let his eyes fall to the floor. The servant returned with the coffee, which he diligently set on the table, refilled Rosanne's empty cup, and poured Nelson his before leaving no less than a minute after he entered.

"If I must be frank, yes, I am out of my mind. I have no one to turn to with this matter, and I need someone willing to take risks," Nelson answered with a wry smile.

"And you believe I am such a person?" She snorted.

"You sail the Grey Veil," Nelson stated.

"Do I?" Her eyebrows rose dramatically. She sipped the hot

brew as she waited for Nelson's spectacular reply. The young lawyer adjusted his glasses and reached for his satchel.

"Even though I am a lawyer, I only deal with the ledgers and numbers. And by that, I mean pushing papers of trade, both marine and sky, yours included. I know for a fact that you trade on the side." This response made Rosanne shift her legs. Her left eyebrow was more rounded than its cousin, giving Rosanne a two-faced expression that either promised friendship or murder depending on which side she presented. They both knit together, forming a unison of uncertainty and hostile provocation, and then amusement.

He produced a brown leather-bound book emblazoned with golden curled script and opened it to a specific page. He set it on the table and pushed the coffee tray to the side. The date was marked on top of each page, and below was a list of aeroships— the columns next to the names listed shipment, tonnage, and approximate value, among other information.

"March twenty-fourth." He pointed to the page and singled out the *Red Queen*. Rosanne's expression was unimpressed. Nelson produced a second book similar to the first one and stacked it on top of the other as the table was far too small to open both at once. "Same date, same ship. I'm not pointing out that you had dual shipments that day. The wares are different. Their tonnage does not match, as they normally don't, but the value of these puzzles me. About sixty tons of wheat were loaded off the docks, as it says right here, but I checked the factory papers and only fifty-five tons were delivered." He brought out a third book, a yearly ledger from a wheat refinery.

The table creaked. Nelson tapped a finger on the same date in this book.

"Your point, Mr. Blackwood?" Rosanne asked.

"The day after you registered, five tons of wheat were delivered to Senland, but none were loaded to your vessel from this port, and you had none registered from before."

"An error in the papers."

"Quite a few errors, in fact."

"Maybe I was trading with an off-hamlet on Senland who was too poor to own an official registration with the trade companies. This colony is built on peasants down-valued by foreign trade companies who ship cheaper materials. What does it matter if I assist with small shipments that have nothing to do with the Magistrate of Trade? Last I checked, it wasn't illegal. My ship is my own business, and I have contracts to back up my claims." Rosanne sipped her coffee without taking her eyes off Nelson.

The spectacles slid down his nose, and he pushed them back in place for the hundredth time. "To be frank, even the RNAA wouldn't look twice at something as small as five tons, especially not wheat which has the lowest gross value of all merchandise in today's economy. Among the wheat you traded at this port, five tons of that were gunpowder. Selling gunpowder outside a Royal port without a license is a criminal offence that can get you permanently suspended and jailed. Your ship doesn't own such a license."

The hot dampness clinging to his forehead only increased at the subtle shift in Rosanne's posture. The only facial expression he could extract from her serene confidence was just that. Had his words reached through her iron hide? Even her naked feet looked more at ease with toes squished into the fluffy carpet than Nelson felt seated on the soft cushion.

"Very well," he said and clamped the books shut, replacing them with a map and small stack of papers, all written trades the *Red Queen* had done the last two years. Again, Rosanne gave no indication of paying as much as half a glance at the pile, but she did arch a brow at the increasing clutter threatening to unbalance the table.

Nelson cleared his throat. "The RDA has conducted a thorough cleanup in the off-trade on the inland over the last couple of years. All confiscated materials are listed and reported to whichever law firm handles the final stage of the material distribution, again decided by the RDA. But here's the interesting part. Among the possessions of several small pirate ships, they found an astounding number of cutting-edge plasma rifles from Haddon across the sea.

At first, it didn't seem like much, considering the pirates could have sailed there themselves. What is interesting is where they acquired the weapons. Of all the ships doing trade to the ports where the pirates procured their weapons, your ship was the only one registered in all instances days before the purchases."

Nelson paused and scanned the captain, whose gaze now rivalled that of an ice queen. She held the cup between stiff fingers, didn't drink it, didn't move it, didn't do anything. Nelson swelled with a hint of smugness that he managed to unnerve the captain, but he also knew if she were as cold as the rumours said, she easily could slit his throat, smuggle his body out of town, and drop his cold carcass over the Black Ice glacier where he would never be found.

The slightest tremble of his hand made him aware of how suffocating the air had become. "And the final piece of the puzzle is how you acquired those guns in the first place. February sixth, 1704: the *Red Queen* took a scheduled voyage to Haddon. Your arrival date to Bogvin was two days earlier than anticipated, meaning you took unconventional routes or had a substantial engine upgrade, which the last ship control didn't reveal. I have a long list of dates, voyages, port registration, and the merchandise you claimed you sold to small inland towns when you had no papers registered for any voyages there, which the RNAA wouldn't notice ... unless I present them this compilation of evidence." He tapped the papers, smiling, an expression which quickly faded upon meeting Captain Drackenheart's glare.

"*This* compilation of evidence?" Rosanne echoed.

"These are only copies." His smirk returned. "Comparing that information with the illegitimate gun trade fits your schedule. You picked up a shipment of tea in Haddon which you sold in Bogvin on the eleventh. You spent maybe a day looking for buyers for the weapons, then sold them on the thirteenth." As

Rosanne set her cup down on the table, the thin and fragile handle broke off with a pitiful *ch-tink*. He attempted to match her gaze but felt like a mouse under the clawed paw of a large and hungry cat.

When she said nothing, he continued, "This is not the way I want to conduct business, but business is the only reason I am here, Captain. This is merely my insurance. It doesn't even matter if it wasn't you who did it. I have evidence enough to put you under thorough investigation for months. Years even."

He could see her tongue moving over her teeth underneath her scarlet lips. "There's the door, Mr. Blackwood, or if you prefer ..." Rosanne gestured with her hand to the closed window.

Nelson did not relent. "Although I'm sure the view on the way down would be spectacular, I must inform you that I have arranged a compilation of this paperwork to be delivered to the Magistrate of Trade as of tomorrow should I fail to meet my business associates. I need your cooperation on this as much as you need your trade freedom, for what I will ask of you is as far from legal as a man of my occupation should poke my nose into."

Rosanne leaned forward and clasped her hands, her lips a thin line. "It must have taken you weeks to find anything remotely linked to the *Red Queen*. Your bookkeeping is unparalleled for a man of your meagre salary." She chuckled and downed the rest of her coffee, then refilled the cup.

Nelson wiped his damp forehead. How a room as cold as this could get so hot was beyond him. "I would never have made the connection had not the warehouse storing the 'wheat' caught fire and caused a massive explosion. Of course, the locals blamed the fertilizers they used, but I knew better when I heard the news." Rosanne stared at him for half a second before replying.

"I'm more interested in how you managed to find my drinking spots." She crossed her arms.

"I never reveal my sources."

Nodding, she pursed her lips, stared at the floor for half a second, then gave Nelson her full attention. "Fine. Let's talk business. What does a lawyer have to do with the disappearance of a warship?"

Nelson's heart leapt, but he contained himself from babbling like a fool. He used a moment to gather his thoughts and got comfortable in the chair. "The Captain of the *Retribution* is Ernest Blackwood, my father. You can imagine why I take this as a personal offence when the matter is swept aside by the RDA."

"Why do *you* think that is?"

At Nelson's lack of answer, Rosanne reached over and picked out a map from a nearby bookshelf. She unfolded it on the table. It showed the soft arching coastline of Noval, the elongated southernmost inland, and the hundreds of smaller islands dotting the coast. She circled her finger around all the landmass of Noval and the sea between the adjacent landmasses of other colonies.

"This is the area the Royal Defense of Aerospace covers, roughly the same as RNAA. First of all, the *Retribution* is a midsized corvette with reinforced armour plates, three square-rigged masts, eighteen guns, two plasma cannons, and a total of thirty-five people operating the ship at all times. A ship like that doesn't disappear without a trace along this coastline, nor is it outgunned or shot out of the sky without alerting the entire country. The *Retribution* was scheduled to return to Salis after finishing its patrol to Bogvin, but it didn't. Do you know why, Mr. Blackwood?"

Nelson was catching up to what the Captain was getting at, but he didn't understand the details of this long list of information. He shrugged.

"Bogvin has frequently been the ship's destination before returning to base in Salis. Take another look at the map. What do you see outside of Bogvin?" Nelson leaned forward and searched the map for the coastal town in the south.

"A reef?" he pointed to a jagged set of rocks slanting outside of Bogvin.

"A good observation, but not quite. Look further."

His eyes fell on the obscured area marked with long lines in a cloud covering the entire left end of the map. The enormous area was more extensive than Noval and revealed nothing of its contents. "The Grey Veil," Nelson said in defeat.

Rosanne nodded. "That is the reason why you're getting the boot. The Grey Veil isn't only outside the RDA's jurisdiction—it's also out of bounds for sanity's sake. You don't enter that place and expect to live. There are no stars or sun to guide you, and some unknown force messes with all electrical appliances, making navigation impossible. There are places you can sail within it, but only if you know the area like the back of your hand." She rose from her seat and gave the young man the briefest glance of sympathy. "Give up this mad quest you have planned, Mr. Blackwood. It doesn't bode well for anyone to dwell on it." His eyes had locked back on the map.

"Two weeks," Nelson muttered. "I only ask two weeks of your time. I have the funds, and considering the gravity of this mission, I'm willing to be gracious. Please."

"Mr. Blackwood, I'm not sure if you're mad or think you have the biggest fish on the market." Rosanne rubbed her temples. "You're asking me to risk my life, my ship, and my crew chasing ghosts who have long since departed this world. Why would I do that? The man isn't my king, nor is he someone of importance to the trade companies or the military or navy."

"Thirty-five people are gone, including my father!" The chair wobbled when Nelson abruptly stood. "You think I like the thought of all those men's families not knowing what happened to them? Not knowing whether they're alive or if there's a body to bury? Maybe it's not even as hard as you think it is. Maybe the ship will be found within days if you just look! I never asked for the Grey Veil to even be an option. I hoped it wasn't!" He straightened his back, trying with all his might to balance his desperatation with directness. Rosanne folded her arms. "You're still docked for a while," he said and reached for his coffee. "Paperwork is slow like that."

"I can still trade with the small towns." She snatched the

coffee from Nelson, emptying it without breaking her challenging stare.

"I can have your license permanently suspended." He tapped the book.

"Now you're being petty."

"No, desperate. Everyone I spoke to regarded you highly as a captain, a merchant, and a sailor."

She took half a turn with her foot, her lips caught in a stiff line. "How much?"

"Basic supplies, ordinary day salary for your crew with an added hazard bonus. All expenses will be covered for two weeks, but I need you to do the actual planning. I also have one more request, and that is that I join you on the journey."

Rosanne sputtered and quickly regained her composure. "I'm not letting a lawyer aboard my ship to poke about my business."

"I need proof of the *Retribution's* fate, and you can't give that to me without towing the entire ship back to port!" A brief silence was followed by the light tapping of fingers against books. Rosanne looked out the window, presumably to the docks.

"I want to cover all my bases before I decide on anything. This is the thick of the Veil you're talking about, a place no one has ever returned from. What you're asking of me is insane, and you're blinded by your own personal agenda. But considering the lengths you go to get results, you make a good case." She tapped the books. "After that, I'll decide if this will be worth my time. No promises."

As she spoke, Nelson's eyes brimmed with hope, and he was on the verge of tears, though he refused to let them fall.

DESPITE THE EARLY MORNING HOUR, Rosanne was already circling the skyport in a cab. They rolled past long queues of passengers boarding ships travelling south to Bogvin or north to Alteen. Exiting the vehicle, she paid the driver and straightened her waistcoat and faded brown hat. A frown crossed her face when she looked at the building in front of her.

The Magistrate of Trade stood like a jewel at the topmost disk. Inside, tall arches separated dome-shaped rooms with red carpets crisscrossing between them, and gilded stair railings were standard for every official trade building as a sign of its numerous years of booming business. On nearly every wall hung life-like paintings and heavy drapery, both of which could kill a person if they were to fall from their golden hinges. Blue uniforms and golden buttons decorated the guards standing on each side of every door. They carried one-handed swords, but the men were nothing more than glorified door-openers paid to look nice.

In the presence of the Magistrate, Rosanne needed to look decent lest she be escorted out by the same handsome men who couldn't avert their eyes from her when she entered the building. She was met by an aging messenger wearing a knee-cut Prussian blue coat. He asked for her name and state of business with a flat, soulless tone.

"Captain Rosanne Drackenheart of the *MTS Red Queen*, here to see Madam Meinstare."

"One moment, please." The man turned on his heel and disappeared behind a double door. Rosanne tapped her foot against the carpet and adjusted the cotton waistcoat that cinched uncomfortably tight around her chest. She blew into her shirt as the chill weather wasn't enough to keep her cool, but the sudden clang of metal inside her coat made her stop and scan her surroundings for people. Reaching into the inner pocket, she adjusted the dagger's position better suited for a noiseless business meeting. She had no intention of using it and extracted the small tin of mints that she placed in her breast pocket. Weapons of any kind were forbidden in the Magistrate of Trade since the Trade Terror of '96, but she wasn't about to take the chance of going anywhere unarmed on the crime-infested skyport.

The door opened, and the glorified secretary stepped aside. "Madam Meinstare will see you now," he proclaimed in a monotonous voice like he had sold his soul to get through another day. Rosanne paid him little attention and went inside. The door shut behind her. She stopped in front of a wooden desk where a small, grey-haired lady was seated, half-drowned in papers to one side, and neatly stacked signed documents to the other.

"Madam Meinstare." Rosanne announced her presence out of formality.

"Captain Rosanne Drackenheart." The past-retirement bag of bones stabbed a quill into the inkwell and folded her hands, her eyes raising to look at Rosanne. Without moving her gaze from the Captain, Madam Meinstare opened a drawer, plucked out the topmost paper, and smacked it on the table.

"Openly resisting official summons by the Magistrate." Her words were sharp like a thorned whip. "Failed to deliver this month's ledger, again, and subjecting messengers to crude violence. My good creator, Rosanne. You didn't have to put them in the hospital!"

Rosanne wrinkled her nose. "Burly and fractious men don't strike me as messengers. Quit antagonizing me. It's irksome and getting old. I have a dozen witnesses who can back me up that your boys pulled their weapons. I responded with less."

"A dozen drunks who saw nothing but the bottom of their ale-cups, I imagine. How difficult is it to send the paperwork to the magistrate, even if you are as busy as you claim you are? Your license will be suspended if you miss another month!"

"Oh, that." Rosanne's eyes wandered over the desk. "An unexpected complication with the last shipment gave me some problems with the traders, which caused the delay. You could have given me a heads-up like you do any other ship registered to this port." Her eyes locked with the Madam's hawklike gaze. "Instead, you have to make an example of me because you believe it will help refresh the minds of those who don't follow the magistrate's rules to the tiniest footnote. Or is this an attempt to put me in my place? I hear that has been a popular topic among the upper class lately. On that note, shall we discuss my pay while we're at it?"

Madam Meinstare rubbed her temples. "For the love of Terra. This is not about any of that. I simply require that you deliver the ledger on time as per magistrate rules."

"We were a week delayed," Rosanne argued. "Besides, my crew is still unpaid for their last job."

"Nonsense. The Magistrate always pays on time."

Rosanne fished a document from her jerkin and unfolded it so the Madam could see. "You see the title, *Notification of Temporary Suspension*? We were banned from sky-trade for two weeks thanks to this. You assured me everything was fine and that my crew would be paid. Instead, I get this nonsense delivered by a pompous bastard with good running shoes. I didn't have time to stop by before we had to leave." Rosanne's livid tone rivalled the madam's, but Meinstare took the document and skimmed through it.

She turned her attention back to Rosanne, her hard eyes only giving the barest indication of defeat. "It will take at least three days for the ban to be lifted. In the meantime, you and your ship sit tight while I go through the ledger. You will get paid as soon as possible." Her tone held nothing close to an apology.

"And here is your ledger." From her bag, Rosanne retrieved a thick, leather-bound book with gilded letters "MT" on the front. The madam eyed it with a smile.

"No more warnings, Rosanne. I have a business to run, and you have a ship to fly or sail or whatever it is you do with it these days. Dual-trade is a sticky affair and doesn't belong here or anywhere else." Madam Meinstare waved a hand as she poured over the ledger.

"Your protocols for trade are insane. I'm grounded too often from your mistakes, and it's costing me more than I earn."

The madam folded her hands and produced her stiffest smile. "If you're so hellbent on testing my patience, go back to your family business in Salis and leave me in peace. Or you can deliver a formal complaint to Queenstown. I don't understand why you bother trading in Noval if our system displeases you so."

Rosanne scoffed. "Trading outside the Queen's Colonies is against the law, and all your laws are the same no matter which colony I visit. Noval happens to have a more pleasant scenery." She swept a hand at the Madam's panoramic windows.

"Glad you enjoy our humid accommodations then."

"Pleasure doing business with you as always, Madam." Rosanne took off her hat in a sweeping motion.

"The displeasure is all mine, Captain Drackenheart."

***

BY THE TIME Rosanne could relax with a hot bath, it was well into the later hours of the non-setting sun. The time spent in archives in both the Magistrate of Trade and the Royal Defense of Aerospace had drained all will she had left to tend to her long list of pressing matters.

The bathroom door stood slightly ajar, letting steam flow to the nearby window. Two glasses sat beside the tub on a stool, one filled, the other empty, the bottle of dry malt whisky stood on the floor. With numerous pins in her hair to keep everything dry, her short stature allowed her to be nearly submerged if she wished.

Her mind churned with the lawyer's words, and the more she thought of it, the less confident she was of worming herself out of this situation. After discussing further details with Nelson, his promise of a payday worth their time was tempting, but in considering the other factors, such as the legality of the work should they be caught, or worse, the danger to their lives, she wasn't so sure. Nelson had appeared weak, but his resolve made Rosanne question his willingness to doom them all.

A quick set of raps came from the front door. She asked who it was, and a servant stepped inside, trudged towards the bathroom door with soft carpeted footfalls, and lingered outside.

"Pardon the intrusion Captain Drackenheart. Captain Antony DiCroce is here." An unfamiliar servant announced the name with great difficulty; his pronunciation appeared to invoke the visitation privileges of a crow.

"Send him in," Rosanne replied without covering her naked form. The bathroom door creaked, and a cold gust preceded her guest.

"That looks nice." His mixed accent rang pleasantly. The Captain of the *Arctic Pride* smiled at her from the doorway, still wearing his blue, gold-buttoned uniform and black tricorn with a golden pin on the side. His hair was a black mess from the relentless winds plaguing the city, but it added charm to his shaven face. The low ceiling made him appear tall, and Antony had to bend his knees to prevent the doorframe from snagging his hat.

"I didn't get you anything on such short notice. Forgive me."

"You are forgiven when you hop in," Rosanne purred. Antony chuckled and shrugged out of his clothing. It took him less than a minute to snake his way into the tub without sloshing water everywhere, and he greeted her like he always did by kissing her forehead.

"How was your trip?" Rosanne asked and leaned back. Antony hadn't changed much since she saw him last, but it felt like a lifetime ago. His olive skin was paler after spending an extensive amount of time this far north where the sun was weak, and the chill spring weather had made his cheeks rosy. She took in his amber eyes, and the tingle in her abdomen deepened. He adjusted his feet around her and took her hand, massaging it.

"It's been quiet these days. Ships with motors unfit for the weather and stranded on mountaintops, settling disputes among upstarts and nobles who do not obey traffic rules ... the usual." He chuckled and grabbed the whisky bottle and filled the empty glass. He took a swig before settling his eyes on her. "I didn't think you would be in town this week. Did something happen?"

Rolling her eyes, Rosanne tsked. "The magistrate fucked up my permit for sky-trade, so we've been stuck here longer than I wanted. I might have a new job within the next few days. Not trade, but something—interesting."

"I'm intrigued. Anything I should know about?"

Rosanne leaned forward and kissed him on the lips. The way his eyes lit up tempted Rosanne to pull him in but knew that any further activities would invoke the wrath of the cleaning staff were they to spill the entire bath's content out on the floor.

"Not if you want to keep seeing me here, but it is new and exciting. The pay is good, the adventures many. We're talking about two weeks tops. Four days if my instincts prove me right. We'll discuss the details later."

"There's always a spot for you among my crew if you'd like to join the navy again so I can see you every day."

Rosanne paused a moment, then laughed. "Me, flying straight? I am much too comfortable running my own business."

"Fair point. It's what makes you unique, and I wouldn't change that about you for anything. My ship leaves tomorrow, and we'll be stationed south for a while. We return on the seventh of next month."

"Is that so? Then I'll see you again at that time."

"You will. And I'll bring extravagant gifts like the shameless man I am for not showering you with any today."

"Hmm. I'm looking forward to it. I do need something from you, though."

"Oh?"

She chuckled and leaned in.

CHAPTER 3

BIRD EYE'S VIEW

As per Captain Drackenheart's instructions, Nelson packed his warmest clothing in preparation for his crazy journey. Stuffed into a large trunk that had seen better days was a pair of stout leather shoes with fur lining, his thickest winter coat, and more wool sweaters than he hoped necessary. He also packed a spare pair of glasses, rabbit fur gloves, enough books to re-educate himself in maritime laws, and a brand-new journal to document the journey. Perhaps he would uncover things that could work in his favour should he encounter any problems.

Nelson still had few to no expectations of the success of this mission. Flying through the Grey Veil was a fool's errand, and hiring Captain Drackenheart effectively put him under a knife's edge. Still, he needed proof of the *Retribution*'s demise, and he needed people who were hardy enough to face dangers, something he wasn't.

He and Rosanne reached a consensus through a signed contract of his own making, promising that no one's throats were to be cut, and no documents were shipped off to the trade associations until the contract expired in two weeks. If something were to happen to Nelson, the same papers he had threatened Captain Drackenheart with would expose her smuggling, and both she, her ship, and her crew would face a lifetime of penalties. The pay for this mission was good, and his generosity about the estimated time for this mission prompted him to pay a fixed salary instead of daily. From what he gathered, the crew had agreed with extraordinarily little qualms when informed about the pay, and for a moment, he thought he might have been too generous.

Nelson disembarked from the cab on a busy street underneath the skyport and retrieved his battered old trunk secured with cracked leather belts. Rain drizzled in wet mist from the overcast sky, and it being the early morning of dark o'clock, which in Nelson's world meant anything before eight, it was too early and too cold. He was a true westerner at heart, though to the northerners, anything south of Orland was *south* regardless of planetary position.

Despite years living north of the polar circle, the scarce hot weather commonly known as early summer was still not warm enough for him. While he was dressed in wool from top to bottom, the northerners donned summer wear and light shoes. They were so one with nature that they adapted the penguin walk or turned into professional ice skaters when they slipped on ice.

The drizzle turned the wooden docks into a slippery mess, and Nelson's shoes didn't agree with his attempt at the northern walk. He slid down the beams as he dragged the trunk behind him, its wheels squealing above the bustle of nearby activity. He passed numerous ships that were too busy unloading cargo to notice the lost lawyer asking for directions. He knew the *Red Queen* was here somewhere, but the docks were a confusing labyrinth stretching halfway across the island's shoreline. All he had to go on was a note from the captain telling him to locate pier seventeen, one of the busiest and crowded docks that could house up to fifty ships.

He approached idle dockworkers and asked if they had seen the ship but only got polite rejections.

"Might be further down the docks in long-term," a stout sailor said, pointing his calloused finger south. It made sense, considering the *Red Queen* had been docked for a while. He wheeled past another three ships loading timber.

Nelson felt a gentle tug on his sleeve and stared down at a blue-eyed boy of about ten. "Mr. Blackwood?" the lad asked with suspicious wonder.

"Yes?"

"Letter from the dragon lady." The boy handed him a wax-sealed envelope with neat curly writing.

"How did you find me?"

"The dragon lady told me about a paper pusher with a large trunk and lost look on his face."

"Ah, that's ... well ..." Nelson couldn't finish his awkward reply. The boy scurried out of sight. Breaking the seal, Nelson opened the letter. "Third to last dock on southern pier seventeen," he read, then set off again.

Only after his feet had developed blisters did he find the *Red Queen* bobbing in the calm sea where the note had said. Her sails were secured, exposing the multi-decked beauty with men and women crawling on the naked masts strung with ropes. She was a magnificent antique to behold, like a weather-hardened sailor's wife. The *Red Queen* was robust, scarred with pieces of ornaments on the low forecastle, and sported an elongated hull accompanied by the faint waft of fish. She was the deepest wooden red Nelson had ever seen on a boat, darkened by the tar used to waterproof the ship for marine trade. She had a single row of gunports on each side with a few cannons on the main deck and a short bowsprit compared to that of modern aeroships. The crow's nest towered above the rest of the ship, and Nelson did not envy whoever occupied it. He noticed a garish red flag with a centred yellow dragon holding an axe at the fore-top masthead fluttering in the scarce winds, a personal design of the captain's, no doubt. The ensign on the sterncastle waved the national flag of Noval in red, white and blue.

"Mr. Blackwood! Glad you could join us," the red-haired

captain hollered from the quarterdeck, her back straight as an arrow and gloved hand raised.

In boarding the ship, one of the trunk's wheels made an escape into the waters below, and Nelson dragged the trunk with difficulty. The captain met him on the main deck with her hands folded behind her back.

"Another thirty minutes, and we would have left without you." Her smirk sent shivers through his back, but he knew this was one of the captain's many faces showing her displeasure. Nelson coughed and balanced his trunk, assuring himself the captain kept her icy stare reserved for later times when he was unaware. He knew what his presence aboard the ship meant for her and the crew, and the crew's unfiltered baleful stares wouldn't shake his decision, not now or during the voyage.

"Permission to come aboard the ship, Captain?" he opened the conversation as politely as he could in a barely audible tone and received a slap on his shoulder.

"Permission granted!" Rosanne's small hand was surprisingly strong and Nelson, again, had to support himself on the railing to keep from falling over. "Everything is as it should be. Crew, supplies, charts, and the lot are all taken care of. Ever been on a marine ship before?" Rosanne's voice bombarded the coffee-deprived lawyer, and her smile grew wider for every moment of his slow response. She wore a wool shirt, faded blue waistcoat, sealskin jacket, and thick trousers fit for rainy weather and chill northern winds. Her boots were heeled but not tall, making the woman half a head shorter than him, yet still, Nelson shrunk under her impressive radiance. It was only under the direct shine of the sun that he noticed her hair was in fact dark brown with a hint of red, a vanity dye he hadn't expected from the same woman who threatened to defenestrate him days prior.

"Does that one count?" Nelson pointed to a Drakkar replica snaking its way down the bay where the waters were calm. Two rows of aristocratic tourists rowed like their lives depended on it by the words of a hollering guide dressed in furs and leather at the longship's bow. The square red sail depicting a snake fluttered in the weak winds.

"The *Long Worm* is a ship, though of archaic design. It'll do. Well then. As our dearly beloved guest, let me introduce you to the crew. Gather around!" Rosanne called, and the crew dropped whatever they were doing and came to stand in front of her without fuss.

Nelson had heard terrifying stories of pirates in his youth, retold in the most fearsome tone by his father and anxious mother who, on life and death, told him to steer clear of any who fit the description of scar-faced, peg-legged, and/or gold-toothed cutthroats. This crew was none of those things but a collection of ordinary people. Most were slender or fit for their frame, except for a round-bellied man with a singular pale grey eye. The crew of the *Red Queen* were slaves to none other than the ship and their salary and didn't appear to have fought many terrible battles in their days at sea and sky. Their uniforms were personalized but well insulated for the frequent shift in weather, and they still had their limbs where they should be.

Some were locals judging by their broad faces, short stature, and pale skin. Others were tall and wiry, heavyset and broad, small and limber, with brown eyes, green eyes, or even gold, and hair blond, dark as raven wings, or red like a sunset. Most of the crew appeared young to middle-aged with weather-beaten faces and a clear distaste for lawyers given their expressions. A mountain of a man had the darkest skin Nelson had ever laid eyes on this far north, his stiff, unforgiving eyes scrutinizing him. A tall, wiry man with equally dark skin stood next to him, relaxed and smiling in stark contrast.

Nelson thought he was looking at the perfect describer's dictionary in human form given the range of skin tones and features in front of him. People from the southern colonies shied away from the midnight sun cities that could only be found this far north, as the sun's rays were weak and left melanistic skin lethargic even in the summer. He was even more surprised to see easterners among the crew, considering the *Red Queen* mostly operated in Noval, a colony notoriously known for little sunlight, strong winds, and bone-chilling winter seasons. Then again, the north stretched around the entire world, and Nelson concluded that he could only blame his ignorance after spending too much time in an office staring at paper rather than people.

A young, flaxen woman with a tool belt slung on her hips smiled at him. Others looked like they'd rather sulk over a strong drink.

"Gentlemen and gentlewomen, this is Mr. Nelson Blackwood, our employer. Mr. Blackwood, this is the noble crew serving the *Red Queen*, and I won't bother naming them all for you. There will be plenty of time for such formalities later. My stout lieutenant, Mr. Farand Duplànte here" she motioned a hand to the large man "will kick your sorry arse off my ship should he catch you sneaking about places you shouldn't, so bear it no ill will if you do get a well-deserved drowning for your curiosity. Speaking of cats, has anyone accounted for Senior Petty Officer Ratcatcher?"

"Asleep in the pantry, ma'am," the round-bellied man answered heartily.

"Very well. If everyone is accounted for, hoist our colours and prepare for launch. Dismissed." And that was that. Nelson's brief study of the lieutenant revealed broad shoulders under a crisp jacket and tightly coiled hair trimmed close to the scalp, suiting his militant and grim face. He didn't even get to properly greet Farand before the tall man's booming voice called the order to unfurl the aether sails, and he whisked himself away to the quarterdeck. A small number of topmen climbed the ratlines faster than Nelson could make them out, and despite the wet ropes, their shoes held firm grips. Ropes were loosened and tightened, flags swapped, and shouts came from all over the ship, but the general mayhem was a highly coordinated beehive. Rosanne spun Nelson around by the shoulders and gave him her most intense stare.

"Let me give you a piece of advice or an official warning if you like: you are aboard my ship only because my crew and I allow it. At all times, you will be under the careful watch of everyone here and even more closely regarded by Mr. Duplànte. And if you were to poke your nose into something you shouldn't and plan to use that against us, let me remind you that we are both under oath to keep every piece of business strictly aboard this vessel and not anywhere else. Have I made myself abundantly clear, Mr. Blackwood?"

"Yes, of course, ma'am." Nelson nodded hurriedly.

"Well then. Right this way to your guest quarters, and when you're done, I suggest you join the rest of us. Oh, and do secure your belongings. Rough weather tends to toss all loose items around for sport." Rosanne pointed to a door leading to the back of the ship and returned to the wheel where she picked up an intercom. Nelson didn't know why he was surprised to see electrical devices by the wheel, but he quickly thought better of it. The technology wasn't altogether unfamiliar to him, but he had never been on a hybrid ship before. It was far more wood and rope than he was used to compared to the standard aeroships made of metal and auto-furling sails.

On his way past the mainmast, he observed two young men in a heated argument pointing to the crow's nest.

A tall, lean woman with short-cropped hair pushed between them, barking in a low voice. "What's this all about then? You lads causing a scene?"

"Olivier always takes first crow! I haven't tried for crow in any port cities because of that, and my eyes are faultless. I can see just as well over these mountains," a stocky brown-haired youth complained.

Olivier scoffed and rolled his eyes. "Because I got excellent hearing and sight," he countered with a pronounced lisp bordering on illegible. He towered over the other two with his tall and wiry frame skillfully hidden underneath layers of clothing to make him seem broader than he was.

Narrowing his eyes, the other seaman stared at Olivier's smug expression. "Dalia, what did he say?"

"Hearing and sight, Norman. You should know it by now. Settle for second crow and get to your other duties. This journey is different than our usual run, so we need you here." The woman ruffled the young man's mop of brown hair and shoved him aside, returning to her post by the mainmast. Olivier climbed into the crow's nest, took out his spyglass and got comfortable. Without the watchful gaze of Senior Watch Captain Dalia, he sent Norman a rude gesture which the youth returned with vigour. Nelson observed this bizarre exchange of flipped birds and simulated throat cutting with strained reservation, yet the others who noticed simply snickered at the commotion.

The guest cabin was small and sparse. Nails protruded from every piece of furniture like they were subjected to a brutal crucifixion. A small window at starboard faced the docks outside. Nelson glanced out to see a small number of children gathering at the foot of the dock, anticipation glowing in their eyes. He secured his trunk underneath the bed, a square with a thin mattress and flimsy covers that didn't qualify as a duvet. He returned to the deck.

Captain Drackenheart spared him half a glance as he approached.

"I hope you are well prepared with shoes and clothing as the high winds can make the ride quite unpleasant," she said without glancing up from the instrument panels on each side of the wheel. While most aeroships had adapted the modern smaller wheel to assist with the complex navigation of sailing the sky versus the ocean, the *Red Queen* still had her original double-wheel, an eight-pegged circle of wood in dire need of new lacquer. It stood on a dynamic wooden block that could tilt back and forth. Two table-like slanted panels stood on each side displaying numerous dials: a compass, the local time, topographical map, and altitude meter, among other things Nelson couldn't recognize. Levers jutted from the floor, and he could only guess what they were for.

"Why are there so many children at the docks?" Nelson motioned to the growing crowd of pre-adolescent youth.

"What? Oh, they are here for the launch. It amuses them. Now excuse me." She turned her back on Nelson and grabbed the intercom. "Mr. Higgs, de-activate the anti-grav engine." She released the button on the side and waited. A shudder resonated from the hull. Nelson grabbed onto the ledge and peered over the side. The waterline shied from the ship's hull as an invisible field formed around it. At the captain's slightest tilt of the wheel, the ship responded by rising from the waterline, the woodwork groaning and dripping with brine. Children by the docks cheered and hopped in delight. Several workers viewed the spectacle, pausing at their posts to catch a glimpse of the pre-flight preparations.

"Cleared!" Watch Captain Dalia hollered from the main deck when the ship was a good ten meters from the waterline.

"Release the thruster ports," Rosanne ordered over the intercom. A mechanical whirring resonated from below the sterncastle, where two trapezoid covers came apart, flipped, and disappeared into their respective sides to be stored within the ship. Two large panels, each with six circular metallic depressions and one triangular at the bottom, contained blackened metallic pins.

"Higgs, engine." Rosanne pushed a few buttons and checked the displays as soon as a small bulb on the panel lit green. Fueled by the thruster engine's power output taken from the aether sails, their hexagonal-patterned grid shone with waves of energy barely visible to the naked eye and brought to life by a reinforced electric conducting fabric.

A clang of metal against the starboard had Rosanne leaning over the rail. She let out a stream of colourful curses. "Which idiot lowered the anchor at port? Fix it!"

Landman Iban hurried across the deck and pulled a lever that retracted the anchor from its watery deep in a series of low clangs. Nelson caught two young men resting by the forecastle stairs as they bumped fists, drawing Iban's sour expression in their direction. Dalia smacked the two men in the back of their collective heads, but it didn't deter their conspiratorial grins. Had the lowered anchor been a prank?

"All clear?" Captain Drackenheart demanded. She received confirmation in the form of 'Yes, ma'am!' from the forecastle to the stern. Higgs confirmed on the intercom that all was clear in the engine department, and Rosanne turned the dial of the short-range intercom to switch the channel.

"Tower, this is the *MTS Red Queen* requesting clearance for takeoff from marine pier seventeen, heading south."

"We receive, *MTS Red Queen*. The sky is clear. Stay below half altitude until Vangam," the radio buzzed.

"Half altitude?" Nelson echoed.

A middle-aged man with salt and pepper hair accompanied by glasses and a mustache came to stand next to Nelson. "Half of the recommended flying altitude to stay clear of oncoming traffic. We have free skies through Vikran, which is the bottleneck," the man replied. "Carson Lyle, Master Gunner, at your service." The man stuck out his hand, and Nelson shook it.

"Nelson Blackwood, lawyer at Parkson & Blackwood."

The master gunner's eyes crinkled. "Keep your hands on the railing until you're used to the motion of the ship. Then, your sky legs will develop fast enough. And come morning, you will feel pain in muscles you didn't know you had." Nelson didn't reply to the man's odd advice but diligently kept his hands within grabbing distance of the rail.

Rosanne put on her shabby hat and tugged the goggles around her neck, securing the straps. Then she fitted her gloves, pushed the safety lock on the tallest lever, and brought the entire rod forward. She stepped her shoes into two depressions on the floor, semi-locking them in place at a wide stance, only to step out of them again. She tested the wheel by giving it a few turns before bringing the *Red Queen* around in a slow pirouette. The ship ascended enough to stay clear of the towering masts from surrounding ships. From the hull, thruster ports hissed to life and brought gentle movements to the ship.

A loud whistle brought Nelson's attention to the main deck where someone waved a red flag, and for a moment, he was alarmed at its implications. By the docks, people waved their goodbyes and kids jumped excitedly as they anticipated a kick-off. Instead, Captain Drackenheart brought the lever forward and eased the ship into a gentle thrust, the back panels brimming with stiff blue flames. The *Red Queen* lurched, increased speed, then climbed. The docks rapidly shrunk as the ship sped by, and to Nelson's surprise, his hat was still on his head.

"Pardon my ignorance, Mr. Lyle, but why isn't the surface of the ship more ... windy?"

Lyle chuckled. "That would be the atmos. It maintains air pressure and stability aboard the ship. Think of it as a protective bubble, much like the air which surrounds our world. We can fly higher with atmos, but not every ship can afford the proper models for higher altitudes. They're absurdly costly. A ship's engine is only as good as its atmos. Fly too fast, and the crew might suffocate at high altitudes." Nelson bobbed his head, but the concept seemed strange and alien.

Mr. Lyle pointed to people's sudden use of goggles. "And those are for speedy voyages when the atmos cannot keep up."

"Can I assume passenger ships have atmos' that are less than ideal? I always have to secure my hat whenever I travel to Salis," Nelson asked.

"Perhaps." The older man gave him a conspiratorial wink.

The *Red Queen* flew just below the peaks of the surrounding mountains until they closed in on the bay past Vikran, a small gap between the islands where the waters from the sea pressed and flooded around a smaller central island every tide. The dramatic spurs of Copper Mountain stood on their left, another set of frosted tops to the right. In the distance, Vangam was nothing but a small plateau, a geographical reference to where the sky trade routes split two ways, one south and one north-west toward the open sea. The fjords were broad and deep, with towns resting in the crevices of these magnificent hunks of rock. When the land flattened out with the occasional mountain, the *Red Queen* climbed altitude. Nelson peered over the railing; the ships sailing the waters became ant-sized and sluggish. He saw other aeroships in the distance, turning southeast to follow a different route.

Mr. Lyle pointed to the large passenger ships and their enormous sails. "Commercial routes are slow and crowded because they primarily rely on the winds to fly."

Nelson nodded, fascinated by all the things he observed, mostly the view, then at the bustling topmen having another go at the rigging.

Captain Drackenheart appeared behind Nelson. "I see you've met my master gunner, Mr. Lyle." Lyle tipped his hat to her. "Can I still rely on you to shoot Mr. Blackwood at one thousand yards?" Her prim and playful tone didn't alleviate the subtle threat she used as constant reminders of who was in charge.

Mr. Lyle nodded. "Indeed you can, ma'am."

"Good. How's the altitude treating you, Mr. Blackwood?"

Nelson noticed the steep climb of the learning curve, but if he didn't acquaint himself with the crew and the captain's banter, this journey would be a long, arduous affair. "Your good-humoured threats hit me right in the heart, Captain. My sky legs will develop shortly."

Again, Rosanne flashed her telltale smirk at Nelson's quick response. "I must pull your leg now and then. Keeps your mind sharp. Speaking of, be kind and join me. I have some matters to discuss with you. Mr. Duplànte, please take the wheel until Salis."

The large man nodded, but his thoughts were hidden behind his stone visage. His eyes followed Nelson as he walked with the captain across the quarterdeck to her cabin.

Then again, Nelson felt many eyes locked on him, including the hawkish stare of the master gunner.

THE CAPTAIN'S cabin often served as meeting quarters for more delicate business and easily fit ten people. The writing desk was large and ornate, and everything on it was nailed down or secured with paperweights. A tall bookcase stood against the far wall, filled with leather tomes, charts, and papers. Rosanne glanced at the markings of each tube in search of the right one, popped the cork and unfolded its content on the desk. She secured the map with glass paperweights.

"I didn't have time to discuss this matter with you, but the earlier we left Valo, the better. Please have a seat." She motioned to the chair opposite the desk, and Nelson sat as suggested. "I borrowed these from the RDA. With permission, of course, in case you wondered. I've looked over the paperwork you sent me about the *Retribution,* and I'll say this while we're early on: this will not be easy."

"Because of the vague nature behind the ship's disappearance?" Nelson voiced, scrunching his brows together.

Rosanne bobbed her head. "Not only that. We don't even know at which port the *Retribution* last docked. All the information we have is still wherever the ship went *to,* as the RDA never requested the paperwork after the ship fell off the planet. Either way, this is the charted route the ship was supposed to take. You have a sharp eye for discrepancies. Tell me what you see."

Nelson stood from his chair and leaned over the map, tracing the *Retribution's* plotted route from Salis to the inland. The route meandered through a complex array of mountains all the way south to Orland and then visited the innermost fjords until it looped back to St. Gerangra to follow the coastline back to Salis.

"This isn't the usual route, is it?"

"I couldn't find any official documents as to why the *Retribution* was to take this arduous path, but I have my guesses. The RDA claims another ship took over the *Retribution's* patrol route from the north, a larger ship. If I were to guess why this sudden change was done, I'd say the *Retribution* was hunting pirates."

"Pirates? Surely, you're joking." Nelson said, unsure whether this was again the captain pulling his leg. However, her firm expression pointed to it being true.

"The RDA updates the trade routes regularly to keep the traffic flowing and the insurance companies happy. I haven't heard of much pirate activity in the inland for quite some time. This whole affair raises more red flags than it should." She rolled the map and stuffed it back into its tube. Nelson's eyes followed Rosanne to the window, where she peered through the curtains to the black waters. "Regardless of their reasonings, we have to stop by the port in Salis to confirm the route. We should be there in less than two hours if I consider my lieutenant's reckless flying."

Rosanne's final remark seemingly went unheard as Nelson eyed the map carefully. "So Salis first. Then we trace the entire route? Won't that take weeks?"

Rosanne shook her head. "We travel to Orland after Salis. If the *Retribution* restocked there, we go to the next destination, and so on. But if I'm right, the ship disappeared after its last planned stop in St. Gerangra, and that is probably why the RDA never issued a search party. A warship doesn't crash or land anywhere in this land without someone noticing it."

"But if you're certain it stopped by St. Gerangra, why bother going anywhere else first?"

"Paperwork and formalities, mostly. Orland is the knot of west Noval and has the largest official trade done in Noval and surrounding countries. Knowing why the *Retribution* was forced to fly this route is for our safety. You gave us ample time to locate the ship, so I use that time wisely to prepare ourselves."

Nelson found himself nodding. The captain had concocted such a thorough yet simple plan on such short notice, and hearing it brought ease to his discomfort. Rosanne leaned back in her seat. "Now then. With that business concluded, how about you familiarize yourself with the ship and its customs before anything else? The crew is dying to meet you properly."

Again, her smile sent shivers through Nelson, and he gulped.

Chapter 4

Be a Potato, Mr. Blackwood

Nelson guessed it was Rosanne's boundless experience travelling the northern coast of Noval made her calculation of the *Red Queen's* arrival at Salis precise. From a tight fit between the coastal mountains, the geography formed a wall slanting southward in the ocean with jagged snow-crested tops for miles. At the end of the wall across the bay, Salis lay on a peninsula facing the open sea. Its exposure to stiff winds made the skyport a bumpy docking station and an often ugly affair.

The *Red Queen* parked at the lowest disk by the wide-spaced docks, and Captain Drackenheart wheeled herself to the RDA's office at the topmost disk. Thanks to a letter from a certain captain of the *Arctic Pride*, Rosanne had access to exclusive information and intended to exploit her connections to the fullest.

Nelson wrung his hat by the gangplank, having watched the docks for the red-haired captain for the better part of the. He turned sharply at hearing Rosanne's brisk walk post-exiting the cab, but her expression was anything but delighted. Her eyebrows were close together, forming the deep wrinkle which scarred her face with irritation.

"Did you find any information pertaining to our mission?" he asked hopefully. Rosanne waved a bundle of documents; a wry smile replaced all vigour.

"Our next stop is Orland. I hope you weren't planning on having tea by the parlour as we're leaving immediately."

She whisked past him without another word, evidently having urgent business elsewhere. Nelson tracked her to the quarterdeck where Mr. Duplànte received the clearance for takeoff. The large man nodded and picked up the intercom, sending orders throughout the ship. Nelson's feeble attempts to catch Rosanne's attention failed as she blew past him yet again. Realizing that this wasn't going anywhere, he leaned on the stern railing, watching the distant ships on the waters. At the fringes of the main docks of a factory refinery, he saw numerous broad-hulled ships, called fluyts, buzzing with human activity.

D. Salis Co. said the red-painted writing on the factory wall. There were many such refineries dotting the coastline, as salt was this town's primary business. Captain Drackenheart's haste to leave port had Nelson wondering where the fire burned. He looked to the captain, who was busy talking with her senior officers.

The *Red Queen* drifted from the dock, guided by the hull's numerous thruster ports. Making subtle corrections, Mr. Duplànte navigated the ship past oncoming traffic and elicited unnecessary honks from disgruntled commuters.

"Mr. Blackwood." Rosanne said. Her firm voice startled Nelson yet again. "We have a long journey ahead, and we will not reach Orland until late tomorrow morning." Her placid face revealed little of her thoughts as if she adopted the expression directly from Mr. Duplànte himself.

"Yes, of course." Nelson straightened himself as he instinctively shrunk before the half-a-head-shorter woman. "But may I inquire why we're in such a hurry? We got here only an hour ago."

"I confirmed the *Retribution* was here as scheduled before it sailed south. I needn't know anything else." She turned to leave.

"While I have your attention, Captain ..." He pointed to the broad-hulled ship disembarking the refinery of *D. Salis Co.* "That's a saltship, isn't it? I've never seen one in Valo."

Her eyes barely glanced at the vessel. "And you wouldn't. Those ships are built for deep waters from the open sea, something the northern fjords do not offer."

"How do they work? I thought importing salt was cheaper."

Rosanne halted her return to duties once more, giving only the slightest indication of a sigh before she turned to the lawyer and leaned on the rail. "Salis has perfected their ships for salt uptake. The ships pump ocean water into a large boiler room, hence the broad hull. The brine undergoes a boiling process which filters the water and leaves only salt crystals. We do something similar aboard this ship but on a smaller scale."

Nelson nodded in fascination. "That saves you a lot in fresh-water wares and storage, no?"

"It does." Rosanne watched the largest saltship sail south for its daily pick-up and averted her eyes to the bustle of the topmen shouting their displeasure as one of the sails was stuck partly unfurled. A sour-faced topman was called to the scene, and he wrestled with the rope which prevented the sail from opening properly, assisted by Norman, the young man Nelson had seen arguing with the current crow.

"You, eh ... brought that knowledge with you from the Drack-enheart Salt business, did you not?"

The question made Rosanne snap her attention to the lawyer, her face a blank mask. "Hard to hide that part when my name is the same. Yes, it's my mother's business. Has been for years."

"Wouldn't that make you an heir?" he prodded.

"With all due respect, Mr. Blackwood, being a lawyer does not permit you to snoop about my family history and business. The *Red Queen* is my heritage and nothing else. Ambushing me in such a manner does not suit your demeanour or reputation."

Nelson deflated under her glaring smile. "My apologies. Consider my curiosity quenched."

"Here's something else for your curiosity then." She thrust

the documents from the RDA at his chest. He staggered and grabbed the yellow-faded sheets before they flew out of his fumbling grasp. The loud clack of her heels resonated on the deck, and it turned more than a few heads as she returned to the quarterdeck. Nelson corrected his glasses, scanning the documents. They were stamped in red on the covers, which immediately had him stuffing them under his jacket and whisking himself to his sleeping quarters where he could study them in peace. Taking the captain's hurried departure, she had no need to know its contents, only their next destination, or had reviewed them before handing it over.

He pushed the thought aside as he sat down in bed. He read each document carefully. The sheets revealed few details about the *Retribution's* official business, which made him think that his father had worked off the books or the correct documents were of higher military classification. Whatever the case might be, he wouldn't find any answers combing through these curly letters, and it only served to drive his thirst for the truth.

THE *RED QUEEN* descended through the low-hanging clouds towards the inland where the winds blew gentler. The aether sails' incessant flapping ceased as the ship came into a northern gale. The ship lurched as she picked up speed. Nelson lumbered about the deck, dodging crew who now seemed more focused on holding their footing than working.

The hum of the sails drew Nelson's attention to the shimmering octagonal pattern. Lights running down the masts glowed brighter as the sun touched the sails, now brimming with energy. Nelson traced conduits down the side of the mainmast, which connected every aether sail into one pipe that led below deck. Aside from metal plating reinforcing the masts at even intervals, the electrical work, the wheel, and the thruster panel below the sterncastle, the *Red Queen* held true to her original state as a waterborne galleon. The ship was older than anti-gravity technology itself, which Nelson had known his entire life. Seeing such a bizarre mix of marine and aero-technology made him appreciate the marvel that was the *Red Queen*. How different this journey would have been if the Queen's Colonies hadn't discovered the precious minerals now lining the hull of every aeroship.

———

CAPTAIN DRACKENHEART TURNED the wheel gently, guiding the ship in a long arch along the wind currents. She squinted against the rays as she fit the goggles over her eyes and fixed the hat firmly in place. They broke through the clouds to reveal an icy plateau with a mountain near-hidden by the glaciers snaking their way around it. The clear ice swallowed the sun's rays in a droopy mirror of black.

"Weather is clearing southward, Captain," Olivier spoke from the intercom. With the conditions pristine for flying, Rosanne set the ship's thruster to cruise control with a simple click of an extra lever. The *Red Queen* flew at a steady speed, following a jet wind flowing south. Shaking off the stiffness in her limbs, Rosanne degloved her hands, massaging her palms.

"Mr. Lyle," she called to the slender man idling by the sterncastle. Locking the wheel in place, she scanned their surroundings for Mr. Blackwood's elephant ears and lowered her voice. "I assume you have backup?"

The man nodded curtly. "Yes, ma'am. One firearm for every second man, sharp utensils for every man. My rifle is polished, and the scope is clear."

"Good. I need you and your team to be alert throughout this journey, especially after we hit Orland. Have two armed sentries by the port and starboard gun ports—no one on the top. I don't want to alert anyone to the fact that we're armed to our teeth. Is the crew trained for this?"

"They are, ma'am. Drilled three times a day, with target practice on the rink and on the fjord. I must say these models are remarkable. Might I ask what we're hunting?"

"Not sure if we're hunting or being hunted once we stick our heads out."

Mr. Lyle's thin lips stretched. "Sounds to me we're dealing with less than agreeable people."

"We might. Inform your team and prepare the shifts."

"One thing, captain, how closely should we keep tabs on a certain nosy guest of ours?" Lyle nodded to Nelson at the forecastle. Given his slack-jawed expression, Nelson was marvelling at the celerity of the topmen conducting their business securing the foremast rigging.

"*Very* close, but not to the point where it's absurd. What he sees aboard this ship stays here, and if he needs a reminder … well. I'll leave that to the crew to put him in place. Unless it's Creedy."

Lyle's mustache rose along with his smile. "If I may, Captain," he began as Rosanne set for the wheel. She stopped. "Mr. Blackwood doesn't seem like much, but the fact that he's aboard this ship tells me he's not someone to trifle with. The pay is good, but still. What did he do to make you agree to this madness? Does the man not fear for his safety?"

Rosanne stared at him in her periphery. Her lip twitched. "A necessary precaution, Mr. Lyle. That will be all."

IN THE CAPTAIN'S CABIN, Rosanne regarded her bookshelves with disdain and frustration. The writing desk was littered with charts jabbed with pencil marks all along the coast of Noval, a long list of names, and a heap of crumpled paper that failed to make it to the bin. With little to no information about what to expect as the RDA in Salis had been beyond useless regarding their current mission, the *Red Queen* was blind.

Having Lyle and his team armed gave Rosanne some comfort, but not much. The papers Blackwood produced pooled into the collective sense of waste of time as they held no hints as to the *Retribution's* mission and whereabouts. After their dead end in Salis, Rosanne hoped to find out more in Orland as it had the largest archive on ship trade and military vessels operating on this side of the colonies. Rosanne scanned the neat documents defiled by her notes.

Compared to the *Retribution,* her merchant ship was twice the tonnage with only a third of the firepower. Rosanne had her fair share of run-ins with greedy buccaneers along the inland trade routes before the RDA tightened their patrols, and more often than not she left kindle for the locals to scavenge from the wreckages of fallen ships. Sending a mid-sized warship seemed redundant. Perhaps the *Retribution* was caught in one of the many winter storms raging along the coastline of Noval, or it simply crashed among the uninhabited mountains and woodlands. If so, how come there had been no reports, and why did the RDA bury the matter altogether? The crew trusted that she knew where to go and what to do, and Nelson paid her to do so, but Rosanne wasn't sure of anything. She had too little to go on. Her best bet was that she would know more once they reached Orland.

"Come in," Rosanne replied to the knock on her door. Farand walked in. The cabin ceiling was one of the few places where the large man didn't have to duck. He sat down in a chair. Pacing around the desk, Rosanne wore an expression caught between epiphany and uncertainty, and he kept quiet until she finally spoke again.

"You've sailed the Grey Veil longer than I have, Farand. What do you make of this business?"

The lieutenant wrinkled his flat nose. "As our drillmaster always taught in the academy: be prepared for any conceivable situation with whatever means you and the ship you board possess. Regarding the Veil, there isn't much you can prepare for that you haven't already done." His deep voice drowned out the murmur of the ship's thruster panels. "Perhaps this is one of those times where your skills will be tested to their limit."

She rubbed the frown off her forehead. "In what sense?"

Farand spread his hands out to the sides. "You have a ship to steer, a crew to protect, a dangerous place to sail, possibly armed enemies or other non-disclosed monsters lurking inside your skull, and a shrewd lawyer sitting on all of our futures. The stakes have never been this high. However, your pride will outshine your fear of failure and wit to your ignorance. Weather's been worse."

Stabbing a finger at the charts, her intense stare pierced into his calm brown eyes. "I don't like going in there blind. We have charted most of the north end of that damned place, but never anywhere else. There's nothing there, nothing at all. Just fog and endless paranoia!" Throwing her hands in the air, she huffed. "In all your years in the sky, did you ever come close to sailing in the thick of the Veil?"

Farand scowled. "Only once. I was a petty officer when thieves still plagued the trade routes. We had come south from Gernera, going straight to Alteen with a shipment of grains. Naturally, we followed the coastline and were surprised by pirates. They chased us into the Grey Veil. We had no firepower of significance, and the captain locked the ship in place, fog surrounding us on all sides. We couldn't climb for the fog reaches so high into the sky our atmos couldn't keep up. We were there for days, unable to move, for we saw no landmark, no sun, no stars to guide us. Finally, on the third day, the fog retreated, and we somehow found ourselves at the outskirts of the Veil. We were lucky, Captain. That's all."

Rosanne groaned and rubbed her face. "Even with the new navigation technology, we'd still go in blind. The only way to ensure we can make it out is to do a square sweep. Have Hwang and Creedy track the winds. You chart our estimated course. Engineering will know the exact speed as a backup if wind directions fail. What do you think?"

Farand's slow, elaborate nod was a stark contrast to the captain's dramatic anguish. "If the winds are in our favour that would be our best bet. I would have all able-bodied sailors on watch and have them compare notes to make sure we stay on target. I'd say an hour in, an hour south, and then back should be safe for starters."

Rosanne chewed her lip at Farand's words. "I agree. I just hope we don't have to go in there at all. I haven't found evidence that suggests otherwise. The crew trusts me to serve them a payday, and I cannot do that if we're trapped inside that damned place. Regarding a certain shrewd lawyer, let's give him something to keep him occupied." Rosanne scrunched her eyebrows together, then turned her stiff lips to a half-smile. "Who's been doing our bookkeeping lately?"

Farand tilted his head in the general direction of Salis. "That would be Martelle, but he chose to sit this one out due to paternity leave."

"Good. Then I know the perfect job for that paper-pusher."

"You want a law-abiding lawyer to straighten our books for us? Captain, you are too cruel." He chuckled and rubbed his cheek.

"It's what Mr. Blackwood earned for putting us through this pain. On the plus side, he can't use our new books as leverage without incriminating himself."

"The contract with the lawyer was a clever move, giving both sides of this business leverage against the other. Have heart, Captain. Beyond the clouds, the sky is always blue." Rosanne crossed her arms as she stared out the window where the weather was as fine as it got.

NELSON WENT DOWN the stairs on the main deck, continued down the corridors, and immediately came into the galley. It was small and snug, tables tight up to each other but large enough to seat everyone for meals. A smoky waft snaked from steaming cauldrons further in. Although Nelson was famished, he was more embroiled in familiarizing himself with the ship's intimate quarters and preventing his lunch from reappearing in a colourful mess.

"Get your arse out of me galley. Come round the back of six for dinner, Mr. Blackwood." The round-bellied man with the funny walk emerged from the kitchen, staring at Nelson through heavy eyelids. He leaned against a support beam with his arms crossed. His accent was thick like a hammer on each word and not local to northern Noval, but southern with rolling r's.

"Pardon me. I was looking around, getting the lay of the land and such. Well, lay of the ship," Nelson replied and shifted his gaze around the room in case anyone else was to jump out and give him a scolding.

The cook threw his arms in a dramatic sweep. "Bah! Just pulling your ears, boy. Everyone is welcome here. But don't steal me potatoes. If you're looking for work, there is plenty to do around the ship. I don't need any. I'm in good company of Senior Petty Officer Ratcatcher here." A lean, grey-striped cat skulked from the pantry and butted his head against the cook's leg. "I am Kurt Hammond, but everyone calls me Ham for short. This here is Fluffypaws." The tomcat swished his tail upon hearing his name and sat down, staring at Nelson with judging green eyes.

"He doesn't bite, but don't disturb him when he's sleeping. He'll be giving you *the look* for the rest of your days." Hammond ran his calloused hand through his thinning hair, and his low ponytail shone in the light.

Nelson let the cat sniff his hand before patting his head. "I'll keep that in mind. Why does the cat have a rank?"

Hammond looked at him oddly. "Are you daft, boy? Little pests have been the greatest enemy to cargo throughout trade history. Most vessels keep a cat or a small dog to deal with rats and stray birds pecking off our supplies. You'll never see a big rat aboard this ship, not as long as Officer Ratcatcher is on duty. Finest cat this ship's ever had." The cat blinked at Hammond.

Farand lumbered down the stairs, stopping low at the frame and the ceiling. "There you are, Mr. Blackwood." The man stood like a giant in front of Nelson, and the lawyer had to take a step back to take him all in.

"Mr. Duplànte, sir. Welcome!" Hammond greeted. "I was just warning this young landlubber here not to steal me potatoes." Farand turned his frame, nodding to the cook.

"Is that so? Potatoes have so many interesting uses. Would be a shame if you didn't put your skills to paper. What do you say?" The way Farand phrased himself, his lumbering demeanour, and only the slightest hint of a smile on his dark face, had Nelson wondering whether he wasn't in too deep of trouble already as it was. In a moment of realization, he concluded that poking about Rosanne's family history was the direct cause of this sudden job assignment.

"Eh?" Nelson uttered, perplexed.

"Be a potato, Mr. Blackwood. I have a job for you."

CHAPTER 5

A DECK OF CARDS

The galley was packed with the crew, and their chatter rose to a deafening volume. A sweet and spicy highland scent misted under the ceiling, accompanied by a good deal of sweaty armpits. The soup was a veggie-broth propped with chunks of potatoes, carrots, cabbage, swede, leek, and ... was that sliced sausage? Regardless of the soup's contents, it was better than what Nelson's cook produced, and he immediately decided to hire a new one upon his return.

Most of the crew avoided Nelson's table. He didn't blame them, considering he was an outsider who held their careers as leverage. Drackenheart and Duplànte were seated with the senior officers for business reasons.

A bowl clunked down at the table opposite his seat. The flaxen woman who had smiled at him earlier sat down. She looked younger than him, but Nelson couldn't be sure under the dim bulb lights that hung from the ceiling. Her fair skin was spotted with soot and grime, yet it added charm to her round freckled face and broad smile.

"Hi there! Ida Simonsen, second engineer," she greeted. Another two bowls clanged in disharmony against the crude wooden table, and a muscled, elderly gentleman with a thick beard and an equally fit but younger man about Nelson's age sat on each side of the lawyer. Nelson wiggled for elbow room, but there was none to be had.

"Artemis Higgs, chief engineer and Ida's *guardian*," the elder announced in a gruff nasal tone that rose at the end, his beard dancing along with his jaw movements.

"Gavin Diggle. Third engineer," the younger man said in a similar accent to Higgs as he eyed his food with a hint of displeasure. Higgs, instead, scrutinized the lawyer.

"Nelson Blackwood, temporary potato-paper-pusher." There was no use undermining his role aboard the ship, even if he was their employee. His reply turned uncaring frowns and passive faces into chuckles from the younger people. Higgs drew a smile at the lawyer's humorous attempt.

"I see the captain is merciless even to the people who pay for our food. At least you won't be bored anytime soon," Higgs said as he dug into his bowl.

"If you ever want some real work, come down to our department, and we'll put muscle on you in no time," Gavin added.

Nelson smiled sheepishly. "Thanks for the offer. But I'm more adept at using my head than my muscles."

"Perfect. Now we got a battering ram in case the engine room door gets stuck again." Gavin smirked.

Laugh it off, Nelson. Laugh it off.

Ida seemed by far the kindest of the three, but between Higgs' disproving grunts and Gavin's stabbing humour, Nelson felt safer observing the situation and playing it by ear in terms of what he said.

Ida poked her spoon against Nelson's arm. "You should stop by anyway. I bet it's more interesting than watching ink dry." Her dialect told Nelson that she was local to the north, but he didn't ask in fear of suffering additional penalties for his curiosity. Ida was well-toned like her counterparts, except Higgs clearly did the heavy-lifting and Gavin, young as he appeared, was still a growing man.

Hammond, the cook, let out a series of puffs from his mouth, which could have been amusement as he sat down with his plate.

"You tinker-tankers at it again? Pardon their frisky balls. The crew of the *Queen* is notorious for stealing labour from other departments."

Gavin's spoon clattered about the bowl. "We'll recruit whoever we damn well please. We're short-staffed as it is unless we get a replacement engine. Besides," he scanned Nelson up and down. "I think he has potential." Nelson wanted to lean away from Gavin's mischievous smirk but was stopped by the bulk at his back called Higgs.

Hammond ruffled the boy's head. "Watch your potty-mouth and eat, Gavin. You aren't putting on muscle with a mouldy face like that." Gavin hissed and swatted the hand away.

"Not the hair!" he complained, tousling his short brown undercut until the hair appeared no different from messy, but on his terms.

"You have engine trouble?" Nelson echoed.

"Leaky Sally is always in a mood. Nothing unusual. We'll get to wherever the captain takes us as long as Higgs breathes," Ida interjected.

"I'll add that to the ship's repair list, then. God knows the ship is already knee-deep in them, judging from your paperwork."

"Devil knows we can't afford anything until you pay us for our work, Nelson. Needles in haystacks are our specialty, or in this case, a ship lost at sea." At Hammond's comment, Nelson felt a tug at the sides of his lips.

Wooden bowls clattered against the floor, spilling soup on other topmen who quickly rose in protest to the scuffling of two men across the galley. Nelson looked over just as Norman jabbed a quick punch into an older man's jaw, sending his attacker staggering backwards into his protesting colleagues. Retaliating, the man pushed off the crowd and tackled Norman, who miscalculated his turn, toppling him face-first onto a table. The crowd grabbed for them, pulling them apart. Norman, with a bloody nose, recoiled from the hands, launching himself snarling towards the other man.

"Enough!" Farand yanked the elder topman away as easily as throwing a rag.

"To the stern with you, Norman. And the forecastle for Creedy," his order rang firm through the disquiet galley, and the two men glared with daggers in their eyes as they stalked up the stairs.

"Second time this month," Gavin said as he slurped the rest of the broth.

Grimacing, Ida twirled her hands around and turned to Nelson. "It happens. Creedy is ... *definitely* moody. He and Dalia are our watch captains. He's responsible for teaching newcomers rigging. They don't always get along." Nelson eyed the commotion with a healthy dose of concern. His eyes travelled to the captain whose steely gaze followed the two troublemakers.

ORLAND'S FOUR-DISK skyport cast vast shadows over the island-dotted coastal town like a sundial visible from the stratosphere. While most of the crew spent their downtime playing cards or dice, some walked around the disk within viewing distance of the ship. Their stay was a short one, but some needed to stretch their legs.

Nelson had been dared up the ratline to join Olivier in the crow's nest. Despite a rocky start, a round of whoops and cheering echoed from below as the lawyer stubbornly made his way up top to prove that he was made of a hardier material than a sea sponge. He understood now why, despite its spelling, everyone called the ratlines "rattlins."

Nelson's ears burned from the attention. Excessive perspiration made its uncomfortable arrival when he spotted a certain blond second engineer watching from below. His arms turned to lead and his legs to lyefish. The rope chafed on his bare hands as he climbed the wobbling ratlines. Olivier stretched out a helping hand which Nelson promptly refused. He climbed ungraciously into the crow's nest and collapsed like a dropped sack of potatoes. The crew broke out in cheer. Nelson peered at the deck below and the massive space between him and safe ground before he swung to the side, his head spinning, face greying, and an uncanny ringing in his ears.

"Hang on, Mr. Blackwood. We'll get you down soon enough." Olivier patted the lawyer's shoulders, congratulating him for completing the dare. It was all Nelson had to muster enough strength for a thumbs-up as he waited for the lack of blood in his brain to return.

***

ROSANNE DRUMMED her fingers on the desk, resting her cheek on the palm of the other hand. The door leading to the Orland archives stood ajar, a cloud of dust visible through a beam of light from the basement window. The shuffling of boxes and a clatter of files came from within, and Rosanne picked up the faintest of coughs. A young man in plain uniform emerged from the dusty room with a file in hand.

"Pardon the wait, ma'am—"

"Captain," Rosanne corrected. The man coughed into his fist.

The anorexic file offered little with its single sheet of paper and the dark backside of an overturned photograph. The desk clerk scanned through the document before disclosing any of its contents. His career could be dismantled in the blink of an eye for giving out privileged information to unauthorized personnel, but Captain Drackenheart's RDA ID was enough to convince him.

"The file is as incomplete as they get, I'm afraid. The *Retribution* docked here on the twenty-sixth of October, 1703, after a wave of suspicious activity from Featherhill. However, there is no information about where the wares came from. This is a picture that was taken in the area, and allegedly they followed it for quite some time. Past Bogvin, it's reported." The young man slid a photograph across the counter, enough for Rosanne to peek at it. He hastily withdrew it.

"But the *Retribution* never docked at Bogvin? And two days later, the ship was reported lost as sea, correct?"

"As I've gathered, ma'am. I can't say for certain they arrived in Bogvin other than eyewitnesses seeing the ship chasing a smaller vessel out to sea. The case was closed. This was in long-term storage. Won't be much longer until the RDA purges the archives."

"May I have the picture?"

"I'm afraid I'm not at liberty to—" his response was left dangling at the additional riksdaler Rosanne slid seductively across the desk, and he handed her the photo, clamping his mouth shut.

"Thank you, dear." Rosanne pocketed the photograph while the desk clerk disappeared in the back with the file. She hailed a cab back to the docked *Red Queen*, and even at a distance, the amassed group of people on the main deck foretold some form of spectacle. Nelson clung to the nest for his dear life, white as a sheet of paper, and Rosanne couldn't resist grinning at the view of the distressed lawyer when she arrived. Rounds of cheers and applauses resonated throughout the ship, some even offering encouraging words.

"Can anyone tell me why our generous contributor is stuck in the nest?" she asked. At the lack of answers and increased breath-stealing laughter, Rosanne waved Creedy over. "Get him down, preferably alive, Mr. Creedy."

"As you wish, ma'am." He snickered and grabbed a spare length of rope before scaling the ratline quick like a squirrel. After a bit of struggle, Nelson managed to attach the makeshift harness. The other end of the rope was cast over the mast to a few topmen working as a counterweight, and with minimal effort, Nelson was lowered to the safety of the redwood deck.

Rosanne noticed hands passing small scraps of betting slips, used by the crew when money wasn't readily at hand; most ended up in Gavin's possession. The man grinned. Shaking her head, she returned to her quarters.

"Great job, Nelson!" Gavin slapped the man on the back, making Nelson faceplant onto the floor in a heap of trembling limbs.

"Nelson!" Ida helped him to his feet.

"I swear I am not this pathetic all the time." Nelson's knees wobbled, but Ida laughed despite his brave front. Gavin wrestled between them and took Nelson's arm.

"I'll take the lyefish back to his quarters. You go do your stuff," he directed at Ida, whose perplexed expression turned into utter confusion.

"You're never this nice!"

"Just making sure our generous contributor will grant me more future riches with similar stunts." He waved the bundle of bills in his hands and dragged Nelson back to his quarters.

"What would the reason be for this sudden intervention?" Nelson asked, building on Ida's surprised reaction.

"Just getting your greedy paper-hands away from Ida, s'all."

"Ah."

SOMETIME AFTER LUNCH, the crew was summoned to the galley. After breaking off into their usual groupings, the air was filled with chatter while they waited.

"Listen up!" Captain Drackenheart bellowed as she entered the room, skirted by Duplànte, who stooped under the ceiling. Ominous darkness clouded Rosanne's features as she came to stand directly under a broken bulb. In realizing this, she quickly took a step to the side where it was brighter. Sweeping her eyes across the galley, she nodded.

"I trust everyone aboard is accounted for and currently present. I got some good news, and I got some grave news for you."

"What we charged for this time? Idling?" Landman Iban shouted from within the crowd, drawing waves of laughter.

"Humorous for someone who skips out on his duties, Mr. Vasilyev." Rosanne stood stiffly, keeping her arms behind her back as she surveyed the amused looks on the crew's faces. "Today at the RDA, I received confirmation about the *Retribution's* route and possible whereabouts. As you all know, there was a chance we had to traverse a location where we had never sailed before. Our last stop is Bogvin for resupply, and then we're sailing into the Grey Veil. I already told you this at the initial briefing, but I'm asking you again. If you have any thoughts about self-preservation, now is the time to get off the ship."

A hush spread across the room, but the crew seemed less than willing to disembark. They merely looked at each other, as if wondering if anyone was brave or cowardly enough to back out after getting this far. Rosanne nodded.

"A word of warning. We need every man available to ensure the highest probability of success and to complete this mission as quickly as possible with minimal damage. Know this, those who step off might find themselves out of a job should we not return, and you will remain unpaid for your negligence. This is a team effort, and *Red Queen* demands cooperation from every one of you." Again, the murmur spread like the plague, accompanied by shuffling feet and furtive glances.

"You heard the captain!" Farand's voice was a booming thunder that roused people from their half-hearted thoughts. "If you have even the slightest hint in your heart that you cannot risk your life for this mission, then stand down! Anyone willing?"

"No, Lieutenant!" The crew's reply came unanimous and unwavering, and Farand was pleased after he scanned the determined faces of the men and women before him. He exchanged glances with Drackenheart, a silent agreement and gratitude for the rousing words. She produced a photograph from her jacket's inner pocket, held it high for everyone to see, and then handed it to Norman, who stood closest.

"Pass this around and take a look. If you see this ship, we're in a world of trouble. The ship might be half our size, but it's packing, and it's vicious. This is the last known target for the *Retribution*. The RDA has named it the *Blue Dragon*, and it has eluded arrest for years. It's a two-spire mayfly hybrid. Very distinct with a ramming spear at the bowsprit and dragon-like Aether sails. Both ships were observed outside the coast of Bogvin days before the *Retribution* was reported missing. We don't have the exact point of entry, but neither ship has been seen since. We'll be doing a standard E-sweep, and I need every single one of you to be on alert. Any change in wind, electronics, gravity, I want it noted. I don't know if we can expect the same as when we sailed the north. We eat and sleep in shifts. Someone always needs to be on watch and alert. Organize your team accordingly." Steeling her gaze, her eyes swept across the expectant faces to that of her crew. "Good luck, and may the blue skies be with us all."

THE BATANSEA'S roaring black waters were less than welcoming after the *Red Queen's* departure from Bogvin. It was their final resupply point before the vast open sea where rough weather and mythical places awaited them. They had no backup should things go wrong.

Nelson drew the furred hood closer to his face as the wind's biting cold was a threat to his sensitive skin. "Will we be alright, Captain?"

He turned to Rosanne, clad in equally warm clothing, goggles, and a hat.

"This is nothing compared to the north during the winter season. Just keep your footing. The decks are slippery after rain and frost," she said.

The wind toyed with the sails and pushed the ship with impressive force, enough to veer it from its course, which Rosanne rectified immediately. She whistled a tune and bobbed her head, her hair a flying tangled mess captured and braided by the wind. Watch captains Dalia, Creedy, and their teams worked the rigging wearing safety harnesses as the winds had the ship swinging from side to side. The topmen tugged at the ropes, checked deadeyes and shrouds, and noted how the sails lined with the winds.

Dalia wobbled to the quarterdeck, speaking into the captain's ear.

Rosanne nodded.

"Fold the sails," she said. "We fly on reserves."

Dalia joined the others on the main deck sharing this new information, and the teams climbed the ratlines. Rosanne caught Nelson's quizzical look. "The wind is erratic. We don't have a tail-wind and use more power to stay on course, so we fly on reserves until it calms down." Nelson nodded, filing this information somewhere in his mind.

The sky was dotted with dark cumulus clouds at midday, and Rosanne brought the ship to lower altitudes. Flying a ship was more than travelling from A to B and having wind in the sails. You had to account for the time of day, the season, high altitude, temperatures, jet winds, what type of clouds were safe to fly through, and many other subtle implements Nelson hadn't realized were a factor for flying.

His hat tumbled when they met winds where the ship's atmos couldn't create a perfect environmental seal on deck, and he discarded it for a warm cap. Nelson was as warmly fitted for the cold as he was on a regular snowy day in the north, except the floor was moving, and if he fell over the railing, it would take significantly longer for him to splash face-first into the ocean and be crushed by the laws of physics.

"Mr. Blackwood!" Rosanne called, waving a hand in a downward motion. "Look down."

Nelson briefly considered the possibility of his untimely and brutal demise, but he had to remind his paranoia that he had taken every measurement to make sure that would not happen.

Holding on to the railing, Nelson peered to the waters. Massive formations of dense coral jutted from the sea like stalagmites spreading out to the north and south in a long arch like a rocky forest.

"This is the Elder Reef? I thought it was normal coral formation!" Nelson stared at the glittering minerals making up the outer coating of the rock-hard surfaces.

Rosanne laughed and did a quarter-turn of the wheel. "It's one of the strangest reefs on Terra. No one knows why it stands out from normal corals or even why it's growing out of the sea. Beautiful, isn't it?"

"And terrifying," Nelson muttered as images of shipwrecks lost in the sea of corals ran through his mind. His teeth chattered in the merciless weather. Although he could hardly pass on such a magnificent view as the Elder Reef, the weather forced Nelson to retreat to his chambers, where he tried to get some decent shut-eye and disconnect from all the excitement.

The uneven rocking and groaning of the woodwork had Nelson tossing and turning. Finally, after what seemed like hours, he kicked off the covers and re-laced his boots. He grabbed his coat and went outside, then below deck. He had already traversed the ship half a dozen times in the last two days, but his options for entertainment in this weather were few, and he sought out the more obscure places of the ship when he had the chance.

A wave of laughter came from the galley, and Nelson followed the source of the merry noise. Around a table in the far corner, a group of people played cards. Steaming mugs sat by each of them; Hammond had concocted coffee for the off-duty crew.

"Hey, Nelson! You good card player?" Iban called out, waving his carded hand and in a moment of panic withdrew it before the surrounding players could see. Both were landmen, but unlike his brother, Kristoff Iban's articulation was so low it borderlined on mumbling, and he often dropped articles and rolled his letters.

"That would depend on the game," Nelson replied.

"King of the hill." Ida's head peeked from behind Gavin's

bulk, shuffling her cards around in hand while keeping them tight to her chest. Gavin and Kristoff shuffled on the bench to make room for Nelson, and he squeezed in. Olivier slapped his last card on top of the pile, hands high in victory. "No cards!" The others groaned and dropped their hands. Iban collected and shuffled the two-deck pile.

"Olivier, if you are here, who's keeping watch at the crow's nest?" Nelson asked.

"Norman wanted a go at crow. I gave him a chance." Olivier grinned.

Shaking his head, Hammond snorted a laugh. "You're an evil sod, Olivier. Poor lad must be seasick swinging from that nest. His first lookout too." No protests were shared around the table save from another wave of laughter and snickering. Iban handed out five cards each, then flipped the topmost card on the deck. Ida slapped down her card on top, then Gavin, and on it went.

"So, this whole search and retrieve business, do you have any hopes?" Hammond placed two equal numbered cards on top of the pile, switching the deck to spades, which had Ida pouting, and pulled three new cards from the deck.

Nelson bobbed his head, but his brow was crinkled and tense. "It's been so long I don't think we will find anyone alive if that's what you think. But I hope to at least learn what happened to the ship and the crew."

"I heard the captain was your dad," Ida said.

"Ouch. That makes this personal, eh?" Kristoff followed up, shuffling his cards around.

Nelson nodded. "With the RDA unwilling to heed my pleas, I had to take matters into my own hands, or, well, yours."

"I'm amazed you managed to get the captain to agree to this mission." Gavin arched an eyebrow. "What did you do? Is there a bigger payout than originally stated?" Nelson let the question hang in the air for a moment too long as the guilt of blackmail came back to haunt him.

"Maybe we're actually hunting pirate treasure. Travelling into

the Grey Veil to find their secret cove and riches. One card left."
Nelson's eyes crinkled at the corners.

"Dammit. You have luck with you." Iban pulled another card
from the deck and placed it.

Hammond eyed Nelson without a word. Scratching his
beard, he pulled three cards, glanced at them, and swore. "Pass."

"Last card!" Ida exclaimed. "It's you and me now, Nelson."
She wiggled her eyebrows in an open challenge.

"Hey, hey! Don't leave me out of the loop. Two cards left.
See?" Gavin protested.

"Fat chance."

The *Red Queen*'s crew was like any other. They worked for
their riksdaler and took jobs where they could find them under
the oppression of the trade companies, which stole most of the
profits and wares. The competition was tough and merciless, and
Nelson imagined even with the *Red Queen*'s dual-trade ability,
their profit was sparse. He had spent hours redoing their bookkeeping, and for months the ship's expenses were in deeper waters
than they could sail.

Nelson took one card and placed it. Hammond tapped his
hand thoughtfully and placed another card on top of the last.

"Hammond's toast." Olivier snickered and smacked two even
cards, changing the colour again. Ida's excited giggle cut like a
knife into Nelson. Had he met any of these people prior to the
mission assignment, he wouldn't even dream of pulling such a
low move as threatening their business with prosecution. Nelson
envisioned what they would do to him if his blackmailing was
discovered. A second thought crept into his mind: Ida's smile
twisting into disgust and hatred upon learning of his ways.
Nelson licked his lips, focusing his attention on the stack of cards.

"No cards. I win!" Ida exclaimed and clapped her hands.
"Take that, paper-pusher!" She grinned at Nelson, who tried his
best to keep his smile from falling into the abyss.

CHAPTER 6

UNDER STRANGER SKIES

The *Red Queen* hovered comfortably at mid-sea. There were no clouds in the darkened sky, and only the waxing moon accompanied them on this quiet night. Rosanne sat on the wide sill, leaning against the glass window. A knock issued on her door, and Farand came bowing through the frame and stretched to his full height upon entry.

"Everything alright out there?" Rosanne asked, studying the bizarre shapes the moon made in the uneven glass panes.

"Quiet, orderly, and well." He took his usual chair by her desk, leaned back, and folded his arms. Rosanne spun around with a groan and flopped into the worn cushion of her seat.

"I hate how quiet it is before a big job. It's always like this. Nice weather, not a fart of wind, and a brooding sense of failure."

Farand let out a bumbling chuckle. "And you on edge, as usual." Her wry smile turned ironic, and she nodded.

"How did we get into this mess, Farand?"

He looked up to the ceiling, pursing his lips. "Was it our first run from Georgetown some ten years ago with the Orwell refugees?"

Rosanne snapped her finger. "Those sneaky stowaways had

the gall to point a gun at me and 'demand to see the captain.' She screwed up her face and haughtily bobbed her head.

"The eyes of that kid nearly popped out of his skull when I said he was already holding her at gunpoint."

"I'll never forget the stink of him either. None of them had bathed in months."

"Desperate people do desperate things."

Her eyes fell to the table, to the numerous notes and calculations of the plan they had worked on for days. "And now it's another one of those situations where we're forced into the uncharted territory of the Grey Veil. I swear if I didn't know any better, I'd say we are cursed."

"At least Mr. Blackwood used well-formulated papers and not a gun to persuade you to do this."

"A true shame he didn't need a bath too. I would have tossed that limp son of a bitch into the fjord if he wasn't so damn prepared."

Farand drew his shoulders. "We still can. Gerangra is lovely at this time of the year, but I believe that will complicate our delicate operation. And frankly, it doesn't look good on paper." Rosanne burst out laughing.

The lieutenant went to the locked cabin, wiggled lose a piece of wood in the moulding, and pulled out a key. He unlocked the cabinet and opened it wide, displaying rows of bottles of different shapes and sizes.

"What will it be, Captain?" he asked.

"Just the one. I'd like to keep my head clear tomorrow."

"Cheap it is." He grabbed a full bottle of brown whisky and two glasses, then set them on the table. Rosanne grabbed the bottle from him and poured the glasses. They clinked them together and sipped.

"I don't recall my cheap whisky tasking like smoky oak."

"That's because I lied. It's Quindecimus, the finest you have." Farand rumbled his laughter at Rosanne's frown when he turned the bottle and displayed the label, but her momentary displeasure quickly grew to that of amusement, and they clinked the glasses again.

"Just in case this is our last drink?" Raising an eyebrow, Rosanne's expression drew one deep guffaw from her lieutenant.

"I entertain no such thoughts."

"Do you ever regret joining the crew?" Rosanne asked.

"Never." Farand shook his head. "The salary might not rival the RDA rates, but I got a cozy spot, never a dull day, and my kid brother got a fair chance at life, all thanks to you."

"Sometimes, I wonder what the hell you see in me, Farand. I am questionable at running this gig at best." She chuckled.

"You do seem more reserved to this job than any of the others."

"That's because the stakes have never been this high."

"The stakes being you have someone to come home to back in Valo? A certain Captain DiCroce of the *Arctic Pride*?"

"No." Rosanne swirled the contents of the glass. "Maybe." A brief silence formed between them, but it wasn't uncomfortable, rather a quiet agreement between two people who knew how to be alone in each other's company. "Is that music I hear?"

Farand listened for a moment, a smile replacing his quiet reservation to keep the conversation going. "I believe the Vasilyevs brought their vodka again."

Rosanne emptied her glass and poured herself and Farand another round. "Can't fault them old drinking traditions before a job. Here's for our headaches tomorrow."

"And our luck be with us." Another clink. Another day. Another job.

NELSON WOKE in the middle of the night to the sound of music. The lively notes weaving with bands of laughter prompted him to leave the stiff comforts of his bunk, which had given him grief and knots from day one. He stretched outside the room, where no ceiling restrained his lanky frame. He didn't see anyone on deck, and he could barely discern the layout in the dark. Without a single lamp lit on deck, the *Red Queen* would be invisible in the night. Nelson fumbled in the dark to the stairs leading below, guided by the scant moonlight and the echoes of his shoes against the floorboards.

The galley was pitch black save for a lamp in the farthest doorway leading deeper into the ship. He followed the light, then saw another lamp, and then another, drawing ever closer to the music and laughter. Down Nelson went, past stairs and the narrow hallway of the outer hull until he came to the lowest deck, a large room cleared of cargo and chock full of people.

He was bombarded with the squeal of concertino and rough-drawn fiddles. People were dancing and swaying to the music, swigging from bottles and cups. Nelson peered back to the empty passage, briefly wondering if the captain and lieutenant would crash the party.

"Nelson!" Iban's heavy accent cut through the music, and the landman dragged him into the room and slung an arm over his shoulder. "Tell me. You drink vodka?" He looked Nelson dead in the eyes, his piercing gaze unfocused but committed.

"I don't normally drink," Nelson squeaked.

"Even better." Iban patted him on the back and thrust a cup into Nelson's hands, sloshing clear liquid on his trousers. Iban hung on his shoulder, swaying them to the music, and Nelson hurriedly drank from the cup to prevent further suspicious wet incrimination of his dry clothes. His face rapidly contorted as if his throat was on fire and cooled to ice at the same time. He shook his head enough for his glasses to take a tumble, throwing the intimate quarters of the lower decks into a blurry mess. Iban swiped the glasses from the floor and thrust them onto Nelson's nose.

"Watch your step, paper-pusher." He grinned.

Frazzled, Nelson made his way towards the nearest wall, dodging the dancing crew and incoming neck hooks from people who really wanted his attention. The sailor next to him clinked his cup against Nelson's. Again, he sipped from the burning liquid and finished with a hoary gasp, the prickling on his face intensifying. Everyone who caught his eye wanted to share a drink, and Nelson clinked cups and drank far too quickly for his comfort.

Now in the centre of the room, Iban folded his arms and squatted, thrust out his leg, then swapped it for the other, and made his way across the floor in time with the music and whoops of the surrounding crowd. He bounced up with his arms outstretched, received a round of applause and laugher. In the far corner sat Creedy, Hwang, and Dalia, smacking their fists into their hands and thrust out with rock, paper, or scissors. Creedy's scissors folded to Hwang's and Dalia's rock, and the older topman took a large gulp from his mug, and off they went again with Dalia's loss and her drinking from her cup.

Nelson spotted Ida and Gavin in full swing on the floor, Gavin spinning Ida in a pirouette. Drumming his fingers against his cup, Nelson drew his lip into a prim smile as he looked around for something to distract him from the foolish thoughts of cutting in on Gavin to ask Ida to dance.

"We had a wager you wouldn't show," Higgs' gruff voice said next to him.

"Who won?"

Higgs' laughter left Nelson confused as the chief engineer disappeared to chat with Hammond. Looking around, he took another swig from the mug, shuddered from the burning sensation and hoped for the best. He was already feeling the floor move under his feet.

"Nelson!" Someone roared his name from across the room. Gavin was waving him over. He wobbled on the oh so unstable floor and meandered past the dancing crowds. Gavin lined them up next to Iban and Kristoff, and the Vasilyev brothers hopped down into their rapid squat leg kicking. Nelson waved his hands in defence, but Kristoff whirled around Gavin, made everyone sling their arms around their side partner, and dragged everyone down.

"Kick your leg, Nelson!" Kristoff prompted and laughed at Nelson's strained effort and slow timing. The boys counted in a chant, rose to their feet, and dropped down again. Nelson wobbled, laughed, kicked out his leg, and swapped with the other. The music grew louder, the claps firmer and crisp, ringing in his ears. Then they all toppled over, laughing hysterically.

"See? Hopak fun!" Kristoff shouted over the noise and patted Nelson on the shoulder.

"Ow, my knees." Nelson rested his hands on his stiff knees, which swore they would never do Hopak again lest they crack under strain. He heard someone singing in the room, the music changed to match the melody, and then everyone joined in, raising their cups.

She came from nowhere in the sky
the Red Queen *slipping by*
A red flag waving like a crimson sunset
No storm can toss her over
No winds too scarce or strong
And if you think different, mate, you're very very wrong!
She's a scary one, that woman
A witch or a bitch, commanding the vessel like an empress.
Her beauty might fade
Blanch to the pale
Greying hair once so fair, posh! What nonsense!
The Demon stands tall and grinning
wicked as it seem
A heart of stone, the sweetest tone to plank us all!

THE WORLD around Nelson started spinning. The thrumming of percussion, squealing fiddles, and roaring laughter stretched his attention to every corner of the room, and every person thrust a new cup of brown or clear liquid into his hands, prompting him to drink. Their faces distorted like wet oil on canvas, their voices incomprehensible and deep. Nelson found himself giggling, letting himself be dragged along for whatever shenanigans the crew had in store for him.

A WALL of thick fog stretched from the murky depths below far out of the *Red Queen's* reach in the sky above.

Rosanne pulled the lever next to the wheel back until it clanked and locked. The ship drifted softly, no thrusters spewing out their blue, flame-like energy. The instruments on the panel displayed a series of numbers which she jotted down in a notebook, along with the local time, weather conditions, and the season.

"Mr. Lyle, please inform your team to be ready," she ordered.

"Yes, ma'am." The master gunner raised a fist in the air, and a seaman ducked below the cargo deck.

"Current observation report, Captain." Dalia handed the captain a piece of paper which was put with the rest of the notes. Tension seemed to weigh the ship down as the disquieted crew eyed the Veil. The risk was palpable. Rosanne took out a second compass and put it next to the built-in display, both needles pointing due east.

"Ready, Mr. Duplànte?" she called.

The tall man clenched his jaw from where he stood on the quarterdeck, hands behind his back and eyes peeled on the swirling fog. "Couldn't be further from it, Captain."

Rosanne's lips pulled into a smile. "Aren't you a ray of sunshine?"

"Nothing but the truth, ma'am."

"Just the way we like it." Rosanne tugged the hems of her gloves and secured the goggles over her eyes. "Here we go," she muttered and released the locking clasp on the lever.

The *Red Queen* slid into the thick foggy bank. All visibility disappeared behind them, blanching the ship's decks into an otherworldly setting of grey and obscure forms. The crew was alert and ready at their stations. Olivier hopelessly pointed his spyglass from the barreled comforts of the crow's nest, Watch Captains Creedy and Dalia on their ratlines with a small team of topmen ready to scramble for the sails should the situation call for it. In the hushed world of grey, whispers would be welcoming.

The thick of the Grey Veil was far different than the north and south fogs which were but mere wisps in comparison. Had Rosanne not been caught trading gunpowder, she wouldn't be in this mess. Although she wasn't sure exactly how much Nelson knew of her side-business, the gallows which waited for them were the type of knot she never wanted to tie. How anyone entered this foggy death sentence of their own free will was beyond Rosanne. She didn't turn the wheel as much as a centimetre; the compass dials pointed to the exact degree as they had upon entry.

Picking up the intercom, she pressed the button. "Olivier, you have a visual?"

"Negative, Captain. No gust of wind disturbing the clouds."

With the landscape locked in a time capsule of never changing seasons, such was the knot in her stomach as Rosanne kept the ship at a steady speed for half an hour. She wasn't used to the fog's inertia, even though she had heard stories of places where the Veil had strayed and left marine ships floating blind for weeks. At this altitude, she expected some movement, but her breath was the only motion swirling the fog into action.

She shook one foot after the other, her eyes returning to the compasses once more. Another ten minutes passed, with the fog remaining unchanged. The instrument panels were silent. If she didn't know any better, she would have said the *Red Queen* hadn't moved at all. The topographical map showed no landscape beneath them or anywhere else, then flickered, static lines of snow dancing across the circular screen. The numbers on the altitude meter jumped between zeros and non-static digits.

"Higgs, anything happening in the engine room?"

"All is well here, Captain." The intercom buzzed.

"Mr. Duplànte," she called. "Note down electrical navigational instrument failure approximately fifty-seven minutes after entry." Farand sat ready next to the wheel, documenting their journey in excruciating detail on a map that was ambiguous at best.

THROUGH THE CRIPPLING headache of a hangover, Nelson observed this activity with increasing narrow-eyed interest. He rubbed his stockinged feet together; they stood little chance of gaining warmth in the cold temperatures at this altitude. He had awoken to the gentle rook of the ship, occupying someone's hammock in the lower levels, and had somehow lost his shoes along the way. A giant black hole existed in his memory where alcohol, dance, and his drunken mistakes should be.

"Is someone missing a shoe?" Able Seaman Hwang popped up from below deck, holding up the fur-trimmed leather footwear Nelson had misplaced. He thanked the man, groaned with the effort, and laced the one shoe to his foot so at least he had some stable grip on the slick deck, and resumed his miserable cradling with the main deck's rail. The crew had made sure he drank his fill and then some during last night's festivities, but as much as the world was still spinning for him, he wasn't going to miss a second of their journey into the potential horrors hidden in the Grey Veil.

To his knowledge, there were no proper maps of the area between the Central Colonies and Cintecha across the Baltansea. Farand's map looked homemade, with pencil scribbles covering substantial portions of the space where the Grey Veil obscured the sea. Nelson noticed a few lines cutting straight through the thinner parts of the Veil to the north and surmised it to be information he had to take with him to the grave.

Farand redid his calculations on a scrap piece of paper, considering the eastern breeze upon point of entry, to determine their estimated travel distance which he marked on the map with a small dot and a timestamp and other useful information. The little dot skirted the Veil's periphery, but then the lieutenant fished out a different map with fever scribbles. Nelson recognized the numbers as their current position.

"You should get some more rest, Mr. Blackwood," Farand commented without lifting his pensive stare, jotting the calculations into his notebook.

"I would love to, lieutenant, but my bunk is occupied." Farand lifted his eyes to stare at Nelson's miserable yet amused frown.

Kristoff burst from the guest cabin and took his place by Creedy, who smacked the man on the back of his head.

"The hell have you been?"

"Sleeping." Kristoff rubbed his face and let himself be criticized for his tardiness.

A SHARP LIGHT broke through the wall of fog, bathing the deck in brilliant sunlight. Rosanne blinked several times to adjust to the glare as the clouds cleared.

"Eastern tailwind. Two meters per second!" Creedy shouted from the mainsail mast. Rosanne's heart leapt at the sudden change.

"Southern breeze at four and increasing!" The wooden boards of the *Red Queen* groaned; her bow forced northwards along with the wind. Rosanne turned the wheel several times to make up for the change of wind, rectifying the ship due west. The wind whistled and moaned. Behind them, the fog remained solid and arched to either side, the wind clearing a massive circular break in the fog turning counterclockwise. The clouds morphed and changed shades of white and grey.

"It's like the eye of a storm." Rosanne marvelled at the surreal weather phenomena.

Nelson whipped his head around and searched the horizon. "I thought these only appeared in the center of tropical storms."

"That's the thing, Mr. Blackwood. The Grey Veil defies the law of physics and nature. The winds are calm enough for us to continue. Note it down. Olivier, what's the size of this thing?"

"Around a kilometre in diameter at this altitude, ma'am. Funnel-shaped, widening at higher altitudes."

"Beyond the clouds, the sky is always blue." Rosanne grinned and nodded towards the top of the massive funnel where she could see the blue salvation of a sky, the first sign of anything in over an hour.

Little happened after their exit of what now was referred to as the "eye." A shudder ran through the ship and disappeared as quickly as it had come. Erratic high winds contributed to this phenomenon on a regular scale, but Rosanne checked her pocket-watch when the intervals appeared fixed, and it happened for a fifth time.

"Five oh three, Mr. Duplànte."

The lieutenant ceased his scribbling, stared at the numbers, and then fished out his pocket watch. "It's twenty-two minutes past five, Captain."

Rosanne stared at her pocket watch, comparing it to the instrument table and Farand's observation. "Time call! Check your bloody watches!"

The urgent holler compelled the crew to action.

"Quarter past five," Norman called from the forecastle.

"Five-oh-nine," Creedy followed up.

"Half past five!" and so on it went as each crew possessing a watch announced their time with varying differences. Rosanne kicked the wheel and turned to Farand, who was as speechless as her.

"We wound every single watch aboard this ship to the exact same time. How the hell did they turn out so differently after less than three hours?" She wiped her forehead on instinct, but Rosanne was anything but hot at this altitude, the chilly fog clinging to their clothes and skin like persistent leeches.

The ship shuddered again, and as it did, Rosanne watched the needle on her silver watch make a slight jump of three minutes forward in time.

"Mr. Duplànte. Note down complete loss of measurement of time."

"Yes, Captain."

"Include manual navigation on that list," she added after a brief pause, the instrument panel compass pointing its needle north while the other pointed south-west.

Chapter 7

Retribution

Rosanne, Farand, Nelson, and the engineering department observed Higgs as he flew about the captain's cabin, clearing the table of any unnecessary junk and replacing it with Farand's maps, a compass, and a device with five suspended metal marbles. He lifted the outer marble and released it, watching it smack face-first into its neighbour and transfer momentum into the marble on the other side, making it pop up and swing back and repeat. He motioned for Gavin to stand next to the desk.

The young man's pensive stare struck Rosanne as curious. He held a notepad and pencil, an entire page filled with lines and crosses.

Higgs rubbed his hands together. "Ladies and gents, allow me to pull a short presentation for you in these otherwise dire times. This clickity clacking marvellous piece here is a Higgs' Principle."

"I'm certain that's a ... what's-his-name cradle?" Nelson interjected.

"New—" Ida began, but Higgs clapped his hands before she could finish.

"That is not what's important right now. Anyhow, we know for a fact that our navigational instruments turned to crapper this arvo. Sometime after that, the compasses went bonkers, and the

75

beautiful lady we have our arses on shivers in her panties. So we currently have no means of navi, no instruments, no stars, no wind, and no sun in the sky since the eye."

The *Red Queen* let out another shudder. The cabin shook, along with a few loose items on the table which clattered to the floor. The instrument upon the desk clacked. The marbles veered off to the side in a wave until they fell still. The compass needle spun madly. Gavin pulled up the notepad and wrote on it with stone-faced concentration.

Higgs pointed at the young man, brimming with excitement. "You see that? Whatever is making the *Queen* shudder is affecting gravity. We're getting closer to the source."

Rosanne folded her arms and shifted her weight to the other foot. "But if it's a gravitational force, it shouldn't affect the ship's navigational instrument, only the compass."

"Very true, my Captain, which is why I'm thinking that these pulses also have magnetism behind them. Consider this: the longer we've flown into the veil, the stronger these pulses have become. While we know from experience that magnetism has a shorter range than gravitational pull, what if our compasses were affected long before the panel glitches, but it just seemed like they were pointing true north and instead towards the source of the pulses?" Higgs hopped over to the maps on the desk, jabbing a finger into the thick of the Grey Veil. "Now that we're much closer to it, instead of a fixed point on the planet, I'm thinking it's a form of landmass with several strong magnetic sources. I might not know much about navigation, but since we've had a shift in the wind and no compass to tell us where in the hooting blazes we are, it's logical that we are further north, drawn closer to this landmass."

"We entered the Veil due west, but if what you say is true, the compass pointed north-west." The captain's thinking frown returned. "So you've had Mr. Diggle count between the instances and shown them to be increasing frequency for how long?"

Rosanne nodded to the third engineer, who was growing paler by the minute.

"An hour and a half, give or take." The older man grinned.

"Higgs is a sadist." Ida chuckled, almost making Gavin lose his control.

"Two hours ago, we only noticed these shudders every five minutes, and they were significantly weaker. Now the instance is down to one minute and ..." Higgs took the notepad from Gavin. "You can stop counting now, boy. Well done." Gavin let out a long sigh and rubbed his face. "One minute and forty-three seconds," Higgs finished.

"By counting between the instances, we can, in theory, escape the Veil when our instruments are out of commission."

"Precisely, Captain."

"Then I say we initiate plan B of the search. Someone do the counting while we continue with our mission. You're off that task, Mr. Diggle."

"Thank you, Captain."

"Hold yer trousers, boy. I still have some maintenance work for ya," Higgs said, stopping him from leaving.

"Always something with you."

"What was that, boy?"

"Yes, Chief."

THE *RED QUEEN* turned her nose to what was a mutual agreement on the definition of southwest and kept that course at a steady speed. As the greatest threat was a pulse of energy and the lurking undertone of that knocking out all forms of navigation, Rosanne posted three sailors to count the instances and compare notes. The instances were stable for forty-five minutes before the time between them decreased, but only a little. It was nearing supper by the time two of the displays on the instrument panel flashed. A soft murmur danced across the glitched blue screen, which showed radio waves on that frequency, and a small dot appeared on the map.

"Bloody hell. Duplànte! We got a distress signal." Rosanne turned the knob to tune in on the signal, but the magnetic pulses made it almost impossible for her to discern anything.

"It's weak but certainly new," Farand commented.

"Aye. You'd think we are alone out here, but we got company."

"Another merchant ship, perhaps?"

"Not a snowball's chance in hell. Either way, we're required to investigate. Give me the best estimate at where we go from here."

Duplànte called over Dalia and Creedy from their posts, and after conversing among themselves, they agreed on a course based on the weak winds.

Rosanne followed the spotty distress signal for the better part of the hour. The instruments were less than helpful as they kept falling in and out of connection, and Rosanne flew more on instinct than following the short-range signal.

The signal was strong enough to advertise its approximate altitude at around 1300 meters. The *Red Queen* kept a steady course, with Creedy noting every single detail so as to aid their return from the Veil. Lyle and his men kept a low profile with guns cocked out from the gunports.

NELSON'S EYES were peeled on the surrounding fog, and he wrung his hands as he wondered how there could be a distress signal this far out and who it might be from. Could it be his father's ship? Six months was a long time under the sky. Should the ship have pulled through its worst peril, even after a month, the chance for survival was slim-to-none in these northern conditions. Maybe the ship found land and somehow was able to get by. Nelson dared not get his hopes up.

"Shouldn't be too long now, Mr. Blackwood," Rosanne announced from the wheel, her eyes narrowed as she guided the vessel at exceptionally slow speed should anything appear without notice.

"Shadow, fore, forty-five degrees up!" Olivier leaned on the railing, his spyglass trained at the source of his excitement. Rosanne pulled back the thruster lever, cutting the engine's power, and let the *Red Queen* drift with gentle nudges. She pointed the bow at a steep angle. The topmen sprang from their seats and climbed the ratlines with impressive celerity. From the hidden compartments of the gundeck, a wave of *tack-tack* followed Lyle's command to ready weapons.

"Straight ahead!" Olivier called. Nelson was learning to understand his lisp easier, like acclimating to a new dialect.

Rosanne slowed the galleon's advance and evened out their keel. With the lowering bowsprit, Rosanne fixed her eyes on the elongated shadow. She engaged the hull's front thrusters to ease the ship into a full stop.

From the thinning mist emerged a floating pile of a wrecked aeroship. Its plated main and mizzenmast were snapped at odd angles with the sails shredded to mere tatters. The military red and blue flag of the RDA hung in limp ribbons at the stern. Long, arched depressions ran from the middle of the main deck's outer hull around to the stern; splinters jutted at the fringes.

"It's the *Retribution*." Nelson grabbed the rail; his eyes fixed on the ghostly visage of the destroyed military ship. A surge of nausea and cold crept across his face. He had seen the beauty that was the *Retribution* many times before: her sleek hull and dazzling woodwork, the glorified, long-haired woman holding a cross at the beak, and the aether sails shining golden under sunlight. While most of the crew watched the ghost ship with reserved professional observation, a few eyes were on the lawyer.

"That is simply not possible." Farand checked the instruments to confirm the distress signal's origin.

"As inconceivable it might be, the ship is still here," Rosanne said, seeing the lawyer's hunched back. It had been clear to her since the beginning that the *Retribution* was no more, but she had not anticipated or wanted to find as much as a splinter, and by the look of Nelson's face, the feeling was mutual. Shaking her head, she went over the instrument panels and levers, securing the ship.

"The top deck is clear. Prepare for boarding and send a scout."

With hooked ropes, the crew hauled the ship closer to the *Retribution* with the gentle help of the *Red Queen*'s port thrusters. A gangplank connected the ships, the hooks firmly secured. Now that they were closer, they gave a short survey of the visible damage to the vessel.

"Doesn't look like they were boarded. I don't see any bullet holes or weapons, and the ammunition for the upper gundeck is still there." Rosanne noted to her lieutenant. The landmen Iban and Kristoff did three rounds of Hwang's game of rock, paper, and scissors, Iban groaning as he lost. Lyle supplied him with a flintlock pistol and a dagger, wishing the tall youth good luck as he walked the gangplank across to the ship's main deck.

"Why are you only sending one man?" Nelson questioned as he saw Iban keeping his head low as he ducked below to the gundeck. Farand spared him half a glance.

"It's a failsafe should there be a threat aboard the ship. It could be a trap set by pirates or the remaining crew. This way, we only lose one man instead of half the crew by a surprise attack."

"He could die?" Nelson said, aghast. His hand ceased fiddling with the button of his jacket.

Farand's gaze flicked upwards and closed. "Mr. Blackwood, every member of this vessel is prepared to lay down their lives should the situation arise. It is in their blood and on their contract. Your generous contribution was most helpful in securing that mindset." He folded his arms. "It is a necessary risk in our trade, and as you know from our bookkeeping, money is a strong motivator." Nelson couldn't argue with that logic. Duplànte merely pointed out what Nelson was prepared for: paying whatever was necessary to get results. In this case, it wasn't all about the money; someone could die.

They all could die.

After a few minutes, Iban emerged from below deck, waving his hands to signal that the coast was clear. Rosanne rested her hands on her hips and beckoned to the crew in a stern voice. "Damage survey, Creedy and Dalia! Higgs and the lot check the engines, the wheel panels, the lot of them. The rest of you do a systematic sweep of the entire ship and see if there's anything worth our trouble." The crew streamed over the gangplank and scattered.

"Stay here, Mr. Blackwood. This is not a job for you." Nelson couldn't go aboard the ship even if he wanted to. His legs wobbled from the shock of finding the ship at all. He observed as the crew examined every nook and cranny; they were rigorous and focused on their work. Rosanne walked aboard, leaving Farand to tend the *Queen*.

ROSANNE TUGGED at the door to the captain's quarters; it didn't budge. She searched for a keyhole but instead found a small box with a set of symbols on little square keys. She randomly punched a few symbols until it gave a disheartening sound of rejection.

"Goddammit. The RDA's upped the security of their cabins?" Rosanne spun around to see the engineers talking among themselves, supposedly deciding who does what. "Ida! A moment." The flaxen-haired woman beamed as she made her way over, appearing to have dodged a cumbersome task.

"You ever crack one of these?"

After a brief glance at the box, Ida produced a set of tools. She inserted an electrical device with a long metallic needle and turned the knob on the box, which produced a sizzling hot glow from inside the lock. Ida retracted the needle and jammed a chisel in two hard raps with a hammer, and tested the handle. The door swung open.

"Easy peasy. These locks are only good if you want to keep the general rabble out. Can I take the box?"

"All yours," Rosanne approved. Ida clapped her hands and set to the test of removing the lock, whistling a cheerful tune.

Rosanne didn't have any expectations for what she might find inside, considering the mysterious circumstances that surrounded the ship. She did recognize the knot in her stomach upon seeing the broken window of the quarters, the coloured glass littering the floor. The desk which should have been nailed down was smashed against the bookshelves of charts and ledgers. Ink splatter covered the red carpet, and the chair was reduced to kindling.

Rosanne ran her hand over a set of uneven gouges in the wood and carpet. The marks ran across the floor towards the window, broad and deep as if claws from a massive beast. A soft breeze fluttered the askew curtains partially ripped from their hinges.

She touched the dried red stain on the broken shards hanging from the windows. Some had only trace amounts, and others were covered. The entire circumference of the broken window was bloody in varying degrees. Had this been Captain Blackwood's final moments? Was this his blood staining the windows red?

A tricorn hat lay in a corner, now covered with dust and cobwebs. Rosanne picked it up and shook off the dead spiders. The pin of the RDA officer showed a dull unsaturated artwork under the dust. She cleaned it off with a handkerchief until the pin sparkled again. Smelling inside the hat, she couldn't detect even the faintest trace of perfume or hair grease.

The crew was already lined up and waiting to give their report by the time Rosanne finished her initial sweep of the cabin. She emerged carrying books, charts, and the tricorn hat. One offered to take the load from her hands, and she accepted.

"Anything?" she directed at the crew.

Creedy stepped forward. "The masts were broken clean off," he said, skipping all theatrics. "Something heavy leaned on them from on low, for no cannon or wind condition can break off the mainmast like that. And the tops don't bear any visible damage like being rammed." Creedy pointed to the low splintered breakpoint. Both masts' metal plating was wrenched apart like a flimsy lid on a can of sardines.

"The hull is damaged from excessive compression, like someone strung a chain around it," Dalia said. "We're thinking it also took down the masts." Creedy nodded his agreement.

Rosanne found their reasoning solid, although she had never seen damage such as this on a ship before, not marine or aeroship. "Alright. Engines?"

"Toast, ma'am." Higgs shook his head. "Not as much as a spark of life. Fuel's all gone. Coolers blown..."

Ida produced a notepad with a long list of parts, all sharing the violent jab of a pencil crossing them out. "All the electrical components were fried from either machine overloading or maybe even struck by lightning. There's nothing we can salvage. The only thing still working is the anti-grav engine. It was protected by anti-electromagnetic plating. Standard issue from the RDA."

"Their atmos was only built to last 1800 meters, so whatever happened most likely went down around this height," Gavin finished.

Rosanne suppressed her need to rub her forehead. "Supplies?"

"Limited or rotten, Captain," Hammond stated.

Lyle shook his head. "Gunpowder storage is soaked. Some weapons are still usable, but the ship's taken in a lot of water."

Rosanne let out the faintest sigh and scrunched her eyes shut for a second, massaged her temples, and took a deep refreshing breath. "Salvage what you can. Anything else?" At this, the crew disheartening exchanged glances.

"We couldn't find anyone, Captain." Norman glanced about nervously. "The crew's things are still in their quarters, jackets, gloves, shoes even. We couldn't find any blood or sign that they exchanged blows with their attacker."

Rosanne waved a hand and shushed him. "A crew of thirty people doesn't fall prey to one rogue assassin. Were they all tossed overboard? Give me something to work with."

Norman looked to Kristoff, then averted his eyes to Captain Dracknheart's stern ones. "As we said, Captain. There are no signs of human infiltration. The crack in the hull, the missing crew ..."

Kristoff continued when Norman was reluctant to finish. "We've heard stories of a beast that plucks living beings from ships and leaves the vessel to decay." The wave of uneasy shuffling feet spoke their shame in the assessed conclusion.

Captain Drackenheart snorted and pinched the base of her nose. "Scared by myths, are we? Alright, enough of that nonsense! Gather up what you can, and let's get the hell out of here. Without the engine, we can't tow this beast back to Bogvin no matter how hard we try. Prepare it for descent." Rosanne hadn't expected the crew to show such a level of deterrence at the sight of the *Retribution*, but she didn't deny its effectiveness at amplifying their theory of monsters. That the ship was in any floating shape at all for such a long time exposed to the elements was a miracle, and Rosanne couldn't help but believe, though briefly, that there was a reason for this. She wouldn't share her other findings with the crew, not now. The way their eyes scanned their surroundings gave her a fair indication of their levels of anxiety. And what if whatever attacked the ship would return? What would the purpose be lest strip ships for parts, or perhaps was it all a lure from an expert angler patiently waiting for them to lower their guard?

NELSON CLUNG to the hat Captain Drackenheart gave him. He had no protests to give as he watched the crew strip the *Retribution* for parts. The ship had served its purpose until the very end. A pyre was raised on the main deck as a part of the final descent. She was weary and broken and soon would rest eternally at the bottom of the ocean.

His moment of apathy broke when Higgs flew out of the warship's captain's quarters in a blaze of excitement.

"For the love of all creation to hold your fire!"

The chief engineer stumbled across the gangplank with a heavy descent onto the main deck and huffed up the stairs to the quarterdeck.

His grin was impeccable. "Ma'am! I found something immensely interesting."

"What is it, Mr. Higgs?" Rosanne cocked her head, perhaps because, given what she knew of Higgs' personality, this level of excitement was rare. Higgs noticed Nelson, and his lips sealed tight.

"It's fine. Speak."

"The ship has a *GPT*!" His excitement ended in a choked whisper.

"A what?"

"A Geographical Positioning Tracker! I've only ever read about those things, but these bastards had one in the cabin! It's recorded the entire journey onto a holographic map. And the best part is that we can use it."

Rosanne blinked, took in Higgs' immense satisfied grin, and, for the first time in weeks, felt excitement light up her smile. "Show me."

Higgs led them back to the cabin, Nelson stringing along behind. At the edge of the shredded carpet, Higgs revealed what red fabric had hidden. A square trapdoor, perfectly snug with the floorboards, betrayed a small compartment with an electrical instrument consisting of a prism base enclosed by arched metal rods. Higgs pushed a button on the side of the compartment. The gadget whirred to life and lifted itself from the hollow just above floor level. Its cylindrical top on the base spun and opened, pushing a rod up which again opened to four new rods bending out like a flower revealing its petals. The ends of the metallic rods sparkled and shot out blue beams, which crossed with each other and moments later produced a holographic image of what appeared to be Terra.

"Bloody hell." Rosanne walked around the device, studying the map with increased interest.

Higgs let out a hoarse squeak. "Far out, innit? The log shows that the *Retribution* employed this for over a year before whatever monster took the captain out for flight." Higgs caught himself, turning his eyes to Nelson. The lawyer stared at the engineer with blank eyes.

"Do continue," he said.

"Pardon my lip, Nelson. Anyhow, they've mapped all the large trade routes and even parts of the Veil! And the best part is that the GPT continued to do so after the crew disappeared. Look how far the ship drifted." Higgs turned a dial on the panel at the bottom of the GPT, highlighting a square area on the map. The Grey Veil was marked as a blue wavy line covering a large area, but as the picture zoomed in, the dotted line of the *Retribution's* course ran in an oval several times.

"It looks like the ship was caught in a constant current. It's been pushed up and down in circles for months," Rosanne remarked.

"Aye. Along its entry point here." Higgs wrung his hands excitedly.

She whistled. "This is military-grade equipment."

Higgs nodded. "State of the art, I'd say."

"Shouldn't be in our hands."

"Nope."

"We could get court-martialed or even exiled. An indefinite stay in her Majesty's dungeon would be too mild of a sentence."

"I believe so, ma'am."

"Get it aboard our ship, Mr. Higgs, and find a good hiding place for it. You might just have saved our hides."

"As you wish, ma'am."

"Mr. Blackwood, permission to...? Mr. Blackwood?" Rosanne caught the lawyer staring absentmindedly at the broken window, touching the sharp edges with his bare hands.

"He was in here before he died, wasn't he? This is his blood," Nelson said.

Rosanne looked to the floor and blew through her nose. "We don't know for sure, Mr. Blackwood. It might be someone else's."

"Please, Captain Drackenheart. It's not like you to show empathy. I knew full well that the *Retribution's* demise was an old tale long before I employed you. I had just hoped for ..." He looked around, sighed, and shook his head.

"You hoped for better closure. A body at least."

"It's similar to what happened to your father's ship, isn't it?"

At this, Higgs creased his brows and stood. "I'll ... get the kids to help me." He exited the room, leaving Rosanne to stare at Nelson with her arms crossed. She dismissed the notion with a frown.

"I wouldn't know anything about that."

Nelson snorted. "Do not take me for a fool, Captain. The circumstances are similar, although the main difference is that no one wanted to find this ship. Now I almost wish I hadn't." Rosanne bit her lip, letting her eyes wander about the cabin.

"You're ... shrewd. And well informed. But that isn't why we are here."

"Your family history appealed greatly to my cause, and I was placing my bets that you would accept, even without me having to go so far as I did." Nelson stepped back from the window, knelt, and ran a hand over the claw marks on the floor.

Nodding, Rosanne let go of the matter in light of the situation. "Your father left us a message in his books before whatever happened ... happened. I'll have to review it before I can show its contents to you. I apologize, Mr. Blackwood."

"It's quite all right, Captain. I got what I came for." Nelson gave her the saddest of smiles she had ever seen, creating a knot in her stomach. She tapped the GPT twice, as if in confirmation of her course ahead.

"Let's finish up here and give the ship a worthy funeral. We'll have you home in no time, Mr. Blackwood."

IT WAS dark in the foggy world of the Grey Veil before they managed to finish the pyre on the *Retribution's* main deck. With its crew gone and the ship broken, there was no reason for the vessel to haunt the shrouded skies of this place any longer. The *Retribution* might not have lived up to its name, but it had served its purpose. Watch Captain Dalia stood ready with a lit torch on the *Red Queen's* main deck.

"Would you do the honours, Mr. Blackwood?" Captain Rosanne asked the disquieted man clutching his father's tricorn hat. His eyes were tear-stained and bloodshot, his lip a thin line.

He shook his head. "I don't think I can, Captain."

Rosanne accepted his answer and nodded her approval to Dalia. The tall woman crossed the gangplank and threw the torch into the pile of wood which came alive in a blaze of light in the night.

Sailors retracted the gangplank once Dalia returned, and Hwang at the wheel guided the galleon a safe distance from the *Retribution*.

The *Red Queen's* crew took off their caps and bandannas, placing a hand over their hearts. Captain Drackenheart lifted her tattered cavalier in salute to the burning vessel. Farand stood next to them with the ship's ensign neatly folded between his stiff palms, and the lieutenant took three steps to stand in front of the captain, waited a moment, and stiffly handed her the flag. Rosanne lifted the flag to her forehead before turning to Nelson and passing it over.

"On behalf of the crew of the *MTS Red Queen* and myself, we offer our sincerest condolences for your loss, Mr. Blackwood. May your father and his crew sail the skies beyond the horizon and further. May they be forever at peace."

Nelson nodded as he held the flag to his chest along with his father's tricorn. Rosanne stepped aside, and the crew each took their turn to bow their heads, offering their condolences to the lawyer. Some provided soothing words, either heartfelt or merely out of courtesy. Nelson struggled to withhold the stinging of tears behind his spectacles.

Flames licked at the wood from the foremast to the bowsprit, its remaining sails disintegrating from the intense heat, popping and crackling. Chief engineer Artemis Higgs pushed a button on a small handheld box. The *Retribution* gently lowered itself towards the unknown beyond the fog below, its gravity engine losing power to keep the ship afloat. The blaze lit the fog up in an orange shroud and was visible for some time before finally disappearing out of sight.

Hammond lay a hand on Nelson's shoulder. "Come now. I've prepared scran for a wake. It's been a long day." Nelson merely nodded as he let himself be led by Hammond's hand on his back. The other crew members trailed after them to the galley.

Rosanne eyed Farand, who caught her attentive stare. "You didn't believe we would find anything, did you?" she said to him. Farand covered his tight, short-cropped curls with his hat.

"Not at all. I had no firm belief that we could trail the ship, that we would be forced to enter the Veil, or that we would find as much as a shred of its sail. It's a cruel joke from heaven."

"I agree. Something about this isn't right at all. We have seen ships in similar conditions, but this? I now wish I had tossed that lawyer out the fucking window the moment I saw him."

"You cannot truly blame him for the state of the ship. This entire incident could be part of something grand, something which started with a single ship and is now developing into an epidemic."

Rosanne ran a hand through her hair, tossing it out of her

face. She huffed. "You're probably right. I'm letting my emotions get the better of me."

"This makes the fifth ship in twenty years, no?"

Rosanne nodded. "That we know of. Seven years since we found a vessel still above water. If there are more out there, it could make that number ten times higher. What the hell is preying on these vessels? Only trade ships have been attacked so far."

"Something hungry."

"Farand." Rosanne's tone was low and warning.

"I'm merely stating a conclusion from my observation. All ships had crews numbering more than thirty. All had been picked clean."

"I'd rather believe in vengeful ghosts than hungry monsters in the Grey Veil. Come. I'm annoyed and hungry."

Chapter 8

Pesky Pirates and Blasting Bitches

A bottle of single malt whisky stood half empty at the edge of the desk. Rosanne had promised herself that the bottle would last throughout the voyage, but now she wasn't so sure she could keep her word.

The curly lettering of Captain Blackwood's handwriting was unparalleled. Pages upon pages in the ledgers were filled with his beautiful lexicon, each entry carefully dated and coordinated to the extent he could until they were left drifting.

27th November, 1703. The Grey Veil is a place of relentless torment where the majority of my crew's mental state has been touched by madness. Two men have been shot, mistaken as spirits. Erik Hammsund died of his injuries this morning. Knut Varang suffers from blood poisoning with little chance of recovery. Morale is low, our supplies are running short, and we have tried everything to get out of this situation.

The storm short-circuited all our electrical components save for our anti-gravity. Our engineer is unable to revive the thruster engine. It's a miracle we're still afloat. We drifted with the wind currents for four days before we saw any change in the environment. It was the calmest storm I ever witnessed, a wide space where circulating wind created a massive eye that cleared all the way to the sky.

We glimpsed the sun for the first time in days, but we do not know what caused this bizarre phenomenon.

THE EARLIEST ENTRIES of the *Retribution*'s latest mission were sparse with details, referring to a specific vessel merely as 'a bird.' Had Rosanne not bribed the RDA clerk, she wouldn't have known Captain Blackwood spoke of the *Blue Dragon*. The photograph wasn't even a good one, taken at dusk when the sun was still low and the ship at full speed, making it a blurry mess. Rosanne noted the double-deck, the gunports, the abnormal bowsprit, and the extra sails, which were sharp-toothed like dragon wings on the sides of the sterncastle. Two masts for such a ship was more than enough power output, but the dragon wing sails made her question whether the vessel was packing more than it betrayed. She scratched the back of her shin with her toenails before digging her feet into the soft carpet.

Rosanne combed through all the ledgers, scrutinizing the writing and the blackness of the ink, but nothing suggested Captain Blackwood had done the entries in bulk.

28th November, 1703. Knut Varang passed away sometime last night. No change in anything since then. We're somehow still recording our navigation, and according to the GPT we are drifting south into the thick of the Grey Veil. We can't escape it.

ENTRY... Another storm came from out of nowhere. The sky is black with clouds, hail, and rain. We're taking in water faster than the pump's capacity to extract it. The engine room is flooding. I don't know what to do...

The crew have reported unusual activity within the fog, shrieks in the night, and large terrifying shadows. We're driven to madness out here. God save us all.

. . .

SHE SHUT the logbook and rubbed her forehead.

"Monsters." She spat at the notion of any such mythological creature and emptied her glass of whisky before pouring another one. Had she not seen the state of the *Retribution*, she would have thought Captain Blackwood had drunk seawater to cure altitude sickness. The truth was she doubted herself more than the words of a dead captain. The evidence weighed heavily against her logic. This also meant that the longer they were in the Grey Veil, the greater the risk of the crew suffering the same fate.

"Captain?" The short-range intercom on her desk buzzed with a grouchy voice, and she reached for it after a short pause.

"Speak, Higgs."

"I got the GPT working."

"Anything which we can use to get the hell out of here?"

"Aye. I'll give you directions."

Rosanne grabbed her notebook and scribbled them down. "Fantastic. I'll have Hwang and Creedy confirm the course before we leave. Keep this to yourself for now."

The prolonged silence in the intercom prepared her for Higgs's unwanted opinion. "Ma'am, if I may, do you want to keep the crew in the dark?"

"I'll allow them to know our current position, but the *Retribution's* course before this point is classified."

"I understand, ma'am. I'll shut the traps of my younglings. They haven't stopped fussing over the machine. They're like children at the carnival."

"I'd expect nothing less." She smiled at the mental image of Ida and Gavin over the moon for having new toys with which to fiddle.

Rosanne scribbled the coordinates of the *Retribution's* journey onto the map she had of the Grey Veil. Although the depicted area was a large blob of nothing, it still followed the rules for longitude and latitude, and with specific coordinates, Rosanne could plot the course which would lead them home again. Rosanne didn't know what she would have done if Higgs hadn't discovered the GPT, and she briefly wondered if the Royal Defense of Aerospace supplied the *Retribution* in preparation to follow pirate vessels into the Grey Veil. But why the RDA would go to such lengths was beyond her. She had never even heard of this specific pirate ship, and any craft of such magnitude should have been to some degree infamous.

"One hell of a secret you have." She eyed the photograph and snorted. If her calculations were correct, they were less than five hours away from the fringes of the Veil. She would have to collaborate with the able seamen who were more skilled at navigation than her, but she needed to make sure before handing this information over.

Rubbing her eyes, she proceeded to put on her socks and shoes and locked the logbooks into the drawer along with the maps over the Grey Veil. Emerging from her quarters, Rosanne was met with a cluster of people shouting their protests at a pair of individuals fighting on the deck. It was Kristoff and Creedy. Others swarmed and attempted to break them apart. Farand wasn't nearby to take care of the rabble, and the crowd so far had been unsuccessful at stopping the altercation.

Kristoff tackled Creedy, and they both tumbled to the deck. The watch captain gasped upon landing, stunned from having the air knocked out of his lungs. His fist locked in Kristoff's hair while the crowd descended upon them in a heap of chaos. The men snarled as the crew tore them from each other with little success, for the wiry men were stronger than they looked. Creedy swung his fist, connecting with Kristoff's nose, which sent the man staggering. Norman broke through the crowd and rammed Creedy before the older man could retaliate and swing again. Kristoff lunged for the watch captain, his eyes livid. Olivier caught hold of him and locked his arm around his neck. Kristoff struggled against the headlock. The two men continued their fight in the form of a shouting match, throwing insults between them until Rosanne's intervention deflated them both. Her face was contorted fury bordering on maniacal, making the men wince at the sight.

"The two of you in my office. *Now.*"

"WHAT IN THE nine bloody hells was that all about? You know the rules!" Captain Drackenheart steeled her gaze until it was as firm as it was merciless.

"It was Kristoff who—"

"Creedy was being—"

"Enough!" Rosanne interrupted the two men. "If your squabble is personal, take it elsewhere. If it's professional, you deal with it like the bloody adults you claim to be. I will not hesitate to have you evicted from my ship if you endanger anyone again. I'll personally drive you both back to the port where I picked you up! Kristoff, you've barely been aboard on my vessel for six months and already have a strike against you. Next time I'll have you demoted. And Creedy, this is your final warning. Do your bloody job or enjoy the brig for the remainder of the trip. Goodness grief." Rosanne caught her breath and sat back in her chair.

Creedy snorted. "I don't need no woman to tell me what to fucking do."

The silence that followed was palpable. Kristoff looked stiff-lipped at the floor. Rosanne's eyes fixed on Creedy's, and she folded her hands onto the desk.

"This isn't about what's between my legs, Creedy. Feel free to call for a vote to have me booted as a captain, but as long as I'm in charge, you are to listen to my decisions. I'm not running a day nursery or a charity—I'm running a business. It is in everyone's best interest that this hierarchy work. If you have a problem with me, I'll be more than happy to meet you head-on. But as of right now, you are under a signed contract with this vessel and her current mission, and you are to abide by the rules until we return to port."

Creedy rolled his eyes and sneered but kept his mouth shut.

"Your personal vendetta has no room here, Creedy. This goes for you as well, Mr. Vasilyev, so wipe off that smug face."

"Yes, ma'am. My apologies." Kristoff cast his eyes to the floor again and did indeed wipe off said smug face.

"So tell me ..." Rosanne rested her elbows on her desk. "What was the fight really about?" The men exchanged forced glances, then hastily looked the other way.

"The sails Kristoff bound weren't good enough to hold them come due winds. I *may* have pointed out too strongly how his laziness might cost lives," Creedy said.

"What do you have to say?" Rosanne turned to the younger man.

"Creedy is never pleased with my progress, so I acted out."

"Fine. Kristoff, get up those masts and secure every sail ten times. Creedy take a jog around the ship decks fifty times. Dalia can oversee your progress. Any protests?"

"No, ma'am." Their in-unison reply might have lacked conviction, but their defiance had fled, and the men left in an orderly fashion to tend to their assignments. Rosanne heard the quick succession of boots on wood as Creedy made his way down the stairs to the main deck and the calling of fellow topmen bidding him good luck.

Rosanne's exasperated sigh caught the tangled mess of her fringe and sent it flying. From the drawer, she took a small notebook and opened it to a specific page. On it were the names of crew members who served the *Red Queen*, and on the side were notes of misconduct. She added today's incident to the entry and locked the book in the drawer.

"Every goddamn generation of landmen, there is one." She rubbed her temples, feeling like she had aged a decade. Creedy's defiance was the last thing she needed right now. After flying into the thick of the Grey Veil, the crew had been on high alert from dusk till dawn, and it wore their patience thin. The faster they got out of here, the better. Had Rosanne not sent Creedy jogging, she would have him and Hwang assisting with the return at this moment. Creedy, fit as a fiddle, still didn't take to running and would be too exhausted after completing his punishment.

"At least he won't have the strength to hit anyone anytime soon. Maybe I should just have Hwang on this? I'm talking to myself again. Marvellous."

———

THE *RED QUEEN* snaked through the fog at low speed. With her instruments virtually useless, Rosanne had Hwang confirm their position and assist with determining the course which should free them from the Grey Veil's ghostly hold. They had flown for over four hours straight, Higgs and Hwang supplying her with directions from the GPT when the ship began to stray. The little light the fog betrayed told them that it was nearing late afternoon, but Rosanne had timed the journey so they should be clear of the fog before nightfall. At that point, they could return to their classic navigational methods and no longer fear sudden unexpected death.

The lethargic flutter of the sails tightened as the vessel picked up speed. Rosanne left the wheel to Farand and stretched her limbs. Sitting down in a folding chair, she rested her legs on the rails to the quarterdeck. She had allowed herself precious few breaks throughout the journey, but as they closed on the end of the most dangerous part of their mission, Rosanne saw no harm in leaving the rest to her chain of command.

———

THE CLATTER of shoes woke Rosanne from her nap. She straightened her hat as she opened her eyes to find Nelson, who nodded at her. He hung his shoulders as he leaned on the railing.

"We're soon in the clear, Mr. Blackwood. You'll be home the day after tomorrow."

"Thank you, Captain. Your generosity does stretch beyond your crude jokes." Her generosity was part that and part out of Mr. Blackwood's wallet, but she simply nodded. Nelson stood for a while, staring into the thinning wisps of fog. Although Rosanne had her eyes closed again, she sensed the rays of light break through the clouds, and the cheer which erupted around the ship put a smile on her lips.

Over the thumping of feet and loud chatter, an electric, pulsating *zum-zum* wrenched Rosanne's eyes open wide. She leapt from the chair and tore Nelson from his spot. The opposite railing exploded into splinters, and a blue-green ball of plasma disintegrated the chair. The impact pushed Rosanne and Nelson from the quarterdeck and sent them tumbling down to the main. Farand was torn from the wheel, landing on his back.

"To your battle stations!" Rosanne roared. She winced from the impact of landing on her hip but pushed herself to stand.

"Get below deck, Mr. Blackwood! Looks like we got company." Nelson didn't have to be told twice and scrambled to the galley faster than a rat chased by a flock of cats. Rosanne flew up the stairs, giving a quiet cheer at seeing the wheel spinning and the instrument panels unharmed. Fumbling with the spyglass, she aimed it portside. Half a click in the distance and partially concealed by the fog flew a two-spire mayfly hybrid with a massive cannon at its main deck.

"Duplànte, can you stand?"

"I'm alive, Captain." The large man rose to his feet.

"Command the attack. I'll give you as much room as I can lend. They're packing plasma cannons." She slapped the spyglass closed and pocketed it.

"Load the cannons and stand by! Mr. Lyle, get your team on deck and await command." Farand's voice was an impressive boom resonating throughout the ship, and the crew scrambled for the batteries and firearms.

Rosanne put on her goggles and secured her hat, a small but

wicked grin on her lips. "Ladies and gents, secure the sails and brace for reckless flying!"

The topmen pulled at the ropes, which let the sails hang free, and secured each of them within half a minute, starting with the main and fore course sails and clambering onto the mast when the vessel swung. Rosanne gave them as much time as necessary before increasing the thruster power. Another shot rang from the plasma cannon, and she swooped the *Red Queen* forwards and down as the blue-green ball of pulsating energy sizzled past. From the fog, a pair of golden dragon-wing sails glinted in the afternoon sun. The ship's sturdy, wide-barreled cannon spun its circular tip. It was recharging.

"Fucking pirates," Rosanne muttered and stepped on the hull thruster acceleration to gain altitude.

"It's the *Blue Dagon*," Olivier called from the crow's nest, after which he immediately slid down the rigging onto the deck.

The *Blue Dragon's* sails were down, but the power output produced by the sun was strong enough to glimmer the sails; it was blinding in the distance. Rosanne twisted the wheel counter-clockwise, bringing the *Red Queen* portside so to face the *Blue Dragon* and its speartip.

"Fore fire!" Farand roared from the main deck, and the *Queen*'s guns boomed. Puffs of smoke preceded the cannonballs that flew at the ship. The *Blue Dragon* dipped low, but a chain shot snagged the topgallant sail and took the topmast with it. The vessel lurched, the speartip pointing up. "Aft fire!" Farand ordered at the sight of the *Dragon*'s exposed hull. The small ship veered to the side as the guns unleashed again. It took only a single hit to the keel.

The *Dragon's* main deck crew opened fire with plasma guns, the subsonic bullets scorching wood upon impact. Rosanne turned the wheel again, dipped the vessel, and pointed the ship's nose up as she turned the old girl around for the second wave of cannons ready on starboard. The *Blue Dragon* shot another ball of electrified matter which hit the *Queen* right at the gundeck. Two gunports exploded and splintered, and an impact tremor swept the ship. Rosanne heard screams, but she couldn't afford them a second of her attention as she was taking fire from the *Dragon's* gunmen.

Lyle sprang to action with his rifle, returning fire at the men on the *Dragon* aiming for his captain. The *Dragon's* agile build granted them maneuverability, and they easily veered to the side. Bullets pinged off its metal-plated hull, and plasma shots dispersed.

Rosanne brought them circling the *Dragon* the moment she saw the electrifying glow of the opposite deck. "Take out that plasma cannon before anything else. We can't get hit again, and I certainly can't get hit more than once!"

"Then drive like mad, Captain Drackenheart," Lyle said as he crawled past her to avoid the gunfire.

The gun crew of the opposing vessel ducked for cover as Lyle and his team peppered them with bullets, and the ship dared not stay still a second longer, increasing speed and circling the *Queen*.

"I need a starboard dip face-down, Captain. Bait them!" Lyle sprinted to the starboard railing that was still intact and wrapped his foot between the wood, cocking his rifle on the top.

"As you wish, Mr. Lyle." Rosanne sped up the *Queen* and joined the *Blue Dragon* in its circular dance of death. The *Queen* increased her altitude, and the *Dragon* pursued, shooting low at her hull.

"Brace!" The singular command rang throughout the ship only once, and the crew clambered onto whatever they could. Norman and Dalia were still crewing the sails, and even wearing safety harnesses they clung to wood with all their might as the ship began its wicked maneuver. Creedy dangled in a rope and secured himself the best he could, the rope tight above him and the deck disappearing beneath him.

Rosanne wrenched the wheel, bringing the *Queen* at a steep sideways angle overlooking the low flying pirate ship. Ropes and harnesses swung to the side, the people in them devoid of panic despite losing all footing. Rosanne had her entire weight on one leg to stabilize herself, but even she would have stumbled had she not had slots for her shoes by the wheel.

Lyle unloaded the full magazine of his plasma rifle into the glowing cannon on the *Dragon*. The bullets ricocheted inside the spinning barrel, producing putrid black smoke, which had the gunman flying from his seat and ducking for cover as the cannon was rendered inert.

"Clear!" Lyle confirmed. Rosanne levelled the ship, speeding away from the pirate vessel. The instrument panel went black before the *Red Queen* could build any significant momentum, and the ship lurched. It bucked and arched at nauseating speed as it spun out of control. It took all Rosanne had not to lose her grip on the wheel. Lyle lost his footing and slid past the helm, reaching his hands for the console. He managed to hook the plasma rifle between Rosanne and the console table, stopping his rapid descent towards the splintered railing. The galleon didn't fly far, slowed by opposing winds and a good dose of luck. The wheel didn't respond no matter how she turned, and she couldn't activate the fine thrusters.

"What the hell is going on?" she yelled into the intercom.

Higgs responded, his voice wavering in what was likely rage. "Something killed the engine, ma'am. Power isn't reaching it!"

Rosanne shot Lyle a nod towards the rear. The master gunner sped to the back of the ship and leaned over. The jutting sterncastle obstructed the view of the ports, but a meticulously constructed rod stuck out from the port side thruster panel. He called for Creedy, who came running with a length of rope and a safety harness. He was secured in seconds to the railing. The weather-hardened lines on his face deepened as he lowered himself towards the panels.

The *Blue Dragon* lumbered closer at a steady speed, coming at them from behind. The crew pointed standard firearms from the *Queen*'s stern. The gun team's fervent exchange of bullets had Rosanne ducking low as she waited for Creedy to free the thruster engine. A stray bullet struck her hat, sending it against the wheel.

"Son of a...!" Rosanne gawked at the hole in her hat. She released the clamps securing her feet, and pulled her flintlock from its holster.

"Take this, you fucking bastard!" At fifty paces, she opened fire against the opposing ship with little thought towards aiming. By pure luck, a single bullet hit the *Dragon*'s wheel, and the captain lurched as his own hat took a tumble.

"Nice shooting, ma'am." Lyle nodded and fired against the smaller ship, downing a crew member who had his leg exposed.

"They won't damage the thruster ports beyond repair. It's to cripple us so they can come up from behind out of reach from our cannons." Rosanne gnashed her teeth and tossed her spent flintlock pistol to one of the gunners, who reloaded the small calibre triple barrel with charge and balls.

"I would say they're planning to take the ship."

"Over my putrefied corpse."

"As you wish, Captain."

CREEDY, meanwhile, had to place his feet sparingly between the scorching ports not to lose his toes. Like a saw-toothed spear, the rod protruded from between the lower porthole and the circular ones. A light built into the technology glowed blue, evidently sucking the thrusters dry or disrupting its electrical circuits. Whatever the case might be, Creedy grabbed the spear with gloved hands.

"Come on, you piece of shit." He placed his legs on either side of it, pulling with every muscle fibre he could muster. In his periphery, the pirate ship approached. Creedy wiggled the spear from side to side and cursed fervently as it stubbornly held on. He continued to tug, and it slowly released its hold on the metal plating.

"Hurry up down there!" some pretentious bastard from on top shouted at him. The rod was buried too far for his raw power to remove it by hand. He climbed on top of it, then jumped. The rod squealed as the metal around it bent, and Creedy could finally pull it free. The motion made him lose his footing. He swung to the side, grazing his back against the circular exhaust port. Its bite was hot. He yowled and kicked out with his feet to get some distance between him and the roasting metal.

"Pull me up!" he called, and the tug of the rope yanked him faster than he could regain his footing. Seconds later, the ship hummed to life.

"Creedy's up," Lyle announced.

ROSANNE SPRINTED for the wheel and received the all-clear from Higgs on the intercom. She turned the *Red Queen*. Farand complied with Rosanne's flying and fired the cannons at the approaching ship. Again, the ship ducked out of harm's way.

"We can't gun them down. They're too fast." Rosanne looked at the instrument panels, hastily crunching the numbers of the altitude, the weather, and the winds. They might not make it out of this fight without massive losses.

"Where the hell did they get their dirty hands on a Sub-theran Y48?" Gavin mused through the spyglass, admiring the pirate ship's state-of-the-art thruster panel. Rosanne hadn't even noticed the third engineer had arrived. Gavin received the spear from Creedy, his eyes gleaming in wonder at the piece of foreign technology.

"Why are you here, Mr. Diggle?" she asked.

"Higgs sent me for the spear and to let you know you're overheating Sally. Also, looking at the pirate ship's make and model, their energy output is about a quarter more to their half size," he said without taking his eyes off the spear.

"Do I *look* like an engineer, Gavin?!"

The young man flushed. "It means that they're quicker than us because of the size of our ship and their superior engine."

A million questions ran through her mind as she scrambled for any feasible ideas that might save their hides. The wheel was cold and slick from the fog, but her hands were locked and unco-operative. She blew out a cloud of cold air, though her insides were boiling.

Cannon ports revealed themselves on the *Dragon*'s hull, metal nostrils of lead ready to fire directly at the galleon. The glow of their plasma canon stuttered, but there was no mistaking it. It was operational again.

"Captain!" Farand called from the main deck, holding on to his hat and pointing. "The Elder Reef!" Her eyes followed his finger to the calm seas below; partially obscured coral columns jutted from the fog. She hitched a breath and wiped the sweat from her face, blinking away its salt sting as she checked the map on the panel. Although they were at the fringes of the Grey Veil, the massive fog was much further out than normal.

"We can't fly through it," she said to herself, watching the pirates pepper the topgallant sails full of bullet holes. "If we're idle for even a moment, they'll hit us with the plasma cannon." A scream resonated from the bow.

Creedy ran to secure the canvas flapping on the mizzenmast.

"What's the wind direction and speed?" she hollered as he passed.

The topman pulled at the spanker sail, which had come loose. "East. Can't say much of the speed with the way you're flying."

Rosanne gave herself a moment to observe the ongoing activity in the rigging. Dalia's voice was a whip as she coordinated the topmen who repeatedly had to traverse the masts. Fast and nimble, Dalia unhooked the safety harness from the rigging and climbed across to the other end of the mainmast sail to assist. A few sails remained flapping so to provide auxiliary power. This was especially important now, as the instrument panel lights were turning orange, indicating the ship's power reserves were spent.

Rosanne knew it wouldn't last for a drawn-out battle such as this. The mizzen sail was riddled with bullet holes to the point of decommission. If they lowered the others, they would suffer the same fate.

Picking up the intercom, Rosanne regarded the circling pirate ship once more. She couldn't make out any individuals, but knowing the pirates had the advantage they needed to pick the *Red Queen* clean was the extra push she needed. "Prepare for emergency. Shut off the thruster engines and start the anti-grav."

A metallic clatter screeched in the speaker. "What in the blazes are you on about, Cap? The port covers will melt!" Higgs protested.

"Just be ready and start up the anti-grav no more than three seconds after the ports close. Just crank the thing to full power. It's imperative!" The intercom smacked against the instrument panel, drowning out the first engineer's stream of grumbles.

"Mr. Duplànte! Secure all sails and brace the crew!"

"Fold all! Prepare for brace!" Cannons were unloaded and secured on their rails, and whatever idle crew were left ran to secure anything that wasn't nailed to the floorboards. Rosanne pushed the wheel forward as far as it would let her. The ship dipped her nose towards the smoky waters below.

The *Blue Dragon* followed in a wide arch like a hunter flanking its prey. Rosanne glanced at the numbers on the altitude-meter drop, the ocean drawing closer at an alarming speed. She ground her teeth and pulled the wheel back, keeping the speed steady and levelling the ship with the waterline. The jutting corals rushed past the portside. Her eyes were on the topographical scan of the surroundings, searching for their one hope.

"Sail input," she muttered as she flipped a small switch. "Engine power line." She flipped another in rapid succession. Rosanne stepped off the foot levers and drew the tall main lever back. "Atmos. Hull thrusters. Speed." The sails' hum ceased their song and shimmer as the thruster panel went dark. She hitched another breath during the few seconds it took her to prepare.

"Cut the thruster engine and close the ports!" she yelled in the intercom. The hum of the engine disappeared. Within seconds, Rosanne heard the stern covers emerge and unfold, sealing the thruster ports in a watertight compartment. Every second felt like a thousand years.

"Brace!" Farand's booming voice called out to the crew, who clambered on to their safety harnesses, the rails, and the masts.

Just as the *Queen* came within a stone's throw of the massive jutting corals, Rosanne steered the ship's bow into the water. The anti-gravity, which kept the ship hovering, cut abruptly as they hit the water. Crewmen lost their footing, and crates stored on deck tore free from their bindings. A belaying pin snapped and whipped a deadeye free from the ratlines, narrowly missing several of the crew in its path over the rails. The *Red Queen* let out a massive groan as she bobbed on the water. Rosanne tumbled against the wheel, but her feet were still firmly locked in place. Her teeth rattled, hat dangling loosely around her neck. Regaining control, Rosanne utilized the speed the ship already had and veered the *Red Queen* into a narrow passage of massive corals. The ship's starboard scraped against the passage wall, but Rosanne's deftness at the helm freed them from the grind. Behind them, the thruster ports steamed hot in the cold seawater, leaving a trail of smoke.

Topmen scrambled for the mainsails and unfurled them just after the turn, and the mizzen and mainmast sails caught the wind, which carried them further into the maze of the reef. Only for a moment did Rosanne spot the *Blue Dragon* pass by the reef opening. Its wide sails rendered them unable to fly low enough to enter the passage without hitting the water. The tangle of rock-hard minerals shielded the *Queen* from above. The crew fell silent, and Farand gestured with hand signals for the battle stations to standby. They returned to the hushed world of ghostly torment with the thickening fog around them.

Rosanne allowed the ship to slow, and she navigated between the thick columns of pink coral.

"Bet they didn't expect that." Rosanne had to congratulate herself. She honestly hadn't thought it would work. Farand arrived from the main deck.

"We've lost two cannons. Three are injured, but Doc is already looking after them."

His grim demeanour was a never-ending reminder of danger, but even so, Rosanne allowed herself to grin. "We cut it too close this time. I'll get us out of this, so be ready for—" The rumble of cannons from above made everyone duck. In the distance, they heard the impact of metal and coral.

"They're shooting blind. They can't keep that up forever," Farand said, eying the distant corals.

"It's a scare tactic. Unless they drop a column on us, we won't sink."

Farand raised an eyebrow.

"We've been through worse, Duplante." She grinned.

"I'm not sure we have, Captain."

DESPITE GOING BACK into the Grey Veil after emerging from their eerie trip, the sight of the corals of the Elder Reef were a relief for the crew. The reef was not unknown sailing grounds. The deafening silence told them the pirate vessel had given up the pursuit, but Rosanne wasn't taking any chances and kept both crew and ship on low profile until they emerged on the other side some two hours later.

"Alright. Let's make our lady fly again." They were out of the water in minutes and steadily climbed to an altitude surpassing the reef. Rosanne steered the *Queen* further into the fog, as she suspected the pirates still patrolled the area.

The sound of cannons resonated again. A massive blow caught them to starboard, woodchips flying.

"How in the blazing hell did they find us?" Rosanne barked as she turned the *Queen* nose-first eastward and increased speed. The *Blue Dragon* fired from deep within the shroud, but even without any direct visibility to the *Queen,* they still came straight at them. Rosanne drove the ship starboard and then port, attempting to shake the hail of metal.

The wind tugged at the sails, and Rosanne was about to have them secured when the ship veered due to a strong gust of wind.

"This is definitely not normal," Rosanne said as the cannons fired again. The *Blue Dragon* was *above* them! Caught in the powerful gales, the pirates flew with their starboard leading. A crackle resonated in the distance. Rosanne wrenched the wheel around, and somehow, the *Queen* obeyed and stayed stable alongside the winds. Gavin ran up the stairs, spear in hand.

"This is how they found us, Captain. It disrupts electrical activities but it's also a tracking device!" Rosanne stared at the spear for a moment, then directed her eyes at Lyle and his men.

"Mr. Lyle! Time to hunt a dragon!" She took the spear and raised it above her head.

"Yes, ma'am." His eyebrows shot up at the sight of the spear.

THE RENEWED exchange of bullets drowned out the howling wind as the *Blue Dragon's* relentless chase of the *Red Queen* brought them within firing distance. Rosanne veered the ship from side to side, purposefully increasing and decreasing speed as the thruster panels stuttered.

Lyle emerged from the cargo deck with the spear, skirted by two men who carried a crudely cut cylindrical tube and filling. They lined themselves up beside the mounted sterncastle cannon.

"You have a solution for everything, don't you?" Rosanne said and shook her head at Lyle's passing. His eyes held the spark of mirth.

The men encased the spear in the tubing and shoved it into the cannon while a small team of Lyle's men covered their actions with a vigorous spray of bullets.

The *Blue Dragon* dipped to go up and alongside the *Queen's* port. Lyle aimed the cannon as his men lit the fuse. The spear shot out of the barrel in a spray of wood splinters and whatever he had used to seal the spear with. The cylindrical tube broke apart mid-air to reveal a saw-toothed head. The spear lodged itself right at the base of the *Dragon*'s right wing. The attack was so swift and unexpected that it produced a wave of panicked shouts from the pirates, their ship spinning and ascending with the winds. A man was wrenched from the deck and fell to his watery death, screaming. Rosanne raised her hand in a rude gesture, pushing the engine into gear in pursuit of the uncontrollable ship.

"Take them out, Mr. Duplànte!"

"Broadside!" Farand hollered.

The cannons emptied their bore at the ship's hull and gundeck. Rosanne grinned at the sound of splintering wood and shattering windows and even more at the cries of pirates scrambling for cover and flying overboard. The main mast shattered in the middle, bringing all the rigging with it tumbling onto the deck. The ship should have fallen right out of the sky. They somehow remained afloat even as the relentless eastern wind grabbed hold of the *Dragon* and carried it away at an alarming speed. The fog stirred at the shift in weather and broke into wisps.

Rosanne fought against the monstrous winds, but the downed sails made it impossible. Dalia already had men crawling on the ratlines, but they were dangerously exposed. The ship followed the current as it veered in a long arch, spinning around.

The rain came in buckets, washing over the deck and the sails, hammering against them as hard as rocks. Rosanne attempted to steady the ship enough for the topmen to get to the sails, but the wind was too strong. She spotted the *Dragon* in the distance caught in the same current. They still hadn't recovered the power to fight the winds. Lightning sparked above them, followed by a deafening rumble. The *Queen*'s mainsail tore right across the middle, flapping uselessly against the wind, and the fore top-gallant had the mast bending in loud protests. Hemp snapped under stress and flew wild.

Dalia and Creedy's teams worked fervently at securing the sails, fighting against wind, rain, and stubborn ropes. Minutes that felt like hours passed before the sails and crew were secure. Rosanne anchored herself to the base of the wheel. Farand assisted on the other end, but there was no power in either of them strong enough to get the *Queen* out of this erratic storm.

A pitched screech followed by a deep echoing rumble made Rosanne turn her head. She squinted at the fog as rain battered her face. Lightning briefly outlined a distant lumbering shadow. She blinked, but there was nothing there other than perhaps her imagination. In the torrential rain, all she saw was the storm swallowing them whole and carrying them deeper into the unknown hell that is the Grey Veil.

CHAPTER 9

CREATURES OF THE NIGHT

The sudden cold slap in her face woke Rosanne with a start. She lay sprawled around the wheel, still secured to it with the harness, and knocked her head against one of the pins as she sat up.

"Captain!" She recognized Farand's voice.

The dampness of her clothes made her shiver. Her hair was matted and clung to her skin.

"Bloody hell." She massaged her forehead and squinted against the weak light illuminating the world around them. Patting the top of her head, she scanned her surroundings.

"Where is my..." Duplànte reached around her and twirled the hat around. "Oh, thank you. Thought I'd lost it."

"You were out for a while." He held out a hand and lifted her to her feet without straining as much as a muscle. His hand, as strong as a hydraulic press on her hands, made her gasp loud enough to catch everyone's attention. She peeled her gloves off gently to find her hands were a patchwork of bruises and swollen fingers.

"That explains a lot." She turned them over, thankful her palms escaped the vicious beating.

"I'll take you to the sickbay. You can't pilot the ship like that."

"We have more pressing matters to discuss than a few bruises. What's our status?"

Farand's uncanny silence as he scanned the deck made Rosanne follow his gaze. Pieces of the mizzen and foremast hung cleaved in half, barely connected by thin fibres of wood. The mainsail hung limp with a tear running along the middle, bonnet and all. The main topgallant sail was missing, along with the uppermost part of the mast. Whatever supplies they hadn't secured on deck now lay on the bottom of the ocean for the marine life to enjoy.

Pointing at the mainsail, Rosanne huffed. "This is exactly why I didn't want to go cheap on the sails. Fuck me sideways ... when we get out of here, we're investing in a six trim mainsail so we don't lose the damn thing." Farand smirked despite the situation.

A few crew members lumbered about picking up useful parts and sorting them into piles. The topmen surveyed what remained of the rigging and shook their heads.

Rosanne let out a snort. Turning around to face Farand again, her heart clenched. "How's the crew? And secondly, how are you?" She nodded towards the crusted red trail running down his neck from a cut on his forehead.

Farand put a hand over his wound and looked away. "Most of us got banged up pretty good during the storm, but nothing fatal: bruises, some concussions and weak bowels. I had the crew retreat below deck after losing most of our sails. I think I received a piece of the foremast sometime during the storm." His eyes turned to the dangling ship piece in question. "From what the crew told me, the storm disappeared as fast as it had come, and we drifted here."

Rosanne released herself from the safety harness and grabbed the wheel to support her wobbling knees. "And where in the bloody blazes is *here*?"

The silence accompanied them like a ghostly presence, for as far out at sea as they were, she expected some form of noise: wind, the crashing of waves, a gull shrieking in the distance perhaps. As she listened, a sharp crackling and deep rumble resounded, albeit obscured by the fog. Rosanne stared at the massive wall of rocks hunkering on the ship's port side.

"Are those ... gravity stones?"

Duplànte shrugged, staring at the wall. Fog snaked around the hunk of boulders and into every crevice. Just above the main mast was the underside of a massive boulder. The *Red Queen* bobbed gently up and down, prodding it in the process and making dirt and pebbles rain onto the deck. Rosanne scanned the ship from bowsprit to stern. All around them, rocks of varying sizes floated about and bumped into each other, creating a cascade of faint rumbles akin to a landslide. When the ruckus settled, not even the faintest breath of wind penetrated the silence.

"Are we somewhat secure?"

"Aye. We're tethered to that large boulder over there. We seem to be moving along with them. We've floated about three hundred meters from when we arrived here two hours ago. The GPT shows that this wall is but a small fragment of a much larger mobile network." Rosanne nodded, kept nodding, rubbed her chin and did a half-turn sweep before scratching the back of her head.

"We need an emergency plan. Gather all the seniors and ... *what* are they doing?" Rosanne threw a hand towards Ida and Gavin.

The second engineer leaned out from the ship, secured by a single hemp rope and Gavin's muscles to hold her in place.

"Shut up and hold it steady!" Ida yelled, stretching a landing net to capture a fist-sized rock floating by. Gavin leaned back as a counterweight but struggled as Ida swung the landing net, precariously balanced while outstretched on the tip of her shoes. .

"Got it. Woah!" She lost her balance and smacked into the side of the ship. With Gavin's help, the second engineer made it onto the deck in one piece. Her face was red from a first encounter with the lip of the deck.

"What are you doing?" Farand crossed his arms at the unusual sight. Ida untangled the net and shook out the rock with a grin. It floated before her.

"Mr. Duplànte, sir! Orders from Higgs. He theorized these rocks had magnetic properties, which is why navigation is impossible. Look at this. Amazing." She bounced it between her hands. "It's rich in raw anti-gravity minerals. Probably the same we use for our ships. Isn't it cool? Who knows how far these rocks go?"

Farand dismissed them with a wave, and Ida disappeared alongside Gavin below deck.

"Anti-gravity stones with magnetic properties? This place is a curse that keeps on cursing." He shook his head at the notion of Higgs' scientific mind playing a larger role than his team's security.

Rosanne untangled hair from her face, combing it back under her hat. Her fingers were stiff and swollen, pulsating with every heartbeat and worsening with any attempts at flexing. For a moment, the floor underneath her feet flowed like ocean waves, and Rosanne grabbed hold of the control panel to steady herself. Her head pounded as she shook off the dizziness. She spent a moment reconstituting herself, drawing deep breaths. Farand seemed well enough to take the wheel, but there wasn't much more of this the ship or the crew could take. Or herself. Rosanne erred in thinking they would escape the Grey Veil in one piece. Were they now suffering the same fate as the *Retribution*? How long would it be until the ship was picked clean or the crew is driven mad to the point of suicide? She shook the dreadful notion away and scanned the instrument panels.

"Ah!" Her excited outburst brought Farand to her. "There's a landmass on the other side of this wall." The big man looked down at the panel screen. At the moment, there was nothing but green snow.

"You can barely see it between the pulses, but it's there. I saw it moments ago. There!"

"Holy Mosaiha," Farand muttered in amazement.

The topographical map showed the flying rocks scattered all

around them. They converged and floated around a specific point. The signal wasn't strong enough to detect anything further out than a mile, and the wall was thicker than that, but the other navigational instruments showed greater promise. The wall stretched perhaps two or three kilometres in width, often disrupted by gravitational and magnetic energy waves, stronger and more frequent now than ever. The space between the wall and the edge of the landmass appeared empty.

"Gather everyone who can still stand in the great cabin."

IT WAS ONLY after the persistent insistence of Farand that Rosanne got her hands checked out. They were soaked in hot water, then cold, then hot again, and lastly cold. The gash over her left eyebrow received stitches, and the waves of nausea she experienced passed without much fuss. Duplànte escaped with a cut that didn't need stitches and insisted he didn't suffer any compromising injuries. There wasn't much else their doctor could do but urge them to rest, which was out of the question.

The galley was in disarray, with overturned and broken furniture, but Rosanne had everyone gather there anyway. Hammond sat on a chair, wincing as he rubbed his bad leg. Fuzzypaws rested on his lap, ears down, eyes stiff and judging. The poor cat was found lodged to the ceiling beam in the pantry after the storm but hadn't sustained any physical injury. Dalia's arms were covered in bruises and rope burns of varying sizes from the safety harness. Her hard face didn't betray an ounce of discomfort as she stood with her feet firmly planted and crossed arms. Slumped against the wall, Creedy's ashen face was a droopy affair mixed with blue bags and a not-so-subtle hint of sleep deprivation. Nelson's pale and sweaty face betrayed ongoing seasickness.

Rosanne clapped her hands, calling for attention. "Thank you all for coming. Let me begin by saying we got royally fucked over." A murmur of agreement went through the room, along with displeased sneers and shaking heads. "Our situation as of right now is grim at best. Mr. Duplànte and I have discovered a landmass across this wall. Navigating through it will not be easy, and we do not have much power. But the truth is we're in a dire situation—we have two choices which I will leave up to you to decide. We can either attempt the return trip as-is or reach land and gather the resources we need to patch up the ship. But here's the downside: we don't have enough power for a speedy return to Bogvin, nor do we have the armament to defend ourselves should we be attacked again. If we're caught in another storm, chances are we will not make it. On the flip side, we do not know exactly what is across this wall. We might not even find the resources we need. What we have is enough food and water for another week, but our mizzen mast and the mainmast are firewood. Our sails are torn, and we're running on reserve power which might last us two days if we conserve it and fly slow." The crew shook their heads, hung them, or simply stared with nothing to contribute.

Rosanne stretched out a hand to the left side of the room. "We go beyond the floating rocks, or," she reached out her right hand, "we fly straight for Bogvin and hope for the best."

Shoes tapped against the wooden floor. Glances were exchanged. Ida crossed her arms and looked for her engineer team for approval before moving to the cabin's left side. Dalia and several topmen joined them. Creedy and Norman went right. The overall result was a close vote. Nelson, although voting for unknown lands, fidgeted and corrected his glasses.

"Anything you'd like to say, Mr. Blackwood? I realize this is not what you're paying us for."

"Not at all, Captain. I trust you and the crew's judgment. But the question still stands: What if? This has become a greater deal than originally planned, and now more than ever do we face the possibility of never returning home."

"What if, indeed. But I'm afraid that is a chance we must take. The vote is clear, albeit close. Uncharted land it is. Rest up for now. We leave at first light."

"Excuse me, Captain!" Kristoff called out, his hand raised. She turned her eyes to the young landman. "Has anyone seen Iban?" The hesitation in his voice and scrunched eyebrows spoke his true anxiety. Iban was nowhere to be seen.

THEY DISCOVERED Iban's lifeless body buried under broken barrels and crates on the cargo deck. He was stiff and nearly cold to the touch when they pulled him from the room and wrapped him in white sheets in the sickbay. Kristoff shook and wept over the corpse. Between his sobs, he muttered incomprehensible words, from the raging torrents of emotions or simply in a different language altogether.

"What do I tell Mother? You stupid bastard! You *had* to secure our provisions!" His fist slammed against the table, but the white shrouded corpse remained silent.

The doctor approached Rosanne and shook his head. "Lad cracked his skull open during the storm. A pointless accident and a true tragedy."

"Misfortune was our only fortune this round," Rosanne said.

"Indeed. Hopefully, the lad will be the only one. Which reminds me, he's from Katshov, no? We can't bury him at sea then."

"We'll conclude that business as soon as we find land. Take good care of them both in the meantime, Doc."

"Will do, Captain."

Leaving the infirmary left a frozen vacuum in her chest, the incoherent sobs of Kristoff following closely behind her steps. She ran a hand through the tangle of her hair. As she replaced her hat, her finger brushed the newly formed bullet hole in the fabric. She examined it, the hole just above where the top of her head would have been. Her brush with death was trite against Iban's tragedy. How many bullets had she dodged, shielded by mere luck, while Iban, a young man from the inland of Katshov with his whole life ahead of him, had his days cut short at the hands of a freak accident?

"That is the life at sea. May his spirit forever roam the blue skies or walk the grassy fields of his mother's land." Her voice was but a whisper, and no one saw the glistening in her eyes.

———

DAYLIGHT HARDLY PERMEATED the thick fog among the floating rocks. Despite recent tragedies weighing heavily on everyone's shoulders, Rosanne had no choice but to press forward through the maze. With the ship's reserves running low, she routed the power to the fine thrusters around the ship's hull, gentle in guiding the *Queen* through the rocky masses. With help from the sonar, she had a decent idea of the path ahead, but often she was forced to change the route as the boulders were too large to circumvent.

Rosanne stepped on the pedals gently and turned the wheel, pushing the ship's broken bowsprit against a medium-sized boulder obstructing the path. It budged from the weak impact, and the crew assisted with long poles to push smaller rubble aside. A rock the size of a small ship floated in from the side. Rosanne pushed the wheel forward as hard as she could and forced the *Red Queen* down. The boulder banged portside against the ship, making Rosanne lose balance. The ship pushed against the boulder. Grinding her teeth, Rosanne turned the wheel again. The frequent fizz of the thrusters hummed loudly as they worked furiously to free the ship. She pushed the ship onward, scraping against the rock, and managed to get ahead and down. The boulder floated on above them. Rosanne's hands shook, swollen and painful, on the pegs she tightly gripped.

Farand appeared from the main deck. A single white patch of bandages covered his cut, but the injury didn't deter his brusque expression. "Do you require assistance, Captain? How are your hands?"

She frowned, cut the thrusters, and set them in reverse to avoid a frontal collision with another stray boulder. Sweat beaded on her forehead, but in this fog, everything was covered in pearly drops of water. Rosanne blinked the drops out of her eyes. "We're almost through. Don't worry about me and help the others as much as you can."

"Captain, I must insist that your state of well-being—"

"I said to assist the crew, Mr. Duplànte."

"...Yes, Captain." He bowed and didn't waste his efforts against Captain Drackenheart's iron will.

The density of the rock belt tightened, suffocating and claustrophobic. Fine dust polluted the air and obstructed their view. Rosanne tied a scarf over her mouth to shield her lungs from the dust. The particles were somehow undeterred by the ship's atmos which told her their technology now worked less than ideally after the storm. The ship struggled to heed her commands of the wheel, and Rosanne wasted more time and power than she hoped.

The rocky belt cleared ahead of them, and a final push from the *Queen* freed them from the obscure world of floating geography.

"God bloody dammit!" Rosanne's outburst was met with groans from the crew, who was equally disappointed in seeing the renewed view of absolute grey nothing.

Rosanne smacked the wheel, felt the acute shooting pain course through her hand, and through gritted teeth said: "Duplànte. You're up!" He took the wheel without a word, and she felt his eyes on her back as she stalked off below deck.

Her shoes thumped against the wooden stairs as Rosanne descended into the *Red Queen*. Her short stature allowed her an upright position navigating through the maze. At the back of the ship, the engine room was linework of varying pipes running across almost every available surface. To her left, the saltwater filter worked overtime, steam escaping macroscopic cracks around the unsecured lid—a slush of brine accumulated along the sides and slopped onto the floor. Valves hissed, and boilers groaned. Rosanne broke out in a sweat and fanned herself with her hat.

"Captain Drackenheart!" She spotted Ida's feet, the rest of the woman hidden underneath the block of the thruster engine as tall as Rosanne and four times as wide. The top row of exposed pistons encompassing the power output thrummed with movement. Ida rolled herself out, and still wearing the triple-layered glasses, which made her eyes appear enormous, she grinned. Rosanne chuckled at the humorous sight despite recent events.

"Is Higgs here?"

"Dunno. He said he was doing rounds, but he probably found something to fix since he's not back yet. We're working overtime like mad down here. The engine is still not behaving like the lovechild it is."

"Anything you can tell me to lighten my day?"

Ida pointed a finger up, then shook it. "Hmm. We might be able to conserve enough power for a return trip if we only use cruise control from here on. The power output to the hull thrusters took more than usual, so we're looking for the leak. We can't shut down the engine for complete maintenance until we have solar power. Batteries are as shot as Creedy's mood. Restarting the engine will purge it completely." Hitching a short breath, she continued the string of information with impressive speed. "*If* we're really desperate, we can temporarily rig the engine to skip a lot of steps that normally would use power, but at the cost of certain goods, like lights, the fine thrusters, perhaps even the atmos. Then there's the safety issue ..."

Rosanne smiled. "This is why I have the three of you. As we have no idea of what is ahead, I'd say go for it. But check with Higgs first."

"I thought you hired us all because we came with Higgs?" Ida chuckled. "Be careful not to stress the engine any more than necessary. If we re-rig it, the ship might blow unless you fly exactly like we tell you to. That's not even a choice, ma'am. Pardon my frankness."

"I get it. And to confirm your suspicions, the ship was a bitch to navigate. Her thrusters are not up to speed. She was leaning to the side as well."

"We'll send Gavin to check the grav-ports. But as things are now, there isn't much we can do. We need power, time, and a lot of tinkering." She grimaced.

"You'll have it all hopefully within the day."

"I'll inform Higgs." She started for the door, her steps light and playful.

"On another note..." Rosanne fanned herself and scanned the room, noticing the condensation buildup on the ceiling and Ida's sweat-stained shirt. "Anything else broken in here?"

"We might have cut the ventilation pump to the room to conserve power." She laughed and ran the back of her glove over her forehead.

Rosanne chuckled, appreciating every moment spent with the team that would bend heaven and expend comfort to make the ship work. "Don't kill yourself now."

"Yes, ma'am."

"*MERDE. I ain't seeing shite*," Olivier growled. Pointing his spyglass into the fog proved futile. It was dark, and not even the faintest light illuminated the fog on any hold. Around the upper decks, the crew lit lanterns to chase the darkness. Without the proper lights, finishing the evening shift proved a tedious task which left the crew bored while the *Red Queen* parked for the night.

"What did he say?" Norman called from the forecastle as he sawed off broken woodwork.

"Shit and that he isn't seeing anything, Norman," Dalia said as she weaved hemp on the shroud and cut the torn ropes. Two of the fittings had broken off during the storm and weakened the rigging's attachment to the mast, but after replacing the snapped ropes, it would suffice for now. When Dalia was satisfied with the tightness of the shroud after running them through the deadeyes and securing them, she added ratlines to the remaining ropes, climbed aboard and rocked back and forth with all her strength. "Yuss. That should do it."

"Whoosh!" Norman called out and dodged a broken peg thrown at him. "Shouldn't we have someone heavier than a stick insect test it?" he said.

Dalia snorted. "I'd be happy to let you try it out, but I'm afraid it will snap under the layers of fat on your face."

"It's called baby fat! I'm just late at losing it, s'all."

Dalia cackled. Creedy was silent, running an extra length of cloth along the split of the mainsail and applying thick glue. After threading an enormous needle, he proceeded to sew the cloth from one end to the other while the glue was still drying.

"You want a hand with that?" Dalia offered, seeing the frown on his face.

Creedy hung his head low close to the seam barely visible in the candlelight. "Nah, I'm good," he grumbled.

"What crawled up your arse and died?"

"This entire bloody trip!" He threw the needle, and it clanged against the deck. Staring at it for five solid seconds, he reeled it back in and continued to push the needle through the thick canvas. Along with the lack of light, to make matters worse, Creedy had to avoid damaging the conductor patterns which absorbed sunlight. The loss of a single hexagonal piece was equal to a whole solar Photo Voltaic module; the extremely thin, vertically stacked planes increased the surface area many times over despite its small size. Each column was connected to a mainline running vertically through the sail and into the support mast, suspending the sail before connecting with the mainline in the masts.

Dalia left Creedy to his misery and shrugged at Norman, who stared at them oddly.

"Night!" Olivier called, making Dalia raise an eyebrow at his heavy lisp.

"Yeah, we know it's night. It's dark, and we can't see a thing," she teased.

"No no. Nnnnnnight!" He pointed towards the sky.

"I don't follow..."

"Nnnnnllllllight!"

"Light? You kidding? Where?"

"LIGHT!" Dalia, Norman and Creedy swarmed Olivier, who leaned over the railing by the anchor. They followed the direction of the spyglass. Against the dark gloom, there wasn't anything obvious grabbing their attention. A minute passed, maybe two. Then a faint blue glow whisked in and out of existence.

"I saw that!" Dalia called out.

"Me too." Norman pointed to another glow at their two o'clock.

Creedy looked above them. "They're everywhere." Hundreds of tiny blue globules blinked around them. Some appeared near, others so far away they were barely visible. "What are they?"

"I dunno."

"Nothing I saw before." A low growl from behind them caused all the little lights to vanish.

Dalia stared at her teammates. Norman answered, "Are you thinking...?"

"Get the lights. Get all the bloody lights!" Dalia hissed, and they sprang into action, scrambling to blow out all the lanterns on deck. Dalia stumbled onto the quarterdeck and grabbed the intercom.

"Whoever is down there cut all of the lights! Something is hunting out there."

"Wha? You're kidding, right?" Ida questioned.

"Just do it!" The lights illuminating the lower decks died out over the next ten seconds. The strange glowing orbs around them resumed their night calls, but the growl had transformed into a giant ball of red illumination swimming back and forth just above their heads. It scraped its underbelly against the topmast, tipping the ship, and swam on to devour the lights in front of it. Rosanne burst from her cabin.

"What in the bloody hell is—"

Dalia, Creedy, Norman, and Olivier shushed her. In the darkness, they couldn't appreciate her profoundly confused expression. They heard her shoes against the deck as she approached.

"Over here, Captain," Dalia whispered and gently grabbed Rosanne's outstretched arm when she was close enough. "Look. We think something big is hunting those lights. It nearly crashed into the ship." Rosanne stared at the distant glowing objects and the large red orb which consumed them.

They watched a stream of flitting lights converge and scatter, then gathered again, shooting like an arrow. The stream passed just above the deck and out of sight. There was a blur of movement, and an unfortunate creature was torn from the others. It flopped against the deck underneath the paws of its predator. The reflective glow of Senior Petty Officer Ratcatcher's eyes brightened as he swatted at the glowing creature he had caught, then scooped it in his mouth and skulked below deck.

"Get that cat!" Rosanne ran after the tomcat. They caught up with the feline before he disappeared with his spoils into the pantry. Hammond's momentary surprise at their intrusion had him turn after the glowing creature, which was the only source of illumination in the room. He lit a lamp and waved it around, bemused at the trail of people descending the stairs to his domain.

"Evening! I assume this is about the fish?"

"Fish? Is that what it is?" Norman asked. Hammond pried the scaly vertebra from the cat's mouth. Fluffypaws meowed and stretched up his legs, swatting at its prey. The fish was silver, long and thick like a shark without the top fin, with a black line running across the tailfin. A transparent sack on its belly stored the fluorescent bacteria, which allowed it to glow.

"Extraordinary. It's like a fish but dry. Not the kind of cured kind you find in Valo." Hammond's laughter was as dry as the fish.

Dalia scrutinized the creature. The fish sucked air through its mouth, but the slits for where the gills should be remained shut. Two pockets on each side turned white as they expanded with each breath. "Look at that, Captain. Never seen anything like it. It's like it came from the sea to live in the fog."

"Makes you wonder what else is out there," Creedy said.

The comment hung there.

Hammond tossed the fish back to Fluffypaws, who caught it and whisked it away into the pantry. "If you see glowing stains, you know where he marks his territory," he chuckled.

The others drew faces of disgust.

AFTER THE CONFUSED buzz around the *Red Queen* had quieted down, the crew rested on the main deck and enjoyed the bustling light show unfolding around them. Shoals of fish flew around the ship, creating an almost whimsical aura. People cried out in delight as the creatures passed over the deck and between the crowds. Bulbous forms rose from below, unfolding like umbrellas and lazily pulsing themselves to higher altitudes. They were as large as longboats, and trails of green light ran along tentacles that danced with their movements.

"They're like jellyfish!" Ida clapped her hands. Nelson was sitting next to her and was equally caught up in the display of beautiful terror as prey and predator circled.

"They are far larger than the jellyfish from home," Ida said absentmindedly. "Once, I got stung by the tiniest little bastard at the size of my hand. Besides the usual fever, vomiting and sense of doom, it felt like my brain was on fire. I never swam in the ocean as a kid again." She laughed while Nelson's face screwed up in horror.

"You think these are just as dangerous?"

Ida bobbed her head. "The stingers will probably kill anything it comes in contact with. Or at the very least paralyze them. It's like the marine life here adapted to the minerals in the stones, and a chemical reaction creates the glow," she said, wearing the thinking frown which arose whenever she had a theory about something fascinating.

"You think the fish are *high*?" Gavin's comment was met with deprecatory and queer looks, their silence close to having its gravity. "Tough crowd." He leaned back, disquieted as Ida and Nelson continued what he perceived as an intimate conversation without him.

"WE CAN ONLY DREAM of seeing something like this at home," Ida said to Nelson after another moment in thought, her eyes fixated on a sizeable shark-like creature with red glowing lines on its back.

"Certainly not in Noval or Queensland. The only marine life I ever saw was at dinner or in the ocean."

Her bright-blue eyes turned lively. "You're not native to Noval?"

Nelson shook his head. "Born and raised in St. Derford. I graduated from law school there and was posted in Valo."

"What's St. Derford like? We've been to Kvenschester, but I hear St. Derford is more prestigious than the crown city."

"Hmm. I would say it's similar to Valo but packed and spacious at the same time. If a bit snobby. It's not as vast as the crown city, of course, but the ports are almost as impressive as Valo's."

"I'm putting that on my travel wish list. We don't get to travel much off trade season, and it's always the same ports I've seen hundreds of times before."

"Once you have seen one port city, you have seen them all, but it is an interesting place for sure. I can only imagine the places this ship has visited. I don't exactly earn enough to travel the world. Still, my small law practice in Valo keeps me happy. It's a beautiful city."

Her smile was fleeting before Ida cast her eyes down. "I'm not entirely local to Valo either. Times were hard, and my parents couldn't do much for me, so they sent me to Higgs, my uncle, to train me in a skill. And then Higgs brought me halfway across the world to give Gavin and me a better life when he lost his machine shop. I took to Noval, being my birth country and all, but Gavin doesn't like it much. 'It's too dang cold!' he would say. Just like us, Noval, Valo, and many other Novalian cities were named something else before the colonization, as a way of uniting us, they claimed. What a load of horseshit. The Queen can call us united all she wants, but we'll never take to the name she gave us. The colonies lost their identity in the cultural purge and were left wandering. Like so many of us aboard the *Red Queen* once were lost."

Nelson thought for a moment, reminiscing in the rich history of the United Colonies but finding the Novalian name quite new to time and no one who dared speak the old name. "I've heard rumours about that, but not openly. It's custom, isn't it, though?"

"The Queen's Colonials change the colonies' names to induce power over the locals. Many Valonials that I know still stick to their customs and language, even if the government has been suppressing it. It's only been sixty years since they figured out how to make anti-gravity tech, and in that short time, they changed everything. It also makes me wonder what will happen to this place if the Queen wants to bring it under colonial rule. Perhaps she will mine it free of all these fascinating stones, and it will disrupt the natural habitat of the marine life here ..."

"That's a thought I don't want to touch with my hands bare. But for now, this place is a no man's land. We're the only ones who have seen its beauty, and perhaps we are the only ones who ever will."

"I like that thought better." Ida smiled, and Nelson's heart burned as bright inside him as the glowing fish around the ship.

CHAPTER 10

NO MAN'S LAND

The jagged black cliffs of volcanic rock stretched for miles to either side of the shoreline. Granite and slate rested between rivers of porous, solidified lava running down the walls and into the sea, connoting that a catastrophic event had once overturned the entire peninsula of the landmass. A beach of ebony sand cropped short by the wavy sea rested below. Boulders hovered against the cliff's face, captured by crawler vines emerging from the grassy top and preventing the hulking masses from drifting off. A few crooked birch trees grew in the thin topsoil of the rocks, leaning awkwardly with the coastal wind.

The strange geography and monochrome colours delivered a deafening calm aboard the *Red Queen*.

"You think them rocks came from the belt?" Norman noted to Creedy, who tugged at the fore course's rope.

"Shut yer trap and work."

"Yes, sir." Norman grabbed the end of the rope and tightened it, watching the sail fold in on itself. His eyes turned towards the hovering rocks as if he feared the wind would blow them in their direction and capsize the ship.

As dawn crept, the sun hung low in the horizon, shrouded by receding fog on the other side of the Grey Veil. At first glance, there didn't appear to be much else occupying this surreal scenery other than a wide grassy plane and a couple of smooth rocky tops in between the volcanic formations.

"We may have to fly further to find wood," Farand noted.

Rosanne pursed her lips and tsked. "We don't have much of a choice as usual. Let's get our bearings before mother nature grants us another unconventional gift of surprise." Farand nodded and drew the lever back to about half its grade and let the ship cruise to the lip of the cliff. Shallow pools dotted the grassy plains. Fish sprang from the surface with a beat of their long fins, floated above the grass they snapped at, and shot back into the water again, jumping from pool to pool before escaping into the fog.

"Are those floating fish?" Rosanne said as she did a double-take at the stream of bearded silver-scaled cod, so ordinary and bland compared to their marine cousins closer to the rock belt.

"Are those *grazing* floating fish?" Farand raised an eyebrow. From behind a nearby floating rock, a stream of fat tuna swooped over the ridge and snapped at the panicking school of smaller fish. "That is the most unusual sight I have ever seen."

"You mean besides the flying jellyfish last night? Makes you wonder if the Kraken theory isn't so crazy after all." Rosanne shuddered at the thought of a giant squid roaming the skies and ambushing unsuspecting ships.

They affixed the *Red Queen* in place as best they could with pegs around the anchor in the thin soil. The brittle ground gave way more often than it remained, and they depended more on the weather to not carry the ship off should the pegs break.

"We'll make it short," Rosanne proclaimed to the lieutenant. "Get a scouting team on the longboat and have them look for resources. Anything that can get us out of this mess. We can finally navigate again, so give them enough information from the GPT to make the return trip. We'll make a run for water in the meantime."

Farand nodded his agreement. "Midday tomorrow?"

Rosanne concurred. "We need at least three days to navigate

out of this place, but if we are lucky, we can postpone our return trip in favour of the ship's repairs. I'll not let us get caught with our unmentionables down again."

"As you wish, Captain."

"And have Mr. Lyle send some men with them. We don't know who or what is out there."

———

THERE WASN'T much of a grave to dig for Iban. Kristoff spent the coming sunrise assembling the rocks he needed for his brother's final resting place at the foot of a smooth, dome-shaped hill. The body was placed in the shallow topsoil and piled with all the jagged volcanic rocks Kristoff could find, for there was little else of use in the barren landscape. As a rite of passage and to respect the dead, only a handful of selected people were invited to observe the ceremony.

Rosanne and Farand observed the youth's process from the deck. "To be buried in a land accursed with our misfortune and the blood of victims to the Grey Veil; I don't think I could do it," Farand said. Rosanne rested her hands with her hat in front of her.

"His choice, and to be frank, I'm relieved he chose this place. For practical reasons," she said.

Farand couldn't dispute Rosanne's pragmatism and the discomforting possible consequences of storing and returning Iban's body to his homeland without cremation.

———

KRISTOFF RESTED his hands on the rocks, smiling at the bruises and cuts on his hands. Hammond, a close friend of the young landmen, lay a hand on his shoulder. Kristoff sniffed and wiped his face with the hem of his sleeve.

He cleared his throat, easing the tension which made it hard to speak. "He always told me how much he preferred the ground not moving. Wouldn't be right to burn his body on a boat. I was the one who talked him into joining the *Red Queen,* and we loved every moment of it. Half the money we earned we sent home to Katshov to save up for a middle-class life. I can't send Iban's bones to mother from here. What do I tell her?" He looked to Hammond, who, in lack of comforting words, held up a hand.

"You tell her you did right by your brother and gave him the finest view of the sea in a place of adventure and wonder." He swept his eyes over the rising sun in the east, shining weakly over the wall of grey in the distance and beginning to hit the cliffs. He hitched a breath and dusted his food-stained pants.

"This is from the captain and myself." He handed Kristoff a bottle of twenty-year-old Quindecimus whisky. "It's not the ninety-five percent your people use, but it's the finest whisky I could abscond from the captain," he whispered.

Kristoff took the bottle and looked at the label. "This very fine whisky." He let his accent slip between the sobs. "Captain will gut us both when she sees this gone!" He smiled. Hammond snorted.

"She'll live, and Iban will be thankful enough to not haunt us for gifting him shite rum from the keg." Kristoff placed the bottle on the rocks where Iban's chest would be, thinking that somehow his brother could reach it if he stretched out his hand and thus have a good drink before his spirit flew on to the afterlife. The sun had barely peeked from over the horizon but would hit the rocky mound at its zenith.

"Hammond. Thank you for being there for us when we were still green."

"You're still green. And you'll stay green until my cooking is to your liking." It made Hammond laugh, and the older man patted Kristoff's back.

A CREW OF TEN PEOPLE, among them Lyle's armed-and-dangerous men, set out in the longboat a matter of hours after their initial touchdown on the volcanic rock. The boat had a single square aether sail, which was plenty for speedy trips over short distances, and it stored all the tools they needed to gather basic supplies.

While the scouting party sailed northeast, the *Red Queen* sailed southeast towards the lush inland. The rounded mountains merged with surrounding lowlands covered with broad-leafed trees. Wide bubbly rivers of crusted magma converged on nearby mountaintops, indicating these were once active volcanoes having exploded to the skies in the distant past. Not even a puff of smoke emerged from the hardened tops, and the dense woodlands spoke of the peaceful times that followed.

A few miles south of the closed vents, glaciers had abraded the mountains, now almost completely melted and winding their way snaillike between wedges. They fed thick rivers to a shallow inland lake with sand and volcanic rock deposits. The lake was one of the largest Rosanne had seen, reaching almost to the horizon and running towards the sea, dotted with grass-patched islands. Here bountiful fish swam, flopping in and out of the water, but didn't fly like their coastline cousins.

Rosanne landed the ship and released the anchor. The crew threw a thick hose into the water from a gunport, using this perfect opportunity to replenish their fresh water supply.

Untouched by human intervention, the vast lands were uncommon sights for the crew used to villages and farms at almost every nook and cranny of Terra. Even the remotest islands and inland fjords were occupied with people since before the rise of aeroships and the abomination that was the Queen's Colonies' gradual take-over of the western hemisphere.

A few animal paths crisscrossed the grassy plains. Olivier watched a flock of deer break into a wild run through the spyglass upon the *Red Queen's* arrival. Brown-spotted geese glided through the water, and in the shallow spots, curlews and long-legged herons waded and stretched their necks in search of prey.

"If that old hag Pestilence didn't threaten to sweep us all away, I would have built my house on that hilltop over there." Rosanne smiled as the breeze rustled her red locks. She hadn't enjoyed a wind this pleasant since their departure. The dry air tickled her exposed neck, and the uncomfortable buildup of perspiration was lessened. Rosanne felt one with the sky. Had her chair not been reduced to kindling, she would have leaned back, kicked off her shoes, and thrown her feet on the railing. She had to instead settle with resting her back against the railing, fanning herself while the crew's excitement increased.

"I wouldn't be able to rest. I'll sail until the day I die," Farand announced with a grunt. He turned the wheel five degrees to keep the ship level with the wind.

"And haunt the skies well beyond that, too." Rosanne cackled, but it was a joke Farand couldn't dispute, and he smiled.

The moment they were in the water, fishing rods lined up against the railing, and although Rosanne hadn't heard of any shortages of supplies from Hammond, the crew's hunger for fresh food was understandable after days of dried and smoked goods. Hammond rubbed his hands at the fat, red-spotted salmon dropping into a supplied barrel.

"I got another one!" Gavin reeled in the line while Ida stood ready with a net. The entire row of people hauled fish quicker than they could free the nets.

"I want to throw out some bread, but that would be unsporting of me and unfair to the dinner." Hammond let out a hearty laugh. "Look how they're swirling. The lake's boiling!"

"Good for us, I assume?" Rosanne smiled.

"We'll feast tonight!"

She turned from the fishing spectacle to her stout lieutenant by the wheel. "How about it, Mr. Duplànte? Do we chance a quick look before returning? If we climb a little higher, we can scout further."

Farand bobbed his head. "I wouldn't advise we stray too far, but I'm not against it either. Rather we busy ourselves than twiddle our thumbs."

"Or haul so much fresh fish aboard the ship it starts smelling?"

"Or that."

THE *RED QUEEN* detoured along the uninterrupted coastline until she hit the volcanic river mounds, which made out the familiar cliff faces of their designated meeting point. As they still had daylight to spare, they cruised north towards the masses of floating rocks which appeared of place.

"Not much of anything on this island but forests and anti-gravity rocks," Farand said, drawing up their route on a new map, making out the mysterious island's coastline.

"You expected treasure and sirens, Mr. Duplànte?" Rosanne jested, drawing a chuckle from the lieutenant. The compass on the instrument panel spun in all directions as if the entire landmass was one great magnet. After she tapped the glass, the needle spun even quicker, and Rosanne didn't know what she expected and left it at that.

An excited but near incoherent bustle rang from the crow's nest.

"Ship. Ten o'clock!" Olivier called over the intercom. Rosanne cast her eyes to the heading, a gathering of floating boulders donning the cliffside like a staircase.

"I don't ..." Rosanne began, but Farand's keen eye caught it before hers, and he pointed.

"On top of one of the largest boulders."

She squinted and caught glimpses of reflected light.

Locking the wheel in place and slowing the ship to a crawl, she took out her spyglass. What remained of a ship's deck lay broken in three pieces along with scraps of wrenched metal. The double masts were broken like twigs, and not a scrap of the sails remained.

Rosanne handed the spyglass to the lieutenant to survey the damage. "What do you think?" Farand scrunched his eyebrows together.

"Looks recent but doesn't seem like a trap. I suggest we play it safe."

Rosanne nodded her agreement. "Mr. Lyle! Prepare to board and bring the guns. Kristoff! Two cannons port and starboard ready to fire." Echoes of "yes, Captain" and "aye, ma'am" resonated on the main deck.

They approached the wreckage with guns and cannons armed and pointed, but no activity came from the other vessel. Farand levelled the ship alongside the rocky surface. A handful of people, among them Creedy, Lyle, Gavin, and Rosanne, disembarked to survey the wreckage. The top deck was a series of gaping wounds of splintered wood and dented metal plating. The beak had seen better days and was buried beneath the topsoil of the boulder.

Rosanne touched the scorched wood riddled with small bullet holes. She took a knife and jammed it into the hole, digging out the lead bullet.

"These are ours, aren't they?" She handed the bullet to Lyle, who nodded after a brief inspection. "Those sons of bitches made it this far? The ship's beyond recognizable." Rosanne spat at the deck.

"Whoever survived cleaned out the supplies. There's nothing left," Lyle commented, a small flintlock pistol ready in his hands.

"Captain!" someone called from the cracked stern. Rosanne ducked under the hanging shreds of what used to be the main-course, followed the guided lamplight to a crevice in the floor, and peeked inside. An ashen-faced body rested among the broken barrels of soaked gunpowder. Rosanne pushed herself through the narrow crack with difficulty but finally came to stand at the rain-slick floor. She took the young man's pale hand and flexed the wrist.

"Cold and stiff. I have a nagging feeling the pirates have been here a while already."

Lyle put his gun away. "Considering how they abandoned their dead and took all the supplies, they must have sought shelter. We found a ladder leading to the cliff, and trails in the grass say they went north." Her prolonged silence seemed to unnerve him as he fidgeted. "You think they have a cove or hideout on this island?"

"I sure hope they're as big of trespassers as we are. If they are prepared for these living conditions, we need to get out as fast as possible." She shook the dripping water off her hat and stared at the hole running through it. "How many do you estimate from our initial encounter was aboard this ship?" Lyle's silence lasted only a moment as he scanned the deck and stared at nothing in particular.

"Ten gunmen, the captain, the lieutenant, the master gunner undoubtedly, six cannons below deck all were fired, and if we assume they had one man per gun ... nineteen to tops twenty-five."

"As many as us then. How many dead?"

"Five so far."

"Plus the ones cast out when we speared the ship. If we're lucky, there are less than a dozen left."

"I wouldn't ride my luck on that *if*, Captain. If every man is armed, they have us outgunned."

Rosanne chewed her lips. "Let's rendezvous with the scouting party first. Leave everything as it is. I don't think the pirates will come back, but if they do, we have to keep our presence hidden unless they've spotted us already." Lyle nodded and had everyone meticulously return everything they had touched to its former state.

Rosanne met Farand on the quarterdeck, the man wearing his brooding and questioning expression.

"This is what a decommissioned *Blue Dragon* looks like, Mr. Duplànte," she said. The man pursed his lips and nodded.

"It's a beautiful sight. Anything noteworthy?"

Rosanne surveyed the landscape. "Someone survived, and they are out there."

Farand leaned against the wheel, thinking. "Let us hope the survivors are complaisant and not volatile. I'd hate to see what they could do to our brig if this is what remains of their vessel."

"Always the *Red Queen*'s best interest at heart, eh Mr. Duplànte?"

"Always, Captain."

The *Red Queen* returned to the designated meeting place well before the appointed time.

"Longboat three o'clock. It's empty," Olivier informed the captain, pointing to a longboat parked by the lower mounds only visible if one approached from the sea. Again, plasma rifles and flintlocks clacked and stood ready to fire.

Rosanne couldn't help but frown.

"This has the stink of a trap." Farand's grim comment encouraged the unsettling paranoia already growing in Rosanne's mind. From over the rim of the hill, a blond-haired man peeked out, waving his arms. He rose his left arm straight and touched the elbow with his other.

"It's Norman. He's alone?" Rosanne questioned, slowing the ship until it rested above ground level on the cliffs. Norman jumped in the longboat and flew up to the main deck. He scrambled over the railing and banged his foot against it.

"What happened?" Rosanne demanded.

Kristoff caught Norman before he faceplanted on the deck. "People! They came out of the woods while we were working!"

"How many?"

"I— uh. I can't—!" The youth's face blanked along with his reply.

Grabbing his vest, Rosanne shook him. "*How many,* Norman?"

"Seven, I think! They were all armed with plasma guns. I was on boat duty, and I came to warn you as soon as I saw the commotion. I didn't hear any gunfire." The young man panted and rested his hands on his knees.

Rosanne turned to the lieutenant. "We need to assume it's the same bloody pirates and that they are after our ship."

He grunted his agreement. "I should be the one to go and negotiate."

"Not even an option. I need you here."

"Not to pull a very obvious card, ma'am..."

"Don't give me that sexist bullshit!" Rosanne's steely gaze cut into him. "It'll be worse once they realize that you're not the captain. I'd rather have them meet a behemoth if they try to take the *Queen* by force than someone they won't fear until I shoot at them. Norman, Lyle, we're going. Give me a gun. I'll take that dagger too."

"Captain." Farand laid a hand on her shoulder and leaned close, his brows crushed together. "Please tell me you have a plan."

"I have a plan," she stated, then paused, and met Farand's questioning look. "I do. It's forming." He released her with a slow, hesitant nod.

Belting the dagger and the flintlock gun, she made a mental check that she had everything she needed. "We don't have enough people for an assault, nor do we have anything but the ship to parlay with. I'll have to use my wit, and if all else fails ..." she bobbed her head. "I'll figure something out. I always do." She muttered curses as the group descended into the longboat. Farand watched it disappear into the distance, sighing and crossing his arms as he ran a strategy through his mind for the ship and the remaining crew. Nelson emerged from his cabin, confusion written on his face as his gaze followed the captain's departure. Farand let his arms rest and prepared himself for a lengthy discussion with their generous contributor.

CHAPTER 11

PARLAY?

Norman guided the longboat along a tall ridge where the landscape dipped into a deciduous woodland that stretched for miles. The canopy made it impossible to see any human activity, and the floral spring bloom obscured any trace of the route the pirates might have taken. Rosanne pointed her spyglass at a clearing among the trees, the only viable supply team option for setting camp.

The pirates had hiked quite the distance from the coast to arrive at this spot. Unless there were sentries in the area, Rosanne had a few ideas about how the scouting party had been discovered. They might have used transportation to cover the miles between here and the wreck of the *Blue Dragon*. The possibility of chancing upon the scouting party was also there, but such cosmic coincidences didn't fly well with the sensible captain.

Norman pointed to a vantage point over the surrounding area. "We came down the ridge over there and straight into the forest. Lyle's men didn't see anything out of the ordinary, and we got to work straight away. The pirates came from the north of the woods on foot."

"Was there another way to the camp?" Rosanne asked.

"Not one that I saw. I was hiding the longboat behind that hilltop."

Rosanne fidgeted the spyglass and chewed her lips. "Fuck it. Land the longboat as close to the camp as you can in plain sight."

Norman's jaw fell. "What on Terra are you on about, Captain? They'll see us right away!"

She popped the spyglass in her satchel, pausing before speaking to deposit a withering glare on him. "Exactly. Follow my lead, and no matter what, do not shoot until I say so."

Lyle slung the rifle over his shoulder and grunted. "I'm looking forward to your plan, Captain."

She tousled her tangled locks, forcing them from a bird's nest into presentable, organized chaos before replacing the hat. "Oh, I bet you are."

Norman directed the longboat down the slope and slowed the craft when they got closer to the clearing. Around them, the mixed birch and oak shoots were drowned out by red-berried bushes and young trees. The scouting team had cleared the overgrown shoots and left a trail of miniature destruction of broken branches and felled bushes. The people in question were nowhere to be seen. Saws, hammers, nails, knives, and batons lay scattered on the ground.

Concealed by the overgrowth of the trees, a handful of men waited by the rim of the clearing. Four men reached for the guns in their belts, while a fifth person rested his hands on his hips, seemingly undeterred by their bold approach. Bruises and bandaged foreheads donned the pirates along with their sullen looks. One of them rested against a tree with his gun trained on Rosanne. Behind them, brown, red, and blond-haired heads, some adorned with bandanas, peeked up from the bushes while two sentries walked the perimeter with loaded plasma rifles. The muzzles hummed with blue energy at the cock of the rifles. Stepping into the light, a brash display of confidence radiated from the unarmed man. He cocked his head, bringing his sun-tanned face out from the shadow of his wide-brimmed hat. Weather-hardened lines appeared as he smiled crookedly in a poor attempt to be charming.

"Wits it is," Rosanne whispered to herself as she scrunched her eyebrows together, working on her hastily forming plan. She immediately replaced her frown with an impeccable smile. She climbed off the boat, touching the ground with a bounce in her step. She fixed her gloves and strolled across the campsite to where the pirate captain stood grinning. He held out his arms, twisting his lean body as he swept his sights over his leverage.

"Aros Bernhart." He bowed mockingly, his voice light and playful. "I assume you're the diplomat your captain sent—" His thin-lipped mouth shut abruptly when Rosanne leaned in with her right fist leading, slamming it squarely against his face. The man staggered and held his jaw, his close-set eyes popping. His men were startled awake by the unexpected violent introduction, and now all of them trained their guns on her. Aros raised a hand, halting their fire. With whistles and cackling at Rosanne's reckless boldness, a cheer resonated from the brush.

Straightening, Rosanne's smirk challenged Aros' confidence. "Captain Rosanne Drackenheart of the *MTS Red Queen*." Fixing her glove, she massaged the knuckles. She gave no indication that the move hurt nearly as much as it did.

Aros wiped the spit from his thin lips. "Well, this is perhaps the most impactful introduction I've ever had the pleasure to experience. Captain, you say?" Unconvinced, Aros shook his head. The men exchanged glances and muttered. Rosanne regarded Aros, who couldn't be any older than herself. His haggard face was evidence of a lack of sleep, and he wore the unkempt stubbles of a beard at least a week unshaven. Behind her, Lyle held the rifle across his chest, feet firmly planted. Norman ducked low for cover in the distant longboat, but no one paid him any mind thanks to Rosanne's introduction.

"How was your flight, Captain? Your docking has seen better days," she teased.

Aros scoffed. "Why don't we sit? The heat must be getting to your head considering how much you like to swing your fists."

Captain Bernhart led them to the fire with a brewing metal pot of coffee. They seated themselves on logs facing each other with the fire in between, Bernhart with his three men behind him, and Lyle at Rosanne's right. She leaned on her thighs and folded her hands. A fourth man poured a wooden cup with coffee and handed it to Bernhart. He sipped at it, coughed, and set it down.

"Well then," Rosanne began. "Assaults and face-fulls of cannonballs aside, to what do I owe this pleasure of having my crew at gunpoint?"

The man took off his hat and glided a hand through his oily black hair. "*You*? Captain of that odd aeroship? You who did that batshit crazy maneuver into the Elder Reef?" He twirled a hand with a swooping motion, his eyes vivid. "That was insane, I tell you. But what a thrill it must have been!" He shot his head back and laughed. The surrounding men did not share his enthusiasm, their faces a grim reminder of Rosanne's crippling battle against them mere days prior. "And a hybrid ship! I have never seen anything like it. How did you do it?"

Rosanne couldn't deny the creeping pride swelling within her at the pirate's boisterous reaction. "With the greatest team of engineers and deep, *deep* pockets. I must say I didn't expect pirates to be in the whaling business. That spear you had got us good."

He rubbed his nose and grinned. "You like it? Picked it up from a crazy inventor at the Mahka islands."

Rosanne's impeccable smile didn't falter with her narrowing eyes. "I'm sure you did."

"Hey now. I paid the man well. We might pick off ships, but we still need to keep business flowing."

"Good thing I returned the handsome investment then."

His smile was wry when he shifted his posture. "You know how to fight, lady. I'll give you that."

She straightened and glanced around, noticing the pirates' hypervigilance to her slightest movements. "Forgive me, but are you holding my crew hostage just to retell the two hours I needed to destroy your ship? Couldn't have been easy flying that wreck. I hope you gave your men a proper burial."

The corner of his eye twitched. Aros pursed his lips and lowered his brows. "Thanks to you, half my crew is sleeping with the fishes. Not much burial to give them as we were as good as dead had we not landed. You're in for a world of trouble, lady." He nodded to the sentries. One of them grabbed a hostage at random, stood him up, and cocked a flintlock pistol aimed at his temple. "I don't really need to say anything about that, do I?" Aros finished.

Rosanne's kept her face as calm as an ice-cold mask as she looked at the endangered topman, who appeared anything but frightened; he stared at her with eyes equally hardened by endless peril as she. "And what about the *Retribution*?" she asked.

Aros seized his grin, his face a glowing red fury. "Is that what this is about, some fucking military ship? Took them long enough to get us." He snorted, shook his head, and laughed incredulously. "You're telling me that the military didn't send a warship after us, but a ..." he threw his hand out, dismissive in its awkward waving.

"We found the ship in the fog. The crew was gone. The ship was wrecked."

"Pity. It was a fun chase. They had some sweet guns too." He drank his coffee again, found the grounds at the bottom, and spat them out.

Rosanne picked up on Captain Bernhart's brief disheartened stare and how his eyes barely changed with his false smiles. Rosanne gave a dry laugh. "The *Blue Dragon* went the same way. Although, you weren't picked clean like the *Retribution* was. Makes you wonder what really lurks inside the Grey Veil."

"Damned if I know. My first visit here, and we're leaving the first chance we get."

"And how do you plan to do that?"

"Isn't it obvious?" He swept his hand around again. "We're going to claim the *Red Queen*."

Rosanne snorted and leaned forward, rising. The resonating laughter from the captured crew had Captain Bernhart turn around. "And *how* do you plan on doing that?" she asked.

The man motioned with a hand in her direction. "Simple. The lives of your crew in exchange for the ship. Easy trade, don't you think?"

Rosanne shook her head. "You would leave us to our deaths the first chance you get. You expect me to hand over a ship none of you can fly?" She leaned forward, her impeccable mask now a sneer. "Over my dead, putrefied body."

"That can easily be arranged." Standing, Captain Bernart drew his flintlock pistol and trained the barrel at her skull. Lyle had his plasma rifle pointed to Aros' temple just as quick. Undeterred Aros scoffed. "All I need to do is pull the trigger, and things will turn really ugly. Your ship will have lost its highest authority and a good portion of its workers. We could still take her with the element of surprise on our side, so I suggest you cooperate, *Captain.*"

Rosanne grinned at the pirate's amusing attempt at discouraging her iron will. "You couldn't fly that ship even at gunpoint, my dear Captain Bernhart. The *Red Queen* is the only one of its kind, and you would choke her before you got her airborne." Her eyes remained hard and unforgiving. "*If* you get her in the air, you wouldn't be able to steer her through the rock belt without damaging the masts and thruster ports, and then you would have to navigate through the Grey Veil where dead men sing. Unless you have an extremely skilled pilot, some means for navigation, and new sails and material to patch her up, you'd be better off two metres below ground."

Aros planted the barrel of the gun on her forehead and grabbed her jacket. Leaning in he whispered, "How about I just bring you with me, my *dear* Captain Drackenheart?" Behind him, his three crewmates cocked their guns. Rosanne felt her eyes roll in their sockets at the man's rotten breath and abuse of whatever carcass he used as cologne.

"You have no idea of what she's capable of," she said. "With me dead, the chain of command follows the same principle. We all would die for the ship. Mr. Lyle here, who's ready to blow your third-rate brain to hell, included. What is *your* crew without their captain? How about we cut the crap and find a better solution?"

"I don't negotiate." Aros drew the flint back.

"Neither do I." Rosanne added more pressure to her hand at his ribs, the sharp poke of a knife's edge prodding through his leather jacket. Captain Bernhart ground his teeth and looked to his men.

Rosanne smiled. "You have no option, Captain Bernhart. Your best bet is to surrender under our authority and go with us to Bogvin, except there you would be hanged at first sight. You have a far brighter future on this island than anywhere else in Terra without your ship." Aros returned the stare, biting the inside of his cheek.

A guttural shriek caught their attention at the nearby bushy growth. A man from the bound crowd stood, his eyes wild and panicked. "There's something out there!"

Lyle secured his aim at the pirate captain while Rosanne's grasp caught Bernhart's vest, driving the knife harder against the leather.

"Who else is out there?" she demanded. Aros' gun wavered while his eyes searched the forest.

"No one. We're all that's left. It must be one of yours!"

"I don't trust pirates for a riksdaler in my hand. Who else is out there?"

"Ow, ow! Calm it, lady. No one else is here. By Odin, it's the truth!"

Something cackled, hastily followed by a shushing sound and offended throaty protests. Guns diverted, Bernhart's men all trained on the bush, while Lyle took a strategic step back and turned his attention to the surrounding forest. Aros stepped away from Rosanne and Lyle to avoid getting accidentally shot.

"Behind us." Lyle pointed his rifle to a tree some twenty

meters into the forest. A skinny tail with a fuzzy tassel swished behind the tree, the tip of a flint spear sticking out on the other side.

"Is this some joke?" Rosanne didn't believe her thoughts any more than she believed her eyes. Even Aros had his undivided attention on whatever surrounded them. A clunk followed by a sudden cry tore their eyes to a cluster of bushes. One of the sentries lay unconscious on the ground with a large gash on his skull. A second man shouted and held his face. Then a hail of rocks rained from the treetops above.

Rosanne held her arms above her. "Get to cover!"

The brush around them exploded with life. Short and wide-bulked creatures bombarded them with rocks propelled from crude slingshots. Men shouted all around her, diving for protection behind logs and doing their best to protect their faces. Bernhart's men fired at the nimble creatures blending with the foliage and hiding in the canopies.

Rosanne tumbled over a root and smacked against a tree. She turned toward the movement in her periphery but instead sat frozen at the twisted face of maniacal laughter. It hit her squarely between the eyes, and the world turned black.

CHAPTER 12

THOSE ARE NOT SIRENS

"I s this the one?" Nelson's feet wiggled from under the thruster engine as he shifted his position to release the ratchet.

"I don't think that was tight enough." Ida's bubbling laughter was nearly drowned out by the hammering pistons and hissing steam. She was on all fours, peeking under the massive engine, standing on precarious support frames with only a few centimetres left to squish Nelson flat.

"Still? I'm putting all the muscle I have into this." His neck was stiff and hot. Sweat ran down his face, and his glasses were fogged. Nelson was not a large man, but he was still tight for space among the scorching and moving machinery.

"You can do it, paper-pusher!" Ida's enthusiasm was not met as Nelson's nagging suspicion intensified that he was free labour when Gavin was nowhere to be found. This left Ida hauling Nelson to the engine room like a blue-eyed idiot because in his mind heading off with her, even for chores, was anything but work. Still, he didn't undermine the job and found himself appreciating it as a fresh breath after doing the ship's dreadful accounting and further incriminating himself. And as much as he had grown to live for every warm smile from Ida, every second he spent with her reminded him of the steps he had taken to ensure this voyage came to be.

Oblivious to his blackmail, she was bubbly and enthusiastic about her work, more than eager to show him the ropes, and he loved every second of it. Her level of inclusion and attention to him was not something he was used to growing up, as his previous encounters with women were reduced to berated lessons of his worn suits and spineless attitude. He felt comfortable enough to joke about himself with Ida, and her laughs lifted his spirits. He wanted more moments like these where he knew he could be more than what he was used to.

Refitting the wrench, Nelson turned the bolt with all his power manifesting through a series of loud grunts before falling limp like a dead fish. "How about now?" His breath barely escaped his mouth.

"Perfect! I'll help you out." Ida's small but exceptionally strong hands grabbed his trousers and tugged. The low-wheeled board eased his exit, but Nelson had to restrain his pants from leaving without him.

"Nice work." Ida beamed with her wide grin and stretched out her hand. Nelson's already hot cheeks turned a shade darker. He accepted her hand and stood up in a hurry.

"Anything else you need help with?"

"I think we're good for now. Higgs is still insisting on working the engine alone, and without the all-go from Farand, we're twiddling our thumbs."

"I'll go clean up then." His shirt was greasy and sticky against his skin. No amount of wiping stopped the steady trickle of sweat from running down his face in this ungodly heat. His arms were bruised and covered in soot, and the sleeves he so meticulously had folded for their own protection were coated in grime. He yelped at the face-full of towel he received. Ida stuck out her tongue.

"I dunno. You kinda suit looking like the rest of us." The comment made his insides somersault, and he buried his face in the towel. Then, as a practical joke on himself, he flexed the fish cakes on his arms that he called muscles, making Ida howl with laughter.

"I'm glad I can make you laugh," Nelson said.

Ida shot him a nervous smile. "You're easy to be around. It's nice. As much grief the crew gives you all the time, you're proving that you can take being here with us."

They shared a moment of silence and an awkward smile. Higgs wobbled into the room, supporting his quavering weight along with the machinery. Ida raised an eyebrow at the sight of his legs. "Sat too long again?"

"Aye. The arthritis isn't agreeing with me today. Girl, be a doll and fire up' Leaky Sally for me. Farand is itching to get a move on." He grunted in front of the moving pistons.

"So soon? But the captain hasn't returned yet."

"Yes, girl. It's why I had to pull my weight to patch her up in a hurry. We're going inland."

"I'll get to it then." Ida disappeared into the steam filling up the room. Nelson wiped his forehead for the hundredth time, his arms sore as the sweat kept spilling.

"Say, Mr. Higgs—"

"Just Higgs, boy," the older man cut in. "Sir, mister, or any other fancy smanchy titles other than first engineer, chief, or Higgs don't exist in here."

"Higgs then ... You said Mr. Duplànte ordered an inland sweep?"

The old man wiped his face with a dirty handkerchief, and his bushy eyebrows rose when he looked hard at Nelson. "Not quite. Captain's welcome party didn't go as planned, and we're going for repair materials 'fore she returns to spank our arses."

Alarmed, Nelson fumbled with his hands, searching for words. "Shouldn't we help her if she's in danger?"

"Take a look around, boy. We're royally fucked if we don't get those sails fixed and have at least two full masts." He tapped a knuckle against the plating on the side of the machine. "We're a hair's breadth away from giving pet names to our fruits unless we overhaul this rust bucket. Our captain doesn't take kindly to such negligence."

Despite Higgs' logical reasoning, he didn't offer any words of encouragement to their otherwise hopeless situation. Nelson couldn't help but admire Higgs' faith that everything would sort itself out with divine intervention, skill, or sheer luck. "You sound confident she will return no matter what."

Higgs flashed a yellow-toothed grin. "I've known our captain for many years. She's as protective of this vessel as a dragon to its youngling. And I've seen her pull through worse situations. Now make yourself useful and find Gavin. That bludger's been gone for hours."

"Yes, si–, Higgs." Nelson turned for the exit. Higgs gave him a long hard stare Nelson could feel drilling through the back of his skull. "And stay away from Ida, you sneaky thief! You and Gavin keep your eyes elsewhere."

Nelson shook his head and smiled. "I wouldn't dream of getting on your bad side, sir."

DALIA POINTED to the foresail yard's glaring breakage point, which dangled uselessly in the soft breeze. "We don't have enough rope to string the mainsail or the foresail. Even if we did, we lack yards for both." She scratched her mop of hair, so wind-stricken she resembled a scarecrow. The watch captain had seen better days scaling what remained of the ship's rigging, and with half of the rope snapped, sails shredded, and supports torn, no one would get anywhere. Farand's stiff scowl bode ill tidings as he assessed the sunlight penetrating the tears and holes in the canvas. Dalia observed in reserved silence as his inner clockwork did its work.

Creedy descended from the crow's nest, bundled in heaps of snapped hemp and shattered deadeyes. He dropped the pile in front of Dalia, who responded by pinching the base of her nose at the increasing headaches she faced. Farand scratched his chin and drew a deep breath. "There isn't a chance we can make it work by making it rigid?"

Creedy shook his head. "'fraid not, sir. Without them sails, we're not getting anywhere anytime fast. Our best chance is charging the engine and letting it run." Creedy pursed his lips and shifted the weight to his other foot. "Dunno if we could manually hook the sails to the engine and just leave them in the open. We don't have the energy output we need for anything that will last longer than a goblin's fart. Without a blacksmith, we can't reinforce the new masts either, so we can't drive recklessly." He had worked on the mainsail, hoping to patch it enough for reuse, and while he managed to get it semi-operational again, the support beam was as busted as a bar stool after a three a.m brawl. "I say we're fucked."

Farand fished out his pocket watch and stared at the dial. He gave the deck one final visual sweep and nodded to himself.

"Our captain has been gone for more than sixteen hours. Do we still have the extra tools needed to get the supplies?"

"Yes, sir. Backup of everything," Dalia replied.

"Have all the operational sails out. We leave as soon as the chief is done with the engine." Dalia and Creedy nodded, riled their teams together, and set them to work. Nelson emerged from below deck, soot-faced with a dirty blond bird's nest where his hair used to be.

"Mr. Duplànte, sir? Excuse me. We're leaving for the inland?"

"We're getting the supplies the scouting team failed to deliver. Captain Drackenheart will be back before long, as a ghost if she must. I'm not sitting on my bottom waiting for her to finish negotiating with pirates, or whatever the hell it was she thought out. Once we're set, we'll look for her and the rest, but for now, the ship is the priority." His brusque quick-as-a-master-gunner answer made Nelson take a step back.

"I see." Nelson felt his heart sink to a new dark underground, but he couldn't deny Farand's logic. They were exposed, and with the ship in its current state, they were in more danger now than ever. While he didn't doubt Farand's or Higgs' ironclad faith in Rosanne's ability to wiggle out of the direst situations, Nelson couldn't help but wonder about the consequences should she not return. What if the pirates met them instead? Another battle would break out, and who would lose that fight?

WHATEVER HOLE Gavin had crawled into, Nelson wasn't finding it. No one had seen nor heard from the third engineer in many hours, and at first, there was speculation that he had snuck off with the scouting team. On a whim, Nelson visited the storage rooms at the lowest deck, which had the smallest but also the greatest number of compartments, all filled with hiding spaces. He walked until he heard low distinct snoring. Grabbing an oil lamp from the stairs, he held it high to navigate through the rooms. A low stack of flour had been rearranged into a makeshift bed and on top of it was Gavin with his legs crossed and eyes closed. Senior Petty Officer Ratcatcher snoozed in the crook of his arms. Alarmed by the noise, the feline spared Nelson half a glance before settling back into slumber.

Nelson bent down next to the stack and shook Gavin by the shoulder.

"Whazzat?" The man startled awake, offending the cat by ruining a perfectly comfortable sleeping position. The feline skulked out of the room, no doubt to find himself better quarters. Gavin stared at Nelson for a moment, confused at what he saw and didn't recognize. "Oh. Hey. It's you. You need something?" He rubbed the sleep from his eyes and stretched his limbs, likely stiff from the sacks of flour, which probably felt like it had rearranged his lower back.

"Higgs was asking for you. You've been missed for a while."

"I have? Shit. I was only going to rest for half a moment. That old man has been riding my ass since after the storm. Can't sleep unless I'm dead." Gavin stopped for a moment, tilting his head, listening. "Are we moving?"

"Yes. We left twenty minutes ago."

Gavin jumped from the stack and ruffled his hair. "God-dammit! I was going to help Ida fix the cooler."

A bell rang in Nelson's mind. "So that's what it was? That was the warmest piece of machinery I ever lay my hands on. I helped Ida with it. She said it works fine now."

"*You* did?" Gavin sounded less than convinced, but upon seeing Nelson's haggard condition, he nodded. "Didn't think you had it in you to wield a wrench." Gavin fist-bumped Nelson's shoulder.

"It was only a few loose bolts ..."

"Still. Got some extra hours thanks to you. 'Preciate it, man." A new hesitant slap on the shoulder and out Gavin went. He paused in the doorway, wringing his hands, and turned back to Nelson but somehow not looking at him. "Hey, man. If you'd like, you can help me out later with the grav ports. Ida and Higgs will be busy, and I could use the help."

Nelson's head bobbed, completely oblivious to Gavin's shift in mood. "Sure thing."

"Cool, cool." He turned and began muttering a trail of colourful profanities at his own tardiness. In the lower corner of the doorway, Fluffypaws peered at Nelson with inquisitive eyes.

"Hey there. Thought you had run off." Nelson hunched down and rubbed his fingers. Senior Petty Officer Ratcatcher saw the hand, pounced, and pushed against it, purring like a miniature mill saw.

"See? I'm not so bad. Can't be easy for you living on this flying landmine, now can it?" The cat stared at him with green gleaming eyes and blinked. "Not much you and I can do in these dangerous times either. Can't say I feel especially useful. What about you?" The cat swished his tail a few times. Nelson sat on the flour, and Fluffypaws followed, circling his lap before lying down and nuzzling his nose in his tail.

Nelson listened to the low hum of the *Red Queen*'s steady progress through the inland. This far down in the ship's hull, he couldn't hear much over her constant creaking. The oil lamp illuminated the room in a gentle yellow glow, and Nelson allowed himself to relax and stroke the purring cat. Was the quiet this ear-deafening when his father met his demise? Or was it loud with the bangs of cannons and retorts of bullets from rifles?

Nelson let his mind wander off, rocking to the comforting hum of the *Queen*.

CLOSING ON LATE AFTERNOON, the *Red Queen* passed a long-dead volcano. They climbed the sleek hills to higher altitudes and eventually came upon a vast pine forest. Farand parked the ship at the edge of the forest, surveying a steep cliffside to the east and the sea to the far southwest.

With a retractable crane, they descended a small platform with tools and crew on the lip of the cliff. Creedy and Dalia didn't waste a single minute scratching marks into the trunks while the different teams followed closely with axes and saws, felling trees and clearing branches. Creedy inspected the length of a log, crouching down in front of it and checking whether its plane was straight enough to do the job.

"This for the foremast. We shave off the others before we can use them for the sails. Mr. Duplànte!" Creedy called out to the lieutenant aboard the ship. The large man peered over the main deck.

"How much time can you give us?" Creedy asked, shielding his eyes from the glaring sun.

"How long do you need?" Farand barked in return.

Creedy contemplated their lack of crew, glanced at Dalia whose grim expression penetrated his very soul should he dare make life harder for her, and muttered a curse to himself. "Five hours?"

"Make it four!"

Creedy rubbed his hands together before turning to the men and women on standby and sending them off to work.

Dalia approached him after some time, dragging an impressive length of vine behind her. "Hey! Look what I found. These should do as a replacement for the rigging if we double weave them, don't you think? We need a hell of a lot more, so can you spare me some of your guys?"

"Take two people and gather at least ..." Creedy made a fist, uncurling his fingers one by one in rapid concession. "Five lengths if you can. As much as you can."

"Way ahead of you."

FARAND SURVEYED FROM THE QUARTERDECK, his dark eyebrows nearly touching in his scrutiny. The continuous throbbing behind his eyes had begun after the freak storm fired up all the fuses he had, and his intense need to destroy something only increased with his fear that Captain Drackenheart might never return. The ironclad rules aboard the *Red Queen* rang in his mind: in the event the captain should be missing for a prolonged time, and it stands between saving the crew and finding the captain, the crew and the ship take priority. He'd never believed the words Rosanne had spoken all those years ago would befall them. The rest of the crew knew this stipulation as well. Everything had been cleared on the first day of their employment contract, the rules of the ship and the possibility of untimely demise through storms, pirates, or warships. No one had ever spoken a word against it. The ship was their lifeline, and without her, they would never see civilization again. He knew that if Rosanne returned and found the *Red Queen* in her current state, Farand would be too ashamed to call himself first lieutenant.

Farand's religious belief in Rosanne's ability to survive wavered because this was a unique adventure they foolishly had swan-dived headfirst into. Truly, he couldn't blame anyone for their rotten luck, only the higher will of heaven. Pirates, electrical storms, this strange land ... everything which was as unlikely to occur as Farand being hit by a falling tortoise strapped with dynamite. Yet, the crew didn't voice a word of complaint.

"Surely I'll hear all about it once we return to Bogvin." He chuckled at the prospect of the entire crew marching into Rosanne's office and handing in their resignations in a disgruntled but orderly fashion.

If the captain didn't return at all ... Farand's stomach flipped. He knew his strengths and weaknesses, but he and the captain were two sides of the same coin, two sides of the *Red Queen*. Farand had been lieutenant long before Drackenheart even bought the ship, but to fly the galleon back to Noval without her didn't seem right. Farand tapped the wheel, searching its worn edges and cracked paint with his eyes. It felt *wrong* in his hands.

The intercom screeched to life, and Farand broke out of his trance and picked it up. "Speak."

"Mr. Duplànte, sir. I got my youngins ready for the overhaul in the engine room." Higgs's distinct voice came through distorted. Farand tapped the intercom twice, pushing a few buttons.

"Pardon, the radio isn't doing too hot either. If you can perform the overhaul in less than four hours, you're all clear."

"That soggy scrag has seen the captain's abuse too many times. I'll send Ida to look at it later. Mind that we won't have any power while we get stuck into it."

Farand digested the words, puzzled by which soggy scrag Higgs meant. He looked at the intercom, noticing the rusted screws and dicey wiring, deciding he'd found the soggy subject. "You're good to go."

"Thank you, sir." The intercom clicked and went silent. Less than thirty seconds later, the low electric hum of the ship faded and was overtaken by the constant sawing, chopping of wood, and chatter below. It was a welcoming change. Farand scanned the empty decks. Everyone was either below deck or on the ground while he twiddled his thumbs like a common idler. He climbed down the rope ladder leading down to the cliff.

"Anything I can assist with?" he asked Creedy. The sweat-soaked man looked up from the felled log, carrying a small hand saw. "We're out of tools here, sir. But Dalia might need a hand with the ropework." Farand spotted Dalia and Olivier in the forest, unwinding long sets of crawler vines along the forest bed. "Take this, sir." One of the topmen handed him his knife. Farand discarded his stiff-buttoned uniform jacket and went to join the watch captain.

The sun scorched the hilltops and the cliffs at mid-afternoon, heat currents dancing visible to the naked eye. Under the cool shade of the pine grove, the working conditions were far more pleasing.

"Take that end. One. Two ... pull!" Dalia and Olivier pulled at a vine with everything they had. The stubborn plant persisted despite the added weight of the two workers. Grabbing it, Farand planted his feet firmly on the soft ground and yanked it clean of its earthly restraints. Dalia's eyes nearly popped out of her skull.

"Thank you, sir. Fancy yourself some work?"

"I do. What do I need to look for?"

Dalia held up the latest catch. "No thinner than this, and if you can't close your hand around it, it's too thick. The longer, the better. I swear we look like fools crawling on the ground." Dalia and Olivier laughed, and Farand didn't deny their remark and prayed the rest of the crew didn't have to see him on all fours.

"By the way, Lieutenant. The crew and ourselves made a little bet. You know, about the captain's return and all?"

He turned a wry smile to Dalia, raising his eyebrow. "And I assume you had nothing to do with its origin?"

Dalia splayed her hands in defence. "Not at all, sir! Here's the bet: the captain returns alive, and we get the hell off this island in one piece, we have to rescue her, or the pirates fuck us over royally."

"You realize that if two of those possibilities were to happen, we'd be deprived of any possibility and hope of survival?"

"Of course. That's why we made the bet." Dalia laughed.

"How much are we talking?" Farand quickly asked.

"Fifteen riksdaler on us rescuing her, three on the captain, seven on the pirates fucking us over."

"Three riksdaler on our captain's return then."

"Optimistic as always, sir. I'll write that down." She made a note on a piece of paper from her pocket and headed away to look for more vines.

"Five on the pirates," Olivier chipped in, making Farand scowl.

"Is this how you waste your money? What did I tell you?"

"It's fun, and I make good money on people's gambling issues." Olivier snickered and lowered his tone. "You shulda seen the other bets we—"

"Olivier, get your ass over here and help me with this!" Dalia shouted, her tone suspiciously close to panic.

"How do I look?" Gavin gave a twirl, the treated leather suit heavy on his frame. He wore additional leather gloves, boots, and a hood with a thin glass-covered slit for his eyes. Nelson could see the crinkles of the third engineer's smiling orbs.

"Like you're about to do something dangerous."

"Exactly! Put on that suit and grab that backpack-looking machinery there." Nelson suited up and strapped on the heavy piece of technology with a hose leading to a wide nozzle. Wobbling from the additional weight of the leather and the machine, Nelson followed Gavin down a level to the portside wall.

Led by the subtle screeching of a hand-held device with antennas, Gavin stopped when it the noise became unbearable.

"This is bad."

"What is that?" Nelson asked, clutching the nozzle as if it could protect him.

"You understand the basics of anti-grav tech?" Gavin turned.

"The ships use refined minerals from gravity stones?"

"Correct. Although they're not blocks of floating minerals like those in the rock belt but extremely fine dust. The air in here is full of them, and it's incredibly toxic if you get it on your skin."

"What does it do if you get it on you?"

"The usual: nausea, headaches, blood floating out of your body through cuts. No gravity tends to mess up how the body works."

Nelson crumpled in on himself protectively, staring into the polluted room without seeing anything. Gavin went to a panel in the wall and flipped it open. Inside were ten sockets of glass vials with a thick black fluid swirling around in them. Three of them were shattered. A cable was plugged into either side of the metal depression storing the vials, and Gavin pulled these out with a simple tug and let them dangle free. The black mass fell still in the vials. In his hand, he had a reinforced box that floated on its own. Gavin plucked out the broken pieces of glass, flipped open the lid of the box, and unfasted one glass vial at a time to replace the broken ones in the panel.

"Are those...?"

"Refined anti-grav minerals. Under the right conditions as made in the panel, these vials can make any material they're attached to float on its own. They still haven't figured out how to make it so the container doesn't float away, so we always have to keep on a leash." Gavin's muffled laughter eased Nelson's discomfort. He wanted to take off his hood, for it was unbearably hot under the layers of leather, but Gavin's words haunted him.

"When we run electricity through them, they can be either disabled or strengthened. Since the ship is a hybrid and can sail on water, we rigged the grav-engine to be able to disable these panels when we want to sail on water and vice versa when we want to fly.

On their own, they aren't all that powerful and need an electric current to utilize their full potential."

"Huh," Nelson marvelled. Now Gavin set a small device on the floor, a box with a coil protruding from its top. He placed a metal rod by the far wall.

"You wanna stay back for this," he said and flipped a switch in his hand. A small electrical charge shot into the air and branched out like reverse miniature lightning bolts directed to the rod. Nelson spotted a dark shimmer in the air of the room falling towards the floor and gravitating towards the coil.

"Then what does this do?" Nelson gestured to the nozzle in his hand.

"That is an extremely nifty piece of tech that can suck things into it and store it. It has a built-in device like the electricity-spitting one on the floor, which keeps the minerals trapped inside it."

"So we're literally going to suck up the gravity minerals?" Nelson's voice was flat and unimpressed, but he laughed despite his disappointment at how absurd this job seemed.

"Let's get cracking. We have two ports to check after this one."

Nelson stared at the ceiling, briefly wondering if he'd wasted his talents on law school.

IN THE CHILL shadows of late afternoon, the crew devoured Hammond's grilled salmon with gluttonous enjoyment. Rows of sailors rested in the grass with their hats or bandanas covering their eyes. Others practiced their knots or played card and dice games.

Ida, Gavin, Higgs, and Nelson lounged by the shade of the trees. Nelson nodded as Gavin illustrated how to properly use one of the many gadgets he had on his tool-belt, a device used to detect metal in wood. Higgs lay propped against a tree, sucking on his tobacco pipe and blowing clouds of sweet-smelling toxins. Ida tinkered with the curious lock absconded from the captain's cabin aboard the *Retribution*.

Dalia's distressed complexion caught their attention as she went from group to group, questioning them.

"Have any of you seen Creedy?"

Ida looked to Gavin, who glanced at Higgs. The older man barely cracked open an eye and snorted.

"He's not on the ship?" Ida asked. Dalia shook her head.

"I checked all over; the ship, the camp, I've asked the others. He's been away for almost an hour. He didn't show for supper either."

"Should we help you look for him?" Ida offered.

"Please. He's managing the rigging, and we need him now more than ever. Farand will have my head."

"He's probably bladdered in the forest 'gain," Higgs huffed and covered his eyes with a handkerchief, settling himself in a comfortable position to sleep in the waning light. Ida ignored his snide remark and packed her things.

"Not much we can do as long as leaky Sally is dismantled. We'll find him before the ship can fly again." She stood and brushed off her work pants. "You coming?" Nelson and Gavin exchanged glances.

"Don't see why not," Nelson said.

"You aren't leaving without me," Gavin agreed.

IDA, Gavin, Nelson, and Dalia formed a line covering more than a hundred paces, combing the forest for the missing watch captain. More than thirty minutes passed with no sign of the middle-aged man, and daylight waned quickly.

"I swear if he's back at camp, I'll string him like a scarecrow to the mast so he can sway in the wind," Dalia grumbled.

Nelson wiped the sweat from his forehead, stopping to clean his glasses and catch a breath. "Is this a trend among the crew, or simply Mr. Creedy's tendency to go about his own business?"

Dalia's face contorted into a sneer. "You mean his entitlement to sod off and not tell anyone? A pain as old as Hammond's pickles." Nelson pictured the many jars of fermented cucumbers lining the shelves in Hammond's pantry and shuddered.

The forest was quiet and bereft of animal and bird activity. Cones of light penetrated the gnarled branches and needled tops, reddish against the rough bark and the crusted lines of sap. The soft forest bed was covered in needles and ants.

Ida swatted the little buggers off her leg. "If Creedy's passed out here, the ants probably got to him first."

"If that's the case ..." Gavin couldn't resist smiling. "All we need to do is find the trail of moving body parts."

Dalia shook her head. "Boy, I swear there's something off about you."

"Far out. My mum said the same thing."

The grove cleared ahead, with a grassy field covering the ground between this and the next grove.

"Do you hear that?" Nelson's urgent whisper stopped them in their tracks. They took a moment to look around. Ida shrugged to Dalia, who shook her head.

Gavin cocked his head. "Someone is singing?"

"I don't hear anything," Dalia said.

"It's coming from the clearing ahead. In that field! There he is!" Gavin pointed to an askew silhouette of Creedy. His back was turned to them. They jogged into the grass, palmed it aside, and waded through to the thinner, patchy center.

"Hey, Creedy! Time to get back to work," Dalia called, but Creedy gave no indication that he heard them. He simply stood there, swaying gently back and forth.

"What *is* that?" Nelson shook the swirling sensation in his mind, overcome with a profound sense of confusion. Gavin stopped moving altogether, his eyes transfixed ahead.

"What's wrong?" Dalia asked the lawyer. Nelson didn't

answer. His face was placid, then grew tranquil and smiling. She waved a hand in front of him, but the lawyer didn't react. "Ida! Something's up with the guys."

"The song ..." Gavin whispered. "Can't you hear it?"

Ida shook Nelson's shoulders, but the man didn't react.

"Reminds me of home," he said.

"Nelson, there is no song. Snap out of it!" She clapped his cheeks, but the man smiled stupidly.

"Creedy!" Dalia rushed to the older man and cried out in terror, falling back. She heaved for the breath she lost. Previously hidden due to the angle of their approach, a tall, skinny humanoid stretched out a wiry grey hand to Creedy's face from a hunched posture in front of him. The creature had small flat breasts with ribs visible in her starved torso and bony pelvis protruding under a loincloth. She stood on the balls of her feet with skinny elongated legs, stooping to meet Creedy's stature. The creature's flat-nosed face twisted into a snarl, and she shrieked at Dalia, who cried out upon meeting her black eyes. Thin black hair whipped as the creature threw her head back in an ear-piercing howl, and Dalia kicked the dirt with her legs to escape backwards.

The creature pounced at her.

"Dalia!" Ida called as the monster raked at Dalia's kicking feet. The older woman grabbed her knife and drove it into the creature's shoulder, who screamed and jumped back. She stared at the dripping wound, then sneered.

Ida leapt in front of the woman, pointing a gun with quivering hands. Dalia groaned, holding her shin where the creature had scratched her deeply. Ida drew back the flint, tears streaming down her face. The creature hissed, revealing pointed brown teeth.

"N-Nelson! Gavin!" Ida called out. She looked at the unmoving men. "What are you doing? Help us!" But they merely stood there, dazed and rocking back and forth.

"Shoot it!" Dalia called out, and the sudden outburst startled

Ida enough to pull the trigger. The gun let out a resonating bang, and the bullet lodged itself in the creature's arm. She cried out and recoiled. Then she let out a different sound, a thin loud shriek. Ida backed away until she felt Dalia behind her, and the older woman pulled the girl down and took the gun to reload it. Calls similar to the creature's resounded from the forest in front of them. Ida stared transfixed at the monster—she only now noticed she was swishing a cow-like tail. An excited gleam shone in her eyes.

"I'll shoot it in the leg, and when I do, you run back to the ship and get help. Ida? Stay with me, girl!" Dalia slapped the weepy girl, who nodded through her tears.

"What the hell is that?" Creedy backed away, stumbling over his feet at the initial horrifying look the creature gave him.

"Do something, Creedy!" Dalia pleaded. The man whipped out his carving knife and pounced. The creature caught his arm with ease, holding him firmly as he struggled against her monstrous strength. At full length, she stood taller than him, and with a squeeze of her clawed hand, Creedy dropped the knife. She rammed against him, and the man fell and rolled to his side.

"Go, Ida! *Go!*" Dalia pushed the girl.

IDA SPRINTED ACROSS THE FIELD, her legs unsteady against the uneven ground. The forest was a tear-stained blur, and she grazed a pine tree, scratching her shoulder. She stumbled but regained her composure and continued her mad dash through the forest.

Behind her, gunshots resonated, stirring resting crows into panicked flight. Ida wiped the falling tears, struggling to see a path through fallen pines and broken logs. Her lungs burned, and her legs felt sour and rotting. She gasped for breath.

The camp was just up ahead.

"Mr. Duplànte!" she called out with everything she had left, a hoarse out-of-breath gasp which barely left her mouth.

"Farand! We're under attack!" she yelled again. Through the fringes of the tree line, Ida spotted the crew rising to their feet. Farand barked orders at them and ran for his weapons.

Ida lurched ahead as a powerful force pushed her off her feet. She caught herself with her hands, the sting of pine needles digging into her palms and making her cry out. She rolled over with her arms braced protectively in front of her. A pair of black pools stared into her teary ones.

"No!" Ida sobbed and swung around, kicking out with her legs to get away from her new assailant. The creature opened her mouth, letting out a shrill yet soothing melody.

Ida's flow of tears ceased, and a warm, comforting sensation filled her chest. She blinked the tears away. The creature before her blurred, the pale face and black eyes fading from view. The world morphed into strange colours and shapes.

"Don't be afraid, Ida." A blond-haired woman wearing a summer dress smiled at her with red-painted lips. "Silly girl. You must watch where you're going. You'll tear your clothes if you keep falling like that."

"*Mamma*?" Ida stared at the smiling woman who held out her hand.

"Come now, dear. Your da is waiting for us." Ida took her mother's hand and let herself be guided.

"IDA!" Farand called upon seeing the lank monstrosity reach for the engineer. He drew the plasma gun from its holster. A massive force crashed into him, sending him tumbling to the ground. Farand turned to find a small party of creatures standing wide-legged as if on the offensive but weaving a melody to the crew members they attacked. The men and women among them lowered their rifles and handguns, eyes transfixed and calm.

"Fire! What are you doing? Shoot them now!" Farand wrapped his hand around a broken branch and smacked the creature in front of him with it. She shrieked, held her face, and stepped back in panic. She called to the others, who immediately diverted their song towards Farand.

He swung the branch threateningly and got to his feet. The four creatures knit their melodies into one another's, their eyes never leaving him. Farand's arms grew heavy. Barely holding on to his only weapon, he felt inclined to drop it. He shook his head.

"Stay back, *grande garce*!" He swung the branch again, putting his best effort and strength into the move and yet it barely went above his knees. His vision swam in currents. The song resonated and drowned out all his thoughts. He grabbed his skull, the song, the melody, and now a voice calling out to him, almost screaming.

"Stop it! Stop it! *Putain de merde*!" Farand lashed out and felt the painful smack as his fist connected, but he couldn't identify with what. His feet moved like they had a will of their own. He couldn't stop them.

Farand saw the path ahead of him leading away from the camp and down the cliff. He followed it, unable to stop.

Chapter 13

Frenemies

The pulsating beat of drums and her rising nausea had Rosanne groaning.

"Shhh! Be quiet. They'll hear us!" Captain Bernhart's voice drilled into her skull like a bad migraine, and Rosanne considered the possibility that this was a nightmare. A dark room with a packed dirt floor greeted her as her eyes fluttered open, accompanied by a burning tightness around her hands and just below her breasts. With a strained gasp, she moved her head around to see she was bound and strung up like meat at the butchers. Aros was against her back, sharing the discomfort of the ill-placed rope bondage. They swung lazily. To her surprise, their feet were unbound, but Rosanne didn't deny the effective discomfort brought upon them by concentrated weight on their torso bindings. She suffered another wave of nausea, took a deep breath, and spat out the accumulated saliva.

"What happened?" Rosanne shook her head as if it would help against the dizziness, but the persistent pounding moved with her. Instead, the drumming concentrated on the gash on her forehead, which had swelled and crusted.

"We got screwed over by trolls, that's what." The urgency in Aros' voice didn't outweigh his choice of words.

Rosanne blinked. "By what now?"

"I don't know what they were. They were small and fussy with a mean aim. So, shut up and let me think of a way out of this especially fucked up situation we're in."

Her neck was stiff, and her eyes rolled against her wishes to stem the nausea. It took a few moments before she managed to concentrate on their surroundings. They were in a cave lit by torchlight, about two meters from the ground, with two ways in and out of the musty room. They were suspended under the ceiling by a hook. Along the walls stood assorted fishing rods, nets, small animal cages, and a few poorly constructed crates. A rotting stench crept into her nostrils, blocking out breathable air. She gagged.

"My dear god, what crawled up your ass and died?" She coughed. Wiggling back and forth to the protest of Aros, Rosanne spun them around enough for her to see a pile of animal bones and rotten skins.

"What are the chances those corpses just wandered in here?" she asked, unconvinced by her own words.

Aros looked at the fly-infested pile and bobbed his head. "I wouldn't place my faith in the modern world's new vegetarian wave."

Rosanne, to her surprise, chuckled, then groaned and fought off another churning sensation. "How long was I out?"

"Almost as long as I was. And why the hell am I stuck here with *you*?"

"You weren't my first choice either."

"Well, ain't that just swell," Aros grumbled and twisted his head around. His left orbital socket was blue and swollen, and his hair was filled with straw and dirt.

"Nice eye." Rosanne grinned, a wave of satisfaction filling her at the sight of his mangled face.

"Take a look in the mirror, lady." She wouldn't have wanted to if she could.

"Stop calling me lady." Rosanne lifted her right foot as much as it allowed her, leaned to the side, and tipped their balance point.

"What the hell are you doing?" he hissed and cast his eyes to the hallways.

"Shut up and let me ... just ..." Her face grew hot as she stretched her bound wrist as much as she could, but the rope was too tight. She let her foot drop, leaving them bobbing on the rope. She let out a shallow breath, then caught a guttural call echoing from somewhere inside the cave system. Their heads dropped and eyes shut at the approach of two small creatures. Rosanne cracked her lids enough to catch a glimpse of flea-infested trolls, creatures half their size with barrel-shaped torsos and stubby arms and legs. Their naked pointed ears perked up at the different sounds they made as they gesticulated with their arms and fingers, cackling. Fuzzy-ended tails swished eagerly, and more than once did they scratch the hairy patches on their bodies. Rosanne caught her voice before calling out at the bizarre sight.

The trolls rummaged around the crates as they communicated in a guttural language, and here and there, Rosanne thought she recognized a word or two. One of them stepped on a fishhook and yowled. The other hooted at his companion's misfortune. Unhooking himself, the hurt creature swatted the other on the back of his head as they exited the chamber.

Aros and Rosanne waited a few minutes after the shadows of the creatures disappeared.

"Ideas, you said?" Rosanne looked back at Aros' panic-stricken face.

"Yes, uh. Obviously, we need to get the hell out of here before those things invite us for dinner."

"Can you reach my boot if I lift it?"

"You got a knife in there or something?" He grinned at the notion and let out a painful groan when she managed to kick him.

"Damn straight, I do. Now get to it." She lifted her foot again. Had she been less nimble, she couldn't dream of pulling off the stretching exercise her thigh had to suffer, but she felt a hand dig into the rim of her boot, and two fingers fished out a small dagger. Aros flipped it and started sawing into the first available piece of rope. A faint cackling echoing from one of the hallways made him pause.

"Better hurry up," she urged.

"I'll cut you if you say another word."

The rope around her wrists snapped and forced more of her weight to fall on the torso bindings. She fought to regain her stolen breath, dazed and about to spill her stomach's contents on the floor. She wiggled her arms to the sides as Aros sawed at his bindings like a madman. The fickle knots didn't hold her for long, and Rosanne freed herself one arm at a time, careful not to fall. She grabbed the rope from which they hung, relieving the stress on the bindings around them. They came undone easily. Rosanne lost her grip and fell over a meter before hitting the ground with a thud. She breathed deeply through the pain shooting through her legs. Aros still hung from the wrists and torso of the crudely constructed bindings, which still had him suspended. It was impressive how the knot became tangled to such a degree.

"Don't you dare leave without me, lady!" Captain Bernhart hissed as he pressed the knife harder against the ropes.

When the pain finally became manageable, Rosanne dusted off her pants and stretched. "You look much more comfortable up there. I'll make it easy for myself and take my leave." Rosanne reached for the rim of her hat but discovered it was as lost to her as she was to the crew. Instead, she turned to exit the room.

"I'll shout," he said flatly.

Rosanne stopped and cast Aros an icy stare. "And get us both eaten? Are you really that petty? You still have a knife."

"Be reasonable, lady. You have a higher chance of survival with me by your side. What do you say, Captain Drackenheart?" His blue eyes shone in the torchlight, and his unkempt and weather-hardened face, which had threatened her life mere hours prior, couldn't scare a dog. Rosanne sighed and began stacking crates.

"I knew you would see reason."

"Shut up and stop wiggling." Rosanne balanced on the crates, and their precarious balance increased under her weight. She took the knife and cut at the main rope. Aros cried out as he crashed against the floor. He spat out a mouthful of dirt. The crates wobbled and tipped over, and Rosanne jumped off. As they broke, the contents spilled out on the floor, and Rosanne spotted familiar items among the rubble.

"They kept our stuff." She holstered the only gun in the crate and put on her hat; it wasn't the first time it had gotten lost, but it somehow always found its way back to her. After releasing Aros from the remaining ropes and absconding with weaponry in the form of blades, they crept into the corridor opposite of where the creatures had come from. The ceiling was low, making Rosanne stoop low as she went forward in the gloom.

"Say, Captain Drackenheart? Aside from mad piloting, you possess some other fine qualities." Aros' lighthearted tone made Rosanne's neck hairs stand on end.

"Keep staring at my ass, and I will serve you to the monsters personally."

A familiar cackling echoed in the murky halls, making the two captains freeze on the spot. Aros whipped his head around, alarmed at the side passage teeming with life. Rosanne scuttled on all fours until the passage opened and allowed her to stand. Eager to follow, Aros sped behind her. Both captains stepped as gingerly as they could until they came to a narrow crack in the wall, which was all but black and empty. Diving inside and hugging the walls, Rosanne and Aros listened to the approaching cackling and soft padding. A small party of five goblins waddled past, oblivious to the captains sweating profusely as they kept their presence hidden in the dark.

As Rosanne's heart still slammed in her chest, Aros craned his neck ever so slightly outside of their hiding place.

"I believe we're in the clear," he whispered. Rosanne merely nodded, steeling herself and steadying her breathing.

As reluctant as they were to leave the illusion of comfort and safety, the captains followed the passage and ignored the narrow rooms and hallways branching out to the sides.

A low drumming hum resonated in the corridor, followed by a trail of steam reeking of fish.

Rosanne cast Aros a questioning look. The man shrugged and tapped his lips with one finger, then pointed ahead.

The cave corridor widened with chisel lines and a rougher surface than the natural stone further in. Leaning against the wall, Rosanne craned her neck to the side, peeking inside an opening more than twice her height and wide enough for four grown men to stand shoulder to shoulder. A meaty slap against stone caught her attention from around the bend. A crudely constructed table as tall as her was filled with heaps of vegetables and sharpened stones. Next to it, a fire roared in a pit with a black cauldron suspended on a hook above it. The scent filled the room, and whatever it was, it didn't agree with Rosanne's tastes. Aros pinched his nose and poked his head around her.

"Look at that thing," he whispered nasally, eyes as wide as saucers.

A tall and lumpy being of roiled fat wearing only a loincloth lumbered into the room, holding a large batch of carrots in his clubby fingers. The room was spacious enough to accommodate its enormous size, maybe two and a half meters if Rosanne's eyes didn't betray her common sense. Its legs were covered with thin patches of hair, while nothing grew on its grey-spotted flat head. It sniffed the different vegetables on the table with its round nose, bushy eyebrows so low on its lumpy face its eyes remained obscured. The creature's mouth scrunched at the smell of a potato that was less than qualified for the stew, and he tossed the root vegetable to the floor where it rolled out to the hallway. The brute swished his short, naked tail. He picked up one of the sharpened stones and began cutting. His hands were less than delicate, and unevenly sliced vegetables flew everywhere.

A small troll entered and stretched out his hand to the giant with a positive chitter. It was so small it barely reached to the giant's knees, but the larger creature seemed pleased and received a fistful of herbs. The troll said something, which made the giant let out a series of snorts which could have been laughter while the little one cackled. Another two trolls emerged from a side room, both carrying bloodied buckets of meat.

Aros nudged Rosanne's shoulder once the creatures were occupied with the cauldron. The two humans went as fast and quiet as they could into the hallway. They spent the next ten minutes wandering the passages which split and meandered, then doubled back from dead ends. They chanced upon a sleeping chamber with straw beds and animal skins, storage areas cluttered with all sorts of garbage salvaged from sail ships, and several rooms housing livestock, like chickens and pigs. Finally, they spotted the murky mist of morning light through the cave entrance ahead. No one guarded the opening, and the two captains slipped into the surrounding birch forest, avoiding the trail left behind from troll activity, and ran for their lives.

ROSANNE'S LUNGS were on fire. Every movement was a hand squeezing tighter around her heart. The botched Georgetown trade six years ago didn't come anywhere close to this urgency to escape. She was a quick runner when ushered by survival instincts alone.

They must have covered several kilometres by the time they deemed it safe enough for a short rest.

Rain drizzled from the low clouded sky. The woodland around them was dense and uneven, with jutting rocks and steep, moss-covered hills. Above them, stray boulders hovered and provided shelter from the rain. Rosanne had seen nothing like it before in all her travels and was intimidated by the sheer size of the rocks. She was reluctant to pass underneath one had it not been for her need to get dry.

"Do call me crazy, but did you see those things?" Aros pointed a thumb behind them and heaved for breath.

"I don't know what to believe either. Those small beings were definitely the ones that ambushed us. I can only speculate what the large one was going to do with us." Her knees wobbled as she sat.

Aros overplayed a dramatic shudder. "Glad we didn't stay for dinner. Or breakfast. Or any other damned meal they prepared. Where the hell did they take us, anyway?" There was nothing familiar like the vast forest landscape or the western mountains. Aros lowered his voice and scrunched his shoulders. "Do you even think we're on the same island?"

Rosanne resisted the temptation to shake her head as she was almost positive they were on a different planet altogether but adhered to her better senses. "I don't believe they could transport us off the island unless they had boats. They didn't seem all that clever."

Aros wiped his nose on his sleeve, grinning. "Good thing I got stuck with you, prepared and all that."

"I wasn't nearly prepared enough for being jumped by trolls. I only prepared for a pirate showdown."

"Aye, but we got out alright. We just have to get back, and all will be swell." He did a spin on his heels, snapping his fingers. The motion had Rosanne caught between perplexed and disbelieving.

"Just?" She swept a hand around them. "Have you looked around at all in the last hour? We're screwed out here for many reasons." She closed her fist then lifted a single finger. "We don't have any food or water." She raised the middle finger. "We've got no shelter anywhere on this godforsaken island." Then the ring finger. "We have no one to back up our sorry asses should we be attacked again." Lastly, the pinky. "We don't even have a fully functional vessel to get off this cursed rock! Wipe off that self-satisfied smirk! We have three daggers and a pistol with *one* bullet, and I'll be damned if I don't use that gun to shoot you *just* so I can get away alive!" She finished her tirade off, pointing at Aros, painting him as a target for her rage.

Her outburst had Aros pursing his lips. "Good to know that you have your priorities as straight as your math. I will do the same." His attempt at twirling the knife in his hand, which he dropped, didn't strengthen his resolution. They stared at each other, snorted in unison, and turned away. The soft patter of rain against foliage made for a comforting ambiance. The boulder above them was low enough to provide shelter, but they were both drenched to the bone. Rosanne shivered and sneezed.

"Fire?" Aros inquired and rubbed his arms.

"Yeah." Rosanne nodded.

"I'll get ..." again the awkward wave of his thumb as he set off to find firewood.

"I'll prep a camp."

THE WOOD CRACKLED and popped with sour smoke as the drenched woodlands had little else to offer. Rosanne and Aros hoped the smoke dissipated enough to avoid detection from under the floating boulder. Still, they weren't hopeful and tried as quickly as possible to dry themselves. "Looks like the rain is almost done." Aros nodded towards the breaking cloud layer.

Rosanne eyed the blue sky between the grey. "We should get a move on."

"Ten more minutes. My breeches are still sticking."

"That is ... just *why* would you even mention that?"

Aros chuckled. "My dear captain. You have a sullied mind."

She opened her mouth, only to clap it shut to prevent herself from feeding Aros' amusement. She wondered which god she had pissed off to be stuck with this half-clammed pirate captain robbed of his crew and ship. He wasn't even a captain anymore, just another unscrupulous bastard sticking to her hide like a parasite because the situation allowed him to do so. And she let him tag along. Was it pity? Or her own need to even out the survival odds, which had never been at a lower point in her entire career? That goddamned lawyer ...

Aside from survival, Aros' intentions were as obscure as this island, and she didn't like not knowing what to expect. "Us being in that cave ... makes you wonder what happened with the others."

Aros poked the fire and made a face between a grimace and disgust. "There weren't many of those goblins there, but we were ambushed by a hell of a lot more."

She nodded. "Maybe the others got taken elsewhere."

"And pray to god that they got away."

"Either way, we're not equipped for any rescue missions. We're better off trying to find our way back." She held her hat over the weak embers, turning it periodically.

"And you'll graciously ship us to safe harbor?"

Her sharp eyes drifted to his hopeful ones. "We'll cross that plank when we get there."

"Tough negotiator, ain't you?" Aros wrung his jacket inside out.

"I don't negotiate with pirates. You have nothing of any value to me. Therefore, you are a liability once were done here."

"Same to you, lady."

"Would it kill you to call me captain, *Captain*?"

Her reaction had him smiling. "Maybe I should call you 'iron maiden' instead. Your hide is tough like metal, and your insides filled with thorns."

Rosanne shook her head and sighed. She picked twigs and leaves from her hair, grimacing to notice how grimy it was. Her last bath had been days ago, a sore reminder of how remote from any decent civilization they were.

Stealing a glance at Captain Bernhart, she frowned. This low-life piece of garbage was the sole reason they were stranded on a monster-infested island. Her ship was broken, her crew scattered over the hills. And yet ... he was in the *same* situation. Undoubtedly Aros has similar thoughts about her, as they both were at fault for getting into the situation by trying to earn a living using the only means they knew.

The only reason anyone was on this island was due to her connections to the RDA. It hit her then that she hadn't thought of Antony since their departure from Valo, her mind so embroiled in the mission and life-threatening situations she hadn't allowed herself the thought that she might never return.

Their meetings were almost always planned, as weeks could pass by without any contact with each other. On and off for two years, he didn't ask questions about her business, and she didn't pry into the affairs of the RDA. All they needed was the privacy of their chambers and a good bottle of wine. He always brought calm to her tumultuous life, a lighthouse to guide the way in the dark. The thought of never returning to that small pocket of peace in her life, that extra form of emotional intimacy she never indulged in when on the job, made her insides coil. And yet, they were from two different worlds. Would he even want her as much in his life as she did him? How much was she willing to give up to have him in her life just a little bit more?

She cast the silly thoughts aside with the bitter reminder that her business was far beyond the law. That was *if* she managed to return Mr. Blackwood to town, alive and on time.

The list of everything that had gone terribly wrong since the mission started was enough to give Rosanne a paroxysm of violent outbursts, but she promptly reminded herself that the less she showed Captain Bernhart, the less he knew how to manipulate her. She couldn't afford useless emotions clouding her mind, now least of all. Rosanne tsked and put on her hat, the underside still hot from the fire and a warm welcome to her scalp.

"YOU'RE A WANDERING ICEBERG, Captain Drackenheart. No wonder my ship went down when you keep rejecting my advances so." Aros laughed despite himself. Hazel eyes stared coldly into his, and he changed the subject at the defeat of his attempted banter. "What I can't figure out is why you bothered to accept the fight." He pointed the burnt end of a twig at her as if an invitation to a duel. She rolled her shoulders, eyes on the fire.

"I got cocky. The fight seemed like it would be to our advantage, but your ship had better equipment. The information we had on the *Blue Dragon* paled during the battle, and by the time we knew for sure what we were up against, our engine was shutting down." Her blank eyes were in contrast to the stark of amusement inside him.

He twirled the stick around in the air, tracing a glowing trail. "That's when you pulled that shapeshifter trick, right?"

The corner of her lips tugged, he guessed at the amusement of his enthusiasm "It only closed the thruster ports so we could sail on the water without damaging the engine. And this only proves my point that you have no idea how even to fly my ship." The pride in her tone when it came to her vessel was unmistakable.

"Well, yes. But still. The fight would have been ours had we not been hit by that storm."

"If that's what you think, I feel apologetic toward your crew for not shooting you in the face. Oh wait, I did." Aros snorted but said nothing in his defence. They sat in silence, poking the fire or keeping an eye on their surroundings. Birds fluttered above them, disappearing into cracks in the boulder. The smoke wafted into Rosanne's face, and Aros was amused to see that she refused to move from her spot. Or rather, it appeared her attention was somewhere far away from the campsite. He scratched his beard and cleared his throat.

"Yes?" she asked, without facing him.

"I was thinking of ways how to dispose of you."

She arched an eyebrow.

Aros splayed his empty hands. "I only have a knife. You have a gun that can effectively kill me at a long distance. If we're attacked by trolls again, it's kill or be killed, so going after you in that situation would be idiotic. On the other hand, if the big guy comes for us, all we can do is run. Your tact and your mouth are what have kept you alive, so I'm thinking it's easier to keep you around. At least until the situation changes to my favour."

She smiled at the intriguing scenarios he espoused. "And if it doesn't?" she asked.

Aros pursed his lips. "If all else fails, I'll find a way. I got my wits and my mouth too. That reminds me. Can you disclose a little piece of information to me? Just to keep the conversation afloat, of course."

"As if the conversation was anything but sinking ... Shoot."

"What was your plan when you first met me?"

Rosanne cast her eyes down and smiled wryly.

Aros leaned his head back and ran a hand over his forehead, laughing. "You had no plan? Not even a tiny one?"

Rosanne chuckled, shaking her head. "I was going to stab you and then have Mr. Lyle shoot the closest guards. I was riding my faith in you being too slow to respond. Instead, we got mauled by trolls."

"Those fucking trolls." Aros was in tears despite his head pounding; a fist-sized rock had hit him during the abduction, the wound now a black-crusted tangle of hair and blood, yet it didn't deter his laughter. He stood up and stretched out his hand. Rosanne gave it a meaningful stare before levelling with him. "How about it, Captain Drackenheart? Parlay for now?" Her eyes bore into his, perhaps in search of any indication that he was ready to end her. But Aros kept his composure, He remained relaxed, both hands visible, and he was smiling which made her face twist into a scowl. Captain Rosanne Drackenheart snorted and shook his hand.

CHAPTER 14

NONE OF THAT!

Aros hauled his weight on the slick treacherous vines while placing his feet in cracks on the boulder.

"What do you see?" Rosanne called from below, tipping her hat back to better view the struggling captain as he slipped on the wet rocks. He grumbled, meticulously picking his footing. The shelf gave in. Aros shrieked as he fell a gut-wrenching metre long drop before the vine held firm. Rosanne cursed as she dodged the unexpected rain of debris.

"The sharp end of the stick if you don't shut up," he grumbled loud enough for her just to catch it.

"What did you say?"

He flipped her a rude gesture and cursed as the vine snapped from its hold, teasingly letting Aros drop for half a heartbeat.

"You know I can shoot you from here?" Rosanne jested.

"And invoke the wrath of the entire goblin-infested forest? I think not!"

Rosanne cackled, and Aros let out another string of colourful words.

He spent the next five minutes clambering to a ledge that he could stand on. He let out the loudest sigh as if the adrenaline-induced climb had taken years of his life. The sun hit his eyes like a set of knives. He shielded them and gazed out to the forest surrounding them.

"Forest. More forest. A big oak. A bigger rock. Floating rocks ..." he muttered to himself and wiped the sweat from his brow. The surrounding hills made it difficult to spot anything over the next top, but a distinct haze about two kilometres away indicated the possibility of freshwater. The bushland was thick, and the annoying obstacles in the shape of hills would make the trek long and difficult, but it was the only source of water he could spot for miles.

The flat woodlands where they had first confronted the crew from the *Red Queen* was nowhere in sight. If he judged by how large the Grey Veil looked on a map, he wouldn't dream of a land-mass as vast as this existed within it. Rosanne's voice called from below, but he ignored her, preferring to plan his grand return to civilization. A small rock smacked against his shoulder.

"Oy!" he cried in protest. Rosanne held her arms out wide, expecting an answer. "There's a waterfall not far from here," he replied. "Don't shoot me on my way down!"

Rosanne's smile was mischievous as she tipped her hat back. "I'll let nature run its course if you fall. Less work for me."

"Aren't you just a big bottle of sunshine." Aros' very own specialty at making people lose their marbles was coming back to haunt him because when Captain Drackenheart put her mind to it, she was good at shredding his sails. Rosanne's sudden change in character unsettled him in ways he didn't think possible. In a matter of hours, she had discovered exactly which buttons to push to piss him off.

The gnarly vines gave Aros a safe and steady descent, and by the time he hit the ground, his arms felt like they had rotted. Rosanne merely stared at him, patiently waiting for his guidance. The gash on her forehead had turned a yellow and green hue. Her gloves were off, and he noticed a particular swelling on her digits and the purple bruise on her left hand, which he recognized.

"Lost your wheel, did you?" He nodded to her hands.

She flexed her stiff fingers. "It was one heck of a storm. At least it was only my hands."

Aros brushed off his pants. "Would be better if it was your head." Rosanne's smile widened while her eyes narrowed to slits. He pointed east towards a set of hills. "Spotted water maybe two kilometres that way. Let's go." He strode off before Rosanne could voice her opinion, and she grudgingly trailed behind him with her thin-lipped smile undoubtedly still in place.

THE CLIMB over the heather-covered rocky hills only accentuated Rosanne's urgent need for basic supplies. Parched and impossibly tired, she kept losing her footing or banging against the loose rocks as her vision swam like a nauseating day at sea. Her hands offered little support for the swelling. They prickled and ached. Dehydrated, famished, and wounded, the two captains marched on to live another day.

"Thank Terra! There it is." Aros threw a hand towards the stairstep waterfall. It formed a cove, the wide river feeding the cascade snaking from a vast barren plateau of rocks. He buckled over and fell on his side in the heather, too tired to let his legs support him. Rosanne sat down and fanned herself. The rising spray produced by the crashing water against rocks had been their only means of direction, and Rosanne noted that the waters were bustling with marine activity even from afar.

"We can wash up and catch lunch if the river is shallow enough. This blasted heat is killing me." Rosanne smacked at a horsefly biting her cheek. Aros offered a groan as he succumbed to exhaustion.

The weather cleared by midday and carried a strong scent of petrichor. The rocks by Aros' head looked deadly, but Rosanne had to remind herself that her chances of survival rode on the competence of a certain idiotic pirate.

Besides, the hills were steep and brittle. Anything could happen.

Aros and Rosanne made it to the cove on willpower alone. While Aros dove his head for water, Rosanne took a more refined approach away from the man as her tiredness had her weakened and hyper-alert. The chilly water perked up her senses, and she washed her face and drank her fill. Driftwood rested along the rocky beach on each side of the river running from the waterfall's pool, and from down here, the falls appeared like a wet stairway to heaven. Water flowed in gallons, and its rumble drowned out any noise from the nearby forest.

AROS SAT on the bank as Rosanne kicked off her shoes and rolled up her pants to the knees. She left her hat and sweat-stained jacket on the shore.

"What are you doing?" Aros asked. With the gun still in her belt, Rosanne waded into the river and took a wide stance in the numbing waters.

"Just get a fire going. I'll get dinner."

His eyebrows rose. "How're you gonna do that?" She rolled her eyes and shook her head, but he couldn't tell if it was simply to get her hair out of her face or at something he said. Nevertheless, he gathered dry driftwood into a pile and stacked a pyre ready for lighting. When he turned his attention to Rosanne, she was still as a statue. She must have been freezing from the chill water but gave no indication that this was a problem. Her eyes were on the shadows moving below the surface, and then her hands sprang into action in a swift straight movement. She lifted a silver-scaled fish out of the water by the gills, letting out a victorious laugh. With stiff yet deft hands, she broke the fish's neck and tossed it ashore. Aros stared at the soon-to-be fish fillet.

"What are you waiting for? Get that fire going!"

Aros' doubt turned to awe at Rosanne's jack-of-all-trades

captain skills and got to it. By the time the fire was roaring, Rosanne had caught and mercilessly killed another three fish and had them gutted and rinsed. Aros had gone the extra mile and prepared wooden pikes leaning over the red-hot embers.

THE SUN DIPPED behind the hilltops, and the cove chilled considerably. Rosanne rubbed her hands together and attempted to resurrect heat in her icicle hands. The cold helped with the pain, but she felt so very little she almost thought her hands were dead. They ate in silence, plucking tooth-pick-sized bones from their teeth. Little else seemed to matter at that moment as the calm silence of the forest gave little cause for concern. All in all, the two captains were too tired to bother with anything other than digesting their food.

Rosanne wiggled her toes close to the fire, keeping warm while her socks dried on two sticks. Every muscle in her body ached. Her shoulders were stiff, her arms weak, her legs like anvils as she lay on the ground. Aros was equally sprawled on the other side of the fire, not moving as much as a muscle, except for a timely burp to break the silence.

"Thanks for the food, ain't that what belching means?" A distinct rise in his tone made Rosanne peek from under her hat.

"I'll take that as a compliment. Western colonies, right?"

He lifted his hat to look at her. "How'd ye know?"

She threw out a hand and let it fall to her thigh. "A wild guess by your terrible attempt to mask your accent."

"So, you *are* curious about me, eh? I knew there was more to that iron hide of yers."

"Know thine enemies, lest you be dined by them."

"Tsk. Always so practical. On another note, what now?"

"We follow the river east."

"To see if we hit the coast, right?" He seemed to take her silence as approval. "So..." He sat up, and Rosanne cracked her eyes open just enough to catch a glimpse of his silhouette. "Do you often get stranded on monster-filled islands and survive on nothing but a pocketknife and your wits?"

"One time too many."

"You're not much of a talker, are you?"

"Do you often lose your ship, your crew, your sanity, and your common sense?" she snapped at him.

"Fine, fine. But maybe we should get a move on. It's already getting dark out."

Rosanne sat up and felt her socks. "Let us wait until at least our footwear is dry." Aros waved a hand and disappeared into the nearby bushes. "Where are you going?" she asked.

"Where do you think?"

Rosanne snorted and lay back, keeping the inveterate pirate under close observation as he milled about the foliage.

Her mind drifted to the familiar shores of Valo and all its islands and fjords. The industrial fumes of the docks below the skyport. The brackish smell of the sea. She was sitting in a tall-backed chair in her room, sipping hot coffee. Valo was the home away from home, even if she didn't have permanent residence there. Life seemed simple then: deliver the ledger to Madam Mean Stare-, eh, Meinstare at the Magistrate of Trade, wait for her approval and for the crew to be paid, scout new trade in the meantime should the Magistrate provide none, and perhaps even receive a visit from Captain DiCroce.

Rosanne smiled despite the silliness of her wishful mind. Those days were drowned out by her current need to survive while trapped in the company of a man quite the opposite from the charming, patient, and capable Antony. The ruggedly handsome face of Aros and his poor attempt at charms, which probably swayed a working woman if he flashed gold, made Rosanne shudder in disgust.

A brutish tug on her belt threw her thoughts off the skyport of Noval and back to the waterfall in the forest surrounded by trolls. Her hand shot out to intercept the assailant and caught

Aros' hand holding the butt of her gun. He recoiled, and she lurched, refusing to let go of the firearm. He kicked her squarely in the abdomen. She lost her breath for a moment but jabbed her free hand to the soft spot between Aros' chest and arm, making him scream and drop the gun. Rosanne quickly drew back the flint and pointed it at the captain's contorted face as he held his side. She wiped the spittle from the corner of her mouth and caught her breath.

"Fucking try that again, and I'll murder you in your sleep."

Aros raised his hands, catching his breath in defeat. "It was worth a try at least. Bloody hell, lady. Where do you get your strength?" Despite his recent attempt almost ending with his demise, he grinned with what seemed like excitement.

"My hidden Novalian anger, that's where!" Rosanne bristled.

"I dated a Novalian girl once. She wasn't nearly as temperamental."

"Is this a joke to you?"

"No, lady. Just survival." She kicked him over to the side, but there was no real strength behind it, and he tumbled like a rag.

"Fine. I'm leaving." She fit her socks and shoes, tugging at the laces so hard they threatened to snap.

Aros groaned, stood, and trailed behind her. Her tempered scolding didn't help his progress or ease the throbbing pain from her bony hands.

———

NIGHT HIT the two captains hard in a cloak of darkness, forcing them to stop. They didn't chance another campfire no matter how cold the weather bit into their skin, for they knew that anyone or anything could spot the light from miles off. They each leaned against their tree, legs crossed, arms crossed, hats low on their faces as they initiated the standoff of who would fall asleep first.

The cold made Rosanne sleepy, but her adrenaline was still

pumping through her system as Aros' narrow eyes were fixed on hers. She knew if she fell asleep, he would go for her gun or possibly slit her throat and leave her for dead, and it was a risk she didn't dare to test. Pirates couldn't be trusted for a riksdaler of worth, and she knew Aros trusted her just as little.

As the night grew colder and darker, Aros' eyes began to sag and close, only to open abruptly. Rosanne said nothing, but tiredness crept over her as well. She wanted to slap herself but knew the sudden movement would startle Aros, who was so very close to entering dreamland. And then came the low snores. Rosanne bid her time until she counted the steady rhythm of breaths (and ungodly loud snores) as genuine. The river drowned out her movements, and she waved a hand in front of his face. She wrinkled her nose as an idea formed in her mind, her eye resting on the vines hanging from the nearby trees.

A BIRD TWITTERED and hopped back and forth on Rosanne's hat. She cracked her eyes open to see a blue feathery tail wag before it flew off in a flurry of protests. She smiled, feeling rested for the first time in days, and stretched her arms.

"About bloody time you woke up!" Aros' annoyed tone burst from the other tree, and Rosanne had to restrain her obvious mirth.

"Slept well, Captain?" she asked.

Aros' scowl deepened, and he raised his vine-tangled hands. Lianas were strung around the tree, keeping him pinned.

"Like the dead, seeing this warm wake-up greeting I've been given. Now release me so I can take a leak!"

"You must have been pretty out of it not to notice." She chuckled and cut the vines with her knife. He struggled against the foot bindings, and the moment he was free, he fled into the bushes. Through the trickle of the river, she heard him let out a satisfied moan.

The sun shone from over the eastern hills. The low dale they followed was still engulfed in darkness. Above, cumulus clouds dotted the sky. Captain Bernhart tucked his shirt in when he finally emerged from the bushes. His haggard appearance, accompanied by dirt and bruises, was accentuated by his extreme lack of hygiene.

They followed the river with periodic stops to rest and scout the surrounding hillocks in case the miniature monsters were close by. The sun slid across the sky and disappeared behind distant, flat ground mountains. Aros walked a few steps ahead of Rosanne, his hands vigorously accompanying his incessant chatter.

"The best tavern in Georgetown is undoubtedly the *Wicker Man*, aptly named for the original owner who burned down the inn out of spontaneous self-combustion; he took half the block with him. They say his ghost still roams the street, seeking to devour the new housing in his terrifying flames, and serves to light up the dark streets. Legends aside, the *Wicker Man* has ale to die for and excellent service. And the women, hoh." He blew a hot breath.

Rosanne made a conscious effort to give him her best wry smile, followed by a wrinkled nose, to clearly state how little she cared for his unsolicited philandering history. "We're still talking about a tavern and not a brothel, right?" she asked.

"You think so little of me, Captain. I'm almost hurt."

"When you set yourself apart with your ebullient presentation of favoured haunts, it stands to reason you're of higher education."

"No such thing, Captain. I'm but a measly lowborn brat from Oxenstreet."

"Lowborn with an extensive vocabulary."

Aros snorted. "What would even a highborn like yourself know of the Georgetown slums? Oh, you're not surprised that I knew?"

"Highborn and upstart are two different things. My family are upstarts. You, on the other hand, are a terrible liar."

"Yes, because no sensible person would willingly call themselves Drackenheart. Why are you even in the trade? Couldn't find a husband brave enough to chisel your frozen heart from that iceberg you call a body?"

"Would you just please for the love of the almighty and the bloody heavens *shut up*? If you need company so badly, get a dog!"

"The only company I need is your abhorrent passion for myself, Captain Drackenheart." Aros bowed mockingly and then dove out of the way when Rosanne, in a fit of paroxysm and with a shriek, hurled at him the closest fist-sized rock she could pluck from the riverside.

"Next time, I'll rip out your tongue! Now shut up, and let's move!"

When she glanced back, Aros still lay on the ground. He gave a wry smile. "Looks like the ice queen has some fire in her after all."

CHAPTER 15

DIRE TIMES

Nelson didn't know what to make of anything that had transpired in the last few hours. He rubbed his glasses as clean as he could, but grime, rain, and other particulates had lodged themselves to the glassy surface. His touch softened over the crack on the left lens. His spare pair was left in his quarters aboard the ship. He saw enough to manage the trek back to the ship from ... wherever they were. Glancing around, Nelson failed to see Ida's smile or sense her wild-mannered enthusiasm. Where was she? Was she alright?

A dizzying variety of exotic sounds filled the night air under the waxing moon. Fireflies winked in and out of view, flashing their lights to attract a potential mate while entertaining any curious onlookers who merely thought the presentation was pretty. Bullfrogs croaking in a nearby pond momentarily ceased their chatter to snap at passing flies with their sticky tongues, then almost as if saying "thank you for the meal," croaked some more.

The fire hissed from wet logs added to the pyre. Around it, five men sat in silence, their eyes trained on the glow and apathetic to the surrounding forest activities.

From deeper within the woods, a different shriek called out. It could have been a fox or a deer, but it might as well be monsters communicating during their nocturnal hunts. Hammond drew his jacket tighter around him, shuddering more from the sounds than the weather.

"Anyone care for frog legs? I can whip something up," Hammond offered the disquieted party, and as usual, he didn't get much of a response. "At least we're alive," he continued.

"And we're toast," Olivier finished, holding the feet of his crossed legs.

Farand sat with his arms resting on his knees like a quiet giant. His doomed expression was an uncanny change from the otherwise optimistic lieutenant. Rubbing his face, he groaned. "A plan. Anyone?"

Olivier exchanged glances with Higgs, and both shrugged and hung their heads. The large man stood and kicked the dirt under his feet as if somehow that would alleviate his frustration.

"Suppose we know why we were left behind and why the others were taken," Nelson offered, drawing the party's attention. Farand stared at the lawyer, his expression equally as terrified as it was quizzical.

"We're stuck in the middle of nowhere without any supplies, no ship, no captain, no crew, and you want to ponder the logic of why we were kicked out of the herd?"

Undeterred by the lieutenant's condescendence, Nelson cleared his throat. "Everyone else was taken by those ... things, those female creatures, by song. We wandered here of our own free will, but it was like ..."

"It felt like a dream," Higgs interjected. Nelson rose his finger in the air, invigorated.

"Yes! A dream. Aware of everything and knowing nothing about what truly went on around us."

Farand shook his head. "If that is what you saw, I share no part in it. I didn't see nor hear anything out of the ordinary. My legs just wouldn't obey me."

"Which brings me back to the point of why we specifically were singled out, and not only left behind, cast out, even?"

Higgs clapped his hands together. "Boy's got a point, sir."

"I heard the song like everyone else, but unlike you lot who simply stood there like gawking drunks, it took a while before I couldn't resist it anymore. And then we all just ... wandered off." Farand scratched his chin. His eyes averted to his younger brother.

"Dun look at me." Olivier raised his hands in defeat.

"*Go away, and don't come back*, more like it," Higgs said, drawings nods.

"The others aren't as wise and fit like us," Hammond joked, slapping his overgrown belly, but Nelson's sudden exclamation and pointing had him fall back on his log.

"That's it! We were not ideal for what those creatures needed."

"Watch your tongue, boy. We're still in our prime." Higgs huffed. Nelson waved his hands.

"Yes, yes. You know what I mean, but hear me out. We were, presumably, sent *away* from wherever they took the others." Nelson's triumphant conclusion created a wave of questioning faces around the camp.

Farand tapped his foot; then he looked to Nelson. "You're saying we were sent here because they didn't want us close to their hideout?"

Nelson nodded vigorously. "We need to find the others and rescue them!"

The big man shook his head, pursing his lips as he rose a gesticulating hand to state his point clearly. "Listen here, paper-pusher. Our group consists of two retired sailors, a lawyer, and Olivier and I cannot fight against beings with supernatural powers that can make us simply wander off. We don't stand a chance against them. We need to get back to the ship first and arm ourselves."

"Yes, of course. But consider our strengths." Nelson swept a hand over the remaining men who eyed him with narrow slits.

Farand blinked. "Your objections are no good here, Mr. Blackwood."

Nelson licked his lips. "What I mean is we already have a scout, an excellent engineer who undoubtedly can cook something up for our advantage, and we have your brawn."

Farand raised an eyebrow. "And what about you?"

"I can ... I mean ... bait?"

"Out of the question."

Higgs patted Nelson's shoulder. "How come? I think he would be excellent bait."

"Thank you, Higgs."

"He draws out the monster, and we whack 'em good." Higgs simulated a powerful swing with an instrument from the toolbelt he still carried.

"At least you got the cook." Hammond roared with laughter, which had Higgs and Olivier joining in. Farand pinched the base of his nose, squeezing his eyes shut as he wracked his brain for any tangible solution to their unique situation.

"No. We need you safe from trouble. We didn't consider this situation when we set out. That's on us." Farand couldn't openly say the reason they needed Mr. Blackwood safe was because if he failed to show back in Valo before the destined date of their return, the entire crew and the *Red Queen* could be decommissioned. Not only would the crew be without a job and deprived of their home, he and the captain would have to stand trial for ... well, *everything*.

Nelson understood Farand's vague answer for what it was, but the situation had changed, and something had to be done. "Mr. Duplànte, we need to retrieve the others. God knows what's being done to them, and I'm not just talking about their lives. I'm talking about their sanity. The longer we're exposed to this madness, the greater the risk of us never getting off this island. There is a presence here, and it wants us to stay."

"Boy's right. Ever since we got here, the fog, the crazy marine life, and now the creatures we've seen, they all want us here. This creeping cold clutching our throats and noggins bears us no goodwill." Hammond nodded at Higgs' assessment. The lieutenant couldn't disagree that something was off with this place, and he had no intention of staying long enough to discover why.

"Then we return to the ship and gear up. We need to get the engine going, and we can still fly on reserves if we haul the mainsails and wait."

"Aye. I like the sound of that. All in favour?" Hammond, Nelson, Higgs, Farand, and Olivier nodded their agreement.

HAMMOND HUFFED AS he dragged his weight, his knee prickling and shooting waves of knifing jabs with every step he took on the soft, uneven ground. "Are you sure we came this way?" He leaned against a pine tree, then cursed as sticky sap clung to his shirt. After smudging it with a spit-soaked finger, the stain grew and ended up gluing his fingers together. He gave up, as his shirt had more sweat stains than not. He hadn't bothered cleaning his shirts properly in years anyway, and this would hardly make a difference.

Olivier placed his hand over his eyes, scanning the scene. "Not anymore. We walked down from the ridge, but I dunno where. My head's all fuzzy."

"Those wenches did a number on our heads, alright. We saw what they did and couldn't do jack about it. Then they sent us on our merry ways like fools on shrooms."

"I forgot how many times I told my feet to stop."

"Nothing we could have done about it, Olivier," Farand assured. He moved to stand on an exposed rock, surveying the area ahead.

"Not that we have any familiarity to this island anyway. Getting lost is easy," Nelson interjected.

Hammond's eye caught a low branch from an aspen bent out of shape. "Look, a broken branch."

"There's no guarantee we did that. We covered a lot of ground before the spell wore off. No, wait, there! That ridge. We tethered the ship there, didn't we?" Higgs pointed to a steep cliff to their north, and they had to take the ridiculous detour to walk to get up there.

"I don't see the ship." Olivier shielded his eyes from the sun as he scanned the cliffside from the farthest reaches in the north and the forest below.

"She's probably still where we left her. She might have drifted into the trees," Farand assured, but a warble to his tone suggested his unease. Farand took point and led them onward.

The five men spent the better part of the next three hours scaling the steep hill leading to the pinewood resting next to the cliffside. They kept their eyes on the woods, but all traces of the black-eyed sirens were gone.

Whether it was the flight of birds, a rustle in the undergrowth from small animals, or a distant bleat of a deer, every noise had them jumping for their weapon of choice, be it tools, branches, or rocks. There wasn't much two older men, an incoherent boy, and a lawyer in a forest could do.

The men stopped. They were pale-faced, exhausted, and overcome by a sense of dread once the lip of the cliff came into view. The campsite was overturned, and all of the equipment had been left behind, save for one small thing.

"Where's the ship?" Nelson asked. The pegs that had anchored the red galleon had been ripped from the ground and discarded. A trail of scuffle shot through the forest with the occasional crudely felled tree, forming a wide path. Nelson stood on the path noting the numerous far-set footprints.

"They took the bloody ship?!" Farand's deep voice rumbled like an angry bear's roar. Hammond ran a hand over a felled tree, feeling the sticky sap in his fingers.

"The lasses must have worked quickly to cut down this many trees. Or there was a hell of a lot more of them than we thought. I saw only five." While Farand took out his anger on the surrounding foliage, Nelson followed the path with his eyes.

"But if they took the ship, we have a direct path to wherever it's hidden. We can walk there."

Higgs folded his arms. "Had they half a brain, they would have killed us."

"But they didn't ..." Nelson pursed his lips and scanned the abandoned camp once more.

"Forget about the why, and let's go." Farand started on the path. A hand caught his arm, and the lieutenant turned his fuming glare to Olivier.

"We must be careful of scouts. We might get spotted."

"Lad's right." Hammond dropped a broken saw to the ground. "Without any equipment, there isn't much we can do before we find the ship and get our bearings."

Higgs wiggled his mustache as if something were caught in it, or perhaps it was his way of thinking. "Or we'll get served for dinner with a pike up our arses. If not them, the mozzies are in the queue." He smacked at the whining little insect, now a red smear on his hand. "Either way, captain's gone, ship's gone, and the entire fucking crew is scattered to the nine winds. I say we go right now. A ship that size oughta slow those things down. Come on, lads. Unless Mr. Duplànte, sir, has got an idea."

Farand fumed as his eyes threw daggers at nothing in particular over the horizon, oblivious to the men's chattering. He growled, turned around, and tapped his foot while resting his hands on his hips. "Olivier, we need you to scout on ahead. Look for anyone who might be surveying the path but keep us in your sight. If there's any danger, you signal us anyway you can."

Nelson picked up a mallet and gave it a reassuring swing. "The ship was mostly done with the repairs when we were attacked, right?"

Farand nodded. "We were. She should be able to fly when we find her."

"Hold your horses. You forget we weren't done overhauling the engine. The ship might float, but she's not flying until I piece

Sally back together. Why do you think those monsters dragged the ship with them rather than have the crew fly it?"

"So we need to find the ship, repair her, and then escape?" Nelson sounded less than convinced, and Olivier shared his moment of impending doom.

"This day keeps getting better and better."

"Grab all the tools you can carry, and let's go. I'll rather deal with monsters than Drackenheart's wrath," Farand ordered and picked up a hammer.

"I second that. She'll dangle us overboard if the ship is defiled on our watch." Higgs and Hammond shuddered collectively. Unable to keep the imagery out of his thoughts, Nelson pictured the engineer and the cook roped together and thrown overboard five hundred meters above the Black Ice glacier, left to freeze in the northern winds as the ship sailed south.

"You make the captain sound like she's evil incarnate."

Higgs cocked his head to the side, nodding as if he couldn't completely disagree with Nelson's statement. "Captain Drackenheart, while having a nasty bite and temper, is also looking out for the best interest of all, and if the ship isn't in any condition to fly once she resumes command, we'll be dead either way. We just like to make up stories to appease the newbies."

Nelson didn't question Higgs' logic because even Nelson himself had been pacified by the terrifying tales of Captain Drackenheart, the demon of the sky. Her piloting skills were next to none, and her talent for quick thinking was astonishing. Nelson had no trouble believing any of those tales because Rosanne Drackenheart was the queen of her ship and her crew, and people respected her outstanding qualities as a captain. Even Farand heeded her words with the utmost respect, despite being older and far more experienced in sea and airfare.

It then hit Nelson that something similar could have happened to Captain Drackenheart when she and Norman went to parlay with the pirates, an ambush set by the scrupulous men or those female monsters, which was why she didn't return at the time of agreement. They couldn't cover a three-part rescue mission against hordes of monsters. The statistical probability of their survival was astronomical at this point, but if they could at least secure the ship they had a fighting chance, and if the captain had been captured by these same creatures and brought to the others, all the better.

THEY FOLLOWED the cleared path for the remainder of the afternoon, resting in the shade whenever they couldn't go on, with Hammond doing highly experimental things with whatever edible creatures and plants he could dig up for later testing.

The forest thinned out to open grassland with the occasional tree and low bushes. At knee height, the grassy space had them stopping low for cover. Olivier's lack of presence ahead of them was far more optimistic as the man was nowhere in sight. The scout might be tall as a giraffe, but his sleek frame could easily slink in the grass like a snake. Thus if anything should happen to them, he at least had a chance at getting away.

The trampled path stood out like a sore thumb in the field. Numerous patches of dirt had been turned over by struggling feet, and Nelson did not doubt that the efforts of towing the ship had been a trying time for the women. The path veered off to the side in a wide arch towards a set of mountains. Nelson stopped, eyes squinting against the crude sunlight, and saw that the path snaked its way up along the sleek mountainside.

"Mr. Duplànte, that's a volcano, right?"

Farand looked at the mountain, a troubling look crossing his face. "It's a dead one, alright."

"The crater would be a perfect hiding place for a ship that size."

Quiet as a mouse, Olivier emerged from the grass, startling the lieutenant. "I wish you would stop doing that!" he said.

"Sorry, brother. They took the ship that way, but I found another path leading to the mountain. What should we do?"

"We need to go directly to the ship."

"Hold a moment, sir," Higgs interrupted. "Consider that we do go right for the ship. I doubt it's unguarded. We're looking for a hide tanning if we're caught, and I don't want to think twice about what they'll do to us, the *undesirables* which they left behind."

"We're dead either way if we don't get that ship!"

"Aye, but we need to be tactical 'bout this."

Nelson smacked his palms together as he stared into the distance, the noise sharp and loud, making everyone else duck for cover in a moment of surprise.

"What in the nine hells are you doing, Blackwood?" Farand hissed, crouching as he made his way to yank the paper-pusher down into the grass. Farand's rage was completely overturned by Nelson's glowing enthusiasm.

"I know how to get in. We have something they want."

"The hell are you on about, laddie?" Hammond's eyebrows did an arched dance, while Higgs merely looked as if Nelson had lost his mind.

"Mr. Duplànte, we have you. Those creatures took everyone who was strong and still in good health. But the song didn't affect Mr. Duplànte in the same way it did us."

"What does any of that have to do with it?"

Higgs, Hammond, and Olivier huddled closer to Nelson in the grass, still hunched and hidden from view. "What would they do if we offered you as negotiation material to those women? We'll not only get inside, we'll find the others, the ship, and yes, I'm aware that we will be captured, but they still *fear* you."

Hammond shook his head. "That still doesn't stop those vixens from controlling the rest of us."

Nelson's enthusiasm remained undeterred. "But consider this: if one of us can prove that you are under that person's control, they cannot use the song to affect that person because the moment they do, you are out of their control. A loose cannon."

"You're playing with fire, boy. If we do get inside, hell, even if we do find one of these women, how are we going to convince her that one of us is the supreme leader of a deranged pack of humans?" Eyes turned to Higgs. "You know what I mean."

"These creatures are obviously of a higher intelligence level than we give them credit for. I'm positive that what I have in mind will work, but I need all of you to follow my lead."

"We don't have time for this nonsense. If harm is to befall you and we return to Valo too late or without you, we—!" Farand's jaw clapped shut. The others looked at him oddly, and Farand quickly cleared his throat and closed his eyes as he reformulated his thoughts to his calmer demeanour. "Supplies, the ship, the rest of the crew, the captain, you. We need everything to get our payout for this monster nonsense. Else the trip simply isn't worth it, and we'll go broke for months."

"That is very true, sir, but this is the best plan we have. I'm positive it will work. Olivier can stay behind while we make our way to their hideout, home, or whatever it is they live in. Daylight is waning, and we're out of time and options." Farand scratched his growing beard, which was prickly and beyond itchy. He had no proper argument for firing at the paper-pusher's madness, but he had even fewer options regarding their situation.

"Pitting a king against a king, a leader to leader. Is that the plan?"

"Essentially. They need us for something, be it labour, security, anything. We need to show that they stole from another tribe, so to speak. We need to think like them."

"Lad, you're asking two old farts, two weaklings, and a brute to understand women?" Hammond's comment had Olivier bursting with laughter, quickly silenced by Farand's hand clasping over the younger man's mouth and pushing him back. Olivier suppressed his growing mirth as he rolled in the grass.

"I like the plan. When do we do it?" Higgs grunted with a nod.

"Hold it right there—" Farand protested.

"With all due respect, sir, we're screwed if we sit here."

Farand rubbed his temples, letting out a long-overdue groan.

"The full moon is tomorrow night. I say we do it then. First, locate those bastards, find all guarded exits if we have the time of the day, and then dive headfirst into danger."

"You are all doomed, and I get to watch." Olivier grinned and was shoved into the grass yet again by Farand's stony hand.

CHAPTER 16

TROPHY WIFE

"Sing us a song, pretty canary," Creedy prompted. His arm was slumped on the bars of the wooden cage, and he rested his chin against it.

"Go to hell!" Ida sneered, her sudden agitation making the cage swing where it dangled from the ceiling. She leaned against the bars, banging her knees as she shifted her legs to alleviate the stiffness. That she was suspended under the ceiling made for a nauseating experience lest she kept still. The small cage on the floor kept everyone else confined with little room to stretch.

Kristoff continued his meticulous abrading of the flimsy rope of their makeshift cage. The fibres were dry and worn from repeated abuse from previous occupants.

"Leave her alone, Creedy. It's your fault we're in this mess," he said.

"What did you say to me, you cheeky—?"

Dalia threw a hand between the two war-thirsty disgruntled men, flinching as the wound on her leg stabbed her with pain. "Knock it off. Your petty arguments won't help us." She chewed on a piece of straw from the bedding which covered the stone floor. It was dry and tasteless but distracting. "Have they even said what they want with us? Or even where they took the others?"

Kristoff snorted. "If you call 'words,' it was none familiar to me. Those ... *pizdy* opened their mouths, and we dance to their tune. Imagine what words could do to us."

"There was magic in their song," Ida said softly, her eyes cast to the ground. "We couldn't do anything about it. No one could. It was like they had a song for all of us."

"She's got a point," Dalia said. "I can't even remember half of the things that happened after we encountered that first one. Next thing I see is the remaining crew waltzing to their song. Not as much as a shot fired or a knife thrown."

"That skinny bastard Nelson just stood there while the rest of us went." Gavin let out a puff of air as he leaned against the wall, finding the most comfortable position he could.

"He didn't just stand there; he was left behind with the others. They told him to through the song," Ida snapped at the third engineer.

"Why do you think that is?" Dalia questioned.

Ida shrugged while Creedy, feeling up for more arguing, spat on the ground outside the cage as if his spittle would be enough to make their captor slip and fall to a cruel agonizing death. "Maybe because he's a wuss?"

"Then why didn't they take Farand?" Gavin said. A short silence followed.

"It's not obvious?" Kristoff looked to the others, meeting their perplexed faces. "Duplànte is scary. He's ... ox? Only spell strong enough for that would be orders of captain." He chuckled as he tore on the rope. It broke from the wood, and he let out a very quiet victory cry.

Ida nodded. "They left the old, the weak, and the uncontrollable." She looked upwards. "No offence, Higgs, should you hear this."

Creedy's sly grin widened. "And you're in a pretty little canary cage."

"Shut up, Creedy."

"*Shut up, Creedy!*" a raven from a cage across the room cackled. The large bird pecked at its perch. "*Shut up, Creedy!*" he said again in a guttural voice.

"Now, look at what you've done!" Creedy threw a pebble at the bird but missed. The bird cooed and laughed, drawing snorts and chuckles from the others.

Kristoff nodded to their feathered friend. "I agree with bird."

The raven in the adjacent cage called out a series of sing-song words topped with their guttural crowing.

Ida leaned against the bars, eying the birds with wonder. Gavin, following her gaze, looked at her curiously. "Did you understand what it just said?"

"I'm not sure, but it sounded like old Novalian. *Word from the queen*, it said. It's not what the hulder speak."

"Hulder?" Dalia asked, drawing looks from the others who wondered the same.

"You know, like the legends. Women who lure men into the forest, and they have cow tails. You saw those, didn't you? Just like the legends, just ... incredibly ugly."

Dalia looked at the birds, pursing her lips. "They couldn't have flown all the way here from Noval. Maybe they came with a ship or ..."

"Or someone on this island trained them to speak old Novalian to deliver messages," Gavin finished.

As their assessment ended, a silence followed. Ida dangled from the creaky cage, the ropework groaning under the strain. Kristoff's fervent hacking at the ropes was the only other sound until Creedy thoughtfully tapped against the cage.

"We need to get out of here."

The third engineer eyed Creedy sourly. "Oh really? I thought we were having coffee and bikkies as we picked out the floral arrangements for the coming hulder wedding." Gavin spat. Kristoff moved to the other bindings and paused briefly to shudder at Gavin's sarcasm.

Dalia rubbed her arms and looked to the older watch captain. "It's scary how accurate that might be ..."

"Maybe they have a thing for old ladies as well."

"I swear, Creedy, if we get out of this alive, I'll serve you to the next hungry elderly noblewoman with a taste for the macabre."

A hush fell at the soft padding of feet echoing in the hallways. Four hulder women with twisted scowls entered the room, their backs hunched as they walked on the balls of their feet. Their tall statures would have let them touch the cave ceiling had they stood erect.

Their upper bodies moved in slow waves, craning their necks as their black-pooled eyes wandered over the prisoners. One of them sneered at Kristoff's failed attempt to cover up his vandalism. He dropped the stone and held up his hands in a sign of defeat. The hulder reached out a lank arm and snatched the stone from the cave floor, exposing her yellow teeth. Kristoff fixed his eyes on the rocky surface of the floor, his heart slamming against his chest.

The women exchanged garbled words followed by high-pitched screeches and heavy hand gesticulations. Three of them moved to open the main cage while the other took the rope holding Ida's cage suspended and lowered her to the ground. Ida gave the creature a petulant glare, holding her legs as her eyes followed the hulder's every move. The cage door opened, and Ida stared at her jailer with open defiance. The other woman nodded her head to the side, ordering her to follow.

The hulder opened the main cage, dragging Dalia by the arm. She shuddered at the monstrous grip, holding her protests despite her mind screaming to fight against it. She forced herself to breathe, quelling her willingness to panic which was stronger than the hulder's hostility. Yet, their impressive stature and claws served as a bitter reminder of what would happen if anyone resisted.

Ida bit her lip and crawled out of her cage, wobbling as she had trouble standing after the prolonged time in the fetal position. Her legs screamed as they straightened out, and the tall female gave Ida time to recover.

Gavin had to be dragged out of the cage as he refused to exit of his own free will and clambered onto the flimsy bars. A hulder grabbed his leg, pulling the third engineer and the entire cage with him. She reached inside and took him by his burly neck. Gavin squirmed and protested but ceased his defiance and let himself be led out.

Two hulder took point and led the way out of the room deeper into a cave, while Creedy, Dalia, Gavin, Kristoff, and Ida followed with two guards trailing behind them. They passed numerous rooms branching out inside a complex cavern system. Gavin touched the wall, judging its composition.

"I think we're in one of the volcanoes."

"A live one?" Dalia shouted in surprise, drawing looks from the leading females, who then returned to ignore their chatter.

"We saw several dead ones north of the black cliffs. Maybe this is one of them."

They emerged from the narrow caves into a large open space filled with bright sunlight. The conical opening of the volcano's central vent was deep and carved with crude pathways leading to the top. An impressive number of hulder milled about the gang-planks and ropework, materials and supplies being carried and distributed. Others worked on a wide rope bridge crossing the gorge from one end to the other. Many stopped to peer down at the new arrivals, expressions drawn into sneers, while some appeared curious, sniffing the air as if they caught their human scent.

Gavin glanced at a small group of females by another cave entrance, but their sharp-featured faces quickly turned away. A few stood out as tall, while the other short-statured women packed significantly more muscle mass.

Women flocked around them with varying degrees of attention and curiosity. Norman and a few other crew members from the ship were led into the room from another chamber. The young man's face beamed upon seeing the others in one piece.

Above, the bright light of the midday sun disappeared as a large, elongated shape blocked the central vent. Shielding their eyes from rogue beams of light, they peered up to see the hulder pointing and exchanging loud, excited words. Long ropes were cast from above and connected to simple pulleys, allowing the women to pull at the ropes horizontally and to bring down the massive hunk of wood blocking the sun.

The elongated shape was unmistakable, and Gavin almost shouted in surprise. "They bloody took the *Queen*!"

Dalia gaped, resting her hands on the mop of her hair at seeing the vessel being lowered into the cave. The hulder milled all around and on it, everyone working collectively to bring the ship into the volcano. Whooping and cheering, they worked the ropes with ease and showed little fear at throwing themselves over the pathways and onto the ship, agile like primates.

"They fucking took our ship." Creedy balled his hands into fists and curled his lips. A female guard caught on to his violent intentions and kicked his legs. The man stumbled to the floor and glared. The hulder returned the look, daring him to lash out. Creedy mellowed, but the fury in his eyes was ever-present.

"We never finished maintenance on the thruster engines before the attack, so we can't escape even if we could get a hold of it," Ida said, ignoring the fact that they were surrounded by hundreds of hulder, listening to their chatter. She doubted they understood her either way, for they showed no indication of it.

"How long would you need to make it doable?" Dalia offered, eyes fixed on the red wood of the hulking ship tight at the gap in the top.

"Too long without Higgs. But the engine room has a dead-lock on the door. Nothing can get in unless they destroy the room." Having tired of their conversation, one of the hulder snapped at them with a command. Ida nearly jumped out of her skin at the face the hulder made.

They were lined up next to each other, while the taller of the hulder quickly looked them over. She singled out Norman, Kristoff, and Gavin, placing them in a group for themselves. She leaned close to Dalia, taking deep breaths as if smelling her. Dalia drew back under the scrutiny. The hulder's black eyes studied Dalia's lank figure and hard facial features.

"That's right, you grey cunt." Dalia grinned. "Hey! Where the hell are you touching me? Chest's off limits!" She squirmed as the hulder groped the flatness of her torso. Creedy roared with laughter.

The hulder made a puzzled face and sent Dalia with one of the other females; the watch captain offered no protests as there was little malice behind their actions. Ida couldn't return the gaze of those black eyes as they roamed over her form like a predator assessing its next meal.

The older topmen and gun crew were guided deeper into the volcano, while Kristoff, Gavin, Norman, Ida, and Creedy were singled out to a different section of the hulder nest.

On their way they were stopped by two women with crude spears guarding a door. The group watched in silence as the conversation turned heated between the hulder, with several gestures towards the small group of humans. The guards exchanged glances, then nodded and opened the door.

Once inside, they were left to the confines of the cave system. They wandered into the dimly lit halls, free of restrictions and cages.

Skeletons lined the walls; their arms spread wide as if chained. The joints were connected with string or a glue-like substance, the bones thoroughly cleaned and bleached, then arranged with meticulous care. The skulls donned carved runes on their foreheads. Dried wildflowers lay in front of them. Some were afforded more than others.

"These are people ... humans, I mean," Norman noted, touching one of the skeletons to feel the smooth bones. The osteological artwork before him was about the same height as him, and the skull had a squared-off jaw and pronounced nasal bones. "Certainly not those things." A dried flower petal crunched at his feet, making him jump.

Gavin stared into the empty sockets of another skull. "Gives a whole new meaning to trophy wife." Heads turned towards the engineer, faces as blank and unforgiving as the situation allowed it.

"You had to go there. *We* could be on those walls!" Norman pointed to the glorified remains, horrified by the implications they brought to his young mind.

"All these rooms are filled with dead people! We're next." Kristoff grimaced and felt the empty spaces for loose rocks.

Ida shuddered at the sight, her discomfort only increasing with the rotting flowers and defiled bones. "They look like they've been here for a long time. But why would they even do this?"

Gavin shrugged and accidentally broke off the skeleton's ulna, effectually collapsing the arm. Panicking, he hurriedly piled the bones together and covered them with flowers. "Ritualistic murder? Slaves until we drop dead? Doesn't matter why. We need to get the hell out before we end up as wall ornaments."

Kristoff threw his hands up and blew a raspberry. "They're too many to fight. And even if we could, they would sing us our song and make us dream."

"Let's bide our time and see what happens," Ida said. "The captain will understand something is wrong. She and the others have the longboat. She can get to us, and if they bring Higgs too, we'll be out of here."

"You're forgetting one thing, Canary." The older watch captain snorted and pointed to Norman. All eyes turned to the young man. "Why the hell is he here and not the captain?"

Norman stared at them for a moment, then gave a small yell in a moment of realization. "I completely forgot! The captain, Lyle, and the pirates were attacked by something and taken away."

"By what exactly?" Gavin asked.

"They were small and hairy. They brought me to the volcanoes and made a trade with the women there who then brought me here."

"We're doomed," Kristoff whispered. "*Doomed.*"

Ida groaned and buried her face in her gloved hands. "Who's gonna save us now?"

"We're on our own, Canary. Better use that clever head of yours." Creedy pushed a finger against her forehead, making the girl swat his hand.

At the end of the hallway stood a large circular room with a carved dome ceiling. Every nook and cranny of the surface was covered with multicoloured paint depicting a scene. Hundreds of skinny, hunched beings lined a black-stained mountain on one side of the room. A few creatures held their hands towards the sky. Ida bent low to better view the drawings closer to the floor, spotting crude imitations of ships with men aboard and the hulder reaching out to them with what looked like ocean waves coming from their mouths.

The mural continued with the hulder walking in front of the men as they were led to the mountains. A dense forest lay on the other side, then an open grass-plane. A river snaked along from higher up the wall, going between rolling hills. Another set of creatures were depicted here, some large and grey with a string of small ones with tails trailing behind them. Ida grimaced as she saw one of the things have its club raised over a man, and the next image was just as gruesome as it could be in its rock-grained low quality. More forest, then water and numerous ships. After that, a swamp with a skull painted on it. The colours were faded and appeared to have been there for a long time, though not without periods of maintenance, as one section of the wall seemed newer than the others.

"I think this is a map," she said after completing the course. The others studied the pictures intensely.

"Look there." Gavin pointed to the middle of the dome, where a sun and moon were painted side by side. "There's something on the floor too." Right below the day-star stood a cabin. A man was next to the house, but tall, lumbering, and with red eyes and sharp claws. On the other side of the building stood an ordinary man, much like those led astray by the hulder. Ida noticed a white trail of dots leading from the cabin to the hulder nest in the mountains, or vice versa. But on the path was a white-painted woman with long golden locks and a golden flower in her hair.

"I really don't want to know what this all means." Creedy made a face, going for the exit as he felt more comfortable among the dead.

Norman stretched his neck, stiff from scrutinizing the imagery. "Maybe it's a recounting of their tale. Or, as you said, a map."

Ida nodded. "It's like people lived here, or whatever this thing in the middle is."

"It's a prank. That's what it is." At Gavin's attempt to divert the gravity of the situation, Ida rolled her eyes.

"The white lady kinda looks like you, Ida." Kristoff pointed out, and she punched his shoulder.

"That's not funny!"

"Then this guy here is Creedy," Norman pointed to the black monster in the middle and giggled. Ida studied the figure, noting the house and the man. "Everything about this mural seems taken from folklore and children's stories, but with twists I'm not familiar with. The hulder can sing, and I have no idea what this thing is supposed to be."

Dalia hopped closer, supporting herself on Ida. "Some sort of demon who lives in a house in the woods?"

"Could be a devil; the one who use fiddle song to lead people astray. Or another version where he is a demon who seeks a companion." She shuddered.

Kristoff took a few steps back, looking fervently around, then navigated between his crewmates to study the floor. "Yes, yes! It is a map! These mountains surround the house, and this is where we are right now." He pointed to the mass of hulder on the mountains, then took another few steps back. "This here is riverland we visited after dropping off scouting team. And that's south, the black cliffs. The captain and others went to this forest surrounded by the hills." Norman nodded slowly in agreement.

A cold sensation crept through Ida's bones as she studied the lurking monsters in the forest. "You mean this is why she never came back?"

"Okay, so these things *eat* people. What do the hulder do then?" Gavin's question had everyone staring at the trail of humans being led by the tall black things in the mountains, but it didn't show anything else. No one spoke for a moment.

"Do we have a plan at all?" Norman threw out his arms, glancing at the others who seemed as lost as livestock going to the slaughterhouse.

"How do we get past hordes of singing nightmares?" Kristoff asked.

Gavin clapped Norman on the shoulder. "We throw handsome Norman here to the witches. Take one for the team, mate."

"That's not remotely funny."

"Jokes aside," Kristoff began. "We need to draw them away from ship long enough for Ida and Gavin to fix engine."

Ida blinked hard. "Fix the engine? I dunno what hole you pull that trust from, but it's far more than we deserve. Gavin doesn't have that level of expertise in the engine yet. We need Higgs."

The door opened, and the same tall hulder from before strode into the bone-filled sanctuary. They didn't say anything, merely holding out one arm to convey their wishes to their captives to leave the room and follow them wherever they were going next.

The five humans ambled after the skinny half-giant females. The ceiling through almost every cave-section they entered had purposefully been chiselled to accommodate their height. No matter where they went, they met other members of the hulder clan, each eying the humans with mixed emotions.

Gavin almost ran into the hulder in front of him when she stopped. "Is this...?" They were led to a queue of hulder, and at the very front, a couple of women distributed food among their clanswomen.

"They're feeding us?"

"Good. I'm starving." Kristoff rubbed his hands together, his stomach voicing its rumbling satisfaction as the delicious scent floated in the air.

The room bustled with chatter, but more often than not did the five humans seem like the hottest topic of gossip going around. A couple of women waved shyly at Gavin, tittering as they turned away. Ida's cheeks inflated with air as she resisted the laughter-now-turned-snort.

"Aren't you popular?"

"Jealous?"

"Hell no. I'm good."

Feeling a pair of passing claws stroke his neck, Norman turtle-shelled his head until it touched his shoulders. "I'll think twice about such beastly company even if I do get a wife out of it."

"Not even I'm that desperate." Creedy glared at the passing females.

Gavin snickered. "It's the only thing you'll ever get with that attitude."

"I don't even swing that way. I'm good," Kristoff excused.

"Hold up. There's Dalia and the others!" Ida waved to the emerging mass of people being led by another two footsoldiers. Dalia chanced a wave in return, catching up with them in the queue.

"What happened to you?"

Dalia's face was pale and glistening. Her eyes darted from Ida to the sentries by the room entrance, and the milling women minded their own business. "I uh ... can't say much for the others, but they treated my leg and then they... examined me."

"They *what*?"

"They did a fucking...!" Dalia dropped her voice as it attracted a hulder's attention, who quickly turned away again when Dalia toned down her fervent response. "They did a search of me. Like touching me. And at least four of those things smelled me up and down." Ida's perplexed face only mouthed a silent "what the fuck."

"As crazy as it sounds, I think they checked if I was still fertile."

"Are you?"

"Long past that stage, hun."

"That is ... good? We were in a room full of skeletons. Human ones."

"Human bones? Here?"

"Yeah, and a mural. Almost looked like a map or a story of the island. It indicated that these things aren't the only ones here and that people have visited this island before."

"That's scary." Dalia took the bowl she was given, waited for the rest by the quiet order of their captor, and was led to a table with a couple of conversing hulder women, who were quickly evicted from their seats. The female guards sat on each end of the wooden bench with their meal, squeezing the humans between them. It was crowded but doable, and the women paid little attention to the group once they were all seated.

Creedy dug into his bowl with a wooden spoon, starvation as evident as his foul mood. Ida shot him a distasteful look, swirling the spoon around in the chunky broth.

"Eat. It's fine. Tastes like Hammond's Sunday gruel," Creedy said through a spoonful of stew. Taking his word for it, the rest dug in; it was their first meal in almost a day.

"Tell me about this mural you saw," Dalia said to Ida, who was seated next to her. The young woman swallowed her fill, readying the spoon for another go. After explaining the painting in detail and their original assessment of its contents, Dalia slurped the bowl empty, smacked it on the table and burped.

"Oh god, we're all gonna die."

"Not unless they want us for some other interesting activities." Creedy waggled his eyebrows as he drank from the bowl.

Picking out the remaining chunks from the bowl, the watch captain bobbed her head. "That does make sense. I didn't see any men."

"Not a single one? Nothing remotely close to a male ... hulder?" Gavin leaned forwards in his seat. Dalia shrugged.

"Not a single man, elderly or child. They all look like they're from the same generation. Only a few stood out to me as old."

"Suspicious if you ask me." Norman slurped from his bowl, his other hand deftly at work attempting to pocket the wooden spoon. He received a whack on the back of his head by one of the guards who hissed and spoke to him in few harsh words. He discarded the spoon on the table, where it clattered in defeat.

As if on cue, two young hulder women came up to the guard closest to the exit, exchanging a few words with her and gesturing in their direction. The guard rose her hand, shaking her head, and gave her reply. One young woman's face fell, while the other, eyes as black as night, looked pointedly at Gavin. The young man nearly choked on a piece of meat, and Ida slapped her hand over her face, wishing to be anywhere else.

Dalia pointed the spoon at the older man. "I think you're right, Creedy."

"I hope I'm wrong because, again, I'm not that desperate."

Dalia turned her attention to Ida. "Come up with a plan yet?"

"We're pulling a Captain Drackenheart."

Dalia let out an amused laugh. "We're so fucking dead. I like it. Don't forget to pick us up when shit hits the bricks. I'll see what I can figure out in the meantime. I think we're being put to work somewhere."

They were split into their respective teams and led to another part of the volcano, a room full of straw beds and crudely woven wool as covers.

"More spacious than our quarters." Gavin picked a bed at random. Ida took the bed next to his, patting the bedding flat.

"You think we'll be alright?" Ida looked at Gavin, who poked his head from under his arm to respond.

"I'm tempted to say we've pulled through worse situations, but we haven't. We're still alive, so that's gonna count for something. We'll be alright, Ida."

"I just hope Nel—the others are okay."

"I'm not stupid, Ida. That paper-pusher signed your heart alright. Look, your cheeks are all flushed now! Higgs is gonna murder him when he finds out."

"Look at the pot calling the kettle black! You've been awfully chummy around Nelson too. You jealous?"

"Shut your hole."

"It doesn't matter when he isn't here. Who knows what those monsters did to him!"

"Could you two take your lover's quarrel elsewhere? Trying to get some shut-eye here," Creedy complained.

Sitting up, Gavin huffed under his breath. "Shut your face, Creedy. We're all equally fucked. We might as well talk about it before we're split and scattered in the nine winds."

"Your yap is awfully loud, kid. There are no quartermasters or senior officers here to cover your hide when you step on my toes." The older man returned Gavin's steely gaze. Tired and sunken as his eyes were, they still cut through him.

"Leave him alone." Ida sighed. "We don't know what's going to happen. You don't have to make our lives more miserable than it already is by being such an ass."

"Higgs let you work with that mouth?"

"Excuse me?"

"Knock. It. Off!" Norman shouted. "Everybody shut up and sleep if you can. We'll find out what those things want from us soon enough. Let's not ship our whales to the market before we catch them." He buried himself under the blanket, facing the wall as if it helped shut out the commotion. Creedy snorted and turned on his side. Ida and Gavin settled in the best they could on the thin layer of straw on a rocky surface. The night would be a long one and even longer once Creedy started snoring like an incubus was sitting on his chest and preventing him from breathing.

CHAPTER 17

MY, OH MY, MR. LYLE

Swallows swooped for the low-flying bugs below the treeline and in dangerously close reach of Aros' hands swatting at their dinner. The mosquitoes made quick work of Rosanne's exposed sweaty skin, and the captain smacked her hand against her other arm, squashing another bug just as it bit her. Red spots dotted her arms, more on her neck, and the running sweat stung on the wounded flesh and itched like mad.

"Can you slow down? My feet are killing me," Aros whined a short distance behind her, his footing awkward and trembling as if his legs didn't obey his will.

"And I'm being eaten alive. You should have worn better shoes." Rosanne's quick reply was laden with annoyance as the woman repeatedly scratched herself, leaving a trail of nail-bitten red lines.

Aros snorted and tilted his head. "Excusez-moi, lady. I didn't anticipate long walks in the rain. And you know tomato plants are good for keeping those pesky creatures away?"

"You expect me to wear tomatoes? I'd rather wear wine-corks."

"I like that idea. Join me for some wine-drinking?"

She nodded towards the black leather on his feet, now coated with mud and clay. "You pilot in those?"

Her negative implication had Aros slap a hand on his chest, mouth open. "Best driving shoes in Terra, I assure you. Made from the finest Cintechan leather and hand-sewn by a master shoemaker." Rosanne shook her head and climbed down a set of rocks as the river dropped from a ledge. The waterway rushed past, deepening and amassing at the steep geography. Aros let out a series of pitiful noises for each step. He raised a hand, sitting down on the rocks. "Timeout. I need to fix this ungodly pain."

Rosanne looked around them, seeing the river too deep and fast for an easy catch of fish. "We'll have to continue a little longer if we're to find food. But we have time before the sun sets."

Aros pried off his shoes as delicately as he could, given they refused to budge from his feet. The procedure left him whimpering and cursing. Numerous white blisters had formed at his heel and around his toes, the surrounding flesh was red and worn. His ankle and calves protested the awkward strain from gingerly placing his feet in favour of avoiding pressure on the blisters. Several had already popped, and the stench of his shoes grabbed at his nose like something from a bucket of chum. He drew back at the slightest whiff, his nose wrinkling. He let his feet dip into the river, and the cool water, although stinging like a beehive's revenge, was far more forgiving than his footwear.

ROSANNE SCANNED THE RIVERSIDE, noting the dense bushland and uneven ground with jutting rocks, the thousands of milling ants in the sandy patches, and considered her escapee partner's feet.

"This ought to slow us down good," he noted after following her gaze. He gave her a look that dared her to follow up on the topic.

"I'll give you the gun and leave. At least I'll live."

"Hey, I'm not saying no to the gun. But please don't leave me here. One bullet isn't going to keep me alive for long."

"You should have worn better shoes then because I am not slowing our pace to accommodate your lack of foresight. Or should I say footwear?"

"Cold and merciless as always. Alright. Five minutes is all I'm asking." He whistled a nonsensical tune as he washed his feet with meticulous care.

Rosanne went to the riverside, had a drink, and washed her face and arms. Days in the wilderness left her in a rather unattractive state, and the uncomfortable sharp smell coming from her could undoubtedly be caught from miles off. Aros leaned back and shut his eyes.

Rosanne used the opportunity to relieve herself in the bushes, and spotting the rich variety in foliage gave her an idea. Returning to Aros, Rosanne dropped off large leaves, soft moss, and makeshift rope made from sapling bark. "If you use your shirt sleeves and these, you can make pretty decent shoes. Should keep you going for a good while longer."

Aros's face lit up, taking the items. "My dear Captain Drackenheart, you *do* care. You have my thanks."

"Anything in the name of survival. Be quick about it. I don't like it here."

While Aros spent an ungodly amount of time rigging his new footwear, Rosanne climbed to the topmost point of a nearby hill, still in the vicinity of the paranoid and loud Captain Bernhart, and she surveyed down the river. She saw only as far as half a kilometre before the meandering river and creeping forest obscured the view.

Between a pair of hills to their east, the river cut across the scenery again, and a new fork led to their northeast. She chewed on her thumbnail, then spat. She looked back the way they had come. The waterfall was long out of view, and the hills branched out around them on all sides, but considerably less so in the east. "Give me a god damn reference point," she grumbled and seeing nothing familiar, she climbed down the hill to find Aros beaming, wiggling his toes. The soles were made from moss, the leaves kept them gathered, and he had wrapped his sleeves around it all and secured them with rope.

"Don't you look comfortable," she noted, smiling.

"The herbs soothe my blisters and ease my soul. Captain Bernhart can walk another day."

On the ground, she placed a few rocks and blueberries that she found growing on the hill and made a rough outline of what information she had of the island's geography. She waved Aros over, who observed her handiwork with interest.

Rosanne ran all the information through her mind. When they first hit the shore, they came from the south, the volcanic cliffs marking the island's southernmost point, depicted by a straw. They had then flown northwest to the low wetlands, and they had a set of dead volcanoes and mountains making up the north of the black cliffs and east of the lowlands. Then they had discovered the wreck of the *Blue Dragon*, marked with a blueberry placed on top of a pebble, about thirty minutes from the cliffs.

Rosanne closed her eyes, tracking their position to the best of her memory. Norman had driven along the coastline, a long and unnecessary detour, which gave her a good idea of the scale of what she thought could only be the southern portion of a much larger landmass. She remembered seeing the mountain chain to the west of the dense woodland where they had been attacked, and she marked it with a flat rock and piled up pebbles in the middle of the map.

Post-fleeing the hill trolls, they had walked for a day and a half north and then gone east until they hit the waterfall, another blueberry marking the far side of the map.

"But where the hell is here? We were taken to the hills, but where are the hills? They're not in the south, nor west of the volcano chain, so north of the woodlands? If so, the rivers should take us to the coast."

Her muttering had Aros draw a smile. "If your information is correct, we're most likely north of the woodlands here. So, after we hit the coast, then what?"

Rosanne looked to Aros, the man taking in all the details he could from the crude map and committing them to memory. His point made sense, and Rosanne placed the blueberry marking the waterfall north of the woodlands and what could be the hills. "We have procedures in case of emergencies like these, and we'll try to locate the ship at the pre-planned area."

"And where's that?" he asked.

"I'll let you know when we get there."

"Your misguided judgment of me as an unscrupulous bastard hurts my soul, Captain. My personality is quite infectious and pleasing."

"Yes. Like the plague with same end results."

Aros scowled.

A sharp snap of a twig close had them catch their breaths, and their eyes whipped to the suspicious bush. Rosanne reached for the gun and her knife, holding them in each hand.

"Is it those bastards again?" Aros whipped out his knife and grabbed a rock in the other hand. He gave each of them a quick glance and sorely felt his arsenal's shortcomings.

Rosanne's eyes scanned the forest ahead of them, but the movements seemed to have stopped. "I don't know. Maybe it was nothing." A flash of light burst behind her eyes. Her vision darkened as she fell to her side with a cry, grabbing the new hot wet spot on her skull. Rosanne glimpsed Aros' blurry silhouette as he swung his arm towards her again. She caught it, snarling as she swung him around, making him lose his footing and overbalance.

"Give me the gun, or those monsters are gonna get us both!" he ordered.

"Don't you fucking dare!" Rosanne lashed out. Aros caught her fist with his jaw and fell in the river. His head broke the surface, and he cursed and sputtered as he scrambled for the rocks.

Rosanne groaned and held her bleeding forehead, her vision a blurred mess as she lost her footing. "You son of a bitch!"

In lack of proper defence Rosanne grabbed the next rock by her feet, hurling it at the moving blob by the riverbed. The rock bounded and hit Aros' shoulder, making him lose his grip. The ground morphed and came much closer. Rosanne held out her hands, eyes wide open in a desperate attempt to regain balance and sense of space. In seconds, a tall quick-as-an-arrow shadow sprang from the bushes, crossing the open space between the forest and the river. Rosanne reeled, grabbing for the knife close to her hand. The shadow ran right past her, smacking into Aros, who ascended from the riverbed right back into it.

"You better hold your pose right there, sir, or you'll get a bullet in your skull!" The prim, stern, recognizable voice rang in her head, and it calmed her immediately.

"Mr. Lyle! Is that you?"

"The very same, Captain. You've been less than fortunate, I see."

"Shoot the bastard if he tries to kill me again. And when I get my wits about me, let me shoot him first." Lyle took a few steps back without moving the nozzle away from its target, ushering him from the river.

"Over there, by that tree. That's it. Get that vine and bind yourself. Nice and taut." Aros shook his dripping jacket, grumbling as he followed Lyle's command. After a few minutes and the repeated protests of a frazzled and disgruntled decommissioned pirate captain, Rosanne felt Lyle's hand on her shoulder, stabilizing her.

"Are you alright, Captain?"

Rosanne could make out Lyle's trim mustache and often-coiffed hair which had now lost its slickness, falling over his face. His glasses were still on his nose, whole and glinting. His white shirt was covered in dirt, and the vest he normally wore under his jacket was missing along with his outerwear.

"It's getting there. Bastard got me good." She swayed her attention to the pirate. "I should have left you in the cave to be troll food!" she screamed at the bound man. Ignoring his string of protests, she waved a hand dismissively and held on to the ground as if she feared she would fall off the planet.

"Better?" Lyle asked after a while.

Rosanne nodded. "Yes. Bernhart, this is my Master Gunner, Mr. Lyle. Our first introduction was rather hostile and half-hearted. Not that this is any different." Rosanne introduced the two with her eyes shut as the light was blinding. Lyle nodded to the man by the tree.

"A pleasure."

"Same," Aros replied through thin stretched lips.

"What happened with you, though?" Rosanne continued. "We're miles from the camp."

Lyle led her to a sitting spot and made sure Aros was secure before returning to the confused captain's side. Tearing a piece of his shirt off, he soaked it in the river and pressed it against Rosanne's head wound. She flinched at the cold rag, muttering a string of colourful curses. She picked up the hat, keeping it in her hand, and gave the bullet hole a meaningful stare as she pushed a finger through it.

"I see you had your fair share of adventures. And with this cretin of all people." Lyle chuckled despite the gravity of the situation, and Rosanne's lips thinned into a prim smile.

"Indeed. You should have seen where we escaped from. Those trolls weren't this island's only occupants."

Lyle nodded. "While we're on the subject of escape, pardon my tardiness. We were hopelessly overrun, and I saw it prudent to slip away. I followed the little people as they dragged you off to the hills north of the forest. We're approximately a mile away from the camp. I lost track of you during the dark hours, and by the time I found the trail, they had split up the party and scattered to the winds. I picked a trail at random and followed it to a guarded cave. There were some ... hideous creatures there. I couldn't find anyone resembling humans, so I returned to the fork. But halfway through the day, I encountered a ... *troll* hunting party that forced me to take cover. Me being here is completely by accident. Dear Captain, your scream was quite loud."

"Dammit. If those things heard us, we're screwed. We have to go." Rosanne rose to her feet, quickly subdued by Lyle's gentle hand guiding her down along with her falling blood pressure.

"I concur, but first, you need to rest. You're no good in your current condition. They're not around here anyhow."

"What about me?!" Aros cried, having only heard the gist of the conversation. He struggled against the tight bindings that were draining the blood from his hands.

Rosanne threw another rock at him, but her aim was terrible as her eyes unsteadily swept over the forest. "I'll tan your hide and draw the attention of the trolls, then leave. How about that?" That effectually shut Aros for any further protests. He squinted against the light to better view the master gunner and looked away when he couldn't match his stare. The older man, although meek-looking in stature, had piercing eyes that were razor-sharp and silencing.

"Captain, if I may?" Lyle offered.

Aros' naked feet pattered against the rocks as Lyle's rifle pressed against his back. He led the way down the river and suffered for every step on the needle-strewn and ant-infested riverside. Rosanne looked worse for wear, but her head had at least stopped spinning, and she no longer relied on Lyle's support to get around. The sun dipped closer to the horizon, long past the surrounding hillsides but still providing light enough for them to continue their travels a while longer.

Lyle adjusted his glasses while keeping a firm grip on the rifle. "Now, recount to me your epic exploits and breath-taking dangers. Spare no details, as we have quite a ways to go."

Rosanne's malcontent was palpable, and she waved a hand dismissively.

Lyle bobbed his head. "I see. Good that you're both in half-decent health, and now we got ourselves some cannon fodder for the monsters. I'd say that will work in our favour."

Rosanne nodded, smiling. "Indeed, it shall. What about you, then?"

"Can't say there's much else to add to that tale, ma'am. I followed, I saw, and I got the hell out of there." Rosanne considered the dark bags under his eyes, the deeply sunken wrinkles, and his normally pristine hair, which was now scattered like a wet privy mop. "Those things, though, seemed to serve larger monsters living in caves. I never saw them leave their dwellings, only letting the little ones run around like errand boys. And they speak too."

Rosanne recalled the trolls entering the room where she and Aros were strung up and ready for slaughter and the guttural melodic twist of the few words she had recognized. "It almost sounded like the tongue the Indigenous settlers of Noval spoke but bastardized."

"Indeed. These creatures use poor grammar and are not too bright, though they can hunt and navigate the forests and the hills. Dangerous critters." Lyle scanned the surrounding hillsides for activity, pointing the rifle wherever his eyes landed, only to dismiss the notion of danger at the wildlife flitting about.

Rosanne shook her head for no reason other than to dislodge the feeling of dread at being in those caves. "Trolls. Who would have thought that children's stories were even remotely real?"

"Yes, I suppose trolls are a good description for those lumbering giants. And the smell carried a fair distance too."

"Oh god, the smell." Aros and Rosanne said in unison. Lyle raised an eyebrow.

"I take it you were in one of those dwellings, seeing your rope burns and keen recollection of their odour."

Aros threw his head back. "We were invited for dinner. These things eat whatever they come across. People, animals, you name it."

Another mental image of a pile of carcasses and gnawed bones popped into Rosanne's head. She shuddered. "We need to find the others. Getting back to the ship is our priority, then a search and rescue. We already know they're here somewhere among the hills, but we don't have the people for it yet."

"As long as the ship hasn't sailed away."

"Don't you jinx us, Mr. Lyle!"

"Pardon my humour, ma'am." His trim mustache stretched with his smile.

They passed a fork in the river and continued south to the grassy shores. The Grey Veil danced in the far distance across the sea, and the river exited into a large bay surrounded by sharp cliffs. The sun's low position cast the southern part of the bay in deep darkness, and in that darkness, something rested among the crashing waves and the thousands of screaming seagulls.

Only when Aros stopped the rifle pressed against his back, did Lyle and Rosanne pay him any attention.

"Your feet tired already?" she said with deep mockery.

"Hilarious, Captain. My feet have been in heaven ever since we came to this patch of paradise compared to the rocky river, but that's not what I want to bestow upon you. Look at the southern cliffs, among the rocks. It's hard to see, but it's there. The seagulls make it easier."

Lyle and Rosanne stood on each side of his outstretched arms, squinting against the pinkish hue of the horizon. In the low tide, the bottom of the bay was riddled with jutting rocks and pockets of deep water, and in them, the seagulls formed a series of straight lines seemingly in the open air. They made out broken remains of marine sail ships, rotten and sunk, exposed hulls and torn sails. The innermost part of the bay was littered with hundreds of smaller sailing ships, corvettes, two-masted galleons, and larger and particularly looming moss-covered hulks and passenger ships jutted from the deeper waters.

"There are so many of them. How did they all end up here?" Rosanne asked.

Aros threw his shoulders. Lyle directed his rifle at the ships, staring through the magnifying scope.

"There are a few trade ships there," he said, letting out an extended "hmm" as he directed the scope across the bay. He shook his head. "All the ships are permeated with rot. They must have been here a long time."

"Before the travelling ban, you think?" Rosanne questioned.

"Safe to assume they are. I haven't seen some of these models in all my career."

"Let me see." Aros leaned his head over to the scope before Lyle could pull away. "A little down to the left. There, excellent. Woah."

"What do thine pirate eyes perceive?" Rosanne voiced mockingly. Aros snorted and rolled his eyes.

"You sky traders might not know this, but marine vessels sailing around the Veil have been the rage since the dawn of trading. They were never discovered because sky trade and the RDA flew routes different from many of these ships. I've seen my fair share of sailing ships around the Veil, and honestly, they're the best pick. Their cargo is mostly unregistered, and they carry their weight in gold and only trade with towns outside the Queen's jurisdiction. Those two up against the south cliff are retired tea and coffee ships that ran south to the Queen's Colonies at the height of the colonization. What was it, thirty years ago? Anyway, you see that five-decked hulk in the deeper parts? That's no ordinary passenger ship."

Lyle retook the scope with his eye, scanning the designated ship of Aros' interest before handing it to Rosanne. She saw the ship's main-, fore- and mizzen-masts were all broken, slung across the intact main deck. In the gloom of the oncoming night, she could still spot the submerged decks. The mermaid carving was lavishly detailed with hints of gold flakes and bird feces. Why the faded facade of a once fabulous ship lay on this island was a puzzle indeed.

"It's an upper-class sailing ship," she concluded, lowering the butt of the rifle and returning it to Lyle, who let it rest on top of his foot. Aros made a dinging sound.

"Not just any rich man's passenger ship either. It's *Anima*, the passenger ship that disappeared with full cargo." He grinned with excitement.

"Cargo being people, you mean? Wouldn't the news of a fully-loaded ship with nobles disappearing make the headlines in every city in Terra?" Rosanne gave an inquisitive look, which Lyle responded to with a shrug.

Aros wagged a finger. "My dear Captain, this ship disappeared sixty years ago. The loss to the trade and factory companies was huge as many families were left without heirs and faithful contributors."

"Then the question begs, how did it end up here, and why a ship graveyard at such a remote location? It's almost as if ..." Rosanne let her statement hang, Lyle's face darkened, and Aros didn't speak another word.

"Down!" Lyle hissed, smacking his arm around Rosanne's shoulders and pulling Aros' rope, so they all tumbled into the tall grass. "Trolls," he whispered, his eyes trained just above the grass towards the cove. On the cusp of waning light, dark shadows of the small lumpy creatures with their spears walking in line along the cliff. They were less than two hundred meters away, but in the gloom, they hadn't spotted the humans. Yet.

"There's a forest and some hills west of here. We can take cover and continue west." Aros whispered, and Rosanne nodded.

"I concur. Let's go. Crawl if we have to."

Down on all fours, the party of three crawled in the grass through the cover of the coming night, spending a good portion of the time complaining of the undergrowth wearing on their knees and hands. Only when the darkness was complete did they dare to walk the remaining distance to the hills where they set up camp, but without the warm glow of a fire to stave off the creeping cold, it would be a long night. The moon was absent behind the clouds, and no amount of light in the sky offered them any comfort or hope of finding more suitable living accommodations.

As a meagre comfort, Rosanne reminded herself that they were all still alive and that perhaps the worst of the dangers had passed. She hoped.

CHAPTER 18

ANGLER

Aros received explicit permission from the captain of the *Red Queen* to put his shoes back on. His blisters no longer shot waves of pain with each step that he took on the sodden turf, but the sour waters stung nonetheless.

A thick fog snailed across the marshes in the early hours of dawn, and Rosanne and Lyle strolled behind the pirate captain, finding it easier keeping him under control with the rifle at his back. Should he fall into the waters and suffer a slow and agonizing death by drowning, they would also know where to step. With the troll-infested cliffsides preventing their swift return to the *Red Queen*'s meeting point, crossing the marshes had been a practical choice.

The landscape was a patchwork of precarious tufts and ponds that didn't betray its hidden depths. One small mistake could easily be their last. Aros picked a route based on the largest, most secure tussocks for their footing with minimal acrobatic stunts. He couldn't outrun them on this type of ground even if he tried, and the patrolling trolls reduced his chances of survival to none. With the marksman of the *Red Queen* at his back, he felt as safe as his bravery allowed him, and he kept his profile as low as he could to avoid invoking the wrath of the wandering iceberg named Rosanne.

The tufts let out a series of bubbles under their added weight, the small waves sending the murky water into disarray. The rotten smell only increased the deeper into the marshes they traversed, but it was nothing compared to that of the trolls. Rosanne counted her lucky stars that the den of the decomposing wild game had burnt what remained of her sense of smell. She stepped on the far edge of the grass, and her foot plummeted into the water. She just as quickly grabbed at the foliage for a hold with panicked curses hidden under her breath.

"I'm alright. Just wet." Her boot let out a sucking sound when extracted from the mud. She emptied the shoe of brown water, shivering in disgust when she put it back on.

Aros and Lyle waited patiently for her, Aros paying more attention to their surroundings as he picked out the path for them to take.

THE SILENCE of the surrounding grove and twisted birch trees was eerie but more comforting than the rush of the river obscuring nearby activity. Bubbles rose through the waters up ahead, a common phenomenon as trapped gases from swamped, rotting undergrowth turned the soil into a smelly deathtrap. The antlers of an elk penetrated the surface not far from them, the top of the skull reduced to bare, brown-stained bone. What was left of its body was obscured by a cloud of mud, but there was no doubt the corpse was nothing but skeletal remains.

"Where to, Captain Bernhart?" Rosanne asked. Aros' eyes snapped to attention as if he had been in a daze. He hopped to the next tuft, slipped and fell on his knees but got up immediately on wobbling legs. More bubbles rose to the surface and popped loud and clear in the silence, along with a rumble so low it made him chuckle.

"Okay, whose stomach was that? Because we just ate." He said as he hopped to the next one. Rosanne crossed the wide gap, losing her footing just like Aros did, and faceplanted on the crowberries.

"Probably me," She replied after she spat out the spicy leaves.

"Nice landing, Captain," Aros kidded. Her gaze in response could seal a small town in permanent winter. Lyle took a few steps back and gave himself running speed before he made the jump and landed perfectly, swaying around before he managed to stabilize himself. In the fog up ahead, a high-pitched tune made them stoop low. The tune morphed into a soft faint sound, swinging the pitches into a sorrowful song, higher and clearer.

"It's moving," Lyle whispered, his eyes peeled toward the source of the noise.

Rosanne also listened. "If that's a fiddle, then it means there are people here."

"That, or trolls can play," Aros shot in from the nearby tuft. Another low grumble had Rosanne holding her stomach, but the lingering hunger she felt had dissipated into nothing. She turned her head to Lyle crouching behind her, who shook his head. The tuft in the water behind them sent out gentle waves, catching Rosanne's attention. It bobbed up and down with its grassy knoll. Rosanne's breath caught in her throat.

"You're white as a sheet, Captain," Lyle commented, furrowing his brows.

She rubbed her temples. "I must be seeing things. Let's continue."

His gaze returned to the hushed world of the marshes. With a gentle ripple in the waters near his foot, grey fingers reached from the murky depths and encircled his ankle.

Lyle jerked his foot back, but the monstrous grip toppled him to his knees. He dropped the rifle just out of reach.

"Captain!" He scrambled for a hold on the soft knoll when a single powerful tug ripped him from his meagre safety and dragged the master gunner helplessly into the waters.

"Lyle!" Rosanne called out at his sinking form and then screamed when she saw what held him. A gnarled face, with large, milky-white eyes framed by grass-like hair, sneered at them from the black waters. Rosanne fumbled for Lyle, who was clambering to the roots jutting from the knoll, her heart quickening at the form of the creature breaking the surface. Gurgling, it grabbed the back of Lyle's shirt with a pale hand and pulled with enough force to drag the man underwater just as Rosanne caught his arm. The creature's face bobbed above water, black and mud-stained, with gaunt cheeks. Its large maw opened and sucked in air as if taking a breath for the first time.

Heaving its weight on Lyle's shoulders, the force dragged all three into the marshes.

Aros jumped across the floating knolls and nosedived for the plasma rifle. Just as it threatened to disappear into the depths, he caught it. The creature's growl intensified. Hollow. Hungry. Unearthly. Rosanne held on to the roots with everything she had. Without any means to draw as much as a single breath, Lyle held on tight to her arm. She gagged at the sour water entering her mouth but pushed the discomfort aside as she managed to twist the roots around her arm to strengthen her hold and keep her head above the surface.

Aros struggled with the unfamiliar reload mechanism, which refused to budge no matter how hard he pulled. Cursing, he worked it repeatedly as his fingers trembled uncontrollably. The waters stirred violently, urging him on.

"Who the fuck designed this thing?!" he cried out in frustration. After pushing the pin on the side of the battery chamber, the mechanism came loose, and Aros could pull it down and back and return it to its original position. Aros let out an astonished cry of victory at the bluish light from the reload chamber.

The slimy creature sucked its breath, staring at the pointed rifle with an empty expression. Aros fired. The bullet zizzled into the creature's head. Milky eyes narrowed, and it gave a wet growl, undeterred by the high-energy bullet dissipating somewhere in its grassy head.

Lyle thrashed under the weight of the creature pushing him down, tangled in its bony limbs and tattered cloak. Rosanne spat and gurgled, unable to hold her head above water and feeling Lyle's fingers slip from her own. She threw her weight towards the tuft but was hopelessly overpowered.

"Shoot it!" she shouted the moment her head broke the surface. "Aros, shoot it!" Aros lowered the rifle, staring at them, the creature, what remained visible of Lyle's blonde hair swishing in the dark, and Rosanne letting herself be dragged along for the feast. His heart nearly burst out of his chest, and he struggled to breathe.

His finger rested on the trigger, and the churning in his gut only increased. He considered the weak light at the side of the battery of the rifle and knew he couldn't possibly have more than two or three rounds left. The last shot didn't slow the monster in the least, and Aros' shaky hands did him no favours. He couldn't swallow the lump in his throat as his mouth was dry as sand.

Rosanne's screaming and thrashing, the splashing of water, and the guttural roar from the monstruous creature sunk into a deathly silence as if drowned. Captain Bernhart pulled the reload mechanism back and down to the side to charge the chamber with a ball of plasmic energy. He aimed the rifle at Rosanne.

"No hard feelings, Captain," he said. The tuft bounced and shifted behind him. Aros unintentionally swung the rifle with his finger still on the trigger before he was smacked aside by a tremendous force. The zizzling crack of the rifle filled the marshes along with Aros' panicked scream. He landed across the bank, scrambled from the water, and climbed onto land.

Through the heavy particles clouding the waters, Rosanne glimpsed a blurry silhouette. Still holding on to Lyle's hand and without a chance to breathe, her lungs burned like molten lava. She yearned to draw breath as her heart quickened and her limbs were sent into paroxysmal spasms. She breathed, and every part of her being was on fire as the water entered her lungs.

A hand grasped her wrist, and with ease, dragged her clear out of the water, suspending her in the air.

A man, it must have been a man, for he was tall and broad-shouldered, held her. But Rosanne noticed little else through her exhaustion and the water burning her eyes.

Coughing and sputtering, Rosanne heaved for her breath. "L-Lyle!" she called out. The creature in the water closed its milky white eyes, buried itself in the mulch, and disappeared.

The burning sensation crept from Rosanne's chest and spread to her body, followed by a numbing cold and acute weakness.

THE THICK PINE forest threw deep shadows in the waning evening light.

"Boy, you had me going for a while there. Your plan worked against odds and reason." Higgs elbowed Nelson. The lawyer's spectacles tumbled off his nose, which he caught with a deft hand. He slipped them back on immediately to chase away the blurry forest but frowned at the fingerprints gracing his vision.

Trailing behind a tall, grey-skinned woman, Nelson led the party of grumpy older men. Up close, the creature was less terrifying than when she and her coven had attacked the crew in the fields. Her gait was straight and relaxed, arms resting by her lanky hips and feet padding softly on the turf. Thin, matted hair whipped around as she glanced back at the men. Her face lacked the pronounced nasal ridge, making her cheekbones and sharp eyes almost striking features.

Nelson turned to the others. "Call it instinct or improvisation. At least we're still alive." He looked at the woman who didn't pay them much attention other than the occasional glance. She wasn't as tall as the party of hulder that attacked the camp.

Hopefully, Nelson would never have to do anything as ridiculous as getting Farand to obey his every word to prove he was in charge again. While this female was easily impressed by Nelson's power over Farand, her clan sisters might not agree.

Farand's stoic expression was less than impressed than his elderly coworkers, who praised the young man's exploits to the high heavens. "For all of our sakes, I pray this plan of yours will see us safe to harbor, Mr. Blackwood."

"So do I." Nelson fanned himself and loosened his collar.

"Lad's doomed us all." Hammond chuckled. "I say we throw him to the witches as a distraction when everything goes to hell."

Farand sighed. "This is no time for jokes, Mr. Hammond. We don't leave our payroll behind."

"Your conversation brings me to tears, gentlemen."

"I don't think our paper-pusher is up to their standard either way," Higgs commented, scratching his thick mustache.

They followed a flat-trampled trail through the pine forest, which transitioned into crooked birch at the foot of the volcanic mountain. Among the trees, black eyes stared back at them. Nelson's insides leapt at the sight of the ebony pools, and with crumbling reassurance, he told himself they were all safe from harm. Relatively.

At the foot of the mountain, a wide fissure led into darkened halls. Camouflaged by the growing foliage, Nelson jumped at the sight of the four moving sentries skirting the cave mouth. One of them crouched down and drew her lips back to expose her yellow teeth. The scout replied with a similar wicked sneer, and the sentries nodded their heads towards the entrance.

Their scrutiny, which had eliminated him and the others from the pack in the first place, was intense. With the way his heart slammed in his chest, he was surprised the hulder hadn't sniffed out his cowardice yet, for they terrified him, and surely any who snuck up on him would make Nelson unleash his most primal scream.

Nelson, Farand, Higgs, and Hammond found their way through the gloom by touching the walls inside the cave. Nelson stumbled over his own feet and smacked against the floor but hurriedly regained composure. As he straightened his jacket, his sheepish laugh brought a headshake from the scout. She drew her clawed hand along the cave wall and let out a series of high-pitched noises that guided them onward.

The blinding light which met them as the narrow corridors opened to a magnificent grand hall stole Nelson's breath. The domed ceiling stood supported by columns of fused stalagmites and stalactites, crudely carved with pockets of glowing blue crystals. The ceiling was a starry sky of green writhing glowworms.

The grand hall didn't hold much of anything resembling furniture, but the walls were covered with effigies of horned animals in skins and bones. Several hulder erected these ornaments, fastening the pieces with rough hemp. Other hulder emerged from adjacent caves carrying sticks and logs. A third group sorted out colourful flowers and braided them into banners.

The hulder faces staring at them were mixed reviews of awe to sheer horror. They clustered around the men, keeping an arm's length away and heeding their sister's warning hisses. The scout drew a breath before communing with a taller sentry wearing a colourful stone and bone necklace.

The men huddled closer at the uncomfortable intimacy the hulder forced them into. Some touched their shirts and jackets, fascinated and skittish at these new individuals. Higgs smacked a hand away as they went for his glasses, making a few of the curious hulder giggle.

Farand leaned over to Nelson. "Can't say I expected this."

Nelson nodded, just as confused and in awe at the unexpected welcome they received from the curious and somewhat civil hulder. A sudden, sharp slap caught everyone's attention. The necklace-wearing sentry hollered at the scout. She pointed feverishly back and forth between the men, letting out a string of words. The sentry's eyes shone with murderous intent, her twitchy nose turning into a sneer stretching to her ears. She grabbed the scout by her jaw in a swift movement and pressed her onto the rocky ground, screeching in her ears.

Nelson was sure they were all about to be killed. He was right when he thought the hulder they'd followed was the weaker link in the hulder hierarchy, a mere scout who had no say in their ways. The opportunity must have been too good for her, as she perhaps saw a chance to place herself in a more favourable position with her superiours by bringing in the men. Or perhaps they were wrong, and these women weren't nearly as civilized as they hoped.

Something the scout said made the sentry cease her hail of insults and eye the men with increased suspicion. Nelson saw this opportunity to step forward, showing a hand to Farand, who came to tower next to him. The other hulder gave way, observing the spectacle with wide, lively eyes.

As per Nelson's instructions, Farand bent the knee and bowed his head alongside Higgs and Hammond. The hulder's eyes were barely visible through thin slits of suspicion. The men stood when commanded. At this gesture, the sentry's sneer softened to intrigue. She grinned, then opened her mouth and let waves of melodies flow.

"Farand!" Nelson called, and the brutish man delivered a slap across the sentry's cheek so powerful she tumbled to the ground. Nelson blocked the man with his authoritative arm, holding his breath as he observed the sentry hold her jaw in wide-eyed surprise.

Around them, the women hissed but cautiously gave the men more space. They craned their necks and observed the situation with wonder and fright.

The sentry stood and massaged her cheek. Then with one clawed finger, she pointed to Nelson and said a few words in their guttural language. Her intrigued grin sent shivers down his spine.

The sentry waved a hand for them to follow, and Nelson knew they now had a fighting chance to get out of this mess.

"I'll never bow my old arse for you again, boy. Just so we are clear," Higgs said gruffly.

Nelson suppressed a laugh. "I am under no such delusion. We wouldn't have gotten this far unless we all cooperated. It seems to be working."

Higgs agreed. "Their song has power over most of us, but only your words have power over Mr. Duplànte. I would never have seen that coming from such a scrawny lad as you. No offence."

Nelson smiled despite the comment, knowing full well his worth in their mission to deliver the rest of the crew and the ship from the hulder prison. "Perhaps that is why it made such an impact."

They were guided to a room deep within the volcano. The corridors were numerous, and at every turn, they met other women of the hulder tribe. The sheer number of women living in this mountain was daunting.

"One of these halls must lead to where they stashed the ship. Can't be many places they could do that," Hammond said.

Farand nodded. "They probably mined the entire mountain. We need to find our way back at least."

Higgs tapped a finger against his forehead. "I got it all in me knocker. Half of it, at least."

Nelson sat on the straw bed, freeing his shoelaces. He regretted taking the shoes off, for the long walks had left their stink. For a moment, he could relate to Rosanne's dislike of footwear. Higgs laid back with a long-drawn painful groan.

"They lit a torch for us." Nelson nodded to the room's only light. "They don't seem as feral and savage as I thought they would be."

"We can certainly expect to be treated as unwanted guests," Farand said. "They have eyes and ears at every tunnel, and I don't want anyone to get the wrong idea about our intentions. We don't move until we see signs of the others, got that?" His words carried an air of superiority Nelson could only dream of, but their hopes rode on a lawyer's capability to lie himself to victory, which wasn't far from his original job description anyway.

"I say we get some shuteye. My back's been giving me hell since we got sacked. Leave tomorrow's problems until then." Folding his jacket, Higgs buried his head in it and closed his eyes.

Nelson folded his glasses and put them next to the bed. He couldn't see much in the gloom of one single torchlight, and somehow the room became the analogy of their current situation. He looked to Higgs, who was already fast asleep. Farand was a statue where he leaned against the wall, lost in his thoughts. Hammond laid belly-up without a care in the world.

When he closed his eyes, Nelson saw Ida's blond hair whipping in the high winds. A pair of goggles covered her eyes, but her smile was unmistakably bright behind her scarf. He hadn't known her long, but that girl made him drop every precaution he had for his own safety just to see that smile again.

Behind her stood Dalia, Olivier, even Creedy. The older man could be a real bastard, but he was still a part of the crew like everyone else. Captain Drackenheart was their heart, the *Red Queen* their soul, and the skies their home. Nelson wanted it all back in its rightful place. He wanted to give all these people their old lives, rewind time to before he proposed this mad quest to Captain Drackenheart. He hadn't even found his father's corpse. What good was this journey when all he gained was his father's hat and memories of a sunken warship? None of this was worth it; it wasn't even worth the money he promised them.

"You are braver than you look, Mr. Blackwood," Farand interrupted Nelson's train of thought. The lawyer looked at him, giving a smile that carried no conviction. "You do your part, and we'll do ours. Everything will correct itself in time. Sleep. There's nothing more we can do today." Nelson nodded and turned to the wall. The straws rustled across the room, and soon Farand's rumbling snore followed.

Nelson would rest more comfortably if he hadn't been in a room full of snoozing men with snores that matched the noise level equal to the pedestrian district of Kvenchester at two o'clock in the afternoon. He closed his eyes and tried to forget about the conundrum which he had gotten them into.

CHAPTER 19

QUEENS AND FLOWERS

The steady crunch of footfalls against the forest floor made Rosanne's eyes flutter open. She glimpsed a pair of broad and dirty feet, suntanned and calloused. With each step, they dug into the dirt, confident and undeterred by the crossing ants and protruding roots. The steady pace induced a cooing rocking so gentle Rosanne could lose herself in it.

Carried like a backpack, she studied the white-lined scars peeking out from the worn, rolled-up shirt sleeves. Her legs were around his hips, secured comfortably by strong arms. His hem-torn breeches were curiously simple. Balanced between three digits on his left hand, he held a fiddle, an old thing that must be close to retirement, given the dark spots in the wood. She wrinkled her nose at the dark hair tickling her chin but smiled; his scent was euphoric and familiar.

Columns of shadows lined the path ahead, and Rosanne was blinded as they went through the following beams of light. The ultramarine sky and rising sun brought with them a humid warmth. The forest around them was alive with activity and undisturbed somehow by their passing.

Rosanne wanted to move, longed to straighten her slumped

sore back and stretch the dead numbness in her body. Legs and arms alike were aflame and drained, a rotting sensation crawling through her muscles. And then she saw it. She let her left-hand stroke over a large bruise on her right forearm. The motion made the man turn his head and view her in his periphery, but Rosanne's eyes were fixed and tearing up from the loss in her heart.

"He held on so tight he left a mark," she murmured uneasily. "Why couldn't he have held out just a little longer?" She caught her breath, subduing her overflowing emotions.

"*Khora ki eme da?*" The man's tone was lyrical and soft. Her eyes narrowed as she didn't recognize the language.

"I'm sorry, I don't understand." The strain of talking spent the little energy she had. Her face felt hot, her core boiling, her lungs like they couldn't draw the air they needed. His eyes sparkled green and copper.

"*Ist dette und spraak for dig?*" he prompted. Rosanne shook her head weakly, only understanding a few words. "My Novali is rusty at best." He considered her words for a moment, his mouth opening. He paused briefly, as if he realized something.

"Novali? Not heard this one before. Long since I hear someone speak." His slow, accentuated dialect was jumbled, and she struggled to place it. "You are far from home, Dragonheart."

"How- how do you know my name?" She exhaled and realized how hot it must have felt on his neck. Her eyes rolled in their sockets, the foliage and light reduced to a bokeh haze. She shook her head.

The man halted their progress and gently sat her down. He laid a hand on her forehead. Even when he was right in front of her, Rosanne couldn't make out those subtle details that, somehow through her haze, seemed familiar. Her eyes were so tired they couldn't focus, but somehow the shape of him, the darkness of his hair, and the way he smelled reminded her of Antony.

"The waters got inside you and is making you ill. Poison for man, life for Nikor."

"N-Nikor?" She echoed and attempted to shake the spinning world away.

"The beast that dwells in the marsh. Now hush. It's far to the cabin, and you need rest. The waters inside you will make you sicker." His soothing voice prompted no arguments from the feverish captain. Rosanne didn't think she could respond, even if she could somehow summon the energy from the muddy marshes where it undoubtedly remained. His hand brushed the rogue hairs from her face, his fingers cool and gentle against her skin.

She almost told him to stop, as, despite how soothing the motions were, her insides recoiled, and her breath hitched at the proximity of his hand. He slung her arms around his neck and grabbed hold of her legs, then stood without drawing as much as an extra breath. Rosanne lacked the strength to do anything about it and rested her head on his shoulder. Everything turned into a cloudy warped confusion caught in a raging inferno. Breathing was hard, the light of the forest was like knives in her retinas, and the rustle of branches grew painfully loud, like cannon fire in her ears.

The man's chest drummed as he hummed a tune.

"Not long now," he said, or had she imagined it? The forest seemed so dark and cold. Her skin was damp, but he appeared unchanged by the weather. Did it rain? Her thoughts were as murky as the depths of the marshes, and for a moment, a pair of large white eyes stared back at her, reaching for her with its gnarled grey hand.

"No!" Rosanne slapped the hand away and flinched. She thrashed against the pale hand which came to subdue her, Nikor's face so close to her own she felt its breath.

"You are dreaming!" The deep voice with the odd accent flowed through her. Warped images danced in her eyes. Nikor's saggy face melted away, replaced with that of green eyes shining in the candlelight. "You are dreaming," he said again, then smiled once her tear-filled gaze re-focused.

Backed into a corner, the fibres of rough-hewn walls tugged at her hair. Candlelight betrayed that she was in a living room in a log house with a cold stone hearth. Through the shutters of the glassless windows, darkness spoke of night. She cast her captor or saviour a look, trying to steady her breathing. He left momentarily, returning with a wooden cup. He placed it in her hands and ensured she could hold it.

"It's water. Drink." Rosanne looked at the contents, a black pool of liquid indistinguishable from any other in the scant light. She spilled it as she gulped it down, and the cup slipped from her weak hands and clattered on the floor.

"S-sorry." Her mouth was still parched, and her eyes stung as she looked around. The cold tightened its grip on her hands. "What is going on?" She crushed her eyes together as the candlelight hurt her eyes. The man refilled her cup, and she drank that too.

"The fever is making you hallucinate. You are very ill, Dragonheart. You should change."

"What?" She looked down at herself, filthy and grime-stained, the leather jacket torn at the sleeve. Her shoes stood by the door under so much mud they were barely recognizable. A few incomprehensible words escaped her mouth, and she realized it was all gibberish. Not even the words formed in her mind. Why was everything so difficult?

The man placed a long shirt in front of her, nudging her shoulder. "You should change before you faint. The fever will come back, and I do not wish to invade your privacy."

Rosanne saw something between his smile and aged empathic eyes; the sense of calm which overcame her was unfamiliar and terrifying.

"Come back? Those things too?"

The stranger nodded. "The fever brings nightmares that scare you. Nikor poisons the waters, so any who drink it get sick."

"What *is* it?"

"Nikor? Just another creature of this land," he said with a hint of disdain. "He is slow and patient. He goes long winters without any food. He sits there in his muddy home, looking for prey to come close enough for him to drag into his jaws. He's a patient angler always on the hunt and only shows himself when he strikes."

"An angler..." It was more of a statement than a question, and a shudder ran through her body, making her tighten her fist and jerk her head to the side as if it moved of its own. "Will ... will I live?" she finally uttered.

His silence unnerved her, and the way his eyes swept over her, from her gaze down to her clutched hands, indicated he didn't seem so sure. The smile that spread on his unshaven face calmed her, nonetheless.

"I've drawn a bath for you in the next room. Wash off before the fever returns. I'll be outside if you need anything." Rosanne only nodded as he exited the cabin. When the presence of him vanished, only then did she notice her burning cheeks.

"Poison, you say ..." Her hand gave a spastic curl when she grabbed the shirt, the muscles in her body screaming at the minimal strain. On wobbly knees, she supported herself on the wall. The floor was cold but dry, decorated with a few brown and grey-speckled animal skins. A small kitchen and a few crudely constructed shelves occupied the opposite corner, along with a homemade dining table and two stools.

A staircase ran to the second floor, and through the cracks in the ceiling floorboards, there was indeed another room. A door stood across the stairs, and she went inside as instructed. The washroom was decent for a cabin, even if it wasn't a proper tub but a large washing basin. Half full, the water steamed in the otherwise chilly room.

Rosanne fell to the floor. She let out an incredulous laugh at her unsteady legs as she crawled on all fours to the basin. Her thoughts spun like she had drunk a bottle of O'Malley's down at the first disk on the skyport. Even then, this experience wasn't nearly as pleasurable as her stumbling piss-faced to the Captain's Quarters with her pockets full of quick-earned riksdaler she had cheated off the gambling table. She pried herself free from the stiff grime-covered garments in an unrefined manner and left a trail of clothes from the door to the tub.

The warm water chased away the coldness in her limbs and loosened the mud from her hair. Even then, her insides and extremities burned with relentless fever sending waves of chills and boiling sensations throughout her system. She studied her hands, arms, torso, and legs; bruises covered large portions of her skin. The handprint on her arm had darkened to blue-black and felt sore to the touch. Her joints might as well have been filled with sand, and her muscles were so lethargic they were left non-functioning. Every thought felt foggy as if her head was filled with cotton, and every memory seemed a hazy lifetime ago. She couldn't remember the last time she slept well, the last time she hadn't been on edge, a time when death stood further than two steps behind ...

She opened her mouth, withholding her scream, refusing to let a single sound escape as she clutched her head. Through her tears, she saw the water around her stain with dirt, her wounds and contusions pronounced and daunting.

When was the last time she cried? She hadn't even cried when Iban died, so why now? She scrambled her thoughts for any logical answer. Lyle had been dragged underwater by that thing right in front of her eyes ... She hadn't hesitated, plunged herself straight after him, holding on to him. Had she even felt the moment his hand slipped? She stared at the five-fingered bruise.

Lyle wasn't the only one lost to the wicked wilds of the land inside the Veil. Where was everyone else? Had Farand brought them all to safety, and what about the remaining crew in the hills?

"I should never have left." Her voice trembled. "I should never have left!" And then she cried. "This fucking island is madness!" She felt hot, muddled, and nauseated. Was the fever spiking already?

Biting down her sorrows, Rosanne scrubbed herself clean and dressed in the provided clothes. She paid the odd fit no mind and exited the room once she felt stable enough to hide her grief and shame. Two steaming bowls of soup stood on the kitchen table. Her stomach rumbled.

"Ah, good. You still have the strength to stand," the stranger greeted her from the kitchen. "Please, come eat. You must be famished." He pulled out the rickety chair, his hand stretched towards it. Rosanne sat without a word, took the spoon, and dug in. She couldn't taste much as the fever had done a number on her tastebuds, but she ate with vigour. nonetheless. She caught his eyes on her then sat up straight as she had forgotten her manners.

"Oh, don't mind me!" he defended. "I didn't imagine your hair had such a beautiful hue and shine underneath all the dirt." She chuckled at his quick, honest answer, then felt a wave of nausea churning her stomach. She held her mouth, grabbing the table with her free hand. The man stood so abruptly he knocked the stool over. He dove for the bucket across the room, and he barely managed to get it to her in time before Rosanne keeled over and emptied her stomach. The mess had her flushed with embarrassment, but Rosanne could spare no decency as the vomiting persisted, each time more difficult than the last, the contents darker and thicker. It didn't even taste like stomach acid, but mud-like and earthy.

When she felt well enough, Rosanne eyed the contents of the bucket carefully. "What the hell is happening to me?" Her voice had turned hoarse and deep.

The man studied the bucket. "It's the poison making you sick. Some came out. I'll help you to bed." Taking Rosanne's arm around his neck, he let the weakened woman lean against him as he guided her up the stairs and into a room. He set her on the bed, tucking her in as the fever returned in full force and made her ramble. She saw his worry through the morphing scenery of her fever-riddled brain and was terrified of her loss of control. She was lost in the dark, fumbling for something to hold on to as the sickness took her mind out for another unwanted ride into a frightening madness.

———

NELSON and the other men stared with a mixture of horrified expressions at the *Red Queen*.

"Captain Drackenheart is going to kill me," Farand said.

Higgs nodded, the engineer crossing his arms and smiled flatly with a frown.

"The captain will tan all our hides," Hammond stated.

Bobbing his head, Nelson shrugged. "I think she looks beautiful."

The three men stared at him.

"Exactly." Their unified voices were perfectly synchronized.

The *Red Queen* floated above ground level, tethered to nearby pillars. Numerous hulder milled about its bulk. Wreathed coloured cloth, flower ornaments, and bouquets covered nearly every surface of the ship. A wide bridge with braided daisies and dandelions ran from a perch on the volcano wall across to the main deck. Four women emerged from a tunnel to the perch, carrying a tall, gnarled root shaped like a throne. After wobbling across the bridge, they set the root down on the main deck between the stairs leading to the quarterdeck.

"Whatever they're preparing for makes this a lot harder for us." Farand shook his head. "If they're occupying the ship twenty-four-seven, we need to distract them from getting aboard at all."

"Nelson? Mr. Duplànte?" They turned at the high-pitched voice that could only be Ida. The young engineer made a full sprint from across the room straight into Nelson's arms; he barely stopped her momentum from toppling them both. Dalia, Creedy, Gavin, Norman, and Kristoff followed right behind her. A soft murmur grew from the onlooking hulder. Nelson quickly shed his disbelieving look and pushed Ida away, every movement paining him as he wanted nothing more than crushing her against him.

"I'm sorry, but I need you all to bow down to me," he whispered.

"You ... what?" Ida asked.

"Just do it!" Farand hissed and did so alongside Hammond. Higgs bent his knees with a groan, bowing his head. Ida glanced at Higgs' apparent pain from the gesture, then to the hulder, whose frowns betrayed suspicion. She cast herself before Nelson's feet. Dalia quickly followed, dragging Gavin and Kristoff down with her despite their protests.

"The fuck is wrong with you all? I ain't bowing for some scrawny paper-pusher!" Creedy snorted and folded his arms. Nelson looked to Farand, his eyes pleading as he threw his head in Creedy's direction. The lieutenant was by Creedy's side in a blur and grabbed the able seaman by the scruff of his hair, effortlessly pulling him down to all fours.

"Do as he says, or you'll jeopardize the plan," he hissed to the older man. Nelson could see Creedy's inner clockwork working overtime to make sense of this bizarre situation, as his jaw muscles danced as he repressed his frustration.

The hulder chatted excitedly, throwing looks to the lieutenant, and somehow found their gazes towards his master. Nelson gulped at the attention. Seeing the crew on their knees in front of him like this was something he'd never imagined even in his wildest dreams.

"Rise and gather around."

Ida's face was stiff as a plank. "What in the flying blazes is going on, Nelson?" she said through gritted teeth.

"Not here," Nelson answered. "Don't say anything until we know we're unsupervised."

Creedy shook his head and spat, then his jaw dropped. "Fuck me sideways with a Milanian street banger ... The captain is going to kill us."

Gavin pulled the skin on his face upon seeing the beautified horror that awaited them, letting out only the tiniest shriek.

Dalia grabbed Creedy's shoulder to steady herself.

"This changes things," she said and then blinked and turned to Farand. "Since you are here, that means you have a plan?"

Farand bobbed his head, eyes locked on the hundreds of flowers they had to remove before picking up the captain lest she bombard him with a million little curses at his inability to protect their livelihood.

Chapter 20

The Hulder Queen

A starry sky filled the volcano's gaping maw, and light from the full moon slid closer to the grand hall's center. Torchlight ran from every crevice and gangway, the lanterns on the *Red Queen* shining brightly from bowsprit to the stern. The ship was almost beautiful in the orange glow and adorned with colourful flower braids. The gnarled throne-shaped root sat empty among the sentries guarding it.

Having spent most of the day under lockdown, Nelson, Farand, and the rest of the labelled undesirables were pleased to breathe the air flowing in from the volcano top. Nelson figured they must have been kept separate from the rest for the same reason they were left behind in the first place. They merged with the other group led by equally stern-faced sentries with stone-tipped spears.

"Where's Ida?" Nelson inquired to Dalia, who limped up to him.

She shook her head. "They took her maybe an hour ago. To where, I don't know. We've been at work in the mines all day."

"Mines? What are they digging for?"

"Unrefined grav-minerals. They have a workshop full of the stuff. It looks like they're trying to make use of it the same as us."

"Are they successful?"

Dalia shook her head, stumbled, and caught herself on Nelson's outstretched arm. "Not by a longshot. They don't seem coordinated enough to know what to do with it, yet they're digging for the stones like their lives depend on it."

"How's your leg?"

"Fucking great," she said through gritted teeth, and Nelson let her lean more heavily on him. "What about you guys?"

"Same as the rocks, I guess. They don't quite know what to do with us, so we've been locked in our room all day."

Farand followed behind Nelson and the rest of the human procession in an orderly fashion as they were herded up the gangways and crossed the bridge over to the ship. They were seated on the floor facing the throne while the surrounding hulder sat and bowed their heads, hands stretched out in front of them. The pale light of the moon crawled over the ship, casting shadows from the masts and fluttering sails. Small specks of light escaped from deep within the roots, flitting around the twisted branches.

One hulder began to sing in a low ethereal tune. Slow and melancholic, the melody invoked familiarity and delight. The sentries around the throne pitched in with a lighter melody, weaving their song into deeper tones.

A soft tingling teased Nelson's mind, drawing forth images and scents, unfamiliar sounds, and soft whispering voices. He felt gratitude, contentment. He wanted to smile.

"You're feeling that, aren't you?" he whispered to Farand, who nodded, his hard chiselled features softening. Nelson let his mind wander as the song continued, even when he didn't want it to.

Another group of hulder crossed the bridge, and in their midst, Ida walked with her head down. She was fit with a tight blue dress that barely kept her modesty in place, along with bracelets made from animal bones and a multi-layered necklace featuring a small feline skull. Her hair was combed and braided back, which couldn't hide the redness of her cheeks. Nelson wouldn't have been able to tear his eyes off her even if he were under a knife. He had never seen the tomboy donning anything other than her working clothes and tool belt. He forgot how to breathe.

Ida was led to the throne, where the hulder prompted her to sit. Her protests were met with frowns and sneers until she gave in, sitting as far out on the edge as she could. Her round eyes darted over the hundreds of onlookers surrounding the ship. Occupying every pathway and cave opening, the hulder kept coming.

As lost as Nelson was in Ida's beauty, his face turned red at the implication of whatever ritual this was. He was not a violent man, but his eyes inevitably wandered to the sentry's spear and wondered if he could even spill the blood needed to free Ida, liberate the rest of the crew, and fly as far away from these religious fanatics as he could. Why would they put Ida on the throne for any other reason than to make her stay? The chanting grew louder, and his thoughts muddled.

The moonlight danced across the twisted branches of the throne. The air filled with otherworldly echoes of the song for a while, the sentries swaying as they continued their melody. In the spotlight, Ida wrung her fingers, keeping her eyes down as if catching direct eye contact with someone would make her lose what little composure she had left.

The armrests on the throne crackled. Ida watched for a breathless moment as they moved, broke apart from the wood, and grew sprouts. They moulded into gnarly fingers, making Ida shriek when they grabbed at her. The fingers turned into hands, and lastly, arms. Ida tore free from the wooden hands, which became more alive with each passing moment, and escaped the chair, tripping over her feet in front of the throne.

The chanting ceased, and the hulder merely observed in silence. The chair morphed and crackled, its twisting branches taking on distinctive shapes resembling hair around the backrest. The wood weaved and moved. A figure pushed itself out from the seat, taking on more delicate shapes and details, carving out a nose, eye sockets, and a mouth. The final stage changed the grey and brown wood to pale white skin, vibrant and faintly aglow. Brown locks flowed down to rounded hips, and the figure took two steps to free herself from the roots.

She stretched long thin arms, twisting her back to chase the stiffness away. Her face was delicate with soft blue eyes and lips which parted into a yawn. She shared the sharp features of the hulder. She also appeared more human with a pronounced nose. Her firm, rounded breasts were covered by an elaborate necklace of colourful beads and teeth as large as a grown man's thumb. She wore a berry blue cotton skirt, and her partial nudity didn't shame her in the least.

Looking at Ida, who seemed too stunned to move from the floor, the serene woman stretched out a hand. "It's okay, Ida. There's nothing of which to be frightened." Her euphonious voice was a welcoming change from the horrific scene of which she had made her appearance.

Rather than fainting, Ida took the woman's hand. Long fingers encircled hers fully, and with one simple tug, she had Ida standing. The sentries on each side of the throne stood taller than both women, but they bowed their heads deep.

Drawing her gaze over the ship, visiting the faces of her subjects, and finally resting on the humans, the hulder queen's gentle smile turned crestfallen.

"*Se kor vi lider!*" her voice rang loud and firm, sweeping her hand around the room. The hulder responded by stomping their spears and feet to the floor, their voices calling out in a soft, mournful tone. The hulder queen's hand rose sharply, and all noise ceased. "*Med ett, der eit håp.*" Her hand shifted to Nelson. With lips stretched into a smile, her serene mirth returned. The hulder broke out in cheers.

"Look how we suffer. Yet, here there is hope," she told him and took a step closer. "Forgive me. We haven't had visitors for a long time. I hope my children have treated you well." Her voice remained soft and welcoming. She nodded to Nelson, who stood and bowed his head like a gentleman in the presence of a lady. "I hear you are the leader of your pack. I am *Skogsdrotningen.* But you may refer to me as the hulder Queen."

A woman came out of the chair. Nelson's brain buzzed with activity as he attempted to regain his focus on the situation but was constantly drawn to the fact that a stroke of magic or divine intervention had occurred before his very evidence-needing eyes. A queen came out from the root shaped like a chair. She was wood, and now she was flesh. He wasn't even sure he had felt this dumbfounded before. The root retained its shape, very much the chair it was even after its occupant had left. Her smile caught his attention, and he coughed.

"We are honoured by your presence. I am Nelson Blackwood of the *Red Queen*: this ship and its crew. We eh ... had a falling out with your children." The hulder Queen placed a hand over her chest, drawing a surprised breath.

"On behalf of the clan, I sincerely apologize for my children's behaviour. They do what they think is best in my absence, imperfect as they may be."

Gavin elbowed Dalia gently. "Her articulation is better than Kristoff's."

Dalia shushed him.

The hulder Queen craned her neck around Nelson to look at the other two. "I take pride in conversing with all sapient species. Humans are no exception." She chuckled, and Dalia and Gavin stared at the floor shamefully. Turning her attention to Nelson, she beckoned him to follow her to the captain's quarters.

"I understand that we have quite a lot to discuss. Come, let's have a private audience."

Ida's panic-stricken eyes begged Nelson to stay, but he heaved his shoulders—he was at a loss at what to do. He closed the door behind them, and the hulder Queen sat down at Rosanne's desk. She gave the room half a look before dedicating her attention to

Nelson. Seeing her behind that desk felt eerily familiar to when Nelson extorted Rosanne's cooperation.

Nelson wouldn't let himself be fooled by the hulder Queen's charm and grace, but she intimidated him at a level on par with Captain Drackenheart, if not more.

He let her take the lead on the conversation, and Nelson told her about their untimely clash with the pirates and how they had ended up stranded, split, and hunted.

"I see. My children took something that was not theirs to take. How unruly of them. You can have your ship back, Mr. Blackwood," she agreed. "The ship and crew will all be returned to you. But I have conditions." Her expression was as disarming as a white flag, and her eyes shone brightly for every spoken word. She was clearly intrigued by his tale and mannerisms, but even more so, she kept him chatting of matters big and small, things she couldn't possibly know unless she had visited the world beyond the Grey Veil. Nelson thought he was in a dream, or his brain somehow forgot to recall everything going on in this room. He knew she had said something but couldn't remember what, and he knew that her knowledge of the outside world bothered him, but not why. Was this another hidden ability of the hulder people?

"Before that. What were you going to do with Ida?" he asked.

"The young female? We need her assistance with a delicate matter. She is a beacon of hope to my children."

The implication made Nelson's guts churn. The hulder Queen might be showering him with promises that no harm would befall Ida, but the brimming hope in her elated eyes foretold something malevolent and forbidding. "In what way?"

Her eyes crinkled, withholding her answer far longer than Nelson liked.

"Word is that the Forest Devil has shown himself, and we need to honour him. He is the reason we are all here."

"The Forest Devil? Are you going to sacrifice Ida to him?"

She let out delicate laughter. "The Forest Devil doesn't

demand sacrifices in the traditional sense, but Ida and Mr. Duplànte will protect us from him. We haven't given him a reason to fear us for a long time."

"That doesn't make any sense. Ida is the least threatening person on this island."

Tapping the table, her face took on the look of silent deliberation. "Mr. Blackwood, I'm returning everything that is yours, even if *yours* by definition is a farce. Captain Drackenheart will have her ship and crew, but Mr. Farand Duplànte and Miss Ida Simonsen stay with us. That is my only condition."

Nelson struggled to pinpoint why her words bothered him. "You have no need for them for this ... Forest Devil. Your people are more than equipped to handle such a threat on your own. Mr. Duplànte, I can understand, but Ida? Release them back into my custody. If not both, then at least Ida." A cold disembodied hand encircled his throat and stole his breath.

He realized what had bothered him. It was the list of names and the mention of Rosanne. Where had she heard all of this? How did she see through their deception so easily? Nelson fought his instincts to demand answers, fought the muddled thoughts in his head. The hulder Queen merely smiled.

"I refuse. You trespass on our land, steal our resources, and expect more than what's fair? I am ensuring your safe return to civilization, and you do not accept because of two people? It's a small sacrifice." She accompanied the statement with a head tilt.

"It's a price I'm not willing to pay. What is it that you really need them for?"

Nelson imagined them as slaves for the hulder clan for the rest of their days, Ida toiling away in the mines, or strung up spread-eagled in the forest, gutted and bleeding as a sacrifice for the monstrous devil. Farand ... he wasn't so sure that Farand was worse off between the two of them.

The woman brushed a speck of dust off the table. "She is not yours, and he is not your guard. You have no power over anyone on this island, not even the people who bowed before you in a very convincing act. Your game stops here, Mr. Nelson Black-wood. My children are naive, but I am not."

Was it Creedy, so unwilling to play along with the ruse, who had given them away? But even so, how could this woman know anything of what went down when she was still a root? She spoke the language so well and behaved according to human norms; it was unnatural considering her circumstances on this island where no other human lived. "How can you possibly know anything of what you've been claiming?"

Her eyes took on a predatory gleam. "I know that you black-mailed Captain Drackenheart into finding the *Retribution*. I know that no one else but her and Mr. Duplànte know of your selfish reasons behind this expedition. I know that you love Ida so much that you want to risk it all just to save her."

A cold tightness crossed his face, and he struggled to speak properly. "Who told you? No one here could have told you this unless you spoke with Farand or the captain. Unless ... You have her, don't you?" The hulder Queen cocked her head slightly back, smirking as she regarded his panicked eyes. She ran a fingernail across the table and then locked gazes with him.

"If you stay here any longer, all of these people will lose what lives they have. How will the crew look upon you then, knowing that you set them up for failure because you couldn't let go of one girl? It's not worth it," she cooed. "Miss Simonsen and Mr. Duplànte stay here to ensure our survival, and there is nothing you can do to stop it. You do not have the power or the resources to do anything against my children or me." She slid her hand across the table, squeezing his hand gently. She caught his panicked eyes with hers. "We are not evil, Mr. Black-wood. We seek our own survival, as you sought peace of mind when you asked Captain Drackenheart to find your father's grave."

A wave of nausea prevented Nelson from keeping his calm. He wanted to lash out, to vomit, to scream in frustration. It was as if someone had driven a pickaxe into his skull; such was the pain. He retracted his hand, burnt by the gentleness of her touch; the electric prickling her skin left on his terrified him.

"You ... you're in my head? You can see it all?"

The hulder Queen cast her eyes to the table and gave him a moment to recover. She stood and walked around him, running her hands across his chest as she hugged him from behind. Nelson didn't resist, couldn't reject her advances, but clenched his jaw to prevent his anger from lashing out. Her breath was hot on his ear, and he found himself in a cold sweat at the implication of what she might do to him. Her aura, the very air surrounding her delicate features, was languorous and menacing. Her claws could tear into his abdomen or slash his neck wide open.

"You are not a strong man, Mr. Blackwood." She whispered into his ear. "You have been stepped on and beaten your entire life. No one has looked at you twice. But you are cunning, and you made your place in the world, although but a small piece. You can accomplish more by staying here. *We* can make you stronger. We can give you whatever you need. We might even let you have Miss Simonsen."

A needle pricked at his thoughts, playing a thousand memories at the same time. He saw Ida's shy smile when she had told him how he put her to ease and felt anew how his heart had thrummed when she seemed so vulnerable at that moment. He saw Noval under his feet as they sailed from Bogvin and the ships of Salis lazing by the coastline, dropping off shipment. He recognized the heavy smell of stale beer at the bar where he met Captain Drackenheart. He saw himself sitting in the dusty office of Parkson & Blackwood, skimming through records and signing endless stacks of documents of small matters. It was all pointless how he went about his day-to-day tasks only to end up staring at the people on the street below his office and wondering how they managed to smile as if their lives were worth living. Why couldn't he achieve that?

"Get out. Get out of my head!" Sweat beaded on his forehead, and his jaw trembled as he couldn't force out any more words. She scraped at his thoughts, pulling them out in the open with a hook. His shame and guilt were laid bare in his own mind, and all Nelson wanted was to forget the measures he'd taken to ensure this mission saw the light. Ida would hate him. The crew would toss him overboard if they knew of his betrayal. They had been respectful in the sense that he would pay them handsomely but also received him well enough to not exclude him. Nelson's rotten insides were black and thick as grime, and no matter how much he rubbed at it, he couldn't get it clean. A permanent black stain on his consciousness.

The nails on his throat drew deeper ever so lightly, teasing his skin, stirring his insides.

"Stop. Get out. I don't want you in there," he said.

Her lips drew back to a smile. "See?" the hulder Queen whispered into his ear. "You are stronger than you think you are." She released him and stepped back. "We will borrow Ida tonight. Tomorrow I'll make sure the rest of you leave safely." She gave him a final look before bowing and taking her leave.

Nelson placed his glasses on the table, wiping the tears from his eyes and wanting to scream until he had no voice left.

CHAPTER 21

THE FOREST DEVIL

"Please don't do this," a trembling feminine voice called out. Shadows flickered past orange light shining through cracks in the wall, forming strange angular shapes. Flame-like, they went around each other, stretching, morphing, and blending.

Rosanne sat still as a mouse, observing the commotion through a gap. Her thoughts spun, and her eyes couldn't focus on anything outside the scene. Another nightmare, she concluded, another strange monster-induced scene playing in her head. Rosanne wanted to shout but her throat seized.

She was grateful in a sense that it wasn't another dream of Nikor's cold dead eyes and Lyle's usual calm facade twisted into calamity. Too many versions had played in her mind already, but no matter how she twisted it around, the result was always fatal. She was forced to watch Lyle being dragged to his doom in the putrid marshlands and Nikor sucking its breath in a cry of victory.

Rosanne listened to the disembodied voice, beams of light dancing before her eyes.

"I want you gone," another shadow growled, his tone deep and hoarse. He towered over the woman. A dark clawed hand reached out to touch him, but the shadow moved out of the light.

Hissed mutters whispered to each other, the shape morphing needlepoint edges on its back and twisted legs.

The shadow invoked a new fear in Rosanne, and she fought every instinct to cry and cower. The rough wooden fibres grated her fingers, and the heat of the room burned her eyes, yet she kept them peeled on the dancing shapes.

"We will all die if you don't do this! Please, just this once, and you'll never have to see me again." The distraught woman grabbed the man, and he, the shadow of him, looked down and shook himself loose with ease.

"I gave you a gift out of love, and you lost it. There's no trust in your words, only the voice of a pathetic, begging creature who can't exist in this world on its own. You and your kin are parasites upon this world!"

She gasped and let out a single sob. "It is my fault he is gone, and I know that! But I loved him more than anything. Without him ... we will turn to dust."

"Your existence, your ancient customs, sicken me and bear me no fruit." He was close to her now, touching her face, but not out of gentleness or from violence. She twisted away from him as if his hands burned. She faced him once again, and for a moment, a pair of eyes glowed green.

"Please. We will die, and then you'll be all alone in this accursed place with the trolls and sprites."

"Begone!" He sneered, his face a vicious scowl, stretching, changing. The flat shadow opened a maw, exposing rows of elongated teeth able to entrap any victim it chose. Undeterred, the woman reached out again.

"'Take the girl then! At least you won't be alone." The shadow motioned behind her while the other leaned forward, craning his long shadowy neck to better view the merchandise.

His head reeled, and he snorted, shaking his head. "She's only a child. You would stoop so low?" He disappeared from the light. The other followed him.

"She's a woman. We made sure. Please, take her as my gift of love."

"I don't want your gifts. And you have never loved me. I was only necessary for your kin's survival. Now take her back to where she belongs. She is missed."

The female raised her head, turned around the room, and took a few cautious steps as her head kept nodding, drawing her quick superficial breaths. "What's that? You ... you already found someone?" The woman sneered, a shrill growl of disgust. "She reeks. She's *tainted*."

"That is none of your concern. Now leave me be."

"How will she feel when she finds out about me? Shall I come for her when you're not around? You can't protect her all the time. Not from us, not from the trolls, not from the beast you stole her from! Do I truly have to go this far to make you understand?"

He stood over her now, cocking his head. His back popped and shook, his shoulders reeled and twisted. His arms swelled and elongated. "You'll be wise with your threats." His voice was even deeper now, inhuman even.

"Then give me what I want!" she pleaded. "I'll even take the girl back; I will leave you alone for the rest of my days."

"If I give you a child out of hate, will it live? Will it save you all from damnation?"

"Yes! And I'll be gone."

Rosanne tried to shut her eyes as the implication became clear. She didn't want to see this, but her mind wouldn't allow her to deviate from the path it had set on. What did this all mean? Gifts, extinction, loneliness, loss, what kind of story was this?

The voices, the shapes of these people, if that's what they were, didn't even seem remotely familiar to her. Why was she dreaming this? Why the surreal puppet show of two broken creatures?

The wood on the floor groaned under his weight, creaking with every step, every turn. The woman cried out and snarled, wrapping her arms around the larger shadow. There was no love, no moans of pleasure, no exchanged kisses, just the dissatisfied grunts of two shadows melting into one.

Why couldn't Rosanne avert her eyes?

ROSANNE GASPED AND SAT UP, kicking the sheets off her. She buckled over and emptied her guts over the bedside, where conveniently, a bucket awaited her nauseous awakening. She wiped the spittle from the corner of her mouth and held her forehead as it pounded. She cried and fell back, grabbing her skull as if it had split open. As fast as it had come, the throbbing pain ceased. Rosanne opened her eyes, her breathing hard. The shirt clung to her skin; rancid marsh-stench and black sweat soaked her very being. Her muscles ached when she sat, and generally ... *Holy hell*. She groaned and wanted to weep.

The door creaked when it opened, and Rosanne, in a moment of panic, drew the covers over her. She must have looked like a living corpse, for the man made a face upon seeing hers. For a moment, Rosanne didn't recognize him, but his gentle eyes calmed her immediately, and she recalled the walk through the woods and his words.

"Pale hues aside, you lived through the night. How do you feel?" He closed the door behind him. Rosanne wiped her forehead and let her muscles relax from the momentary panic. She survived the Nikor attack and all its nightmares and fever, the strange shadows, and the twisted sickness.

"Like I was ... dead." Her mind filled with Lyle's fear-stricken eyes, and her face contorted as she desperately pushed it aside.

He glanced into her puke bucket. "I imagine you did. Ah, it's cleared up considerably. Most of it is gone now."

Rosanne let out a short laugh. "I don't think I'll ever be comfortable about anyone evaluating the quality of my stomach contents."

He chuckled and took the bucket. "I have been lucky, too. Come now. I've prepared breakfast. Your clothes are still not ready yet. I apologize that you have to endure my tasteless garments for a little while longer."

"No, not at all. Thank you for saving my life from that ... thing."

He stopped by the door; a faint, considerate smile crossed his features. "Sometimes, I wonder if it had been mercy to leave you there instead."

Rosanne's breath caught in her throat. "Because of the other creatures out there?"

His face lit up. "Oh, you've seen them?"

She nodded. "Short creatures with long tails and good aim. And big trolls ... I think."

The slight turn of his head made her think he waited for more answers, but he merely nodded. "Then you have been very lucky." As if his answer had been satisfactory, he exited the room without another word, and Rosanne wondered if it meant that there were other things on this island she hadn't encountered yet, something worse than trolls and swamp men.

An image flashed in her mind, a room bathed in orange light and two shadows dancing, and the female voice promising blood lest she was given what she came for.

ON THE PORCH of the little log cabin in the woods, the morning sun made its warm appearance. Bundled in a blanket, Rosanne rocked the chair softly with her feet, gently pushing against the floorboards. The foggy weather dissipated with the coming heat, but the air remained chill and moist. She wrapped the blanket tighter around herself to ward off the cool air and the clammy clothes she still wore.

She observed her rescuer take down the laundry, a sight she never thought she would appreciate until she first spotted it.

The man stared at Rosanne's custom-fit pants, turned them around and cocked his head to the side as if it was the strangest thing in existence. "I don't believe I have ever encountered a woman wearing ... what do you call these again? My vocabulary is not vast, I'm afraid."

Rosanne suppressed a laugh. "Breeches. Not the traditional of men's wear, mind you. These are snug for me. Wool layered and almost water-resistant."

"Ah. That explains the odd cut, for surely no man would ever wear something like this. That would prove a tight fit in certain places." He flicked his eyebrows and gave an embarrassed cough. "When I got you out of the bog, I almost thought the Nikor's poison had made you change skin colour." He made another face, eyes as round as plates, then chuckled to himself. Rosanne shook her head, hiding her grin under the blanket.

"Here you go, Dragonheart." He came to the porch and handed over her folded clothes. Breeches, shirt, sweater, vest, and jacket had all been cleaned and looked vibrant, almost new. Certainly cleaner than when they left for Salis. The shoes stood next to the hearth, the insoles still soggy. She took the clothes and let them rest in her lap.

"Say, how do you know my name? You translate it, but still. I don't think I told you." Rosanne didn't remember much of anything for the past twenty-four hours, but her pride in her heritage made it so she never forgot when she gave someone her last name. The swamp, the monster, Lyle and Aros, then the mystery man somehow saving her from the Nikor; it was all a blur, and for a while, she believed she had imagined it all.

"That is easy." He sat down on the steps and took out a small pouch. "One of the men who were with you in the swamp called out to you. Your name and your words have different origins. I find that curious." He fished a wooden pipe out from an inner pocket of his jacket and added a few pinches of the pouch's contents into it. Rosanne resisted the urge to ask about the snuff, mostly out of her own need for tobacco in the events of soberness.

"People move around a lot. It's quite common these days. Pardon my curiosity, but where did you come from?"

The man flicked a small firesteel, which sparked and caught fire. He lit his pipe, sucking in a breath. "I speak many tongues, but I have never travelled from here. This island has forever been my home."

"You've lived here, on this island, your whole life? Family then?"

He shook his head. "Have none that I can remember. But tell me. I've seen the ships in the bay, and then I saw that beautiful galleon flying above the mountains. Do they all fly?"

Rosanne laughed. "No, not all fly. But it is common after the Queen's Colonies created anti-gravity technology."

He sucked another breath, blowing out rings, which stretched and grew bigger, and then blew another smoky trail through those. "Sounds exciting. I could do with a history lesson."

Rosanne sat up, folding her hands in her lap. She noticed a sparrow twittering on the grass and how it took flight almost as fast as it had landed. "Some monarch sixty years ago decided to unite the central lands under one banner and one constitutional democracy, but it changed everything. Trade opened in every major city, unifying but at the same time destroying the cultural identity of many locals. People change cities like they change clothes, and names are no longer associated with nationality. We lost our roots in the process and our names. And many looked for better lives elsewhere when the economy collapsed." She stared at the pipe.

He nodded, seeming fascinated yet perplexed at her tales as if it was a world of which he could only dream. "Just in the last sixty years?"

Rosanne nodded.

He blew out an incredulous breath. "Your world is so different from mine. Admittedly, I didn't understand half of the things you said. Democracy, nationality ... all are so foreign to me. But this major change that happened in the world made people leave their ancestral lands and seek out good fortune?" He motioned with the pipe, and Rosanne's eyes followed it.

"My family moved around a lot and settled in Noval, but my Novalian is rusty. Is that tobacco?"

He smiled. "Would you like some?"

"Yes, please," she whispered and stretched out as he handed over the pipe. She took a long deep breath and let the sweet fumes fill her lungs and calm her more than anything had been able to for many days. For a moment, her mind was quiet. When she was done, she handed it back. "That was wonderful. Made it yourself?"

He nodded, showing her the pouch. "Ground weedlefair leaves. Only grows in a small cove over the mountains." He took a whiff and blew a set of smoky rings.

"I didn't ask, but what is your name?"

Raising his hands, he motioned to everything and nothing. "I have no name. The locals have nicknames aplenty for me, but I never had a name"

"Locals? There are other people here?"

"'People' would be a stretch as they possess the linguistic communication abilities of a toddler. For the most part, they only growl and curse."

"Last time I checked, I was troll food."

"Ah yes. Those things." He spat on the grass in contempt. "They discriminate little between their meals. Not to worry. They will not come to this side of the island."

"So, what do I call you since you so adamantly insist you have no name?"

"What would you like to call me?"

"That's not fair."

"I suppose it isn't, but I have no name. The creatures call me The Dweller or Forest Devil."

"Forest Devil? You seem anything but a devil."

"I must be a handsome devil then." He gave her his sliest of smirks which had Rosanne burst with laughter. The joyous strain had Rosanne grimace as her muscles shot waves of pain with every movement, and she leaned back in the chair to rest.

"Yerrik," he said.

"What?"

"You can call me Yerrik." The man emptied the pipe's contents on the side of the steps, cleaning it thoroughly. His facial expressions were open and relaxed, and even the slightest movement of the forest critters in the grass had his smile present.

Rosanne cast him a furtive glance, noticing how his trimmed beard framed his sun-tanned square features. The first times she had seen him, he resembled Antony, but they looked nothing alike up close. There was a slight slant to his eyes, with gold-rimmed pupils droning out the green. His hair was a darker brown and unruly, so far from the familiar look and feel of Antony's trimmed black cut. The man wasn't overly tall or muscular, and the possibility of him dragging Rosanne clean out of the bog now seemed impossible. He must have done something else to pry her from Nikor's grasp, but again, with the ever-stacking questions, she kept her silence in reservation for what mattered the most.

"Did you by any chance see what happened to the people I was with? You haven't mentioned them."

He looked at her for a moment, then cast his eyes back to the sparrows in the grass. "I was distracted with your recovery and didn't think I could bring you the news when you were still so out of it. I realize it was selfish of me to wait this long. My apologies." He bowed his head to her. "I did manage to get both you and that man out of the marshes from Nikor's grasp. However, I could only take care of one of you. I arranged for someone to care for the older gentleman, but I do not know if he survived."

Rosanne's eyes teared up, and she felt like something grasped around her throat. "Mr. Lyle's ... alive?" She was sure she had seen the monster drown Lyle. She could still feel his grasp on her arm, almost crushing as he desperately clung on for his life. She touched the bruise. No, she hadn't imagined anything. Nikor had dragged Lyle under. How did this man get both him and Rosanne out then?

"I don't really know. I merely left him in someone else's care."

"And ... and the second man?"

"Miss Dragonheart, he almost killed you. He was about to shoot you as he failed at killing Nikor. I don't know where he went." In the heat of the moment, when Nikor had both Lyle and Rosanne dragged under the surface of the marshes, Rosanne's eyes were filled with the sour waters, stinging and blinding her. She remembered calling out to Aros to shoot the beast, and she was positive he had fired multiple times. She considered the situation in Aros' shoes, one rifle, too few bullets, a monster strong enough to drag two people into the bog. He had no way of getting them both out of there, so in his eyes, it might have been the only option considered morally right; the only time Aros had attempted to kill her had been for the right reasons.

"It would have been mercy, and that's probably the only time I will consider him a decent human being. That fucking bastard's been a pebble in my shoe even before we landed here."

He hesitated. "Would you like to find him?"

Now it was Rosanne's turn to spit over the railing. "He can burn on a pyre as troll food for all I care. It's his fault we're here in the first place. I need to see Mr. Lyle. I need to know if he's alive."

"Pardon, miss, but you are in no condition to move. The poison turned your muscles into lyefish. You will need a few days to recover, at least."

Despite his warnings, Rosanne knew she had no time to rest. Their time on this island was limited, and she had a crew to retrieve and a ship to fly, perhaps not in that exact order, but she had to do something. Staring at her trembling hands, the weight of her arms alone where they simply hung in the air above her thighs, screamed even when not in use. She wished to curl up in fetal position and sleep the day away, but she couldn't afford that luxury.

Yerrik caught her worried stare and stood.

"How about I draw you another bath to ease the pain, and you can tell me your story after that. Everything will be alright." Rosanne didn't have the strength to reply. Would everything truly be alright? His words bore such conviction that Rosanne almost believed them, yet this dark undertone concealed by the island's peaceful exterior hid terrible creatures.

Captain Drackenheart had to get her crew and ship far away before the island swallowed them all.

CHAPTER 22

DEAL WITH THE DEVIL

D alia paced in front of the entrance to what would be the closest equivalent the hulder had to an infirmary.

"Is he going to make it?" she asked, nodding towards a makeshift stretcher.

"He's a tough geezer." And yet Farand didn't sound so sure.

"Look at the claw marks on his legs. What could have done this?" Ida studied the deep putrid gashes, and the smell made Dalia wrinkle her nose.

Two hulder crushed and mixed herbs with spices, then applied them to the wounds. Lyle heaved and reached out, throwing his head back. One of the women held him as the others applied the mixture and bound the injuries with leaves and hemp.

The master gunner's pained screams echoed in the halls. Dalia couldn't understand how any of this happened. Lyle had left with the captain and Norman, but now he was here, sick and possibly dying, with Norman having found his way here by chance. Captain Rosanne Drackenheart was nowhere to be found.

The hulder Queen had left the ship with a procession of sentries. Hours later, Nelson, Farand, and Dalia had been led to this room where they had been met with Lyle's fervent muttering, the hulder begging them to assist. The hulder Queen herself and Ida were gone.

The hulder exchanged words, pointing at the wounds and shaking their heads at the fever ravaging his insides. Lyle was as ashen as the hulder who treated him. Dalia chewed on the nail of her thumb, barely able to catch the little that remained of it.

One of the hulder looked to Dalia, shaking her head. "Nikor," one of them said grimly.

Dalia didn't know what that meant, but it was killing Lyle.

He flailed his arms, and the hulder rushed to restrain him. "The Captain! It took her," he cried out. Dalia was next to him, grasping his cold hand.

"Who took her, Lyle?"

He coughed and drew his breath. "It. The creature."

"The one that did this to you?"

"No. A different one ... Intelligent ... Inhuman one moment, human the next. It took her into the woods." Dalia didn't know what to make of his words. The hulder's expressions were puzzling and distressed, and the lack of communication skills between her and them frustrated Dalia even more.

"The mural!" she cried out, drawing Farand and Nelson's attention.

"What mural?" Farand demanded.

"The hulder have a mural, or a map, painted on a wall somewhere in this cave, and it showed the different creatures living on this island." Dalia rushed out of the room, leaving worried calls of the hulder behind her.

Nelson and Farand followed Dalia to the main hall, almost losing her as she ducked into the cave system. The two sentries guarding the chambers of bones held out their hands in surprise, stopping their advance. Dalia smacked her hand against the wall, then to her eyes. The sentries stared at each other in confusion.

"In there, you oafs! I need to see the mural!" She pointed at the door. After several moments of repeated gestures, they were let inside under supervision.

Dalia threw herself to the walls in the innermost chamber in search of anything matching what Lyle mentioned. She turned to the sentry, uttering one word she might understand.

"Nikor?" She pointed to the wall. The sentry's face contorted and cast her eyes down. "Where is it?" Dalia prompted. The sentry gazed hard at the mural, then pointed to a swamp on the floor south of the mountains surrounding a house. A pair of black eyes under a tuft of grass peeked out ominously.

"This place truly has a gift for surprise." Farand frowned and studied the mural.

"Mr. Lyle said another monster took the captain into the woods. What's the closest monster around this area?" Dalia searched around the map. Farand and Nelson followed her lead.

"There," Nelson tapped the house with the creature outside. "He said it could look human, right?"

The sentry shrieked and took a few steps back, making Nelson jump out of his skin.

"What is this?" Dalia asked, even when she knew the hulder didn't speak a word of English. The female shook her head and sneered before making a hasty exit. A cold sense of dread rushed through Dalia's insides, making her stomach flip. "Even the hulder are afraid of it. Have you seen it?"

Farand shook his head. "If this is a map over the island, we wouldn't have encountered it. The captain and Mr. Lyle must have cut through the marshes to get to the grassland where we were supposed to meet." Farand studied the mural, taking in the hill trolls, Nikor, and this central creature that terrified an army of well-equipped warriors. "We're in much deeper shit than what I thought we were."

"What's the plan then, sir?"

Checking the hallway for anyone who might listen in, he turned to the watch captain. "Olivier is outside and will cause a distraction to draw the hulder away from the tunnels. Ida, Gavin, and Higgs will fix the engine while we seal off the entrances with the cannons when we get aboard. We hope that it will buy us enough time to get everyone out of here."

Nelson's eyes nearly popped out of his skull. "What about Mr. Lyle? He's in no fighting condition."

"We leave no man behind. If he's dying anywhere, it's aboard the *Queen*. We have until tomorrow to figure everything out. Notify the rest, get familiar with the caves, and, if possible, don't get caught."

"Yes, sir."

THE SENTRIES RETURNED with a small party of equally terrifying hulder warriors who looked like they could liberate limbs from their respective body parts. Dalia, Farand, and Nelson were quickly escorted back to their sleeping chambers, telling them all too clear that something had changed since Lyle's arrival. What were those painted creatures on the floor that sent terror through a tribe of warriors capable of pacifying their enemies with song alone? The thought of Ida meeting any number of the creatures depicted in the mural made the hairs on Nelson's neck stand. He hadn't considered that the hulder Queen could have lied simply to appease his anxiety. Now that Nelson knew she could read their minds, how much of the plan had been exposed? Did the hulder around them understand their words? Was there a shared consciousness of this tribe, or was the hulder Queen's mind tricks making him paranoid and distrusting? Nelson looked to Farand and dreaded the moment where he had to tell the terrifying lieutenant that he possibly had ruined them all.

YERRIK HELD the door open as he peeked inside the bedroom, greeting Rosanne with a smile. "Sleep well?" he asked.

"I ... is it morning already?"

An early afternoon sun shone through the window, and only then did she notice how unbearably hot the room had become. A strange sensation she couldn't place haunted her. She couldn't remember going to bed. They were smoking on the porch, and then ... shaking her head, Rosanne dug deep for the memories of that morning, but the scene following that conversation turned hazy and dark, drowned by the subtle intrusion of fiddle music. It dug into her skull, and she cried out in pain.

"Rosanne? What's wrong?"

As soon as the icepick cluster headache had passed, nausea followed. Did Nikor's poison remain in her system? She held her mouth and resisted the involuntary reaction.

"Feels like someone stuffed my head with cotton. Can I please have some water?" she uttered through her hands, shaking violently as she suppressed another painful spasm.

Yerrik turned in the door, his footsteps loud as he exited the cabin. She gasped for breath, the bruise on her forehead throbbing. Was it even possible to feel this terrible two days in a row? Rosanne grabbed the bucket before another unfortunate accident befell the bedsheets.

Yerrik came through the door with a cup and sat on the bedside, then carefully helped her drink as her hands trembled too much to be of any use.

"This bloody better be the last of the poison. I'll be damned if I have to wake up another morning feeling this shitty." Rosanne caught her words, and her face flushed red. Yerrik chuckled at the amusing turn of her manners, or lack thereof.

"You speak your mind, Dragonheart."

She returned his smile wryly. She had never been conscious of her words before, so why now?

"I believe my manners rest at the bottom of the bog." She arched an eyebrow and finished the cup.

"If so, I should return there and get it back for you."

"Please don't. Wouldn't want another soul to get eaten."

"My dear Dragonheart. I am fully capable of defending myself from whatever this island has to offer, monsters or damsels in distress."

"Rescued many damsels, I take it?"

"Not out of habit, no. I just got lucky." He winked a green eye, and the unfamiliar heat returned to her face. She looked away, blowing a short burst of breath.

"Come now. Let's eat." Only when Yerrik was out the door could Rosanne feel her face. A silly grin replaced her embarrassment.

"The fuck is wrong with me?" Rosanne drew up her legs and buried her face. She hadn't blushed in front of a man since her coming-of-age ball at fourteen. She had as much difficulty breathing now as back then, donning a tight corset, a choker, and meters of ridiculous frills. Fiddle music played in her mind, slow and joyful, like the quartet at the ball. Champagne glasses clinked. She bit her thumb and tasted the white silk of the gloves.

Her father's trim mustache and kempt beard stood out to her in the crowd of clean-shaven faces and elaborate prim costumes. "Honey, if your mother catches you biting, she'll renounce your riding lessons." Rosanne looked up to her father's crinkling eyes. He raised his glass to the crowd and, in a clear, firm voice, said, "To my little girl, Rosanne. Happy birthday, sweetie."

"To Drackenheart," the crowd cheered. .

———————

THE WET LINENS swayed as Rosanne shook them with a distinct "crack." She fixed them in place with wooden pincers, and no matter how the wind tugged at the fabric, it couldn't steal it. She brushed her hand over the once sweat-filled bedsheets, taking care of the unsightly creases.

"You should be resting." Yerrik shook his head, standing next to her, untangling her fancy vest still wet from the wash. She snorted.

"I feel much better. It's not like I can let you do everything when you endangered yourself to save me."

"I couldn't stop you even if I was a magician." The remark carried a truth that made Rosanne laugh. She stopped.

"Is something wrong?" He cocked his head to the side. His green eyes appeared almost blue in the sunlight, and she stared into them, caught in a daze. She dismissed his question with a wave, straightening the sheet.

"What else is there on this island?"

"What are you referring to?"

"Besides the swamp thing, Nikor, I mean."

Pursing his lips, he thought for a moment. "Well, there are the hill trolls, as you've told me you met. Sprites live in this forest right here. I can't say much else for other creatures. I tend not to stray too far."

"Are the sprites dangerous?"

"Not at all. Harmless little creatures of light. But don't follow one if it wants you to. They might be small, but their mischief outweighs their size."

Rosanne swallowed and bit her lip. "No flying marine creatures?"

"Your imagination must be running wild."

"It sounds ludicrous, but on my way here, we encountered some strange creatures living in the fog. They came out at night in ribbons of lights, then devoured each other."

"This I must see. You are a captain of a sky-vessel, no? Would you mind bringing me along to see these ... flying fish?" He took his pipe, creating wave-like motions in the air with it.

Rosanne snorted good-naturedly. "You should have seen the largest one. It glowed a dark deep red and devoured the smaller lights it came across. It scuffed against our mainmast too. It was huge!" Her hands stretched up and to the sides. She caught his contented gaze and stopped. Again, a strange sensation filled her insides, crawling from the pit in her stomach, squeezing her heart and her lungs. "Of course, we wouldn't be here at all if it were for that storm. You haven't by the slimmest chance seen a flying boat somewhere, have you?"

He arched an eyebrow. "Can't say that I have, but the island is big. Would you be able to find it if you looked?"

"We have our ways. The masts needed to be replaced, so a forest with tall, straight trees would be their first stop in my absence. Raw spruce works as a patch job, but pine is preferred as they grow taller."

"Tall, straight trees, you say? I don't know of any such trees here."

Her hand ceased working the creases, resting on the fabric. "I know they're out there somewhere." She looked to the blue sky. "My crew and my ship, and I'll find them."

He nodded, pinched his eyes to slits and bobbed his head. "... after you have recovered enough not to turn green when standing up?" He pointed at her, and she felt the sweat on her face. Then she buckled over and retched the little food she had eaten.

"Oh god. Please tell me I didn't hit the linen."

"The linen survived your green-faced faucet." He stroked her back. Rosanne spent a moment regaining herself.

"You're wearing your expression again," he said.

"My what?"

"That face. What's wrong?"

She shook her head. "I'm having the strangest sensation of *déjà vu*. That's all." She dismissed his comforting hand and stood.

"Deiza what?"

"Déjà vu. The feeling that you have lived through this moment before."

"Seems like every time I draw breath," he jested.

"Life is but a clockwork of repetitions." She laughed. "But some are so identical it overlaps with your past."

FARAND MARCHED behind Nelson as they descended deeper into the depths of the volcano. Led by two friendly-faced hulder, they were guided through numerous halls, bridges, and rocky paths.

"I don't want to know," Nelson said, shimmying against the wall along a thin ledge. A rope bridge awaited them ahead on a wider shelf, and the two women kept perfect balance from start to finish. Farand wobbled, his considerable bulk unbalancing him with each step. Beneath them waited a deep chasm engulfed in darkness. Torchlight illuminated both sides of the bridge, but Nelson was ill-adept to the meagre light.

After the previous night's conversation with the hulder Queen, Nelson remained trapped in a state of enervated discordert. He didn't know whether the hulder Queen had told her subjects, her 'children,' of his ruse and powerlessness. If she had, the women leading them didn't show any indication of mauling Nelson and Farand until they had no breath left to take.

"There must be a reason why only we were chosen," Farand said, not bothering to whisper as the women chatted freely among themselves, oblivious to Nelson's and Farand's concerns.

Nelson shook his head. "That woman, she who came out of the throne, she knows I'm a scam."

Farand arched his eyebrows. "You only tell me this now?"

"I am observing the situation. The other hulder don't appear to know that anything is amiss."

"Is this related to Ida's disappearance?"

Nelson nodded. "The hulder Queen told me she needed Ida and you as insurance and that if I didn't comply, she would tell the rest of the crew about my blackmail."

Farand's eyebrows nearly touched as he scratched his growing beard. "Who could have told her?" The ensuing silence as they trudged through the dark tunnels unnerved Farand.

"I did," Nelson said at length.

"What do you mean?"

He tapped his forehead. "I felt her in there, inside my skull, poking around. By far the most terrifying feeling I've ever experienced. I couldn't stop her from looking at my memories, and no doubt she's searched the others to find leverage. She could tell me things only the captain and I discussed! I don't even know if she's seen through our plan or not." Nelson wiped the sweat off his brow. His heart a thumping pain in his chest at Farand's deafening silence.

"Have I led us all into ruin?"

The large man brooded through the echoes of their footfalls and the chatter of the two hulder up ahead.

"I'm not so sure they know," Farand said, nodding to the women. Nelson followed his gaze. "Look how relaxed they seem. If they knew, wouldn't we all be under supervision?"

Nelson let his shoulders fall. "You're right. I haven't noticed any changes to their behaviour or their treatment of us. Maybe the hulder Queen believes the leverage I have over you is enough for her to keep me in check."

"She's a terrifying foe."

"You believe me?"

Farand bobbed his head. "I'll take your word for it. We've seen stranger things."

They descended on a pathway to a jagged dome-shaped cave with stalactites and glowing blue crystals clustered about the walls. The woman in the lead put her torch on the ground, stomping out the flames with ease. Nelson tripped on a rock and tumbled forward but caught himself.

"Do you feel that?" Nelson turned to Farand with wide eyes. Farand pushed his feet from the ground, remarkably light in his movements.

"Anti-gravity stones," he concluded. "They are even more concentrated than on the rock belt."

"Higgs would have a field day."

"Suppose this is the source for our navigational issues. And in such quantities ..." Farand shook his head and skipped down the stone steps. A small party of women already occupied the room, standing around a cluster of crystals discussing matters Nelson could only assume had something to do with their arrival. They waved to the guides, excited as they came over. Nelson and Farand put some distance between them, observing the situation with alarming reservation. One of the hulder handed Farand a pickaxe and a hammer, stolen from the ship no doubt. Pointing at a cluster of crystals jutting from the cave wall, she motioned, swinging her arms down, a look of optimism in her eager black eyes.

Farand glanced at Nelson, who was as perplexed as he.

"I honestly have no clue why they can't do this themselves."

Farand complied and gave the pickaxe a swing, planting it firmly at the base of a crystal thick as a grown man's fist. "It's the low gravity," Farand said. The pickaxe gave a reassuring clink and buried itself into the crystal.

The tool remained stuck. "Blasted thing is tough as a diamond." Farand grunted as he planted his feet on the ground and heaved with all his might. The crystal gave a pathetic shatter, broke from the base, and floated away. Farand flew back, bouncing on his rump. The women cheered, picking up the crystal and studying it with increased chatter.

"Are you alright, sir?" Nelson looked at the man. He waved a hand and stood.

"That took everything I had." His eyes were wide with surprise. The hulder amassed around the crystals, eagerly pointing for Farand to break a few more. He dusted his pants and readied for another round of break-a-war.

"Rosanne. Come. I want to show you something." Yerrik shook her by the shoulder, urging her to follow him outside. Torchlight lit the courtyard in the night gloom. Beneath the tallest oak stood a pyre packed with logs and sawdust, and a gruff-looking man dangled from a rope slung over a thick branch. Rosanne's insides somersaulted.

Bound and gagged, the man struggled against the bindings, kicking with his legs. His eyes were wide and pleading, glistening in the torchlight.

"Captain Bernhart?" Rosanne couldn't believe her eyes. The pirate captain had run like a coward from the marshes, and she hadn't seen him since, not that she wanted to. "Do I want to know?" she turned to Yerrik, whose grim expression remained malevolent. His grip remained firm on a torch, but Rosanne could tell it was not for luminous purposes.

"He left you and that man for dead, Rosanne. He came for your ship."

She shook her head, blowing a raspberry at the ludicrous idea. "That's absurd. He couldn't have pulled that off even if he had a crew."

Yerrik's eyes cast to the ground, then closed them. He took a deep breath, laying eyes once more on the squirming captain. "His crew is still alive. Scattered in the forest, but still very much a threat. I've seen him collaborate with them."

Aros was a pathological liar and would do anything to stay alive for just one more day. He must have rallied his men after he fled from the marshes, thinking the *Red Queen* was easy pickings with Rosanne out of the picture.

"What are you proposing by ..." she motioned a hand to the pyre, scared to confirm its obvious implications. Yerrik's brows furred, and his eyes turned steel blue. Aros' muffled scream was barely audible. He swung on the rope; the bindings were tight around his torso.

Yerrik handed over the plasma rifle, Lyle's choice of weapon in any fight. This weapon had taken so many lives of late. It had even been intended for her. Rosanne cocked the loading mechanism back, seeing the chamber light up with a blue charge in its chamber. She locked the mechanism in place, keeping the barrel down. "Even with this, he couldn't take my ship. Me being dead or alive wouldn't make a difference."

"He knows where your ship is. He confessed so."

Rosanne's blood ran cold. Had the pirates already discovered its location? Then why was Aros here? Unless he needed her to pilot. Then what of the crew? What of Duplànte and the others?

Aros frantically shook his head.

"Where is my ship, Aros?" Rosanne aimed the muzzle at the pirate captain, swinging frantically on the rope. He shook his head so hard tears flew from him.

"In the wetlands, no?" she said. "How the hell did your men get all the way over there? Was it Norman? The kid in the longboat? Answer me, dammit!"

Aros spat out the gag. "I swear by the broken keel of my ship. I do not know!"

Rosanne whipped the muzzle aim from his head and fired off a shot. The bullet hit him in his right thigh, making the man scream.

"Yes, yes! The wetlands! It's there ... fuck that hurts, lady!"

Lowering the rifle, Rosanne shook her head. "The ship isn't there, Aros." She turned to Yerrik. "He doesn't know."

"If it's a lie, this will make him talk." Yerrik grabbed a torch and held it to the dry wood. Aros kicked and flailed, shaking his head frantically. "Now then? Anything you would like to share?"

"Yes! By God, yes!"

"Last chance, Aros. Where is my goddamn ship?" Rosanne pressed.

"I don't know where it is. The hulder took it with them into the forest. They killed the rest of your crew. They're all dead."

She spent a moment processing his words and snorted. "As if

I'll believe that. One more lie from you, and I'll put a bullet in your other leg."

"It's true! Tall, lanky, and terrifying women sang to your crew and slit their throats when they couldn't resist. It was like they were under a spell. They couldn't do anything! I beg of you; it is the truth!"

Rosanne lowered the rifle. "They can't be dead. Nothing could ever ..." she muttered to herself.

Yerrik laid a hand on her shoulder. "Rosanne, I'm sorry."

"They're not dead!" Wrenching herself from the touch, she looked to the pirate captain. "Mr. Duplànte, a dark-skinned man big as a mountain, what happened to him?"

Sweat beaded on his pallid skin. Blood oozed from the leg wound onto the dry logs. "He fought against the song, but they overwhelmed him. It took a while, but they got him too."

"What did they do with the bodies?"

More tears accompanied his crestfallen face. "They just left them all there for the wolves and crows ... I couldn't stay any longer, or they would have gotten me too." His words choked through quivering lips.

Rosanne's hands felt numb. His words were a noose around her neck. "Why did you survive, Aros? What the fuck did you do to survive that!? You're nothing compared to my crew, so why did you live and not my crew?" she screamed, her face contorted into disbelief and rage.

"I don't know!" he wailed. "I truly don't know ... Just please, don't kill me."

Rosanne grabbed Yerrik's torch. "Burn in hell, you bastard." She tossed it to the pyre. The wood caught fire immediately, hissing and crackling as the orange flames spread and consumed the dry wood. Aros shouted his pleas, kicking with his legs to swing away from the growing flames.

Smoke rose in a thickening funnel, engulfing the man in a blanket of putrid and suffocating toxins. Squeezing his eyes shut for the smoke and heat did nothing to stop the rising temperatures blistering his skin.

Inhaling smoke as he cried for mercy, Rosanne and Yerrik merely stood there, observing with extreme reservation. Rosanne's eyes were blank and unblinking. She didn't see anything happening before her. Her head lowered, and she fell on her knees and sat in silence as Aros' screams filled the night.

CHAPTER 23

IN BETWEEN ALL THE MESS

"Well done, sir." Nelson applauded Farand and the bag full of glowing crystals they brought from the mines.

"Don't push it, Mr. Blackwood." The lieutenant's white tunic had seen cleaner days, with rolled-up sleeves covered in sweat and soot.

"My apologies. I really had no intention of things lasting this long."

"Yet here we are, carrying moon crystals for fabled shamanic creatures."

"Is that what they are? It reminds me of anti-grav minerals since they float, but I always thought they were extracted from rocks." Farand kept his discontent along with his silence as his muscles ached from the gruelling work. Emerging into the grand hall, the hulder took the bag with crystals and made their way towards the ship.

"Suppose those are for decorative purposes?" Nelson suggested.

"As long as people don't come out of them, I couldn't care less what they do. I've had enough mumbo-jumbo for the rest of my days."

At supper, Nelson and Farand rejoined the others. Creedy,

Gavin, Dalia, and a few others were covered in volcanic ash and grime, sweat-stained with dark rings around their eyes.

"Have you been working all day?" Nelson eyed them up and down.

Dalia shot Nelson a tired eye as she banged her head on the table beside the bowl of stew. "Those cow-tailed sirens have miles of tunnels. All sorts of mineral and metal deposits are in this mountain, and the hulder wanted it *all*." She motioned with her arms wide and rested her head on the table. Creedy deftly swiped Dalia's bread when she wasn't looking, munching it down.

"Did you just nick my bread? Bloody bastard, give it here!" She swatted at Creedy, who dodged her hands with ease and stuffed his face with the bread. "You arse... I'll dump Hammond's pickle juice on you in your sleep," she cursed with a hiss.

Nelson slid over his bread. "Have mine. I've worked the least of all of you."

"Bless you, Nelson. Oh? Hold up. There's Norman and Ida." She nodded to the duo emerging from the queue. Ida was a right mess alongside Norman, her blond hair uncared for, and soot spots dotting her pallid complexion.

"They give you mine work as well?" Dalia prompted.

Ida could barely nod, plopping down to her seat.

"After last night, I was placed in a different room. I don't think whatever it was the hulder Queen had planned worked, but they did send me to work the mines like you."

"What exactly did she do?" Gavin prodded.

Ida's morose expression remained fixed on the food.

"I can't really say. It was bizarre. We went to this cabin in the woods. Someone was living there, but it was like ..." she looked up, gesticulating with a grabbing motion, something intangible. "They said he was the Forest Devil, but I couldn't tell what he was. I think it was a man, but I couldn't make out his face even when I looked at him up close."

Nelson's eyes searched the food, not for its chunky contents, but for that thread of information about what Ida said which bothered him.

"The Forest Devil," he whispered. Judging from her words, her ignorance might have kept her safe from the hulder Queen's plan. A man living in a cabin in the woods and Ida dolled up and presented as a gift to appease him. Nelson kept his silence, pocketing that piece of information as not to alarm anyone. Also, she hadn't mentioned seeing Captain Drackenheart there. What did all of this mean? Nelson tore off a piece of the bread and paused and stared at it, for he was sure he had given his to Dalia. Sure enough, she was eating it with satisfaction. Nelson looked around the table, finding Gavin's head turned away and fingers drumming the table, but no bread by his untouched bowl. Nelson didn't know whether to feel flattered or shocked.

"All the better, you're back in our care then. Ain't gonna let anything happen to you, hun." Dalia ruffled Ida's hair. The watch captain looked to Farand, leaning in closer and whispered: "When are we gonna do it?"

"Anytime soon. Hopefully, before more of us disappear." Dalia nodded, returning to a now half-empty bowl that she hadn't touched yet.

"Creedy!"

YERRIK OPENED THE CREAKY DOOR, a bright smile accompanying crinkling eyes. "Good morni—"

Rosanne sat up in alarm, breathing hard. "It's morning again!"

Yerrik shot her a questioning look.

"What did we do to Aros?" Her nightgown was drenched in sweat, her eyes wide and frantic, searching Yerrik's puzzled expression.

"Who's Aros?"

Rosanne threw the covers aside and ran barefoot to the porch.

The heavy door slammed against the wall, and Rosanne scanned the clearing, breathless and dizzy. No pyre had been erected or burnt, and no charred, carbonized corpse of a former Captain Bernhart hung from the oak. She sat on the stairs, grabbing her forehead. The courtyard was moist from morning dew, the grass tall and untouched.

"Where is the pyre?" She turned wild eyes to Yerrik. "Where's the ..." Her hand lingered in the air towards the oak. "Body?"

Yerrik placed a hand on her shoulder. "You are exhausted, love. You've been having nightmares again."

Shaking her head, her eyes were hard and unforgiving as she felt the betrayal of her memories. "Am I losing my mind?"

He gave her a sympathetic head tilt and stroked the hair from her shoulders. "I had nightmares for months after Nikor poisoned me. I assure you, this is normal."

"You're saying this will pass? That these fucked nightmares will eventually fade, and I won't feel like I've lost my sanity?"

He nodded. Rosanne buried her face in her hands, digging her nails into her skin as she resisted the urge to claw her face off. Was her mind truly this twisted to wish such a horrible death upon her enemy?

"What did you dream?"

"It ... it doesn't matter. Something horrible. *I* was horrible." She sniffed and wiped her tear-stained eyes.

"How about we take a walk today? Get you some fresh air, and perhaps new sights will help you clear your mind?" Standing, Yerrik stretched out a hand. Rosanne shielded her eyes from the rising sun and saw his smile was genuine. She accepted his offer, her heart skipping a beat as the burden suddenly became lighter.

ON A NEARBY HILLTOP, Yerrik and Rosanne sat on a bare spot of rocks surveying the low birch forest. The grass thatch roof of the cabin blended with the trees, making the building nearly invis-

ible in the ocean of leaves. Behind the hill stood towering mountains, once live volcanoes now covered in grass and snow-crested
tops. The forest morphed to a prairie rolling over the plateau and
disappearing into the horizon to the west.

"It's beautiful out here," Rosanne said, breathing in the warm
breeze blowing in from the south.

"This is a great spot for game. Look over there." At the base of
the hill, a pair of thick antlers protruded from the brush. Rosanne
had to squint to make out the elk grazing in the bushes. Two
calves followed her. Their front knees bent to reach the green
foliage. Yerrik directed his hand towards the horizon. "The ocean
lies beyond that grassland. It doesn't seem far, but it's more than a
day's travel to get there."

A deep gurgle called from above where a pair of ravens circled
the hills. Their wide wingspan gave them plenty of drift to stay
afloat with minimal effort. "They must have caught the scent of a
carcass," Rosanne said.

Yerrik nodded. "Ravens are the skirt of death. They follow it
intimately and leave nothing but bones."

Rosanne chuckled. "Carrions, on the other hand, consume
skin, intestines, sinews, and bones. Nothing is left when they're
done."

"Now you're being pessimistic." He laughed, drawing a smile
from Rosanne.

Yerrik rubbed his index finger with his thumb, pausing for a
moment. "Would the pessimist in you deem it possible to stay?"
he began. "If you can't find your ship, I mean. Or would you stay
if you had a choice?"

Rosanne shrugged. "I don't know if I could. My crew is still
out there, and I don't care much for your neighbours." She gathered her skirts and pressed the scarf tight to her chest despite the
heat. How long had it been since they landed on this island? "But I
already think it's too late to save whatever life I had built for myself.
I don't want to give up, though. I've come too far, fought too

many pretentious bastards. Fought far too many pirates. But I'm forced to face reality as it is, and me and my crew's future is looking rather bleak. Yet I must try. I must fight until I can't anymore."

"Do you mean that pirate who tried to kill you?"

Rosanne chuckled. "He's the least threat of them all. A small thorn in my side, but it stings nonetheless."

Yerrik drummed his hands, pursing his lips. "It's clear to me that this Aros person is bringing you a great deal of distress. You have nightmares about him trying to take your ship, much like he attempted in the past. We can do something about it."

"It wasn't him that did something to me. I dreamed I burned him, right there in the courtyard."

"Didn't you also say he tried to kill you?" Yerrik countered.

"I guess. I can't remember. Everything is muddled. It's like I can't trust my thoughts anymore. These nightmares take everything I know and turn it into lies and doubts." Rosanne rubbed her temples and gave a wry smile.

"Perhaps Nikor's poison had a stronger hold on you than we thought. It will fade with time, but you need to accept it as part of your life for now. What we can do is make sure the pirate captain never reaches you again."

"Those pesky pirates, eh?" Rosanne shook her head. Yerrik stroked his beard and let out a long, purposeful "hmm."

"You're not thinking we hunt him down, are you? Aros is as harmless as a kitten."

Yerrik rose a finger. "Yes, but a kitten has claws."

Rosanne swept her arms out to the sides, taking the whole landscape in her embrace. "Say we find him somewhere on this extremely vast land. Then what?"

His face lit up. "The hulder will benefit from the pirate captain. We could make a peace treaty by using him." Rubbing his hands together, he grinned.

She arched her eyebrows. "And what's stopping you from doing the same to me?"

"My dear Dragonheart, what those women need are men, not more women."

"That's... Is *that* what you meant? You would subject your kind to such a fate?"

"I do not count honourless scoundrels as part of my 'kind.' A thief will always be a thief, a pirate a pirate."

Without the words to dispute his logic, Rosanne snorted a laugh. Yerrik's eyes found hers again, and Rosanne's heart clenched in her chest.

"We find Captain Bernhart and give him a beating for stranding you on this island. Then we deliver him to the right creatures. Peace and equilibrium established."

"Spoken like a true trader."

"These women can be dealt with if we do things right. It's how I've survived for so long. I have something they need, and they leave me alone. Living here is perfectly feasible as long as we have the right bargaining chips. What do you say, Captain Rosanne Drackenheart? Would you like to join me on a little pirate hunt?"

She nodded to his eager smile.

"For better or for worse, I still need to teach that bastard a thing or two about clubbing me twice and leaving me for dead. And I have a ship to find."

CHAPTER 24

MY CURSE IS YOU

A harsh whisper came from outside Rosanne's bedroom window.

"Psst! Lady!"

She rubbed her eyes, yawning the sleep away. A tuft of matte brown hair jutted from the windowsill, barely concealed by the shutters. Rosanne opened one of them, staring down at a pair of distressed blue eyes.

"What are you doing here?" Her voice was like acid, but Captain Bernhart's iron will wasn't corroded by her displeasure. The pirate captain clung to the sill with precarious balance on an expired ladder with more than a few rungs missing.

"You got to get out of there. That thing will come back soon. It's safe to leave. I got you covered."

She snorted. "What the hell are you talking about? The swamp monster is far off and won't leave the marshes."

"Not *that* monster!" His outburst unbalanced the ladder, making him wobble, catch his breath, and look around for anyone who might have heard him. He leaned closer, lowering his voice. "I'm talking about that thing that lives in this cabin." His eyes darted around again, and he checked if the rifle at his back was still secured.

Rosanne studied the frantic captain, noticing his unusually dilated eyes and hypervigilance, constantly looking around like a terrified animal. "You've been on amanitas, haven't you?" She chuckled.

Aros straightened his hat. "Lady, you're the one who's high for not seeing that thing that's been circling you for the last few days. And I know how to avoid those 'shrooms, thank you. I haven't slept since the attack, and I've barely eaten while you're out here having the time of your life."

"My dear Captain, I've been here a week already, and no monster lurks about these parts. *He* is making sure they stay away, as should you. Go back to wherever you came from. I'm tired of your games." Rosanne straightened her posture and reached for the shutter.

"I am not joking here! You've been here two days, and you can't see the beast for what it is says enough. He's huge, and he's got claws. He is not human, I say!" The ladder wobbled along with his agitation.

Rosanne paused. "He a man, not a monster. Don't let others' chivalry make you jealous. It doesn't suit you. A pirate should stick to what he does best: souring other people's lives with their greed."

"You're off your rocks, lady! With the things we have seen on this island, you won't believe what you call a man is, in fact, something entirely different? How long has he been living here? Why wasn't he eaten by trolls? How in the nine blazing hells did he have the strength to pull you and that old-timer from the marshes? He threw me across the bog like a doll!"

Rosanne stared at his panic-stricken face. Aros was a confident man, but what he had seen clearly frightened the black out of his breeches. She rested her arms on the windowsill. "Let's say he is a creature. What does he want? Why does he look human? Why does he treat me kindly?"

"You've known the guy for a night and a day, and you're ready to bed him already? I knew Novalians were loose, but that isn't the point! Listen to yourself. You're ... you've *changed*. You're mellow compared to the woman who shot me out of the sky. He's changed you. He's *grooming* you!"

The soothing tunes of Yerrik's fiddle replayed in her mind. Its undefined and alien melody swept through her in tranquil waves and ethereal crashes. Time had flowed in nicks and stops, unrefined and strange until now when she saw Aros in the flesh. He felt genuine and not intangible like that of a dream conjured by her poisoned mind. How many mornings had she lived through already, in a dreamworld and otherwise? Who was the true liar?

"Look at this then." He pulled the side of his shirt, exposing thinning ribs coloured in various shades of purple. "I got this when that thing smacked me across the bog. Had it been a week ago, that bruise would be yellow. And what about when you kicked me into the river? I have the bruise on my butt to show for that, too."

Rosanne let out a snort and rolled her eyes in open disgust. "That doesn't prove anything. And I have no need to see your backside."

"He's got you under a spell! I don't believe in magic for the life of me, but his fiddle must've put you in a trance. His music is cursed, just like the legends. This person, this thing, he looks human most of the time, but I have seen his true form. He becomes something of a nightmare, a predator. Not like those trolls or the bogman. A shadow."

Aros ducked low and awkwardly hugged the cabin wall. "Shit, he's coming back. Listen, lady. I found a working ship so we can get off this bloody rock. I'll be on top of that hill there until midnight. If you want off this island, there's an open spot among the crew, but I'm not sticking my head out for anyone else."

Rosanne caught Aros' arm before he descended the ladder. "Why?" she demanded. "You didn't have to come back, so why did you?"

Aros' steel gaze held her own. "Because you're bloody marvellous, Cap." He wrenched his arm loose. "That hill. Midnight."

He tipped his hat and scurried down the ladder and into the forest with his head low. Rosanne stared after him, watching his inconspicuous movements in the bushes disturb half the wildlife in the area.

She looked at her still bruised hands. They retained a blue tint. Why hadn't the swelling gone down? Her clothes rustled when she moved, a sound unfamiliar to the trouser-wearing captain. Her vest had been replaced with a loose cotton shirt tucked into an ankle-length skirt. She couldn't remember the last time she wore anything half as ladylike. Her heart quickened. She stroked her curls, soft and untangled to the touch, and tied in a low ponytail. She wouldn't wear anything like that for practical reasons, but she couldn't deny she was comfortable.

"My father's hat …" The lack of headwear around her neck made her look about the room. The hat rested on a chair in the corner along with her other clothes. The trousers were damaged beyond repair, and she couldn't recall how that had happened.

The front door creaked open, and Yerrik's feet padded their way over the floorboards. He stood next to her, a hand on the windowsill.

"What are you looking at?" He smiled at her. The scent of heather surrounded him. It was familiar and comforting, almost alluring, or was that something else teasing her brain? Rosanne shook her head.

"There was an elk. I must have scared it."

Yerrik observed the trail of fleeing birds then met her gaze. "You look tired. Shall I play the fiddle for you?"

She shook her head. "I'm good. Perhaps I should take a walk. It's a bit stuffy in here."

"It's not safe out there."

"Just to the outskirt over there. That should be safe enough, right?"

He stroked a rogue strand of hair behind her ear and nodded. "All right. Just call out if there is anything." Her chest tightened when he left, suffocating like something prevented her from breathing. His soothing demeanour and comforting presence had snuck under her skin quicker than she thought possible, and she couldn't understand how he had broken through her barriers. The redness in her cheeks returned, and she patted them gently.

"Must be hysteria," she muttered. And yet, the thought of something as absurd as a scientifically unproven diagnosis didn't sit well with her emotionally.

It was a feeling akin to being in her room in the Captain's Quarters in Valo, how her heart fluttered with excitement whenever the *Arctic Pride* docked to the skyport. How every knock on her door, while it was berthed, had her in emotional turmoil. Yet she retained discipline over her feelings around Antony, controlling the scene, the play, and the duration. Where had her sense of restraint run off to?

NELSON WRUNG his hands and shifted uncomfortably in his seat. It wasn't his first visit to Rosanne's quarters aboard the ship, but he dreaded how the negotiations would end after his last meeting with the hulder Queen.

"What will it be, Mr. Blackwood?" The hulder Queen's smile didn't appease him in the least, for he understood the malignity and desperation hidden behind her beautiful facade. In the dim light of captain's quarter's, the hulder Queen shone radiantly. Nelson didn't let it affect him as much as during their initial meeting, reminding himself it was a trick related to whatever mystical substances allowed her to transform into a person.

Spending the greater portion of the day watching Duplànte gather crystals in the mines, Nelson had time to think and ponder about this ethereal creature, this woman who preached peace in exchange for lives. Ida's return puzzled him even more, and her lack of answers only deepened the mystery regarding the hulder Queen's true intentions. Peace offerings to anything with 'devil' in its name usually ended up in human remains resting on an altar.

"The Forest Devil didn't want Ida," he stated, watching her eyes twitch as they narrowed. She crossed her legs, straightening her back. Nelson struggled to maintain eye contact as the woman, this incredibly beautiful woman, was far under-dressed as his professional aesthetic generally allowed him to keep a straight face.

Her eyes caught his furtive glance. "Like your quiet actions right now, so will the Forest Devil accept Ida, whether it be his intentions or not. I can see to that."

The hulder Queen's smile widened, but Nelson scoffed and shook his head. "I by no means underestimate your seductive ability to achieve your goals by using whatever means necessary." The hulder Queen threw her head back in laughter, hiding her mirth with a delicate hand.

"Oh, I am beginning to see a far greater potential in you, Mr. Blackwood."

Nelson merely nodded his gratitude. "Presenting Ida as a gift but having her returned tells me there's something grand afoot. You're all women here, and the mural tells your story of how you sing men into obedience. You are by far the most breathtaking of them all and the most clever. You have no need for songs. You're tailored for someone, and you are desperate for his affection."

Her delicate features contorted. "This is for something far greater than mere affection!" Her whole body began to tense but instantly she regained her composure. "My children are sick, Mr. Blackwood. Degenerate, impure. Seeds of their fathers created them like this. Your arrival presented an opportunity for us to atone for the mistakes which led us here."

A bell rang in Nelson's mind as he finally understood what this was all about and what was at stake. "And I want everyone to return to their homes alive and well. We're not so different, your majesty."

"My offer no longer stands, Mr. Blackwood." She jabbed a fingernail on the table, never breaking eye contact. "The Forest

Devil's refusal changed the terms. To ensure the safety of my people, I need your captain's beautiful ship as well."

Nelson blinked. "Forgive me, but you are far more adept at survival than you give yourself credit for. You have no need for the *Red Queen* if it's a matter of security."

She scoffed a laugh. "Her firepower outweighs her beauty. With a ship like that, we could make the entire island fall to her knees."

Nelson scrambled his brain at this new information. With the hulder Queen's ability to read minds, Nelson had no doubts that she would be able to teach her minions to control the ship as long as she kept the right people in her custody.

"Why now of all times?" Nelson asked.

The woman knit her eyebrows.

"Your hurried decision about having Ida and Farand do your dirty work, your sick children, and this Forest Devil who poses a threat to the point of bringing you to the offensive ... why *now*?"

The hulder Queen stroked her abdomen. Her eyes lit up, bright like fire, sharp as knives. "I have something new to protect. If the Forest Devil wills it so, he could destroy us all. I can't have that."

Nelson rubbed his temples. "That doesn't answer the question."

"He too has something to protect now."

He watched her serenity wither away at the admission.

"You all fear him yet revere him as a deity. But now you will fight with whatever means necessary?"

The hulder Queen stood, her calm demeanour replaced by an uncanny tension. "Captain Drackenheart was clever to fear you. Knowing the lengths you had to go to ensure her cooperation inspired me, Mr. Blackwood. But I will not be intimidated by your words. As long as you remain in my home, you are at my mercy. I see it in your thoughts." She pointed a clawed finger at his forehead, trailing it down his cheek and under his chin. His throat bobbed as he swallowed, but his eyes remained firm and fixed.

The needle poked in his mind, digging around and drawing out conversations between him and Captain Drackenheart like a hook. Nelson tried to push the hulder Queen out and fend off her soothing voice and cooing, which so easily cracked his mind open. He could not stop her from seeing the forest where he, Farand, Higgs, Olivier, and Hammond had camped following the attack, the words slowly being dragged out of their mouths.

"You can have Ida and Farand," he said as the prodding needle twisted around.

Her pristine smile returned. "And the ship. The rest of you can go," she added.

Nelson nodded. "And the ship. But our lives are guaranteed." The salty sting of sweat ran down his forehead. He found himself panting for air.

Folding her arms, the hulder Queen gave him another thoughtful look. "You have yourself a deal, Mr. Blackwood. I suggest you leave on the morrow."

Nelson stood and went for the door, feeling her piercing eyes in the back of his skull. "You can always return when you tire of the island wildlife." Nelson fought to steer his thoughts away from Farand's plan, knowing that the longer he stayed within probing vicinity of the hulder Queen, he was jeopardizing everyone's safety. He made his hasty exit, ignoring her playful calls, and left the ship. Hopefully not for the last time.

ROSANNE SCANNED the opposite bluff at the foot of the western mountains. "That hill at midnight, eh?" Captain Bernhart would be foolish to bring the ship in plain view of the cabin and would most likely be waiting there in person. She had no weapons and only the words of a two-faced pirate to abide by.

"I must be out of my goddamned mind to trust a pirate," she muttered, chewing her lips.

She rested on a rock a little way up a jagged hilltop surveying the crooked birch forest. She hadn't gone far, but far enough to regain a sense of freedom and sense of self. Up here, the air was fresh and welcoming and didn't throw her emotions into a bitter battle for affection from a stranger. It was a different toxin than Nikor's, which made her insane without it requiring physical contact or disfigured limbs. Everything Yerrik did and said, the sound of his voice, the scent of him filling the room, all contributed to spinning her thoughts around and around in a vortex of confusion.

The very notion of her being attracted to Yerrik, physically and mentally, terrified her. It was a power not given to any before him, and the prospect had her desperately seeking refuge among the quiet wildlife. If Yerrik had put her under a spell, if such a thing was possible ... She groaned and buried her face in her palms.

What would Yerrik's purpose serve by keeping her in a dream? Was he pushing her boundaries, testing her potential and moral limitation? Was he giving her more reasons to stay and abandon her mission? Was it all to please her? Rosanne admitted several of the dreams had been pleasant, free of all the stress she faced as a woman in the skytrade business, free of the grim future which awaited her back in Salis with her family business, free of dealing with reality ...

Yerrik offered himself and his home, and the thought of being far away from her own family and the damned colonies allured to her common sense more than she dared admit. But she wasn't the only one out here. Somewhere scattered across these forests and mountains, her crew and her ship awaited her return and salvation. Somewhere out there was a gold-digging and ship-stealing pirate with a crew and a working vessel. She couldn't let him have any of what was hers.

But as she turned to look at the cabin, her heart filled with unease, and all fight left her.

By the time Rosanne returned to the cabin, the air surrounding the property was filled with the most wonderful aroma. Smoke flew out of the chimney, and wax candles were lit throughout the house. Rosanne stopped in front of the door. Looking at her feet, she couldn't understand why they disobeyed her so.

Perhaps Yerrik was untainted by the cruelty of the world and possessed a profound kindness Rosanne had never experienced, that her intimate dalliance with misfortune and malevolence beckoned her to retreat from close, gratifying relationships. She had held so tightly on to a gun for so many years she didn't know how to lower the barrel.

Reluctantly, she opened the door and was met with Yerrik whirring about the kitchen. The simple clay oven smoked as he removed the lid and reached inside with a thick-gloved hand, fishing out a lump of golden-brown bread.

"Just in time, Dragonheart. Have a seat." Yerrik dashed to the boiling cauldron in the hearth.

"Would you like some help with that?" She smiled as he fanned his hands from the hot bread.

"Nonsense. Recovering patients should rest and enjoy the view of work being done for them." Shaking her head, Rosanne sat by the table and observed his beaming excitement.

"Say, what day is it? It's like I've been here for many days already." She fiddled with the empty cup, rolling it on its base.

Yerrik lifted the pan off the stove, eggs sizzling and sputtering. He swept the spatula out, opening his mouth to speak, but refrained from answering.

"It feels like an eternity," she commented.

He pointed the spatula at her. "It does, doesn't it? Time flies when you're in good company." He sat but caught her disquieted look. "I mean if you do enjoy my company. I wouldn't like to be on your bad side or talk too much or anything else causing you discomfort in any way." He tripped over his words and looked uncertain.

She straightened herself, caught off guard by his crumbling confidence. Rosanne dug her thumbnail under the nail of her index finger, and somehow her eyes found the fibres on the table wood more comforting than setting her eyes on Yerrik's. Her heart thumped like a drum. "All I meant was since coming here, my sense of time has been off, and it confuses me. I don't mind your company at all. And implying anything else, considering you also saved my life, would be extremely rude of me. Not that I think so little of you. I ..." she looked up finally, finding Yerrik's amused smile on the brink of complete suppression. "I need to lie down for a bit." She stood hastily, making for the bedroom, but Yerrik, quick on his feet, caught her gently by the arm.

"What is going on with you? You're nervous." He checked her forehead. "And very warm."

"Must be the fever," she mumbled to the floor.

"Rosanne, I didn't mean to embarrass you."

"You didn't. It's just my head being silly." Yerrik's hold on her was relaxed but firm, and she didn't protest against his touch. It was like fire, and she didn't want him to let go, yet she wanted to run, far and fast. His scent drowned her, his touch smothered her, and his mere presence shackled her. He leaned close, so close his breath teased her skin. Their eyes locked, and Rosanne found herself unable to break his gaze or even turn away from his gentle but terrifying approach.

"Come with me," she blurted. "To Noval." It was the only thing she could think of to make him stop. Her knees almost buckled under her weight, and she fought herself to stay calm when she was anything but. He regarded her curiously, never letting his eyes wander from her hazel ones. Undoubtedly, he could see through her transparent attempt at stalling the inevitable, but he let it happen anyway. He took a step back, giving her some breathing room.

"Are you sure?" He stroked her hair, and Rosanne finally managed to break eye contact and look down.

"Yes, I would very much like that. I can find you something suitable in Valo, even work if you want. It's the least I can do, and I do know quite a few people who would be able to accommodate you. I would like to show you my gratitude, as I'm repeatedly told I'm terrible at it."

"Will we ...?"

"Yes?" Rosanne couldn't contain her excitement at his comment, filled with anxiety and anticipation for the next few words.

Yerrik shook his head. "It's not time yet. Rest easy, Dragon-heart. I'm not going to whisk you away to the land of dreams. Come and eat, and we can walk later. Perhaps even find that scoundrel you owe a few blunt force traumas to." He took both of her hands and led her back to the dining table, and again, his words made her laugh.

CHAPTER 25

SHIVER ME CANNONBALLS

P anicked shouts echoed from every direction in the hollow mountain. Hammond put his head against the twig-bundled door. His face twisted as he tried to make sense of the commotion.

"I have no bloody clue what's going on, but they're scrambling in their unmentionables."

Farand leapt from his bed in alarm. "That's the signal," he said and snatched up his shoes, lacing them like a drilled soldier.

"This soon?" Nelson fumbled for his glasses.

"I don't know what he did, but he's creative, and by the sound of things, it's working." Farand opened the door as soon as most of the noise had faded and peeked outside. The sentries stationed outside had disappeared.

"It's clear." He waved the men out and rushed down the halls, retracing their steps to the central vent. Ducking low behind stone columns, they searched the room for activity. A few stragglers emerged from deeper within the mines only to rush towards the exit quick as arrows. The *Red Queen* hovered gently above ground level, still ornately pristine and adorned with fresh flowers.

Farand turned to the group behind him. "Nelson, find Dalia

and the others. Higgs, you get yourself to the engine. Only open the door for Ida or Gavin. Hammond, you ... you..."

"I am not entirely useless, sir." The older man fixed his trousers. "I can load a few of 'em cannons while we wait for the others."

"Excellent. Get to it! Nobody fires until I say so."

Nelson rushed down the hallways as quick as his feet could carry him. All the hulder were gone from their posts and the rooms. *Must have been some distraction Olivier made.* He was grateful for the lanky scout, and it would all be thanks to him if they managed to escape with their lives.

Quick, light footsteps approached at an alarming speed, and Nelson, in a moment of gut-wrenching panic, didn't have time to stop before rounding the corner, crashing into a screaming woman.

"Ida! It's me, stop it. *Ow.*" Nelson fended off her mad flailing arms after receiving a sucker punch to the cheek. When, in a moment of wide-eyed horror, she seemed to realize what she was doing, she slunk back to give him space. Nelson held his throbbing jawline, biting back his whimper.

Tears streamed down Ida's eyes, and she hugged him tightly. "Nelson! You're safe. I came looking for you as soon as the guards left. They were frantic. What's going on?"

He fixed his askew glasses, which had miraculously survived without a scratch. "Our plan in the making. Do you know where the others are?"

"Down here. Mr. Lyle is in the infirmary not far from the others."

"Good. Stick to me, and we'll get Dalia first. Dalia?"

"Ahoy there, paper-pusher." The watch captain emerged from a side tunnel, bringing a trail of sailors behind her. "I assume this is the *Captain Drackenheart,*" she referred to the plan and grinned.

Nelson nodded, pleased by the crew's initiative to escape at first given opportunity. "The timing is imperative. The moment

Farand issues the command to seal the tunnels, we will not have long until the hulder return in full force. We need to locate the others before then."

Dalia turned to the men behind her. "You heard the man. You three with me to get Lyle. The rest of you scurry to the ship and prep the sails for takeoff." The five topmen complied with a series of "ayes" and set off towards the central vent in a hurry.

"I'll see to Creedy and the guys," Nelson offered, glancing down the long corridor ahead. "When you retrieve Mr. Lyle, please hurry. We don't have time to idle."

Dalia scoffed. "You take me for an idler, Nelson?" she barked to the man as he ran into the hallway.

"Not at all!" came the echo.

"HAMMOND, this isn't the time to be cooking!" Norman called out to the chef, scurrying about the pantry. The older man grumbled as he rummaged through the crates, heaving his weight around with great effort. He balanced gingerly on his leg, relieving stress from his knee.

"I know it's here somewhere," he muttered and tossed a bundle of carrots. Norman dodged the orange roots flying out the pantry door.

"Sir, we have to man the starboard cannons. No one else is back yet." He clutched the doorframe and glanced behind him.

"Shut yer trap, lad, and get the stove going. And take the small cauldron!"

Norman groaned as he turned on his heel and grabbed the cauldron in his passing. Despite its small size, the pot hung heavy from the ceiling chain suspended above the central hearth. He removed the copper lid and stuffed it with kindling and a few logs. Norman looked around to the pandemonium that was the kitchen counters. Skillets, utensils, crumbs, and canned goods littered the area.

"I can't find the firesteel!" he called to the cook.

"Check the cupboards!" came Hammond's roaring response between the clatter of shuffling items.

Norman opened the first set of cupboards before him, shrieking as he dodged tumbling cans crashing to the floor. Among the pickled cucumber jars nestled the one-handed firesteel in a cob of spiderwebs. The steel rod joined the flint with a single nail and spring, enabling the steel to strike against the flint once pressed.

"What sensible person puts the firesteel there?" Norman shook his head at the row of yellowed pickle jars.

"Now we're talking." Hammond emerged from the pantry carrying a small crate. He grunted as he lifted it and dropped it on a table. He removed the lid.

"What on earth is that?" Norman asked as he fanned the kindle. Hammond picked up a knife on the floor, supporting himself on the table. He then jabbed the tip of the knife into the cache and twisted it back and forth. He went over to the heating cauldron and tossed in several fatty lumps. Norman shot him a questioning look.

Hammond wiggled his eyebrows and cackled. "This ought to keep out those foul tunes." Undeterred by the heat, Hammond scooped up the now soft lump of wax, tearing it into smaller pieces, and stuffed it into his ears. His eyes lit up as he looked at Norman's confused face.

"Aye?" Hammond prompted.

Norman bobbed his head at the wax-stained ears. "That is absolutely ridiculous. But I'm in."

"What?" the older man held a hand to his ear.

"I'll get this out to the others!" Norman shouted after plugging his own ears.

"Hell's bells. This is good stuff," Hammond said with a chuckle.

LYLE GROANED. The men carrying the stretcher were less than gentle as they scurried through the hallways.

"Just a little further, Lyle. You'll soon be aboard the ship again," Dalia reassured him as she kept the pace quick. She looked behind her; the hallway was dark and empty, but for how much longer? The feeble husk of a man was as pale as the canvas. Sweat ran down his fevered forehead, but his thrashing had seized.

"Don't you go dying on us now, you old bastard. Captain won't stand for it, and neither will I!"

They crossed the bridge and hopped onto the main deck. "Get him to the infirmary. Hopefully, someone found the doc." Dalia wiped the sweat stinging her eyes and immediately turned her attention to the people handling the rigging.

"Wax for the ears, ma'am?"

Dalia jumped as Norman stood next to her with a black pot in his hands.

She looked at the gooey mass and frowned. "What on earth for?"

Norman pointed to his already sealed ears. "Now we can't hear the hulder sing," he close to shouted. It was then she noticed the numerous hand signals sent among the crew in the rigging and the lack of yelling she was so used to.

Dalia scooped up a small lump of wax, massaging it around to form two balls. "I will regret this..." she said as she plugged her ears and listened to the world around her go almost completely silent.

"I'M GONNA KILL YOU, PAPER-PUSHER!" Creedy roared as his legs pumped with everything they had to bring him away from the horde of hulder pursuing them.

"You do not pin this on me! You ran into them!" Nelson protested and shrieked as he dodged the swipe of a clawed hand.

"You scream too loud! You attract monsters. Your fault."

Kristoff huffed, his eyes narrow and brows scrunched together as he sprinted next to them, gaining speed with every step he took.

As if his lungs had caught fire, Nelson's lack of breath slowed his sprint to a trot. An alluring tune weaved through the air. He whipped his head around to see a pair of hulder slowing their pursuit and bombarding him with singing. The noise echoed in the narrow hallway, and Nelson shouted nonsensical words at the top of his lungs to drown out the song.

"What are you on about?" Creedy barked.

"They're singing!" Nelson replied and continued his panicked incoherent shouting. Creedy immediately yelled with all of his might, stuffing his fingers in his ears as he sang a Bunnsboroux sea-shanty off-key. Kristoff joined in the song as he ran ahead, exiting the cave into the central vent where the galleon awaited. They dove into the nearest tunnel, scrambling up the steep path to the exit in front of the bridge. They collapsed onto the deck, heaving for breath.

"Where's Nelson?" Dalia called to them.

Kristoff threw a pointy finger in the direction they had come from, grabbing his stomach. Dalia peeked over the railing, seeing a frantic Nelson shouting as he exited the tunnels, hands covering his ears and huffing like his life depended on it.

"For the love of Terra, seal the tunnels!" he yelled.

FARAND SPOTTED Nelson exiting the tunnel and aimed the main deck port-side cannon at the tunnel and pulled the string. The cannon let out a deafening boom, intensifying in the funnel of the volcano, and it rolled back on the tracks that kept it tethered to the floorboards with a metallic clatter. The cannonball rendered the lip of the entrance to pebbles. Rocks piled up, leaving gaps around the crumbling ceiling. The cannon's metallic blast reverberating through his skull like clattering gravel.

Around the ship, the cannons fired in rapid succession, each aimed at their own tunnel entrance. Rocks exploded on the walls all around them. Amplified by the circular vent, the noise hit the lieutenant like a wall.

Farand grabbed the small sack of gunpowder mix from the supply cache, stuffing it into the barrel followed by an eight-pounder shot. The next blast he made collapsed a large chunk of the ceiling, sealing off the main tunnel.

He didn't bother counting how many more they had to defend once the hulder realized they had been lured away. He kept firing at the largest exits, praying that sealing them off would give them enough time for the engine to reach working condition.

Between the firing, the distant echoed snarls forebode of an oncoming horde. Limbs flailed and clambered through the piles of rock by the main tunnel entrance.

The *Red Queen's* sails unfurled, but they lacked the usual shimmer in their octagonal pattern. Farand scanned the panels for signs of electrical activity. Save for the intercom, all the screens were as dead as the sails. The topmen on deck exchanged hurried arguments while pointing at the defunct sails.

Farand turned towards the busy quarterdeck and signalled at anyone who looked his way to get Creedy's attention. The message circulated, ending up with the watch captain. Quick on his feet, Creedy joined Farand on the quarterdeck, removing the wax plug from one ear.

"Arm everyone and hold them off as long as you can." Farand roared to the topman through the thundering of cannon fire.

"Aye, sir!" Creedy rushed towards his bickering team, catching Dalia on his way below deck. Not half a minute later, they emerged with two teams armed to the teeth with plasma rifles and flintlock pistols. Through the excessive noise and chaos, they abandoned the earplugs as close combat became imminent.

A flock of livid hulder poured into the main hall from every unsealed tunnel. They leapt from the ground floor and clambered onto the hull, crawling up the woodwork like spiders. Two hulder emerged onto the quarterdeck, hunching over and ready to pounce. Farand abandoned the small deck cannon and cocked the flintlock, aiming at the closest hulder growling at him. Another one joined it, undeterred by the weapon. He pointed the barrel up in the air and fired off a warning shot, then redirected his aim at the two hulder.

"For the love of Terra, please back down," he whispered to himself, feeling the teasing pull of the trigger under his finger. Farand glanced to the main deck, where another three sentries emerged over the railing. Without hesitation, they pounced at Creedy. The crackling shot of his plasma rifle rang through the air, and a hulder let out a pitiful cry. She fell face-first to the deck, unmoving. The two others jumped back, seemingly confused by what had happened. Farand's heart nearly stopped as the blood-thirst in the hulders' eyes turned to him. They could not be reasoned with, he realized with a heavy heart.

"Shoot to kill!" he announced and fired the moment the two hulder attacked.

LEAD BULLETS ZIPPED at their targets, followed by the rumble of cannons and spray of volcanic rock. Nelson sprinted out of the tunnel, his glasses hopping on his nose. He wobbled across the bridge as the ring of a stray bullet passed by his ear. The hulder pounced from the cave behind him.

"Lords almighty. Do something!" he cried and wobbled faster. Two cannons fired simultaneously, whizzing past Nelson and connecting with the entrance. The blast sent three hulder flying off the ledge, another one a direct hit; she died upon impact without as much as uttering a syllable. The tunnel collapsed with ease, but the women relentlessly clawed at the rubble, determined to break through.

Nelson fell onto the deck and crawled to Dalia—his legs had all but given up. A sentry climbed over the ship railing, having followed the ladder from the hull. Dalia shot her in the chest, and the creature shrieked and dropped down.

"Take this, Nelson." Dalia shoved a plasma gun into the lawyer's hands, and he stared at it without knowing how the mechanism even worked. Dalia smacked him aside as claws swiped at him, and the bang from her offhand flintlock rang in his ears.

She grabbed his gun and drew back the rounded top piece. "Aim and pull the trigger. Draw this up and back to recharge the gun. Wait for the blue light," she barked and pushed him aside as another sneer-faced hulder climbed down the mast.

A hand grabbed Nelson's foot from over the ledge, and the man cried out. His finger jerked the trigger and fired off the gun without much regard to where he was aiming. The hulder clawing on the ledge next to his attacker yowled as the plasma bullet seared into her shoulder, and she lost her grip. Nelson fumbled with the rounded top piece, drawing it back and counted to three. A toothy grin spread on the hulder's lips, and she dragged him right past the railing.

"They got Nelson!" Dalia cried.

Creedy swung his rifle, butting someone's face to an even surface. "Leave him!"

"We don't leave without him!" Farand ordered, firing another cannonball against the masses clawing their way through the partially sealed tunnels.

A powerful fist knocked down the topman, but he shrugged the pain off and shot the hulder without a second thought. He leapt to his feet. "Screw the money. It ain't worth our lives!"

"We might as well die here if we can't return with him!" Farand regretted his words as soon as he said them.

In the midst of chaos, Creedy did a double-take. "Whaddya mean?"

Farand abandoned his cannon, shoving past a sentry blocking his path to the quarterdeck. He grabbed the intercom. "Hurry the bloody up down there! We're getting swarmed!"

"So are we, in loose screws and foul tempers!" The shouting voice in the intercom turned Higgs' voice to static.

Farand dropped the radio with a snarl. The hulder pounced at him, claws leading with a wicked sneer. He caught her bare-handed and promptly tossed her overboard. Another raked at his arms, and the man growled from the sharp pain. The forces coming at them were overwhelming, even with the cannons dropping lead and rock and the plasma guns and the rifles critically wounding the women in their dozens.

Their numbers only swelled.

"GET YOUR BACKSIDE MOVING, BOY!" Hammond yelled between the ear-shattering shrieks of the hulder clawing his arms wrapped around her. "I can't hold her for much longer!" Throwing his bulk against her, the only reason the hulder hadn't escaped the cook's grip was due to his sheer weight alone.

Norman scrambled inside the room, raising a shovel high above his head, and whacked the iron straight against the hulder's back. She shrieked and tumbled aside. Before she recovered, Norman summoned all the muscle he could muster into his swing and smacked the shovel at her head. She swayed for only a moment and spun around on one leg before falling flat to the floor.

"Dear God. I didn't mean to ..." Norman stared at the dead hulder and held his mouth.

Hammond groaned and rolled to his feet with some effort. "Forget about it, boy. They're after blood. We can't reason with 'em any more than we can convince the pig roast to jump to the pyre."

"Yes, I know, but ... I didn't have to hit her so hard." Norman's eyes wandered from the blood pooling around the creature's head to Hammond's hand holding his side. "You're injured!" The seaman grabbed Hammond's hand and pulled it off. Three gashes gaped, dripping blood with each breath the man took. Hammond pushed Norman away, hands resuming to stem the flow as he doubled over.

"Don't worry about me. Go take out those vixens that got past us."

"But Hammond—"

"Take the blooming shovel and whack some more heads before I whack you instead," he grunted, leaning against the wall. Norman gripped the shovel tight and nodded.

"I'll be back before you know it," he said and rushed down the gun deck.

Hammond watched the three cannons across the room slide on their rails after emptying their lead. The men arming them were far too occupied keeping the portholes free of the shrieking creatures to pay him any attention. The main deck above teemed with quick footsteps and scuffling, and outside, the pangs and clanks of rifles and guns went off in uneven intervals.

Wiping the sweat off his forehead, Hammond pressed his hand firmly against the throbbing wounds and hitched his breath.

CHAPTER 26

LAST STAND

Wading across the room amongst an ocean of screws, nuts, and tools, Higgs slipped on a patch of oil and grabbed the table next to him. Small boxes came crashing to the floor along with the man, spilling their contents.

Ida sat neck deep in parts, assembling the gravity dynamo for the thruster engine. Seeing the added mess through her many-layered monocles, she gave a faint scream.

"Hurry the bloody up down there! We're getting swarmed!" Farand's overbearing voice from the intercom crackled into static.

Higgs grabbed the intercom and supported himself on the wall, feeling the stretch from his fall. "So are we, in engine parts and foul tempers!" he growled and dropped the intercom. It dangled on its elastic coiled spring and smacked against the wall.

"Where are the valve springs?" Ida yelled and shuffled through the parts littering the floor. She crawled around on all fours, studying the many coiled springs so identical to the ones she truly needed.

Gavin rolled out from under the raised engine, the support board catching everything in its wheels. He muscled himself out of the tight gap with a grunt. "I bypassed the backup power, but it's not gonna hold forever. If the engine overloads even a little, the power supply shuts off." Wiping the grime on his trousers, he grabbed the welded scaffolding framing the engine. "Help me lower this, Higgs."

The old man grabbed the other side, and on three, the men put their backs into lifting the engine just enough so Gavin could kick the wooden supports out. Higgs gasped as they sat down the machinery and held a hand to his lower back.

"Sweet Terra, you all right Higgs?" Gavin asked. The boom of cannon fire resonated from upstairs, followed by gunshots and screams.

"I'll be fine. Ida, girl, you done with that? Things are getting hairy."

Ida stared at the block of metal and thumb-sized pistons, assembling the valve springs with quick, deft hands. "Pardon my rudeness, uncle, but kindly piss off."

Higgs laughed despite the shooting waves of agony in his spine. "Atta girl."

On the floor were four large metal clasps designed to hold the bottom scaffolding of the engine. Gavin shut them all and gave the engine a test pull, rocking the hunk of metal back and forth. It didn't budge.

"Alright, engine's secure."

"Finally. You take that side. I take this one." Higgs grabbed a set of thick cables, moving to plug them into a panel on the wall. "Only plug the vital power supplies. No hot water for anyone."

"Don't mix the rear thrusters with the fore-thrusters, and we might all live to see another day," Gavin said and received only the simplest puff of breath from the chief engineer.

A great weight banged against the engine room door, rattling it. Ida shrieked and dropped the rounded piece of metal. Gavin yelled in surprise when it hit the floor, followed by a stream of curses upon seeing one of the piston heads bent awkwardly to the side.

After scrambling for the ball, Ida cradled it. "I can fix this. Just gimme a few." She plucked the broken piston apart. A snarl made her turn around, and through the many-layered monocles, Ida gasped at a flat grey face and black eyes. The hulder grabbed Ida's arm and pulled her towards the door.

"Ida!" Gavin slid on the parts littering the floor and threw himself at the hulder. The creature merely swiped him aside. Crashing against the working table across the room, he caught the edge right on his hip. Gavin gasped from the impact and slumped on the floor.

Ida thrashed against the hulder's hold, but the creature ignored her. Ida glanced at the dynamo in her hand, feeling the small but surprisingly heavy object. She swung her free arm and landed the hunk of metal straight onto the hulder's skull. The hulder staggered and turned around, blinking through unfocused eyes. A mighty clang of metal rang throughout the room when the flat end of a shovel hit her, and the hulder landed among the pipes running along the far wall. Norman rose the shovel, huffing, readying for another swing. The hulder remained unmoving.

"You good?" Norman asked, his eyes wild. Ida took a moment to register Norman's presence and hiccupped a sob. Then she stared at the dynamo in absolute terror.

"Oh, thank God. It's all right." Wiping the blood smear off the smooth side of the metal, she ran back into the room.

Norman stretched out a hand towards Ida, an expression of mild confusion plastered on his face. "Is that thing necessary?"

Gavin sputtered. "Is that thing necessary ..." he echoed and shook his head.

Once Ida finished, she held up the ball, showing the eight pistons jutting from its top half. "Got it." She leaned over the engine and fit the dynamo into a hollow slot carved in the metal block. She retracted her hands, holding them up as if the device would explode if she made the wrong move. The metal ball hovered a centimetre clear of the metal, its pistons pumping in a repetitive dynamic dance. Gavin, Higgs, and Ida all leaned closer to the engine, putting their ears right up against the block of machinery. Norman did the same, and through the gunfire above and shuddering in the wood from cannons, only the tiniest whirl resonated from within.

Higgs gave a self-satisifed grunt. "Fire her up, Gavin."

"Aye, sir." The third engineer pulled a lever on the far side of the block, flipped three switches on the electrical panel on the wall, and pushed a large wooden button.

"Fingers crossed," Higgs said and crossed his fingers. Ida bit her lower lip and crossed all the fingers she could, and Gavin simply stared at the engine.

The engine gave a shudder, and the massive pistons on top of the block puffed slowly. They began rolling unanimously, creaking the valve springs. On the wall above the engine hung a panel of coloured light bulbs and a set of names marking their function.

"Power input," Higgs said as the bulb lit yellow. "Power output is green. Anti-grav is stable. Thruster panel is good. Atmos is offline, but that's to be expected. Fine thrusters connected. Hah, didn't screw up this time, eh?" Higgs elbowed Gavin.

"The sails are offline?" Ida's breath caught when the bulb remained unlit. "We're getting yellow on the input, so why are they still offline?" She grabbed her hair, ruffling it as she was close to screaming.

Gavin smacked his hands together. "I knew I forgot something."

"You didn't plug in the bloody sails?" Higgs roared.

On the decks above them, the commotion grew louder.

NELSON CLUNG TO THE LADDER, close to losing his grip as the hulder pulling at his feet possessed inhuman strength. He hooked his elbow around the rung. With his free hand, he aimed at the snarling monstrosity and fired at point-blank range. The plasmic bullet sizzled through her skull. Her eyes rolled, and she fell limp in a half-turn before crashing to the cave floor with an anticlimactic thud.

Nelson scrambled up the ladder, rolled onto the deck and huffed. In the corner of his eye, Dalia and Creedy fired at hulder descending the rigging or crawling up the hull. The creatures seemed so determined to stop them, using their lethal claws to climb.

Getting to his feet, Nelson stared at the throne of the hulder Queen, knowing she had returned to her cozy realm of safety. "You see and hear everything, don't you?" he said.

On the stern castle, Farand shot down any resistance coming too close to his position. Next to the cannon stood a single torch, flames flickering with all the activity surrounding it.

Nelson zipped past Farand, grabbing the torch by the stern.

"What in the bloody hells are you doing?" Farand asked, his voice alarmed.

"Buying us time." Nelson rushed to the main deck.

"Hey, you bastards! Over here!" he bellowed when he stood next to the throne, holding the torch close to the roots. A few hulder drew to his calls. Their faces wrenched from fury to fear in less than a heartbeat, stopping them dead in their tracks. They cried out, reaching with their arms, and advanced no further. Dalia and Creedy held their fire when the hulder ceased their attacks and pleaded with alien words.

"Any closer and your queen will burn!" He teased the wood with the hot flames. The hulder on the ship withdrew to the ledge, never taking their eyes off their precious leader. All around them, hulder called out in frustration, pacing back and forth.

"Cover Nelson!" Dalia rushed to his side, aiming the rifle at anyone too close for her comfort. Nelson allowed himself a victorious grin, a swelling pride he hadn't felt from his unlucky streak of utter uselessness ever since they sailed from Valo.

Branches grabbed at Nelson's tunic. He swung the torch in panic and dropped it. Twigs twisted around his arms.

"You should have taken my offer, Mr. Blackwood," a crackling voice said. The hulder Queen took shape in the woodwork. Her branch-like arms scraped against his bare skin as they travelled up to his neck.

Her gnarled grin only grew. "This man here betrayed you all." Her voice became clearer for every word as she took shape. Dalia aimed at the hulder Queen, searching for that opening where she could cripple the woman without harming Nelson. The hulder Queen was a slender shape behind Nelson, shielding herself from the crew's weaponry. He struggled to breathe with the wooden hand on his throat. "He blackmailed your captain into finding the *Retribution*." She chuckled, prodding Nelson's mind even as he scrambled to fight off her intrusion. She pulled at Rosanne and Nelson's conversation in the Captain's Quarters, drawing out every detail she could.

"What the hell is she talking about? Mr. Duplànte, sir?" Creedy turned to the lieutenant. Farand's jaw tensed, and he kept his eyes on the floor.

The hulder Queen scraped at Nelson's throat with vines protruding from her fingers. He sputtered and gasped for breath, his face turning a darker shade of red with each passing second.

"If he's not returned to Valo within a fortnight after departure, a certain package containing all the fruits of your labour will reach the Magistrate of Trade." The hulder Queen grinned, tightening her hold on the struggling lawyer. Nelson balanced on the tip of his toes. His glasses tumbled. "Not only will your careers be over, but you will also be hunted and tried for treason against the Central United Colonies."

"That's a load of horseshit! She's messing with us!" Dalia cocked the rifle, peeling her eyes on the hulder Queen with the finger ready on the trigger.

"Is that so?" the leader of the hulder clan laughed. "Your little run to Haddon paid off."

"How does she...? Say you didn't, Nelson. Say it!" Dalia cried out in disbelief. She lowered her gun, forgetting the amassing hulder crowding the gangways and paths surrounding them. They were confident now that their queen had awoken, eying the crew like a predator assessing its prey. The hulder Queen took a few steps towards the bridge, dragging Nelson with her.

"I'll put a bullet through the both of you bastards!" Creedy aimed his plasma rifle, but was knocked off his feet by the mass of Farand yanking the weapon out of his hands.

"We need him, you daft idiot!" Farand couldn't deny the crew's dwindling trust, their divided attention. Only those on the main deck had heard the hulder Queen, but it was effective to seed doubt into their minds and instilled second thoughts about keeping Nelson safe from harm.

Dalia's gun wavered. Creedy's palpable fury had the man gritting his teeth. The hulder crawled closer to the ship, making their way down the masts and rigging from the ledges above. The sheer number of hulder had Kristoff changing targets as he also kept an ear open to the revelation on the main deck.

The hulder Queen's hold on Nelson lessened enough for him to catch a breath. "Nothing was supposed to happen," he uttered between his escaping breaths.

She cooed in his ear. "No use for that now, Mr. Blackwood. Look at their eyes. Read their disbelief from your betrayal, their *hatred*." He did, and he hated every second of it, from Dalia's disbelief to Creedy's seething rage. Farand's eyes rested on the floor in defeat. Nelson had doomed them all from the beginning.

"I'm a scumbag, but I'm not going to let them die here." Nelson drove a finger into the hulder Queen's left eye, making the woman scream. The sentries howled their battle cry, running from the pathways and crawling up the walls. Blinded, the hulder Queen stumbled on the bridge. Nelson tackled her with all the might his scrawny paper-pusher body could muster. He caught her and sent them both toppling over the edge.

"Nelson!" Dalia cried after the lawyer, shooting at the hulder pursuing them. Nelson clambered onto the woman as they fell, tumbling against the volcanic rock, rolling and falling along the rough walls. Cushioning his fall, the hulder Queen landed back first on the floor, crying out upon impact.

Nelson's arm hung limp, throbbing with pain in the shoulder joint.

Dalia and Kristoff peppered the advancing enemy rushing for their queen, Nelson protecting his head with his good arm as the bullets flew around him. He limped toward the ship's hull, and just as he grabbed the ladder, his feet were swept from under him.

The hulder Queen held to his legs, dragging him away from the ship. Nelson had no strength to kick himself free. Farand skipped down the ladder as fast as he could. He was intercepted by a hulder jumping on his back, driving her claws deep into his shoulder. Groaning, he seized her arm and yanked her off.

"Mr. Blackwood!" Farand tossed him the single plasma gun he possessed. Nelson caught it clumsily with his good hand. He fired instantly, the plasmic energy shearing the hulder Queen's exposed back. Recoiling, her unearthly scream drowned out the surrounding clamour. Nelson covered his ears.

The hulder Queen rolled on the ground to lessen the intense plasmic energy melting her skin. Nelson scrambled for the ladder, finding Farand's hand in front of him.

"No time for delicacy. Let go, and you're a dead man," Farand grunted. Nelson held with his good arm around Farand's massive neck as the man skipped up the ladder, feet quick and coordinated. Nelson tumbled from side to side and struggled to hold on with his singular grip lessening. Farand tossed Nelson onto the deck like a dead fish. "Get that damned throne off our ship!" the lieutenant howled the moment he came over the railing. Kristoff and Creedy ran to comply.

"To that broken railing there. On three ..." Farand ordered when he joined them, and the three men pushed the massive root on his command. Nelson was grounded from physical exertion. He reloaded the plasma gun for good measure as he attempted to steady his stolen breath and keep his feet obeying basic commands.

"Take your filthy hands off that!" The hulder Queen dragged herself aboard, clawing towards the throne being pushed the other way. Her back was a gaping hole of smouldering wood like a rotten log, filled with larvae and mushrooms, moss and grime. Nelson recoiled with a scream, pushing himself away from the raving woman who left a trail of chipped wood and insects in her wake.

Dalia grabbed the lit torch scorching the deck. "Hold up!" She rushed to the men and stuffed the torch deep within the roots' wooden network. The dry fibres caught fire.

The hulder Queen erupted into flames, the crackling cutting through her screams. She flailed her arms and kicked with her feet, rolling on deck to put out the fire engulfing her. With a final push, the throne tipped overboard. As the heavy root smashed against the rocky ground, wooden splinters flew and scattered. The throne split in half, with the flames reducing it to ashes.

All around them, the sentries cried and fell over in agony. They pulled at their hair, howling and screaming, patting at their arms and legs as if they were the ones who burned. The hulder Queen twitched and sobbed, blackening and disintegrating. Her final death throe had her charred body come apart, leaving a pile of ashes and embers.

The crew stared, horrified at the smouldered pile.

"What the hell happened?" Dalia asked, assessing the remnants of the throne and then the pile of ashes of the former regal queen of the hulder tribe. The remaining hulder on the ship stared blank-faced at the ashes. No one moved. Dalia waved a hand in front of a hulder's face but got no response.

Through the deafening silence, the sails' electric hum rang out. Creedy whipped his head around, staring at the fluttering canvas catching the silver moonlight and shimmering in response.

"We have power!" he called out so loudly his voice failed him completely, and he coughed in a fit.

"To your stations!" Farand ordered and took the wheel. He barked into the intercom, and seconds later, the engine sputtered to life. Dalia shoved a sentry overboard. The hulder didn't even resist, she merely stood frozen with an empty look in her black eyes.

Farand gently tilted the wheel back, stepping on the pedals for the small hull thrusters, hissing as their puffs rose the *Queen* through the central vent of the volcano. A few hulder recovered from the initial shock and leapt aboard. "Keep them off. Don't let them damage the sails!"

Ignoring the armed crew shooting at them, the hulder locked their eyes on Farand. They snarled, pounced, and clawed in rage. Every bullet they took only slowed them down until a fatal wound ended their lives.

"Captain Drackenheart will have my head." Farand winced when the ship banged against the volcano's lip, scratching the hull. "She'll make me eat my shoes," he muttered to himself, sweating with every twitch of his hands guiding the ship. The slightest turn and tilt of the wheel and pedals controlled every thruster on the hull, and he didn't feel nearly experienced enough to clear the volcano top without damaging the galleon.

The open sky stretched all around them, bathing the ship in the moonlight. A round of cheers erupted on every deck. Dalia raised her rifle in victory and let out her loudest whoop. A clatter from the forecastle drew their attention as Creedy rushed Nelson.

"You fucking bastard! I'll kill you!" Creedy snarled and pummeled the cowering lawyer. People rushed to tear him off. Nelson covered his face and any other part receiving kicks and pummeling, but he had no strength to defend himself properly.

Farand was too preoccupied with the ship's wheel. "Throw Creedy in the brig!"

Kristoff tore a snarling Creedy away from Nelson. "You lying sack of shit!" Creedy screamed and flailed. "We're all gonna hang if we go back to Noval." Kristoff staggered against Creedy's defiant shrug.

"What are you talking about?" Kristoff eyed the topman. The crew surrounding them listened in quiet anticipation.

Creedy pointed at the cowering lawyer. "This bastard has all our necks on paper, and he tied the noose. This sack found out about our business."

"You ratted on us?" Kristoff asked in disbelief. Nelson wiped the blood from his lips, stroking his nose to check for any broken bones.

"That's not how it is," he argued weakly, nursing his ribs. "None of this was supposed to happen. We weren't supposed to get stuck here! I did what I did to get Captain Drackenheart's cooperation. Those papers were never going to see the light of day if we returned in time."

Creedy turned to Farand. "You knew about this, you lying piece of—"

"Calm down, Creedy! Both the captain and I were aware of the risks. At the time, there was no chance of that happening. We did what we had to do to keep our ship, and you lot, safe."

"And that makes it alright, then?" Dalia spat. "Keeping us all in the dark?"

Against his better senses, Farand struggled to keep his thoughts straight, unable to de-escalate the crew's rising displeasure. Mutiny was not an option. "We took every precaution that this mission would proceed as planned. The threat was dealt with ideally. Pirates were not a part of it. If you want anyone to hang, you should track down the scums that stranded us." Farand knew he was fighting an impossible battle. The crew's morale was low enough as it was, and on top of that, they learned about Nelson's betrayal at the worst possible timing. Creedy thirsted for blood. The surrounding crew would quickly follow unless something was done.

"Escort Mr. Blackwood to the brig," Watch Captain Dalia ordered, assisting Creedy to his feet. Kristoff took Nelson by his good arm, and Norman hovered to the other side, remaining quiet as they led the semi-conscious lawyer below deck. If Farand protested, he would fall on the wrong side of the crew's favour. Without Captain Drackenheart to back him, his position was vulnerable and questionable regarding this delicate situation. He simply lacked the words and conviction to do anything about it.

"Mr. Duplànte, sir. How many days do we have left until we're royally fucked?" Dalia asked.

"About three or four days."

"Bloody hell." She grimaced and rubbed her temples.

Farand nodded. "You must understand we did whatever we could to make sure you all were safe."

"I understand that, sir. Nelson's a good guy, but it doesn't make this alright. At least not among certain groups." Dalia eyed Creedy, who was stomping about the rigging, re-checking the ropes for the third time. "He'll be safe as long as he stays in the brig. No one dies today at least," she concluded and nodded once.

"Good call, Watch Captain."

"Thank you, sir. Now how do we find the captain and the others?" On cue, Hwang gave a shout of surprise.

"Sir! The horizon is on fire!" He pointed north to a set of dense forest now ablaze at its periphery.

The internal gears in Farand's head turned, wondering if this was the distraction Olivier had created. "Mother always said pyromania ran in the family." Farand rolled his eyes and turned the wheel.

Shadows flitted around the grass, the crooked birch, and the hulder carrying buckets of water and tossing them on the fire. Away from the rabble, they saw a single torch waving in the darkness.

"That's Olivier. Prepare for a quick descent. No dallying!"

Dalia nodded and rushed teams to coordinate the touchdown.

Olivier was a mere outline in the darkness after ditching the torch. The dry grass smouldered within seconds, and before he even made it aboard, Farand nudged the ship towards the sky. Olivier stumbled over the railing, stretching out his hands and did a half sweep of victory to the applauding crew.

"Not the distraction we expected, but it was hella efficient," Dalia congratulated.

"You shulda seen their faces when I dropped the first torch." He cackled.

"All right. Now we need to find our dear captain," Farand announced. "I want us as visible as possible. Light all the lanterns. Wave torches. Burn the spare canvas if you think it'll help. We have a captain and half a crew to find and not a day to spare!" The crew scattered about the ship, lighting all the lanterns they could find, stealing those from storage and fixing them along the railings with rope and belts. Olivier climbed to his nest on the mainmast, taking out his spyglass to survey the vast forest below.

The *Red Queen* shone brightly in the night with the moonlight to power the sails and flowers donning every crevice and rope. She was a glowing enigma.

Ida emerged from the engine room. Soot and grime already dug deep into every piece of her clothing, and her neatly braided hair had faced the full oily might of the thruster engine and lost, now a tangle of escaped strands.

"How're we looking, Mr. Duplànte?" she asked.

"Considering her state, she flies well enough. What's the situation down there?"

"She'll hold, but I don't recommend any cooling or lights below deck. Or hot water. No water ... The lanterns work well enough, though."

"Fine by us. Tell me, Miss Simonsen, where did they take you?"

Her face paled. "The hulder Queen and a convoy carried me southward, I think. I didn't see much, but we definitely walked for a good three hours. Past those mountains there, I reckon."

"Then that's the way we're heading. You're sure you never saw our captain?"

"Positive, sir. Although the hulder Queen, the little I understood, said there was a woman there."

Farand's eyes lit up. "That is excellent news. I need you to guide us to that cabin."

"Aye, sir. West of those mountains, then we turned southeast. What's happened up here?" She looked at Creedy pacing the deck nursing his knuckles and the crew's general solemn state.

"The crew had a falling out with our proprietor. He's in the brig for his own safety."

Her eyes turned wide. "He's what? Is he hurt? What did he do?"

"Miss Simonsen, this is not the time nor the place. I suggest you put your personal feelings aside in favour of our survival."

"...Yes sir."

CHAPTER 27

FEAR OF BEING ALONE

The low hanging clouds burned red. Rosanne stared at the blazing sky accentuated by low-hanging clouds, bathing the black volcano in a hellish rim of light. An excited jolt ran through her, and she resisted the urge to run off and leave without a word.

"It must be them," she told Yerrik, who minced about the hearth, preparing a fire for the evening.

"It could be the forest inhabitants," he said.

"That's bullshit, and you know it. A fire large enough to paint the sky red isn't for giggles." Shaking her head, she tapped the windowsill. "It's them. I know it is. I need to get to higher ground."

Letting out a sigh, Yerrik blew out the match he held with plans to light the kindling. "If you're that adamant, I can go with you." He opened the door and nodded towards a hill barely visible in the harsh moonlight. "We can get to that hilltop there in less than an hour." The mound in question was a barren rock beaten by cracked boulders and frostbite, giving it a youthful appearance of sharper proportions.

Rosanne gathered her vest and hat. "Then let's go."

Yerrik did not protest as Rosanne jogged into the forest. He shook his head and followed her until she realized she had no clear sight of the path ahead and let him lead with a torch. Rosanne followed as closely as she could. Her skirt caught in the bush too often for her comfort, but considering the state of her breeches, now a shredded sight of indecency, this was the better alternative.

"Are you all right? You are out of breath," Yerrik asked.

"When we get to Noval, I'm taking a month-long holiday to catch it again. All this hiking in the wrong boots kills all feelings my feet should have." She smiled despite the discomfort, fanning herself with the hat.

"If that is your crew, what makes you so sure they would come this way?"

"That fire isn't a small one. I smell a plan, not ashes. You said other creatures live there and that you sent Mr. Lyle their way. Granted, I'm betting more on my gut feeling than knowledge at this point. But I'm certain. It's my Hail Mary."

When they reached the foot of the hill and started their ascent, the top of the northern volcano let out rumbles of odd noises. "Do you hear that?" Rosanne ceased all movement and listened. A sharp crackling followed by a distant boom. "Cannon shots. They're fighting."

"It appears to come from inside their den."

Rosanne stopped. A puzzling thought occurred to her. "Why would they have cannons *inside* the volcano?"

Yerrik shrugged. "If they want something, they take it, be it material means or people. They're especially fond of men."

"I can see why my crew would be there then. But my ship as well? Unlikely. And you have been in there?" She rested her hands on her hips, catching her breath.

Yerrik bobbed his head. "A few times when I had to trade. They can be difficult, but for the most part, our deal is that they leave me alone."

Rosanne nodded, and although the questions buzzed about her brain, she didn't have time to question him. If she missed her chance to get off the island, she would be stranded for the remainder of her days. She had better things to do with her life. Or so she wanted to believe.

The distant sound of cannon fire resonated in the mountains for half the climb to the hilltop. They stopped by a rocky wall crop, having to go around to continue their trek. Only when it was quiet did Rosanne train her eyes in the distance. She squinted against the gloom.

"Come on, you bastards. Follow protocol," she muttered to herself, drawing an amused grin from Yerrik, who said little to break Rosanne's concentration.

"There's a faint light over there." He pointed between the next two mountains slightly lower than the volcano. A stocky conglomeration of lights swooped over the northern mountains.

"That's a ship, all right!" Rosanne let out a whoop of joy. "We need to signal them before they pass us."

He handed over the torch, and Rosanne lifted it as high as she could, giving it a wide meaningful sweep. She waited, then did another long sweep. She repeated this process a few times as the ship sailed closer. A flicker of light waved back.

"They saw us!" she announced and jumped in excitement. "What was the signal again. Uh..." She scrunched her eyes together. "One, two." She flashed the torch up and down. "Three and one." Then she waited. The torch, barely visible to the naked eye responded. "It's them. They're picking us up. Come on. We need to get further up to ease their landing."

Yerrik turned to lead the way. His body cast a twisted shape against the flat rocky wall. Her heart felt like it failed to beat, and Rosanne struggled to breathe. *The shadow.* She was certain it was the same as the one in her first nightmare after Nikor's attack. Aros' words called in her mind about Yerrik not being who he seemed. Yerrik followed the path without an issue in the darkness of night, picking his way between the rocks and placing his feet as if he knew every part of the mountain by heart. Rosanne swallowed her surprise and raised the torch to illuminate the path.

"Y-Yerrik?" she called.

"Something the matter?" His gentle eyes shone when they turned to view her, reflecting silver in the torchlight like a nocturnal creature.

Rosanne forced a smile, lowering her gaze. "Are you sure you want to leave this island with us? You don't know what's out there."

He shrugged. "Can't possibly be worse. Besides, I quite enjoy your company." She nodded and went up beside him. How had she never noticed his eyes glowed in the dark or his shadow didn't fit his frame?

"I'll lead the way. My light's better."

He stepped aside, holding out a hand. "After you." As soon as Yerrik's attention was on the ground, her smile withered away at the notion that he wasn't human. His actions, his words, the very being that was Yerrik; she couldn't read him. Did he seek to harm her and the crew? Or was he simply searching for a way off this island? If so, why bother to ask her to stay? Perhaps she was the target all along, and coming with her was just as acceptable?

You see what you want to see. Aros' words rang in her thoughts again. She swallowed the lump in her throat and took a deep breath. What did she want from Yerrik?

The crackling hum of the *Red Queen*'s thruster engine rang like music despite the occasional sputter. She waved the torch low enough for the scouts to make out the ground, and whoever was behind the wheel didn't compensate for the broken fine thrusters and banged the ship against the hilltop. Nevertheless, Rosanne climbed the ship's hull ladder, struggling to keep her skirt from catching her feet and leading her to a miserable end at the rocky outcrop below.

Dalia and Norman's faces lit up like Constitutional Day upon seeing Rosanne, and they rushed to help her over the railing.

"Am I glad to see you all again." Rosanne smiled. "Good lord, you guys look worse for wear." Kristoff's eyes went to her skirt immediately, and his face scrunched together like something was wrong with the fabric of the universe.

"One word about my attire, and you're scrubbing barnacles for a month." She tucked her ring finger and thumb under the palm of her hand and turned it, displaying the palm-side up to Dalia. Dalia's face blanched and quickly displayed the signal around. The gun crew gathered around the ladder, loading their rifles and pistols. Farand, at the wheel, nodded at Captain Drackenheart's approach to the quarterdeck.

"You've looked better, Captain," he said grimly, but his eyes bespoke his relief of seeing her alive and well.

"Don't I know it." She snorted. "And what the hell happened to my ship? Are those *flowers*?" She pointed to the once beautiful floral braids, now a tangle and loose arrangement of disaster. "Where did that scratch on the main deck come from?"

Farand's brows scrunched together, refraining himself from any sort of reaction which could give away his shame. "I have quite the tale. Now shall we focus on the interesting company you brought?" He nodded to the approaching figure emerging over the railing.

Yerrik paused at the long-barreled welcome party. His face betrayed surprise but also wonder. He climbed aboard with meticulous care, holding out his hands. He looked to where Rosanne stood on the quarterdeck, with both hands on her hips and chin held high.

"What are you, Yerrik? Man or beast?" her authoritative voice called out, clear for all to hear.

He cocked his head to the side as if the question was odd. "Neither."

The crew amassed on the main deck. Half a dozen rifles were trained on Yerrik's head, another dozen pistols on his chest.

Rosanne leaned on the security railing, her eyes scrutinizing his expression. "You did something, and I know you can alter your shape. What is it, Yerrik? If that's even your name."

He splayed his hands. "I am whatever you want me to be."

"Then reveal yourself."

"I am not hiding from anyone. I never lied to you, Dragon-heart. I am what you see."

"Bullshit!" she spat. "You kept me trapped in a dream for days. You made me see and experience things for your damn pleasure." Rosanne's lips quivered, fighting the boiling anger welling in the pit of her stomach.

A flash of confusion crossed his features. "I never forced you to do anything. The dreams were of your making, and I staged the scenario. Everything that happened was of your own volition, to rid yourself of the pains of this world."

Rosanne sighed. "What is it that you want? Why go through all of this?"

"A companion, Dragonheart. As did you. That is all."

She hitched a breath, wanting to dismiss his comment entirely. Only his eyes glowed in the torchlight, a most unsettling sight if she thought he was human, and by all accounts, that is how he appeared to her. Was this truly all he wanted from her, to be with her? It couldn't be that simple. There had to be some deeper meaning to it, a trick to which they would all end up trapped on this island to the end of their days. But his eyes, silver and nocturnal, looked sad as they regarded her. Rosanne's heart clenched.

Creedy staggered back in a yelp. "What the fuck is that?"

The others regarded Creedy's behaviour curiously.

"How did he *do* that? You ain't seeing it?" Regaining his pose, he held the rifle steady.

Dalia, who stood right next to him, shook her head. "What are you talking about?"

"I see it too!" Kristoff burst out. A round of gasps and curses went through the crowd, and many exchanged curious and terrified glances. The crew drew away.

"Absolutely no one fires as much as a bullet without my say-so," Rosanne commanded, drawing the crew's attention so they would not lose their composure to fear. Rosanne stepped down to the main deck, the crew parting ways for her. She stood at the edge of the crowd, surrounded by guns all trained on the man. "You can't hide behind that facade, Forest Devil. I may still see only a man, but you can't fool everyone aboard this ship."

"Captain, I'm not sure what it is I'm looking at," Farand called from the quarterdeck.

"That depends on what you want to see. Mr. Creedy, what do you see?" Rosanne asked.

The older man looked uncertain. "I don't know what he is, but that is hideous."

"His eyes were blue. I'm certain of it. But now they ... they're red," Dalia commented.

"Are you off your rocks? That's a man." Despite his assertions, Olivier didn't lower his gun.

Rosanne laid a hand on Kristoff's rifle, lowering it. "You can't come with us, Yerrik." The Forest Devil's eyes flashed. "You do not fit into our world."

A smile replaced his confusion. "I know your desires, your fears. I know you, Dragonheart. I know *you* and what you need."

Rosanne shook her head. "That doesn't change anything. For your own sake, you will remain here, and we will return to our world, to our homes and our people." As quickly as it had come, his smile withered away, disintegrated by Rosanne's hard eyes. And yet, there was a hint of tears, albeit invisible to most.

The crew's aim remained firm. Unnerved by his silence, the way his eyes searched her subtle change in facial expression, Rosanne took another step forward.

"*I* don't need you in my world, so please get off my ship. Don't make me shoot you."

"Rosanne, I—"

Rosanne yanked the flintlock from Olivier's hands and aimed it at Yerrik's head. "Leave!" Yerrik took a step back in surprise, reaching out a hand as if pleading yet pacifying. Her heart wrenched so hard she thought she would be sick.

"Mr. Duplànte!" She called out before Yerrik could speak

again. "If this man hasn't left the ship within ten seconds and I haven't pulled this trigger, you have my permission to shoot him."

"Aye, Captain," Farand replied.

"One ..." Her lips trembled so badly she almost bit herself.

Yerrik's disappointed eyes locked on hers.

"Two ..." She drew back the reload mechanism.

THE SHIP ROCKED as it disembarked from the hilltop. Rosanne shut the door to her cabin quietly behind her and leaned against it. She listened to the clatter of shoes against the deck, Dalia and Creedy commanding the masts, and Farand calling for updates. It was a comforting bustle, and Rosanne welcomed it.

The curtains to the windows were drawn, and Rosanne ran to them and wrenched them aside. From the window, Yerrik's dark shadow faded fast in the distance, his outline barely visible in the moonlight. She imagined him staring right at her, could almost believe it in her mind's eye, could almost feel his warm longing gaze at her once more. She almost screamed, almost drove her fists into the floor, almost threw the paperweights against the walls.

How did she not see it before? Why couldn't she just ignore what he was? Yerrik would never fit into her world. It burdened her with a profound sense of guilt that she had let herself be seduced so easily, but she had embraced his approach, and she had wanted it. She envisioned him in front of her with his gentle smile and open arms.

All strength left her body, and she simply sat at the foot of the bookshelves, unable to fight the new emotions, unable to process the self-betrayal.

As tears streamed freely, her face contorted, and she opened her mouth in a silent scream.

Chapter 28

I'm Sorry

Located deep in the bowels of the *Red Queen*, a square cell stood in the middle of the room. A window no larger than a man's head provided a limited view of the outside world, now showing nothing but the blackness of night.

"I heard about what happened." Ida sat down next to the cell, crossing her legs and facing away. Nelson leaned against the bars, nursing his swelling eye and lips. "You look like shit." The unspoken duplicity negated any trace of humour in her tone.

Nelson bobbed his head and winced from the sudden movements. "Just about the same as how I feel, then." He flew into a fit of coughs, holding his side and struggling to breathe. He spat on the floor, his phlegm mixed with blood, and his breath gurgled.

Ida drew a sharp breath, turned and looked at Nelson, who seemed occupied with his broken glasses. "Creedy went too far. Look at yourself."

He sighed. "Nah. I'm the fool."

"Nelson, you ... you betrayed our trust." Ida paused, taking in the creaking of the ship's timber, the low hum of the thruster engine. "Now it all makes sense," she said. "When I first saw you, I couldn't understand how you convinced our captain. You seemed so small and harmless. I get why you did what you did. Or is that a part of another lie?"

He looked at her now, the one good eye dull and robbed of will. "All I wanted was to find out what happened to my father. This journey was based on my selfish need for closure. We would have been back in Valo a week ago had we not been attacked. I should have known better than sending a trade ship to find a military vessel that's been swept under the rug. I should have let it rest."

"You didn't know that we were going to be attacked. You couldn't have predicted any of this."

"I didn't want to burden you with the prospect of imprisonment, even the gallows, but your captain ... that god-damned woman drives a hard bargain. I had all the information at my disposal, and I used it against people I regarded as nothing but common criminals. I couldn't have been more wrong." The bars clanged as he slumped back again, having lost all breath and the will to continue the conversation.

They sat in silence, listening to the clamour upstairs. A loud thumping on the deck above told them that there was someone in the storage rooms, but the visit was brief, and the room turned quiet again.

"When do you have to be back?" Ida asked at length.

Nelson counted on his fingers, muttering. "Three ... maybe four days?"

Ida let out an incredulous laugh. "That's barely enough time to make it." She let the sentence hang, hoping Nelson had additional comments to alleviate her fears. "We need the captain and the rest of the crew. Else we don't stand a chance."

"I'm sorry, Ida. I blew this up to the sky. But my apology won't do you any good." Ida turned towards the bars and snuck her arms between them. Nelson eyed her incredulously, then moved to her. Ida embraced Nelson the best she could, resting her head against the cold metal as her arms encircled him. "Let's get home first. Then we can deal with whatever shitstorm is coming.

We're traders, after all. If the market changes, we adapt. We can survive anything."

"I made sure the paperwork was thorough enough to have you all arrested for whatever the fancy term for gun trade is."

Ida laughed at the prospect of how utterly screwed they were. "Trading and abetting foreign state in military warfare against the Central United Colonies."

"Yes, right. I should have remembered that. Not only did I ruin your careers, but potentially your lives as well. I incriminated myself, so when we get back, we're all out of a job. Equality at its best. Ow!" Nelson held his side where Ida's fist had connected.

"Nelson, I hate you," she whispered.

"I know."

"I hate you, and I care about you."

"I ... what?"

Smiling, she squeezed him tighter, their faces inches apart. "You acted how anyone would. Extortion and blackmail are what we do. God knows the captain has gotten us through rainy days for far less but with a larger impact. She's done a lot for us. It's only fair that you are allowed to do the same without being judged. But we came to like you, Nelson. You became a part of us. *I* came to like you."

If her words moved him in any way, he gave no indication of it; instead, he looked away. He moved back slightly and took her hands, holding them firmly to his chest. "What's there to like?" His gaze rested firmly on the floor.

"Why does a man love a woman?" She countered with another jab so he'd lift his head to see her smile.

Nelson stroked her cheek, letting out an elaborate hmm. "Beauty always makes a great first impression."

Ida snorted but didn't shy away from his touch.

"Her bright smile, which lifts my spirit in a storm. Laughter that carries my heart across the seven mountains. Her bubbly personality which enchants me, and her wicked humour which inspires me to not take my shortcomings so seriously."

Ida laughed then, recalling the silly moments they shared during the journey, Nelson's first and only trip to the crow's nest, the many stories they shared about their travels, and how he always helped whenever he could. "Were you always such a smooth talker?"

"You inspired that in me." His smile suddenly withered, and he pulled back. "It was never my intention that it got this far."

"It's not over yet. There's still time, and as long as we can escape the Grey Veil, we can get through this too."

"And if we don't?"

Ida frowned. "Your pessimism is breathtaking. We'll sail the Aurora, of course." She held her arms wide, a bright smile replacing her frown.

Nelson blinked. "What is the Aurora?"

"You haven't heard of it? It's a local tale of Valo, from before the colonization." Her eyes brimmed with excitement. "A southern man fell in love with a woman from the north, a powerful priestess. She controlled the sun and the moon and the stars and the bridge to them, the Aurora Borealis. But to be able to walk among mortals and her beloved, the shaman had to give up all her powers to live a normal life. For a while, they were happy, but then war brewed in the south and the man was called to arms. She was unable to stop him, and he set off to assist in the war. As time passed, the woman's longing and grief from their separation grew so strong she begged the stars to return her mystic abilities. The stars took pity on her cause, granting her the powers she once gave up. She called to the aurora and made a bridge to her love, and she walked to the battlefields upon ribbons of green and purple lights and retrieved her beloved. But the man was wounded, so the woman made a new bridge to the stars and became one of them. They're there to this day and for all eternity. For she loved him too much to give up on his life."

For the first time in what seemed like an eternity, Nelson smiled. "That's a wonderful tale."

"My grandmother used to tell it to us when we were kids. She was a native of Valo and her husband, ironically, a man from the south."

"Pity there aren't any northern lights this far south."

"Our captain might not possess the mystic abilities of a shaman and summon the heaven's bridge to get us home, but she cares about us too much to give up, and she will see us safe for as long as we live. And for as long as we're under contract with the *Red Queen*, but that's beside the point." Nelson chuckled painfully; his laughter caused waves of stabbing agony to his side.

Ida slid forward and hugged him again, keeping her hands away from his broken ribs. She pressed her face between the bars but couldn't slip past. "Come closer, Nelson."

"Why?"

"The steel bars are cold, and I want to kiss your dumb face." Seeing Ida's cheeks squished against the metal and her soft, forgiving eyes, Nelson couldn't help but lean in and press his lips against hers. The metal was cold, but Nelson's head buzzed with fireworks. For the moment, the outside world didn't matter. Nothing else did.

Ida's blue eyes fluttered open. "Don't you dare give up already," she whispered. "We're all survivors here. Don't apologize for doing what we would do."

"I'll keep that in mind the next time I'm betraying a crew of terrifying and skilled individuals."

IDA RETURNED to the comforting squalor of the engine room after ensuring Nelson's wounds were treated. Tools and tubes, wires and screws were littered about the place after she, Higgs, and Gavin had raced against time to patch up Leaky Sally to make their escape.

Higgs wasn't around; no doubt occupied elsewhere with new problems arising from their patchwork. She picked up the screws and sorted them into the wall of little compartments next to the door. Only then did she notice the bloody pool creeping from under the open door. Closing it, she saw a hulder slumped against the hot pipes, the skin on her face and shoulder sizzling where they had connected with the metal. On the back of her head was the impression where her skull was caved in thanks to Norman's shovel.

The smell made her gag.

Grabbing the limp body, she dragged it off the pipes with a squelching sound. Another three hulder lay piled outside in the corridor, and Ida dragged the charred remains and dumped them on top of the others.

She attacked the sizzling flesh left on the pipes with a spatula normally used for oil and grease spills.

She put on a funny voice. "Hulder skin marinated in plasmic oil. Available only for a brief time aboard the *Red Queen*! Hammond would be so proud."

She dumped the remains in the waste bucket and covered it with sand to stave off the scent of cooked meat which reminded her of mid-winter celebration pig rind.

The room heated up quickly now that the air-conditioning was switched off, but she couldn't risk turning it on for her comfort when the ship was barely able to fly. She wiped her sweat with a towel, threw it over her shoulder, and then picked up the remaining junk littering the floor.

Footsteps by the door had Ida screaming in fright, and she threw an unlit blowtorch she recently picked up at the approaching creature.

"Easy! It's only me!" Gavin caught the torch before it clattered behind some incredibly hot pipes. His nose twitched. "Do I smell bacon?"

Ida laughed despite her reaction, and then it morphed into a sob. "Fucking hell, Gavin! You ass!" She smacked him on the chest, making him stagger.

"Sorry, sorry. I was just checking up on you when I couldn't find you in the brig. Nelson's looked better."

"I know. I patched him up the best I could."

"And now you're here, sulking."

"I'm not sulking." She attacked the assortment of littered tools on the workbench.

Gavin frowned. "You cleaned the room. You're sulking. Ida, I like Nelson. I really do, but perhaps it's best if you didn't hang around him anymore."

She huffed. "What is that supposed to mean?"

"He cut us good. I heard what happened. I'm not sure what is more shocking: that the captain and lieutenant knew of his blackmail or that the hulder Queen did. How the hell could she know?"

"Maybe she's a mind reader. I don't really care, Gavin. And who I hang around is my business. Now leave me alone."

He took her by the shoulders, forcing her tear-puffed eyes to look into his concerned ones. "Being around Nelson right now will put you in a very bad spot with the rest of the crew." Ida's scowled so deep her forehead hurt. "Okay, Creedy will disapprove," Gavin corrected.

"Then fuck Creedy! He's the reason Nelson can barely breathe. He's already paid the price. Maybe we should focus on getting home and stopping this disaster from happening rather than bickering who the hell I choose to spend my time with!"

"Ida, I only meant—"

"Not another word Gavin." She pointed at him with a wrench, her eyes hard and livid. "You've been acting strangely throughout this entire journey. You don't think I didn't know? You honestly think your apparent jealousy and incessant need to be included whenever Nelson was around was something you could hide from me and then have the gall to tell *me* to stay away?" She smacked the wrench at the table, screws and bolts clinked to the floor.

Gavin paled.

Ida scoffed and rested her hands on her hips. "You never had the courage to speak your mind. Not even when we both shined on the same guy."

"I ... I didn't say anything because he likes you!" he burst out. "*I* don't even know what the fuck I'm doing! Nelson just made everything so easy!"

"He is easy to like, isn't he?" Ida stated with half a laugh.

"Much easier than you." Gavin countered, and Ida smacked his shoulder. They shared a moment of guilt in the form of silence and fallen looks. Ida stroked her arm, calming the unease in her heart.

"I'm sorry, Gavin. I didn't want this to come between us. You mean so much to me."

His prim smile feigned nonchalance as he hoisted his shoulders. "Oh, you know what the captain says. Cut your losses and so on."

"This is hardly the same," she said.

"I'm trying to be brave here. Give me some credit."

Ida embraced him, and he hugged her with equal ferocity.

"It's Creedy I'm scared of, not your dalliance with Nelson," he said after they pulled away from one another.

"I know. I was just mad. Did you say anything to Nelson when you saw him?"

"Hell no. If I'm as apparent as you say I am, hopefully, I won't need to." He sniffed the air. "Can we do something about that bacon smell now? It's making me hungry."

"Skinny bacon that weighs a lot," she quipped, making Gavin chuckle.

"I think the broken gunport would be the easiest way to toss them."

"Gunport it is." Ida grabbed one set of hulder feet and grinned.

CHAPTER 29

GOLD, ME HEARTIES!

When Rosanne finally emerged from her quarters, she was donning familiar garments of trousers, wool tunic, leather vest, and jacket. Her hair was braided and hidden under the battered remains of her father's hat. It was a miracle she hadn't lost it in the bog; the string clung around her throat in a suffocatingly loving manner.

"What's our status, Mr. Duplànte?" She marched up the quarterdeck, standing next to the now haggard hulk of a man.

"Looking better, Captain. Engine is running, sails a strumming, ports sputtering, and we're severely understaffed."

"Marvelous. How're the engine levels looking?" Rosanne scanned the dashboard when Farand didn't respond, locking her eyes on a display of numbers. "Ten bloody perce...?" She rubbed her face.

"Daylight's four hours away," the man tried hopefully. "We can make it to the coastline before that time at this pace."

Rosanne scanned the rigging and the makeshift masts, rough on the edges but doing their job. "How sturdy are the masts? Will they handle my driving?"

"If you treat her gently, she might carry us home." Farand spotted the older watch captain milling about the deck with rope hemp. "Mr. Creedy! Rigging status!" Creedy's face bore an expression as if he had just bitten into mouldy bread.

"Good enough to hang ourselves should we be stuck here any longer!" he barked and stalked off with his rope. Rosanne rose her eyebrows, glancing at Farand who didn't condemn Creedy's displeasure and merely shrugged.

"On a positive note, Mr. Lyle is in the infirmary, albeit in terrible shape. Hammond's wounded as well, but he's receiving treatment," Farand continued, giving the wheel half a turn as they closed on the mountains to their starboard.

Rosanne let out a sigh of relief. "I honestly believed he was lost to us. We have quite the tale to fill your shore leave. But right now, we have bigger issues." She tried to suppress a frown. "The pirate captain, Aros Bernhart. I met him, we negotiated, we were attacked by trolls, and now he's supposedly found himself a new ship. I am certain he wasn't referring to the sorry broken sight by the cliffs. That dragon has been slain."

"How did they find a working vessel all the way out here?"

Rosanne shrugged. "We passed a ship graveyard in the bay due north, but he could have found it somewhere else. He's got a crew more numerous than we first thought. Chances are, if our missing crew escaped the initial attack in the forest, we'd find them by the cliffs or toward the ship graveyard. But to be safe, make way to the landing spot first."

"Aye, Captain." Farand corrected the ship's bow, steering them southeast.

"On another note, Mr. Duplànte ..." Captain Drackenheart began, staring at Norman, who emerged from below deck with a broom. "What is that?" She pointed to the pile of ashes on the main deck.

"I er..." Farand fumbled. Norman noticed Rosanne's narrow stare and hurriedly swept the ashes overboard, grinning sheepishly before scurrying off. Shaking her head, Rosanne let it be.

"Oh, and Captain?" Farand prompted, catching her curious

stare. "Don't ever leave me in charge again." The man smiled despite his words.

Rosanne snorted a laugh. "You're too humble for the big guns."

"True as the sun shines, miss *Demon of the Sky*," Farand mocked.

———

TOPMEN FLEW UP the ratlines to straighten the mizzen and main topgallant sails, giving free way for the moon's rays to hit the larger sails. The *Red Queen* sailed through the sky like a stumbling sailor. With nothing definite to fix or hold together, the crew rounded up the hulder bodies and tossed them overboard, leaving a trail of malformed monstrosities in the forest below. With their claws, songs, and superior strength, the hulder could have easily inflicted mortal wounds on the crew but somehow refrained from killing them even when presented with the chance. Perhaps it was under the orders of their queen, as they were a necessity for their survival, or perhaps something else. Farand spared this half a thought but promptly reminded himself that their survival took priority.

Rosanne made personal rounds visiting the gundeck and rounding up the station captains. The results she expected were worse than she hoped, but considering that they all had escaped the hulder volcano with minimal losses, it was a best-case scenario.

"We have fifteen leads left. I don't think we have ever had that little in stock." Hwang kicked the near-empty crate of cannonballs.

"Gun ammunition is sparse as well, and all the spare plasma packs are now primary." Kristoff shook his head.

Back on the quarterdeck, Rosanne dragged the skin on her face, creating a ghastly blue and black ringed bone-faced monster akin to Nikor. "We don't have time for tact, and if the crew is imprisoned or worse, we need the cannons to make a hell of a noise to scare off the trolls."

"The what, Captain?" Farand asked.

"Trolls. The forests we went to were filled with them. Big monsters as well as tiny fuck-annoying ones. Good throwers, excellent aim, and we're on their menu."

"Duly noted. So, pirates and trolls are what potentially stand between us and the rest of the crew? We've seen worse odds. Frankly, I'm quite optimistic about this one, as escaping a horde of hulder was by far the scariest experience I have ever lived through. Reminds me of why I divorced my first wife."

Rosanne threw her head back in laughter. "Your timing for banter never ceases to amuse me, Farand. Shall I take the wheel?"

"If it pleases the captain."

"Bugger off and rest. I need to hug my beautiful girl again."

Holding out his hand, Farand beckoned Rosanne to take the wheel and stepped back. She stopped him before he could leave. "While you're here, I don't see our notorious lawyer about. Should I be concerned?"

"Mr. Blackwood's ploy was exposed under the worst possible circumstances, and *certain* parties did not take it well." Farand cast his eyes about the ship, sweeping his hand towards Creedy, skulking by the forecastle. "He's confined to the brig where no one hopefully murders him before we clear our return to Valo."

"Well fuck us sideways ..." Rosanne huffed her breath.

"Your taste for foul language has improved, I see."

"That's what being courted by monsters does to you, Mr. Duplànte. I should introduce you to one, so you can explore your mental dictionary of profanities."

"Ah, a language to your tastes."

"Three hours, Mr. Duplànte. Sleep well." Rosanne smiled and stared off into the distance. Dalia came to the quarterdeck wearing the adrenaline-induced expression of someone who had just escaped death. Her pupils were so small the irises were all colour and had no focus.

"I had almost lost hope for a moment there, Captain. Glad you met us halfway."

Rosanne nodded. "I would have missed you completely if the horizon wasn't on fire."

"That would be Olivier's handiwork." She pointed a thumb to the crow's nest, where a pair of naked feet peeked out from over the ledge.

"That explains the commotion. How are the crew doing?"

"Questioning your loyalty to us but very much alive and still happy to see you. Creedy's itching to smother a certain law-abiding blackmailer, and we have too many people crippled from the fight. How are you? Who was that man from before, or whatever he was?"

Rosanne let out a sigh, nudging the wheel gently and bringing them higher over the jagged mountains below them. "That man held me captive under the pretense of helping me return to the ship. He would have murdered us all given a chance," Rosanne lied. The crew was worse for wear, and her personal feelings were far less important than the integrity of the ship's operators.

"We'll make it back to Valo in time. I need you, of all people, to keep the topmen busy. Take everyone you need from other stations. If we're lucky, we won't need to fight again with anyone but the border customs."

"Nothing to worry about, Captain. But you don't look well."

"Your concern is appreciated but unnecessary. Keep Mr. Blackwood alive, retrieve the rest of the crew, and avoid pirates and storms. Getting back is our only priority right now."

"Yes, Captain." Dalia said nothing about the bloodshot capillaries surrounding Rosanne's eyes and scurried off to gather helping hands.

THE BLACKENED shore of the southern cliffs was near invisible in the darkness of night, illuminated by its many pools glowing silver under the waning moon. Marine life crawled across the rocks or flew out of the ponds. Silvery crabs scuttled over the black rocks and grassed at the nearby tufts, snipping them short. Eel-like fish with bulbous bladders flew out of the ponds, grabbed at the crabs, and dragged them into a limb-ripping agonizing death.

"This place never ceases to amaze me." Dalia stared at a crab fighting for its life, and the fact that she could see it so clearly from fifty meters away was another indication of the shelled creature's impressive size.

"The sooner we're off this rock, the better," Rosanne said while peeking at the scenery through the spyglass. "I'm not seeing anyone. Olivier, do you have visual?" she called toward the crow's nest.

"Nun, Captain!"

"I would be impressed if the missionaries made it this far to set up cloister." Dalia chuckled. Rosanne checked display dials, and the urge to destroy something was triggered by their lack of response.

"Daylight is still another two hours away, and we can't afford to wait. Round up as many as you can and have them scout while we go at a crawl. They can sleep when they're dead."

Dalia disappeared below deck, and it didn't take long before her pot holler rousted every man available from their spread-eagled slumbers. Soon enough, every man was armed with as many rifles as were available, and Rosanne turned the ship northeast, heading towards the ship graveyard.

Rosanne performed regular checkups to the engine room, receiving Higgs' disapproving complaints about the captain's merciless torture of the engine's performance capabilities every time.

In the coming twilight, they hadn't spotted any activity on their path. Perhaps the rest of the crew was dead, wound up as troll food for the dirty inhabitants, or perhaps the pirates took them out as payback.

Whatever the cause might be, it was too early to draw conclusions. Rosanne would comb the shoreline and the woods for only a day, and after that, they would be unable to return to Valo in time. Already now, she was pushing their luck, praying the ship didn't fall apart during their journey or that a storm knocked them over with a shrill howl of surprise.

By the time Farand returned from his restless sleep, Rosanne's adrenaline was ebbing. The crew, to keep from passing out, took turns to shut their eyes for a few minutes and then return to their duties. Farand didn't have to say anything and merely took the wheel. Rosanne's eyes were stiff and bloodshot. A gentle push from the lieutenant had her feet automatically returning her to her quarters, where she passed out the moment her head hit the pillow.

"AIM LOWER. GIVE 'EM A DIRT SPRAY," Olivier said while looking through his spyglass. Kristoff turned the little wheel on the side of the cannon, lowering the nose by a few degrees. Then he pulled the string and felt the jolt of the cannon rolling back on its tracks. The cannonball flew into the top of a low mound, exploding the ground into a firework of flying dirt.

The waist-tall grass surrounding the area rustled with life and angry chitters. Mops of shaggy brown hair moved about the field in panic. A pale, gnarled face growled at the *Red Queen*, and with its short stubby arms, it sent a spear flying. The weapon arched and lost momentum before thudding pathetically against the galley's hull, barely scratching the wood.

"That was ..." Kristoff began, bobbed his head, and snickered at the trolls' amusing attempt at felling the ship. Other trolls followed the first and threw their spears with expert precision, but the hull was simply too strong to be damaged by their flimsy weapons.

"Focus, lads. We got people down there." Dalia smacked Kristoff and Olivier on the back of their heads.

Through the dirty lens, Olivier spotted half a score of men ducking for cover in the tall grass and behind boulders, armed to their teeth with rifles and sharpened wooden spears. Dalia aimed her plasma rifle at a small lump of movement barely visible in the coming dawn. Pulling the trigger, the sizzling ball of energy whizzed to the ground and seared the grass. The troll yelped and rolled back, retreating to its waiting comrades huddling behind the mound.

"This isn't even a fight. They just hide," Kristoff said with a great deal of disappointment as he reloaded the cannon. Dalia drew back the headpiece on the plasma rifle. The weapon's low electric hum grew louder for each second of charge before falling completely silent. Aiming at the singular troll peeking out from the mound, she took the shot. A commotion broke out as the troll fell over without as much as a cry.

"Fire just at that spot, Kristoff," she commanded, and Kristoff complied without a second thought. The blast sent the fallen troll flying in pieces, making Dalia scowl in disgust. The remaining trolls retreated with haste, leaving a trail of screams and lost pride as they scurried towards the forest on stubby feet.

"I guess that is that then." Dalia rested the pommel of the rifle by her foot.

"I feel bad for them. They didn't have chance." Looking at the hunched form of a once-living troll, Kristoff shuddered.

By the cargo door, the retractable crane stretched out its wooden arm. Chains ran from the base through the arm and suspended a wooden platform which was lowered to the grass. A wave of cheers and greetings went around on ground level, and men with broken arms and legs, or too beaten to climb the hull ladder, ascended on the platform. Excited cries accompanied the coming sunrise, and the crew, despite the many dangers they had suffered, exchanged hugs and jokes almost immediately.

The spectacle drew Rosanne from her sleeping quarters.

Looking at Farand operating the wheel, she raised her hands in question. The lieutenant shrugged.

"A most anti-climactic battle unfolded while you slept, Captain," he said.

The sun peeked over the horizon, illuminating the bay. Broken masts and split decks were aglow in red. Even the surrounding shallow waters were ablaze in the morning rays.

"What a beautiful sorry sight that is," Rosanne said to the lieutenant.

Leaning on the wheel, Farand scanned the barnacle-covered hulls and the hundreds of seagulls defecating their decks. "We don't have time for this," he stated flatly.

"No, we don't. But what on Terra is that?" she questioned the numerous crates, suitcases and chests piled on the ground. The rescued crew grinned even wider as the first haul was brought aboard and people amassed to witness their findings. They opened one of the suitcases, a battered old thing barely held together with sewn patches and broken latches, to expose its golden belongings. Rosanne sputtered at the sight. Waves of excitement erupted around the ship, and someone smacked Rosanne on the back without her registering.

"Let me get this straight," she began, her tone silencing the bustling crew. "You six went against emergency protocols, knowing full and well that this land is crawling with monsters and pirates, and you decided against your better nature to get some bloody treasure?" Her eyes were piercing. Their response was anything but sheepish with half regretful faces. "You bloody idiots just made this trip worthwhile. Now get it all aboard. We leave as soon as you're done."

CHAPTER 30

THE FAST AND THE PERILOUS

The *Red Queen* was a wobbling sight of wilting flowers and gaping wounds in the woodwork, but nothing could cripple this vessel as long as her integrity and her crew survived.

The Grey Veil stood as a foggy wall in the distance. With the atmos disconnected, they sailed at lower altitudes and prayed none of the sea dwellers reached up to swallow them. The full force of mother nature swept over the deck and crew; they suited up, protecting their hands and eyes from the sour winds.

Rosanne pushed the ship as hard as she could without overheating the engine. Now that the sun shone in a relatively cloudless sky, the *Queen* could fly at close to normal speed.

The hours ticked by. The crew grew restless the closer they came to the fog obscuring the path ahead. Mental preparation was a thing of luxury, and Rosanne pressed on without allowing herself much thought.

"Here we go again," Rosanne whispered and released the lever locking the thruster engine, slowing the galley to a crawl as they entered. The fog snaked around them in ghostlike wisps. The same feeling of dread welled deep in her stomach, and Rosanne had to restrain herself from reliving the hell they went through during the electrical storm.

Dressed in sealskins and knitted wool, the lieutenant successfully warded off the chilly weather. "I've confirmed the route with Hwang and Creedy. We're at least four hours away from the rock belt at this speed," Farand's muffled voice called through his scarf. Looking at her pocket watch, Rosanne raised her eyebrows at the allotted time which had passed since they entered this nightmarish scenery.

"I swear we just reached the fringes of the Veil, yet here we are an hour in." Her teeth chattered. "I can't press on any faster than this, or Higgs will have my head after we dangle from the noose." She chuckled and blew into her hands. "This chill isn't normal at all. The sun was blazing hot back there, but in here, it might as well be winter."

Farand's teeth chattered in agreement. "It's my shift, Captain. I'll notify you when we reach the b-belt."

"She's all yours, Mr. Duplánte." Rosanne rubbed her arms as she stiffly made her way to her cabin. Flopping down on her chair, Rosanne faceplanted on her desk and lay sprawled across it.

"Perhaps we'll make it," she told herself and sniffed through her ice-cube of a nose. Like a bad dream, she wished this entire mission could plunge into the sea of her subconscious and never rise again. A warm, comforting hand rested on her shoulder, and Rosanne instinctively placed hers over it. She grasped only the leather of her jacket. Rosanne sat up and looked around; then, burying her face in her hands, she groaned.

"TO YOUR BATTLE STATIONS!" Farand's thundering voice startled Rosanne out of her bed. She hit the floor hard and dove for her flintlock by the desk.

"God bloody dammit." She nursed her sore bottom and put on the hat. The bell rang outside, an indication of immediate danger in dire need of extermination. She grabbed her jacket and flew out the door.

"What is it?" Instinctively she hunched from the sharp cold, and she fit the goggles to protect her eyes.

Farand swung the wheel and pushed it forward, making the ship dive. A cannonball whizzed over their deck, nearly hitting the mainmast. "Pirates, Captain. They have a ship, and they're loaded."

A small coastal schooner with fore and aft rig zipped haphazardly along the front of the rock belt. Five men on the pirate ship's single deck fired their flintlocks, bullets pinging into the galley's woodwork. The schooner was small and limber, with only one cannon on each side.

"Like dropping bombs to hit a fly. Why do they always choose such tiny vessels? Goddamn you, Aros," Rosanne cursed and waved Farand away from the wheel.

The lieutenant had no complaints as he sprinted down the stairs. "Don't forget half the hull thrusters are offline!" he roared.

Her hand immediately let go of the lever controlling the thruster engine's energy output. "Very well then. Give them hell, Mr. Duplànte."

With a two-finger salute, Farand barked for the gun crew to get moving. "Aim for their sails. It's their biggest target!" The gun crew quickly loaded the main deck cannons. Farand released three shots at the holed remains of the aethersail. The flying metal missed its target, and the schooner answered immediately with its own cannon. Glass from the galley's sterncastle shattered, and a heavy crackling thump alerted Rosanne to the potential that her room might need hefty renovation.

Creedy, leaning over the railing, looked up at Rosanne. "We got a hull breach!"

"Impossible!" Rosanne called. How could the schooner have caused extensive damage? Small vessels didn't have such firepower.

"They have a thirty-two-pounder, Captain!" Creedy's frantic voice was drowned out by the *Red Queen*'s broadside peppering the schooner.

Rosanne shook her head as if her ears betrayed her. But sure enough, on the schooner's deck, she located the cannon with the firing capacity to crack the *Red Queen*'s wooden hull wide open. It was bolted to the deck, and the thirty-two-pounder's barrel was wide enough to fit a grown man's leg.

"They looted the ship graveyard," she muttered to herself, recalling the hundreds of ships, military and commercial, that lay back on the island; most had been armed to the keel. She couldn't bother with how or why the pirates would add such a heavy weight to their schooner, as her own galley was almost out of munition since their last battle.

The schooner flew above them, teasingly, as it was out of reach for their cannons. A dare, Rosanne knew. Behind their wheel, she saw Aros take off his hat in a mocking salute. Rosanne pulled her pistol and drew back the flintlock, firing it without any real intention of hitting anything. Aros ducked out of view but soon returned with the biggest grin Rosanne was determined to wipe off his face.

The *Red Queen*'s gun crew showered the ship with bullets, but the schooner zipped out of reach. Their mainsail was riddled with seared holes, but not enough to cripple the ship's power supply. In the fog, the small schooner quickly disappeared out of view. Rosanne drew as much power to the engine as the ship could muster, pursuing the annoying little wasp laughing at them from above.

The *Red Queen* drew up almost neck-on-neck with the pirates, and Rosanne spun the wheel, slamming the galleon's hull right into the schooner's side. The pirates staggered from the impact. One of the topmen manning the mainmast crashed to the deck. Rosanne smiled wryly and turned the wheel away from the schooner, separating them with a series of cracks and groans from broken wood and splinters.

Having caught the opportunity, two pirates climbed over the railing of the quarterdeck. With her hands too preoccupied dodging the schooner's attack, Rosanne nearly missed the intruders as they came upon her with sabres and guns. A plasma bullet went through one man's chest, and a shrill scream resonated as Nelson pounced on the other. The small lawyer smacked the butt of a pistol into the pirate's forehead half a dozen times before the frenzy died in him, leaving him huffing and puffing from the burst of adrenaline. Then he gasped and gripped his side. Rosanne laughed incredulously at the bloody pool growing under the twitching pirate.

"Where on Terra did you come from?" Rosanne asked, as equally impressed as she was astonished.

Nelson breathed hard as he pointed behind him. "A cannonball broke open my cage and I saw them climb up the hull, so I followed them." He continued to huff his breath, wobbling along with the ship's swaying motions when Rosanne dipped the bow to fly them to lower altitudes.

"Well done, Mr. Blackwood. I'll entrust my back to you then."

Nelson saluted with a shaky wave. His hand slipped at the bloodied handle and nearly dropped the plasmic gun while reloading it.

The schooner flew into the thick of the fog and disappeared, but Rosanne knew they would return to attack from another angle. She noticed the large boulders drifting with the invisible current which encompassed the rock belt. The schooner navigated around the treacherous landscape between the boulders, providing perfect cover from the galley's attack.

"Mr. Duplànte! Bring the dynamite."

The lieutenant's double-take split his attention between ensuring the right canons were loaded and Rosanne's ridiculous request. "Whatever for, Captain?"

Rosanne answered with a single point of her finger towards the rock belt. "Blast them all to hell." Farand blinked, laughed, and shook his head. Kristoff and Norman disappeared below deck. Rosanne kept the ship level to ease the young men's attempt at hauling the box full of dynamite aboard deck. The schooner was presented with time to reload their guns and cannons, but Rosanne could afford that increased threat.

Norman held a stick of brown paper-wrapped dynamite, staring at the dangling fuse. "How many seconds do you think this lasts?"

Kristoff shrugged. "Ten seconds? Maybe less?"

"*Maybe* less? You know we're throwing it, right?" Norman protested and shrieked as Kristoff held a torch under the fuse, lighting it up in angry sparks.

"Throw it, you idiot," Kristoff nodded, unperturbed.

Norman hurled the dynamite. It soared in a long arch and thudded against a floating boulder, then fell. A deafening blast shook the boulders from their tranquil course, creating a cascade of rumbling rocks.

"I counted five seconds," Kristoff said, grinning. Norman's petulant stare drilled through Kristoff's skull. Every indication that the schooner was caught in the floating boulder slide was drowned out by the noise.

Farand ran to Rosanne's side, shouting through the commotion. "Captain, you don't think this is a bit excessive?"

"My patience is spent," Rosanne said and turned the wheel. The *Red Queen's* bowsprit pointed into the rock belt. "We're going home, Mr. Duplànte. Now, clear the way!" Single sticks of dynamite flew ahead of them, timed to explode almost upon impact. It didn't take much to move the rocks with this method. Rosanne steered clear of the largest boulders, stepping her feet on the pedals as little as she could to not overuse the broken hull thrusters. The rock belt quickly closed behind them, and Rosanne urged the crew to continue with the dynamite if they wanted to see daylight again.

"Captain, this is madness!" Farand protested, holding on to his hat as he ducked pebbles raining from above.

"But it's working!" Rosanne cackled, steering the galleon over a massive boulder too stubborn to be bothered by single sticks of explosives.

CLEAR OF THE floating rock belt, the thrusters gave a pathetic sputter, shaking the *Red Queen*. The sails ceased their humming, and most of the panels on the consoles died. The ship fell eerily quiet. They drifted to a painfully slow crawl. The western winds edged them on, the galleon's sails tight enough to move them. Rosanne spun the wheel, but the thruster panels didn't budge.

"... Higgs?" Rosanne tried the intercom.

"That's it. Sally's toast. Dead." The sound of Higgs' boot kicking a hunk of metal rang through the intercom, quickly followed by a stream of curses.

With the Grey Veil swirling thick around them, a rescue was an impossible dream even if they sent out a long-ranged distress signal. The gentle winds kept them moving at a crawl, but for how long? Rosanne put the intercom down and pursed her lips as she tapped the wheel.

"All right, ladies and gents, get comfortable. We ain't leaving anytime soon." The crew's open displeasure was as infectious as their immediate relief that most dangers had passed for now.

Nelson looked to Rosanne, who shrugged. "It's up to the gods now, I suppose. If anything, it was an interesting journey, Mr. Blackwood." She smiled.

"Glad to have been a part of it, Captain Drackenheart." He shook her hand.

"You spilled blood for us, Nelson, and I respect that. Doesn't matter what the crew thinks. I owe you for that."

Glancing at the people milling around deck, those who simply rested against the masts or on the floor, even those who stared apathetically at the never-changing scenery, Nelson knew his actions wouldn't matter anymore. "I can only pray we arrive in time."

"I wholeheartedly agree." Rosanne twisted a few knobs on the radio connected to the intercom, scanning the area around them. The display was a cracked facade filled with lines boxing in the topography below them, except there was nothing there. She flipped a switch and changed the communication range to long distance. She let the ship float as she returned to the wreck of her room. She excavated a chair from the rubble, dragged it to the wheel, and sat in front of it, covering her eyes with the hat.

Then she waited.

THE LAZY SWIRLS of the fog were broken an uneventful hour later as the wind picked up. The thick mist to their starboard amassed into clouds, spinning in their centre.

"Where is it taking us, Hwang?" Rosanne barked into the intercom, struggling to hold the wheel straight as a gale grabbed the ship and took her for a ride.

"The wind currents blow counter-clockwise. Our position puts us straight west of Bogvin."

The wheel smacked over Rosanne's hand. She snarled and dropped the intercom. Diving for the helm, she wrestled with it and ran their statistical chance of survival through her mind. If they surrendered to the storm, they could end up either north into the thick of the Grey Veil or too far south for any chance of a return to Valo. "Isn't this just bloody dandy." She straightened the ship, following the forming cloudless funnel at its fringe.

With the engine offline, Rosanne steered the best she could, coordinating the topmen pulling at the sails in accordance with their orientation.

"Goddamn pirates." Rosanne did half a turn with the wheel, bringing the *Queen* slightly tilted against the wind on the storm's periphery. "Fucking trolls." The mainsail pulled against groaning wet ropes and vines ominously. "Yerrik, you bastard." It tore a protracted line right next to its original damage. "In the nine bloody hells! Secure the main sail!"

Swinging from a rope of the bottom sail, Creedy took a tumble. Norman threw himself after Creedy, latching on to the older man's legs, and brought them both to the deck with a violent crash. Dalia and her crew clambered onto the supports and got to work, tightening ropes and fighting flapping canvas and treacherous gales.

This relentless storm robbed Rosanne of all sense of time and space. They could be anywhere by now, deep within the reaches of the accursed place where so few returned from, or at the very fringes of freedom.

A strong current carried them in a sleek arch. For how long, no one kept track. As quickly as the storm had appeared, it disintegrated within minutes. The clouds swirled lazily around them once more while the galleon sped up, powered by the velocity produced by the storm.

"... *do you read?*" The radio buzzed, and Rosanne nearly missed it. She fumbled with the intercom and clicked the side button.

"This is Captain Drackenheart of the MTS *Red Queen*. We're requesting ..." Rosanne thought of what was most urgent, seeing as they had been caught in fights, storms, monsters, and whatnot. "We're requesting towing to the nearest port. Our engine is offline, and we have numerous people injured from a storm."

"This is military vessel *RDA Arctic Pride* off the coast of Bogvin. We read you loud and clear, Captain Drackenheart. Is it wrong of me to assume you're still sailing?"

Rosanne's heart nearly leapt out of her chest.

"Captain Drackenheart?" the operator prompted at her lack of response.

"Ah, yes! Riding the winds, sir. Expect to slow down soon," she replied.

"Copy that. We will rendezvous with you within the hour."

"We're eagerly awaiting your arrival."

As soon as the radio went silent, Rosanne pressed the call to her chest and nodded to the crew. Their intense stares morphed into rounds of applause and hysteric sobbing. She reached out her hands to silence the crew, and although she was smiling, they couldn't rest yet.

"As you all heard, rescue is on the way. The *RDA Arctic Pride* will be with us within the hour, a military vessel. You all know what that means. Hide *everything*. And for God's sake don't even talk about the gold to anyone for as long as our rescuers are within earshot. Get to work!"

Staring at the intercom with a sigh of relief, Rosanne couldn't believe her chances of running into the *Arctic Pride*. Had she any religious beliefs, she would have prayed to the high heavens, but she settled with a whispered *thank you* to whoever granted her such fortune.

———

THE *RED QUEEN*'S many nooks and crevices, left out of its blueprint, could provide smugglers with ample hiding space. But with the numerous suitcases, crates, and chests picked up on the ship graveyard, the loot proved a challenge to hide due to its sheer weight alone. The crew was more than trained to stash any type of shipment, but if they were to be subjected to an inspection, their tonnage alone would be too different to disregard. Norman and Kristoff carried barrels of dried fruit and potatoes, cracking open the lids and pouring it all into the ocean below, leaving a trail for the fish to enjoy. Flour was tossed by the sack, water poured over the deck, and to Hammond's greatest terror, all the dried meat was either consumed without delay or joined the rest of the goods.

When even their best efforts to alleviate the tonnage didn't work well enough, they cracked open the keel ballast and tossed as many rocks into the sea and replaced them with the gold. It was all a precaution, but a price so low they were willing to pay it if it meant that their precious goods kept the ship straight and buoyant and their pockets filled.

Rosanne spotted Dalia carrying a large jar of yellow-brown

liquid, the watch captain sneaking between the milling crew. Creedy stood hunched over, rummaging through a crate, oblivious to the woman's approach. When she stood behind him, she unscrewed the metal lid and dumped the revolting liquid over the man. He howled in shock and disgust, then stood with his arms out, staring as Dalia's face contorted with laughter.

"I promised, and I delivered! You won't be stealing my food again, you old bastard." Dalia wiped the tears from her eyes. The surrounding crew recoiled in disgust and held their noses.

Creedy smirked. Dalia paused mid-laughter, her face instantly turning to that of regret. The man reached out his arms for her. "I'm gonna hug you good!" he called as she sprinted away from him. Creedy set after her, causing everyone in the vicinity to clear the way in panic.

Farand caught the tail end of Dalia's shenanigans-turned-regret, his face a giant question mark. He shook his head as if it was just another day on the job.

"We have company!" Rosanne called after receiving an urgent call from Olivier claiming to spot a ship in the distance. The *Red Queen* had slowed considerably within the last hour but still sailed at a generous pace. Ten minutes later, the two-masted brigantine caught up with them, sending out hooks to grab the main deck and slow the galleon to a halt. A gangplank was laid out between the two decks. The *Arctic Pride* was about two-thirds the size of the *Red Queen*, but the military vessel was no less impressive. She was as beautiful as a ship on its maiden voyage, without a scratch on her pristine hull and with fresh canvas fluttering in the high winds.

"Permission to come aboard, Captain?" A broad-shouldered man asked from the gangway. He donned a straight blue uniform emblazoned with the winged eagle and trice flagged lines.

"Permission granted, Captain DiCroce." She couldn't contain her smile or the flutter in her stomach, and certainly not the racing of her heart as Antony's relieved smile filled her with overflowing joy. By the looks of it, he was as happy of seeing her she was.

"This certainly is the last place I expected to meet you, Captain Dracken—" The upstanding and decorated captain of the military ship *Arctic Pride*, the state-of-the-art vessel of the RDA, was ill-equipped to respond in kind when Rosanne planted a large kiss straight onto his lips. It lasted a mere two seconds, but Antony was still as stunned as his grin was wide, and his words were reduced to blabbering.

Rosanne rose her shoulders. "I am very happy to see you here, Captain DiCroce." She took a step back to give the baffled captain breathing space. Behind him, one of his men coughed.

Anthony bobbed his head, shaking off the paralytic effect Rosanne's surprise kiss had on him. "And I am elated to have you here with me." He caught the *Red Queen*'s crew's open and stunned faces. "And your crew as well, of course." He took her hands and leaned close, whispering in her ear. "Does this mean we have to stop by Salis on our way to Valo?"

Rosanne giggled. "Perhaps? Wait, no. No, no!" She shook her head. "We have to get to Valo first! It's the topmost priority!" Their conversation was loud enough to be heard by those around them, and the crew hurriedly added their urgent comments about returning to Valo as soon as possible.

"We can arrange that. We'll tow the ship, as we were returning to Valo already."

"That would be fantastic. And any medic you can spare, we'd appreciate, as we're in dire need. Oh, and we're completely out of supplies."

He chuckled at their hopeless state. "I'm sure we can arrange that as well. While we're at it, do you know anything about a rogue schooner? Their captain mentioned a squabble with a flying galleon. I was skeptical at the thought it could be you, but how many flying galleons are there?"

Rosanne's face turned sour. She thought she was finally rid of them for good.

Antony continued, "We picked up the pirate ship about ten miles southwest of here. You're lucky we were in range, or we could have sailed straight away. The pirates were not so lucky. They're currently enjoying the intimate comforts of the brig."

"Give my love to Captain Bernhart," Rosanne snorted. "And tell him I would gladly face him in aerial combat any day."

"I see the reason he no longer owns a state-of-the-art hybrid ship was your handiwork."

"That is a conversation I would love to have over a bottle of Quindecimus whiskey, but it must have disappeared during the attack." Antony chuckled and turned to board the *Arctic Pride*.

"Captain DiCroce!" she called out to him, and the man turned, regarding her curiously. "Let us stop by Salis someday." The smile on his face widened, and his eyes shone ever so brightly. The straight-jacketed sailors behind him lowered their sheepish gazes, keeping their grins and snickers to themselves.

Captain DiCroce tipped his tricorn hat to Rosanne.

"Glad to have found you, Captain Drackenheart."

Creedy elbowed Dalia, still stinking of pickle brine. "You'd think our captain was a cold-hearted iceberg, but she's shining like a sun. It's disturbing."

"Happiness awaits us all, Creedy."

"I thought the only man who ever wanted the captain was a shape-shifting demon."

Dalia planted a hand in his face, shoving him away from her. "Shut up, Creedy."

Civil Misconduct

Three weeks later, spring came to northern Noval in rivulets of late snowfalls and hot winds. The third disk of Valo's splendid skyport was a conglomerate of government buildings and floating docks of all sizes and shapes. As the very heart of all public transport of the port city of northern Noval, ships from north and south, near and far, glided in the queue of the skyport's numerous but crowded jetties.

In the early hours before noon, traffic was no less heavy, and ships lined up above the city's main island, creating a string of metalwork and flapping canvas, all waiting to drop off their precious cargo: passengers.

Next in queue floated a schooner, a small yet speedy ship having arrived straight from Salis. Nelson Blackwood gripped his leather briefcase and tapped his foot as the ship had yet to dock. Fishing out his pocket watch, Nelson broke out in a sweat. Not since his mental battle with a mythological creature aboard the *Red Queen* had he been so anxious.

The ship reared and thrust forward with a jerk, then glided down to a jutting gangway just free of its previous occupant. Nelson placed himself at the very front of the gate while passengers amassed behind him in an orderly fashion. They chatted freely of matters large and small, which filtered out as white noise in the young lawyer's racing mind. The moment the gate opened, Nelson held on to his hat and ran as fast as his stiff legs allowed him, giving him a stickman walk to the amusement of any onlookers. Ignoring the crowds, he dove for the first available cab, which had barely let out its previous fare.

"To the courthouse on the double!" he shouted and pulled the door closed behind him. The driver arched an eyebrow through the window.

"Young man, this is not a race-cab." Nelson shoved a gold coin into the man's gloved hand, turning the driver's sullen look into a gleam. He snapped the reins and guided the horses on a fast trot through the crowds, hooting at them with a nasal airhorn. Pedestrians shrieked in surprise and jumped aside, throwing curses after the renegade cab.

The driver stopped in front of a wide Gothic building with numerous floors and narrow, arched windows. Nelson raced for the front doors where two men in stiff jackets fumbled for the handles at the young lawyer's express approach. His shoes clacked against the polished marble floor, robbed of all carpet cushioning, and his footfalls alerted everyone in the main building about his arrival.

A young desk clerk eyed him curiously, likely considering security detail.

"Courtroom five?" Nelson huffed, staring at the desk clerk with wild eyes. The young man pointed up the stairs to his left, and Nelson tipped his hat before rushing off to the second floor. The building was meticulously mapped out and labelled with signs in cursive letters, and Nelson had no trouble navigating himself to the designated courtroom as sparse as he was on time. The last mass of people drew into the courtroom, and the doorman began to close it off for the session.

"One moment!" Nelson called out as loud as he could without sounding like a maniac. The startled doorman did as instructed. Well inside, the benches from the frontmost seat to the wall were packed with offenders and frill-dressed nobles with nothing better to do. He spotted a red-headed woman at the very front and made his way over to her side.

"Where in God's name have you been?" Rosanne uttered through gritted teeth and a stiff smile. Her curls had been washed, brushed, and arranged with pins hidden under the worn hat, which had seen far too many dangers, including today where it threatened the very balance of court fashion. Rosanne donned a pair of trousers with pleated folds that mimicked a skirt and a high-necked blouse with a corset underneath, smothering every breath she took.

"My apologies, Captain. I was stuck in traffic. I'm glad you followed my advice. Except for *that*." He motioned to her hat. She dusted off the pants, smiling.

"Once in a lifetime, Mr. Blackwood. Savour it. And *this* will save my hide any day." She took it off regardless and let it rest on the table in front of her.

"All rise for the Honourable Judge Thomas," a frill-decorated man by the front side door called out. The entire room got to their feet in a chorus of shuffles, falling silent as a black-robed man wearing a ridiculous, white-curled wig strode in with a leather satchel under his arm. Judge Thomas was short and broad and had seen many lavish dinner plates in his time; his red-cheeked pallor spoke of health issues regarding his diet. He sat down at the centre podium at the very front of the room and took out the case files.

"Court is now in session," his flat voice was completely bereft of soul. The audience sat in indifferent silence. "A fine crowd has gathered here today, by all means for something interesting, I presume. First order of today's agenda is NX5372. Captain Rosanne Drackenheart, are you currently with us?" He glanced over the top of his glasses, which sat perched at the tip of his nose.

Rosanne rose diligently, straightening her pleated pants in the process and giving a courteous dip so expertly trained Nelson believed she was a different person. "Yes, your honour." Her graceful smile erased all the hard lines earned through shady transactions, pirate battles, and monster encounters.

"Come to the front, please." Judge Thomas shuffled through a three-page document, speedreading as Rosanne stood stiffly in the center of the open place between the court and the audience. The man glanced at the documents, then at Rosanne, and back again. Her smile widened, but she restrained herself enough to keep the grace of her facial bone structure. "There appears to be some sort of misunderstanding. Are you aware of what this document says, Captain Drackenheart?"

"Vaguely, your honour," she lied.

"Have you been fully briefed of its content?"

"I have not."

"On May sixth, you were observed performing an act of civil misconduct against this city's upstanding gentry. You have been accused of, and I quote ..." Judge Thomas paused, staring at Rosanne's impeccable expression of confusion, and smacked his lips. "Clobbering General Astor Hughes and throwing him over a bar top, resulting in injuries such as a broken nose, split lips, and a dislocated shoulder. End quote." The buzz following Judge Thomas' pause was that of wonder with sprinkles of amusement. Rosanne rose a hand to her lips, drawing a quick breath, and blushed.

"Are you aware of such injuries?" the judge asked.

"Oh, dear. I might have been too rough on the poor man."

"And what is your explanation to this ... accusation?"

Rosanne threw a nervous glance to the floor and pressed her hands to her chest. "You see, Judge Thomas, General Hughes had been making outrageous passes on me at the Captain's Quarters hotel for some time now, and that day he had too much to drink. I was in the company of my fiancé, Captain Antony DiCroce, when General Hughes ..." Rosanne paused for effect and looked down with a blush spreading to her ears. "He touched my breasts, your honour."

The women in the audience gasped.

"Order!" The judge smacked the gavel. "If I understand this correctly when General Hughes made a pass on you, you proceeded to break his nose, toss him around the bar, and dislocate his shoulder?"

"I am stronger than I look, your honour. And the poor disgruntled man attacked me after I refused his advances. Captain DiCroce vouched for my case as he witnessed the incident," Rosanne's saccharine tone sent shivers through Nelson.

"Yes, it says here General Hughes was unsteady on his legs and is currently hospitalized ... well, Captain Drackenheart. The sentence for aggravated assault, especially against the general himself, and he was very clear on the specifics of this sentence, is that you have your trade license revoked and communal service of two years without pay."

The women in the audience stood up in protest, shouting and throwing hands. Judge Thomas smacked his hammer down repeatedly, calling for order.

Nelson stood from his seat. "Judge Thomas, if I may have a quick word with my client?" Judge Thomas approved with a wave. Rosanne bent down to hear Nelson whisper into her ear. Her eyes gleamed, and she had to suppress her grin. Rosanne returned to her spot.

"Judge Thomas, if I may. All sorts of outrageous accusations were used to harass me that evening. General Hughes accused me of being a cross-dresser frequenting the molly house at Cork Hill, and that is probably why he grabbed my ..." Rosanne made a grabbing motion with her hands over her breasts and coughed. "He's seen all sorts of people there, and I fear the general might not realize just who he's met once visiting Cork Hill." The skin on Judge Thomas' face turned ashen. Rosanne continued. "What is a woman to do but defend her dignity against the superior sex? I realize I was too hard on the poor general. He's probably ashamed of showing his face at the molly house along with so many other *governmental officials*." Stealing a quick breath, Rosanne covered her mouth and looked away from the judge.

The audience snickered. Judge Thomas coughed and looked to his scribe by the podium below, who gave him a questioning look.

"Very well. As of today, the second of June in the year of our Majesty 1704, I hand down the judgment of two weeks trade suspension for Captain Rosanne Drackenheart for aggravated assault against a servant of the crown who..." he stopped himself as he couldn't figure out the proper wording, and looked down to the scribe again.

"For sexually harassing the accused, your honour." The scribe pipped in.

"What he said." He smacked the gavel with a resounding *whack*.

ROSANNE AND NELSON stood outside the courthouse under the sweltering summer sun. Rosanne let her hair loose and put on her hat.

"Mr. Blackwood, as usual, you're full of surprises. How in Terra's name did you know Judge Thomas frequented the molly house?" She loosened the buttons at her throat and snuck an arm up the blouse on her back, pulling at the corset strings. She gasped in satisfaction of being liberated from this torture device. "Dear God, I really should have broken in the corset before wearing it. I haven't bothered with one since I was eighteen." She tucked the blouse back into her pleated pants.

Nelson ignored Rosanne's complete revert of character, preferring the dress-hating captain rather than the innocent woman she portrayed in the courtroom. "When you see him passing by your office window in drag and heading to Cork Hill, you put two and two together. Most people don't care when publicly showing themselves going there. But leverage is leverage if one is ashamed of his actions. I'm just glad it all worked out in the end."

"Different strokes for different folks. His wife might disagree, though." Rosanne snickered.

Nelson dropped his jaw. "I didn't know he was married! That explains his lenient sentence."

Rosanne gave a hearty laugh. "I'm glad that is sorted. Hopefully, I don't have to meet the rude bastard general again. By the way, did you find what I asked of you?"

Nelson fished out a scroll tube from his bag, handing it over. "I did. Had to comb through the entire archive in Salis to verify its origins, but this is the real deal."

"Excellent." She stashed the tube in her lavish purse, another item worn for the sole occasion of presenting as an upstanding lady of upper-class society.

"Was it found among ..." Nelson scanned their surroundings for any prying eyes or elephant ears. "The *gold*?" he whispered. Rosanne nodded.

"Many a treasure on that trip, but this is by far the most precious of them all. Bernhart would be green of jealousy if he knew what he missed out on by backstabbing us."

"How's he doing?"

"Enjoying the rocky comforts of Bogvin's dungeons awaiting trial in Bunnsboroux. Lovely justice system we have, don't you think?"

Nelson snorted and shook his head but didn't disagree with her banter. "The artist who painted that, was he employed on your father's ship?"

Rosanne nodded. "Indeed. R. S. Thompson was a cartographer, but he also painted portraits and other interesting creatures seen on his travels with my dad."

"And the creature on this map?"

Flicking her eyebrows, she gave a secretive smile. "It's probably connected to the ships disappearing off the coast of Noval for the last few centuries. The fact that we found this map in the ship graveyard tells me Thompson survived his final voyage with my father and somehow wound up in the Grey Veil."

"You don't think your father could have —"

"Not a reindeer's chance among a pack of wolves."

Nelson shuddered at the thought of ever returning to the island of fabled horrors. "Don't tell me you're going back to that god-forsaken place?"

"Please, Mr. Blackwood. Didn't you hear the judge? I'm out of a job for the next few weeks. I should get busy with other projects." Her scarlet lips widened.

"Whatever makes you happy, Captain."

"You won't care to join us this round?" Nelson held up his hands in blatant rejection.

"By the gods, no. I have a dinner appointment to meet Ida's parents, and that's an event I do not want to miss even if my life wasn't at stake."

"You're welcome aboard any time, Nelson. You have proved yourself as such."

"Thank you, Captain, but this time I'll happily decline in favour of my happiness. If I survive Ida's family ..."

Rosanne laughed. "It'll be fine."

She saw Nelson off in a cab before returning to the sea-level shipyard where the *Red Queen* still underwent repairs. After more than a month on the ground, she was pristine again. Her hull had been patched and painted, rails replaced, new metal-plated masts and double reinforced aethersails installed, and a new female figurehead donning a crown reached out in passionate fury. Her crew was checked in at the nearest hotel, and she entered the worn building, still in her splendid outfit. They were all gathered in the west wing vestibule, as they had the entire floor just for them, and Rosanne greeted them by slamming the door open.

"I'm off the hook, ladies and gents! Two-week suspension." The room erupted into cheers.

Mr. Duplànte saluted the captain. "I see your deception worked wonders."

"With a helping hand from a certain paper-pusher, the judge was caught wearing a different wig," she teased. "And I got great news!" She took out the document tube, wiggling it in the air, and popped the cork. The crew massed around the large center table as Rosanne laid out a large map.

"Tired of being stranded yet?" she said and flashed an excited grin. The crew burst out in protests, shook their heads, waved hands, or simply turned their backs on the idea of diving headfirst into another mission.

Lyle scratched his mustache. "No more islands," he said when he saw the map.

"Captain, you're not suggesting ..." Hammond leaned forward in his chair, wincing and holding his side that still hadn't healed fully.

Rosanne's smile sent shivers through everyone's spines. "Oh, I *am*."

ACKNOWLEDGMENTS

This story is the product of a lot of work by a lot of people. I would like to thank Tina, my wonderful agent and editor, who took a chance with me and my story. I couldn't have asked for a better match championing my book and bringing it out into the world, from half a world away.

I'd like to thank Alex, and the rest of Rising Action Publishing Collective for all the work they put into this, more than I ever saw and knew.

Thank you, Chris, for your sharp eyes and wit which inspired the dumbest quotes and scenes during the beta process.

I give many thanks to my friends who supplied me with their enormous variety of English-as-second-language grammar and use which made for a lot of hilarious cultural misunderstandings.

And lastly my cat; I could have finished way earlier if he wasn't trying to get me off the computer all the time.

About the Author

Norwegian born and resident Lilian Horn brings life to Scandinavian folklore through her debut *Perils of Sea and Sky*. With a degree as a biomedical laboratory scientist, hobby painter and game enthusiast, she lives in the arctic city of Tromsø with her introverted and demanding cat.

Follow Lilian on:
   Instagram: @ lilianhornwrites
   Twitter: @LilianHorn_

Rosanne Drackenheart and the crew of the *Red Queen* will return in *Journey of the Lost and the Damned* releasing in Spring 2024 from Rising Action.